The FIRST
*V*IAL

The FIRST VIAL

LINNEA HEINRICHS

thistledown press

Library and Archives Canada Cataloguing in Publication

Heinrichs, Linnea, 1950–
The first vial / Linnea Heinrichs.

ISBN 1-894345-84-3

1. Black Death–England–Fiction. 2.
England–Civilization–1066-1485–
Fiction. I. Title.

PS8615.E37F57 2005   C813'.6   C2005-900868-7

Cover painting detail from *Triumph of Death* by Peter Brueghel the Elder —
Courtesy of Art Research
Cover and book design by Jackie Forrie
Printed and bound in Canada on acid-free paper

Thistledown Press Ltd.
633 Main Street, Saskatoon, Saskatchewan, S7H 0J8
www.thistledown.sk.ca

 Canada Council
for the Arts
Conseil des Arts
du Canada
 Canadian
Heritage
Patrimoine
canadien

Thistledown Press gratefully acknowledges the financial assistance of the Canada Council for the Arts, the Saskatchewan Arts Board, and the Government of Canada through the Book Publishing Industry Development Program for its publishing program.

The FIRST *V*IAL

To my husband, Barry, for his encouragement.
To my children, Ryan and Kim, for their patience.
To my editor, Rod MacIntyre, for his kind advice
and sense of humour.

CHAPTER 1

And the first went, and poured out his vial upon the earth;
and there fell a noisome and grievous sore.
                                                    — Revelation 16:2

IT IS SAID DEATH RIDES A PALE HORSE and that when he unsheathes his sword to manifold slaughter he falls on the unwary, for amid the common mortality of man, no one perceives his coming.

In gothic grandeur like the rest of its brethren rooted in the Christian soil of England, the church keeps haughty and unsuspecting watch over the village of Claringdon, while the village rots at its feet in an untidy skirt of rude thatched cottages.

A curtain of mizzle fogs the hamlet while a negligent summer sun inclines its cheerless face toward a human column flowing down one of the meandering spokes connecting the village to its church. At the forefront toils a stooped figure, sweating under the weight of a large wooden cross. Following him, three others carry lighted candles. The square cap atop a tonsured head, singles out the parish priest coming in behind them. Its nostrils blowing at the priest's back, an aged cart horse strains against his harness, ears flat, head bobbing. In his cart bounce two mounds wound in white cloths, black stitched crosses worked the length and width of the coverings. Crows glide on currents of air overhead, their raucous calls strident and mocking.

Well nigh the whole village throngs behind the wagon. The adults walk in silence save for the rustle of their rough costumes and the scrape of their feet against the stones. Children, oblivious to the gravity of the occasion, caper and giggle at the rear of the party.

The procession reaches the churchyard, moves up the central porch beneath a traceried rose window and through a soaring archway. The dead are laid in the middle of the church and the villagers press into the nave, shoulder to shoulder, shuffling and nervous. Small children seek refuge behind their mothers' skirts and peer from this place of safety, eyes round and curious.

The ornate glory of the house of God stands in stark contrast to their own mean cottages and they feel a mingling of worshipful awe and naked terror inside the massive stone edifice. A great gilded cross spans the chancel arch, its arms terminating in emblazoned medallions of the symbols of the four evangelists. Rood lights flicker beneath it.

The priest takes his place on the chancel steps and an expectant hush quiets the congregation. Solemnly he kisses small crosses embroidered on his silk stole. He folds the amice back from his head where it hangs like a small cowl around his mottled neck. Father Simon is ascetically pale and gaunt-cheeked, his faded blue eyes embedded in dark hollows. He stretches thin fingers dramatically toward the biers and opens his lips while his eyes roam slowly over the assembly. He pauses, seeming to await a divine signal to speak, then his moment is lost when a child's shrill voice explodes in unrestrained fascination.

"O-o-o, look at 'em!"

Reluctantly, all eyes are forced to the biers. So tightly bound are the shrouds around the faces of the dead that one can easily distinguish the outline of nose and chin. Those with heightened senses curl their noses at the stench of decay carried on threads of floating incense.

"Look, Jamie," the childish voice goes on. "Them's the lord and lady from the castle. They's dead," it adds with relish.

There is an answering whimper from a second child and a woman hushes them. The priest glowers, a hiss accompanies his sharp intake of breath then he puts on a face of gloom and throws his arms wide, recapturing their attention.

"Good men!" he laments. "Behold, a mirror to us all. Corpses brought into the church. God be merciful to them and bring them into everlasting bliss. Each man and woman that is wise, make ready. For we all shall die, yet we know not how soon."

The assembled company shrinks in on itself, hands clenched at their chests. With anxious eyes they hear the recital for the dead and the sanctuary grows thick with swirling incense and the acrid smoke of many candles.

The black pall billows out of the church after them, accompanying them to the graveside.

"May angels escort thee to paradise," intones the priest. "May the martyrs receive thee at thy coming and bring thee into the holy city Jerusalem."

Father Simon passes the censure over the dead, the bodies are lowered into their dark holes and he raises his voice in the final ancient prayer.

"May their souls and the souls of all the faithful departed through the mercy of God, *Requiescat in pace.* Amen."

Shovels are plied. Providentially, a pardoner materializes, and the proximity of death prompts a hasty purchase of the offered indulgences, duly signed and sealed by the pope, rendering them a true covenant between God and man. Purgatory's torments being imminently alarming, the promise of remission of temporal punishment for the next forty days is snatched by eager hands. The pardons are pushed inside their tunics and hidden next to their hearts, that seat of all evil.

There is much doleful head wagging and tongue clucking among the women as the townspeople return to the village.

"Murder, it was," one whispers to another, hitching her skirt out of the mud churned up by their recent passage.

"Don't I know it," her companion agrees. "And my poor child, isn't she laundress at the castle even now?"

The sun has finally begun to warm the damp day and wisps of steam drift up from thatched roofs. The women hurry. Funerals make men hungry. They will need hot meals before returning to the wet fields. The dead are retired from their labours and may repose in peace. The living are not so fortunate.

Unseen, the pale horse and its dreadful rider loom ever closer. He does not pity the poor, nor regard the privilege of wealth. His command is irrevocable and his sword is drawn.

Much higher than the stone church, Crenfeld Castle straddles a rocky promontory jutting out into the grey waters of the River Wyvern. Lofty cylindrical towers buttress its red sandstone walls, a wide ditch glutted with pink and white water lilies surround all but the north side of the castle. The Wyvern hurls itself with such ferocity against the northern cliffs that a climb from below means certain death. Entrance is gained by a wooden drawbridge spanning the west side of the ditch, terminating in a gateway barred by stout oak doors and a heavy, iron-tipped portcullis.

A lone sentry treads the walls. Upon reaching the far tower he leans against the stones and studies the line of trees to the south. Two figures on horseback separate themselves from the dark wood and the sentry hastens to descend a ladder leaning against the battlement.

The figures resolve themselves into a man and woman. The man sits astride a chestnut mare, the woman atop a large thickly muscled black destrier. The man is thin, fair and hollow-cheeked, with a sparse straw-coloured beard. His hands and his gold and purple cote-hardie flutter about him as he speaks. The woman too is slender, but there the similarity ends. Her hair is a thick, lustrous red and her features delicately turned. She rides proudly, gracefully, a simple grey cloak billowing around her skirts in soft folds. The sun slants lower in the sky and burnishes the castle walls in a molten bath of gold.

"A fine castle, is it not pet?" the man says to his companion.

The woman nods wordlessly, fixing her eyes on its walls.

CHAPTER 2

KATHERINE WAS PLEASED. Perhaps this marriage would not prove such a dismal union after all. With her father's death the previous year, the family property had gone into the hands of her brother, Douglas. He made it plain that although he would not leave her desolate, he expected her to marry and marry as soon as good taste permitted. He reminded her that their father had indulged her in her single state to her detriment, for she was now well past a marriageable age.

After a suitable mourning period and under the guise of feasts and parties, Douglas displayed his sister to a number of prospective husbands, Nathaniel being the least repugnant. She tried to tell herself she expected little in the way of happiness. Yet she had hugged close the hope that somehow Nathaniel would awaken a love that merely slept, the kind of love of which the poets wrote so eloquently. But it was not to be and her heart had shrivelled into a firm little core as she resigned herself to a life bereft of the romance of longing sighs and quickened pulses.

Nathaniel was kind to her in a vague sort of fashion and they lived well and entertained lavishly until eventually the routine of it grew dull and monotonous for Katherine and she craved some new distraction.

Katherine felt somewhat ashamed of herself when the death of Nathaniel's aunt and uncle paved the way for just such a distraction. With no immediate heir, their manor fell to Nathaniel as eldest nephew, who was elated at his good fortune. Although his was a family of considerable holdings, he held no property in his own right. With feverish haste he assembled their belongings for transport and they travelled to claim his inheritance.

Nearing the castle, Katherine heard a shout on the wall and the heavy timber grill was hoisted. The gatehouse door began its ponderous inward pivot. She urged her horse over the lowered drawbridge and after a moment's hesitation Nathaniel did the same. The horses' hooves clattered on the wooden planks, echoing back to them off the castle walls. Below, a cloudy water image crossed with them. Just inside the inner ward they dismounted and passed the reins to two stable lads who led the animals away to drink from a nearby trough.

When no one came to meet them, they made their way across the ward in the general direction of the great hall, the close-clipped grasses thick and soft underfoot, lush from unseasonal rains.

A man in a leather apron emerged from the stable while several horses watched, resting their chins on the stall doors, ears pricked forward. The man rubbed his hands down the sides of his apron as he approached.

Nathaniel frowned and pointed a finger at the man's chest.

"Who are you?' he demanded.

"The marshal, my lord," the man said.

Nathaniel bristled.

"The stableman? Where is your steward? Met by a stableman," he muttered to his wife.

Katherine rested a hand on her husband's arm to stay his flow of words and smiled at the marshal.

"Is the steward in some other corner of the manor?" she asked.

"No, my lady," the marshal answered. "He's gone."

"Gone?" Nathaniel broke in. "Gone where?"

The marshal lifted his shoulders. "Don't know. After Lord Philip and his lady hopped the twig — sorry my lady — he was never seen again. There's some as say the demons snatched him away for failing to save his master. But most think he was helping himself to the master's money and so took himself off before anyone found out."

Nathaniel blinked and his jaw dropped slightly.

"He was overfond of his fine robes," the marshal explained. "And pressing for a house of his own same as the steward on Lord Victor's estate."

"Lord Victor? Who is . . . oh, never mind."

Nathaniel sighed. "No steward. How can we operate without a steward?"

The marshal gave Nathaniel a blank look, shrugged and returned to the stable. The problems of the nobility were of no consequence to him. He saw to the horses. Men's estates were their own affair.

Katherine exchanged a look with her husband, raised an eyebrow and began a proprietary scrutiny of her surroundings. Directly to her right the smith shaped a sword blade, his hammer ringing at each stroke. A young lad worked the bellows and as the smith plunged the blade into the fire, he glanced up and stared a moment, before bending back to his task. A kitchen maid rounded a corner bearing two full water pails suspended from a pole across her shoulders. She kicked at a trio of plump, snorting pigs whose rooting had brought them nearly under her feet. Moving out of the way to let her pass, Katherine admired the neatly fenced-in garden. A small orchard of apple, pear and plum trees sheltered a group of straw and wattle hives. The cool weather was making the bees lazy and they floated aimlessly among the white blossoms of the newly-flowering plum trees. Neat lines of young seedlings marked out the herb and vegetable plots.

Katherine was drawn from this pleasant view by the movements of a young boy at archery practice. She watched him intently, marking how he pulled the taut string and took his aim. Her father had taught her to use the bow. It remained her favourite accomplishment and her father had been proud that her marksmanship rivaled his own. Perhaps she would pursue it again.

Katherine looked up at an exclamation from Nathaniel. His annoyance at the steward's disappearance was forgotten in his pleasure at discovering the small conical building housing the hunting birds. Like a miniature tower it boasted its own tiny turrets and parapets. Nathaniel's hawk had arrived before them and Nathaniel made for the mews at once. Katherine trailed behind.

Nathaniel found the panting bird tied to a weathering block outside the little tower. She was biting at her jesses and bell and stretching her long grey wings in an attempt to take flight. Katherine watched while Nathaniel stroked the bird's head, all the while speaking to her in a gentle singsong. With his free hand he sprinkled her with a few drops of water from a nearby bowl. After a time the bird stopped panting and grew calm.

While Nathaniel spoke in undertones to the falconer, Katherine drifted around the ward. Her husband loved to hunt. He had dogs for deer hunting but falconry was his principle passion. Katherine wished she shared his enthusiasm, but she grew weary of hunting and hunting tales and was more than a little disconcerted that Nathaniel's peregrine, who often accompanied him on his wrist, should even share their chamber on the eve of important hunts. She was always a little afraid the bird might curve its sharp talons around her throat while she slept.

Outside the kitchen doorway, she came upon an old woman vigorously scolding a pair of young greyhounds who had managed to tug a sheet from the wash line.

"I'll cane ye both, see if I don't," the old woman cried, brandishing a short ash pole.

She made a limping advance on the cavorting animals. The dogs hesitated a moment too long, mouths full of stolen booty, and received a sharp rap on their snouts that sent them bounding away.

The old woman grunted, turned to seat herself on the kitchen steps and noticed Katherine. She pointed her pole suspiciously.

"Who are you, then?"

Katherine joined her on the stairs.

"Katherine Fendlay," she answered.

The old woman rapped her knuckles on her thin breast bone. "Eleanor, but most call me Nory."

She winked a rheumy eye at Katherine. "You be she as slips her feet out from under the sheets with Lord Philip, don't ye," she said knowingly.

Katherine raised a dark eyebrow. "Lord Philip is dead."

The old woman blinked and squinted at her. "So he is," she nodded, her creased face collapsing into sad lines. "So he is."

"I am his nephew's wife," Katherine explained. "He is your new master."

"Who is that, then? What's 'is name?"

"Nathaniel. Nathaniel Fendlay."

Nory wrinkled up her nose. "I'd push out all of me teeth sayin' a name as that." She thrust out her bony chin. "See here. Don't he be the one as killed his lordship and puir lady wife?"

Katherine stiffened.

"He did not," she denied.

"You'd know, I expect," Nory sniffed. "Nought to do with me. Which of ye did it only the saints knows."

She crossed herself with pious exaggeration and drew a ragged cloak around her shoulders. Katherine frowned. What had happened here? And why did the old woman think Nathaniel was involved?

"Were you here the day Lord Philip and his wife died?" Katherine asked.

"M-m-m."

Nory was giving her full attention to the sheets on the clothesline. Sitting a little apart from her, Katherine planted her elbows on her knees, cupped her chin in her hands and watched the old woman through a screen of black lashes. So, it was to be like that, was it?

"Why do you say they were killed?" Katherine asked. "The magistrate says they died of a consuming malady."

Nory snorted. "Didn't. Were deathcap mushrooms hidden in with the meadow mushrooms they ate in their chamber for late supper."

Katherine shuddered. "A mistake?" she ventured.

"No mistake. Cook is me own daughter, isn't she. A babe would know difference 'tween poison mushrooms and safe. Them as his lordship doted on has pink gills. Poison ones have white." Nory glared balefully at Katherine. "Mark me, missus. Them as has summat to be gained has done this black sin. Most think it were your husband."

Before Katherine could frame a reply the old woman struggled to her feet and, leaning heavily on her walking stick, limped across the courtyard to disappear behind a stone tower.

Katherine sighed. Lord Philip's own son had been killed in France during the English victory at Crecy. Nathaniel, as the only living relative in succession, had been unaware of his cousin's death until news of the inheritance reached him. Of that she was certain. Her husband took little interest in anything save hawking, hunting and court gossip. No one else could possibly benefit by their deaths. Unless, of course, one of the local landowners, anticipating no heirs, thought to appropriate it for himself. If so, their plans had been thwarted. Katherine shifted uneasily. The magistrate had given out that the deaths were from a common illness. Did the castle servants share the old woman's knowledge? Then the villagers would be equally as well informed. That would tend to explain the peculiar looks shot in their direction as she and Nathaniel passed through Claringdon. She had attributed it to the normally suspicious nature of a small village. But maybe it was more than that. Maybe they looked on them as murderers. Not a very pretty way to gain a manor but it would do no good to dwell on it. They had done nothing wrong and eventually people would learn to accept that.

Katherine rose from the steps, walked round the walls and poked her head into the hall. Next to a great hooded fireplace, decorated with a magnificent pair of stag horns, two young pages fidgeted on a shared bench beside a quantity of cheerily burning logs. Katherine moved through the doorway, suddenly conscious of the coolness of the outside air and the warmth of the great hall.

A chaplain was endeavouring to instruct the pages in the art of table service, pantomiming correct procedures. The boys paid scant attention to his words. They were engrossed in the progress of a spider dropping slowly on a silken thread toward their teacher's bald pate.

Katherine smiled and scanned the room. Thick, colourful tapestries graced the walls and heavy candles gave a good light from hinged sconces. The kitchen staff was busy covering meal tables with white bord cloths. She realized she was hungry and was about to go in search of Nathaniel when he came in behind her and tugged at her arm.

"See here, pet."

His peevish tone dissolved her lightened mood.

He lifted an elbow. "My tippets are muddy. I will need a change of clothes."

The streamers hanging from the sleeves of his waistcoat did indeed look quite grimy. Katherine wished he favoured less flamboyant styles. He caused seamstresses and cleaning women a great deal of exasperation in his pursuit of fashionable attire. It made her uncomfortable to see him so obsessed with his toilette. Her father had been the kind of man that expected his wife to manage his costume. But her husband followed the vagaries of court fashion with religious exactness. French styles were much in vogue and

21

he demanded his clothing reflect the choices of King Edward's retinue.

At the sound of Nathaniel's querulous voice the chaplain left off his lesson and came to meet them. His students were deprived of their fun and the spider fell harmlessly to the floor, whereupon the boys pounced down to scoop it up and amuse themselves by having it climb up their arms by turn.

"My lord, you have arrived!" the chaplain beamed.

"So I have, so I have," Nathaniel agreed absently.

He tugged his sleeves, twisting the fabric and frowning over his soiled costume.

"See here, where is the laundress?"

The poor chaplain looked confused. "The laundress?"

"I think the laundress may wait." Katherine made an effort to speak without sharpness. "I imagine the household has been expecting their new master."

"Yes, yes," the chaplain said eagerly. "You are long awaited."

Nathaniel stood stonily, put out that his request was being ignored but Katherine lay a soft hand on Nathaniel's sleeve and smiled into the chaplain's face.

"Have the castle staff join us in the hall at dinner. My husband wishes to address the household."

The chaplain returned her smile. A charming woman.

"They will be in attendance my lady. I will see to it myself. Your quarters are just through this door. I will inform the chamberlain of your arrival at once. Hurry lads," he said to the two young pages still busying themselves with the spider.

"You must be ready to serve at table. You were paying attention?" He screwed his face into an anxious frown. "Come, come."

The chaplain urged the boys out of the hall while Katherine and Nathaniel mounted the steps to their bedchamber.

The stairway was narrow and winding, the stone walls closing in hard on both sides making progress single file. The sharp wind to the right was a sensible precaution against attack. As all income garnered from the manor was kept in a chest in the lord's chamber, any intruder would have his sword arm to the wall with no freedom of movement while the descending defender would have full use of his weapon.

Of course, Katherine thought ruefully, if the marshal were right about the steward, there may be nothing in the chest to protect. Their footsteps echoed down behind them as they climbed and Katherine found the walls unduly clammy for a summer day. But then, this was no ordinary summer. Spring torrents had given way to summer drizzles and the whole of the country seemed continually sodden.

When finally they reached the top, Nathaniel entered first, clapped his hands, then spun and placed them over Katherine's eyes.

"Whatever are you . . . ?" she began with irritation.

"The bed is arrived, pet!" he cried, dropping his hands.

And so it was. Part of her dowry, the bed boasted highly polished walnut posts, intricately carved with twining vines and fluted lilies. Putting a hand round a post released the perfume of the warmed beeswax that polished them. Fine green linen curtains hung between the bedposts in lavish folds. A maid was just tucking in the edge of a heavy damask quilt. Perfect for this unendingly cold summer. Katherine twitched back the top. Yes, her grey miniver coverlet lay upon the sheets.

She nodded her approval at the red-faced girl.

"Thank you. This is exactly as it should be."

The maid scurried out as Katherine dropped onto the edge of the bed and leaned against its plump pillows. The blue and gold Fendlay crest hung on the wall above the bed, its zigzag of colour and four golden long-tailed dragons climbing up the sides. The bare stone walls were hung with somber, dull-coloured tapestries, the floor planks covered with plaited straw mats.

She would have the tapestries removed and lain on the floor to keep her feet warm. The walls would be white-washed, and . . . She tilted her head to one side to consider. And tiny red roses painted on the walls. There would be wool pillows, trimmed with crimson and green threads, for the cold stone windowsill, making it a comfortable place to sit and overlook courtyard activity.

She noticed their clothes chest had already been placed at the foot of the bed. That heavily chained chest under the window probably stored the manor documents, silver plate and coins. If there were any. A basin and ewer sat atop the chest. There was a tall stand for candles between the bed and the window and, next to the unlit fireplace, a single stool on a skin mat.

"Not that one!"

Nathaniel pushed aside the chamberlain who had come to help him choose a change of costume. He rummaged through the garment chest, flinging out clothes with both hands. The chamberlain stood to one side, his over-long mournful face drawn down even further.

Katherine groaned and reluctantly rose from the bed.

"Wait outside if you would, chamberlain. I will call you when his lordship has made a choice."

The man bowed stiffly, glowering at the back of Nathaniel's neck.

With the door closed, Katherine knelt beside her husband.

"Come, come," she soothed. "We will find something together. Only do not throw everything about." She laid a restraining hand on his arm.

Nathaniel's narrow chest lifted and fell in a deep sigh and his fingers relaxed limply around a handful of fabric. He threw the garment on the bed.

"It is too unfair," he moaned. "Do you know they all think I murdered my own uncle. Me!"

So he had heard the talk. The falconer must have told him. Katherine had hoped to prevent him hearing of it until she could frame the news as trivial gossip, not worth noting. But it was too late now. She shook his shoulders gently.

"But you are innocent. If anything at all has been done, it was not done by you. Ignore their foolish talk. Concentrate on the business of running your manor."

Katherine fixed her determined green eyes on her husband. He looked into their steady depths and seemed to draw strength from them.

"You are right, pet. I am ready, chamberlain," he called out in a firm voice. "Dress me quickly."

The hall was full when they took their places at the high table, the lower tables occupied with servants not directly involved in meal service. Cook was a tall muscular woman whose watchful eyes darted about the room. With her sat the usher, and in place of the absent steward, the chaplain. Other tables seated the long-faced chamberlain, the marshal, the keeper of the wardrobe, the laundress, linen maids and seamstresses, household knights, men-at-arms and watchmen. The pantler brought in hot loaves of bread and thick chunks of butter then took his seat. The butler and his assistants served the wines and beers while squires served the meat dishes all around before being seated. Last of all, the remaining kitchen servers brought out trays of fruit, nuts and cheeses, laid them out and took their own places at the farthest table.

Katherine looked down on them and smiled and nodded while she ate. The bord cloths were clean and neat, the table candles adequate and the bowls filled well but not overly so. Katherine bit into a ripe cherry and was surprised by its juicy sweetness. Obviously, trips to London merchants had been continued despite the steward's absence, and the quality of foodstuffs had not suffered any decline. Katherine enjoyed the delicious taste of fresh fruit and very good cheeses.

Nathaniel sat stiffly and barked occasional orders to the young squires doing service. Katherine smiled. They were clumsy and it was obvious they had not been paying too close attention to their teacher.

"Isn't she handsome," whispered one of the linen maids to a seamstress. "Slender as a reed and skin the colour of milk. And look at her hair. Like shining fire."

The seamstress nodded. "It will be a pleasure to clothe her. But that jacka-napes of a lord. Already he's insulted the chamberlain and Peter is a proud man."

"Yes, he is a sulky one and has a preference for French ways by 'is looks. Hard to please, I expect."

The linen maid winked at her friend. "P'raps you'll just have Lucy do his sewing. She likes his kind, she does."

They smothered giggles and turned innocent eyes to the head table where Nathaniel was just rising with a strained clearing of his throat. Any servants moving about the room froze in place and lowered their trays. The hum of conversation died away. They gave full attention to their new master.

"I greet you all and bid you know my loss is as great as your own. Lord Philip was a fine man, a fine master and a fine uncle. You served him well for the most part and I expect you to do the same for me."

Nathaniel drew himself up and gave a hard look around the assembled company.

"I am a fair man and I count upon a fair day's labor from all. Should you wish to apply to me with any complaint about your present situation you may do so tomorrow after I have breakfasted. However, there will be no wastrels in this household."

He smiled thinly. "I reserve that privilege for myself."

There was a derisive snigger. Nathaniel's pallid cheeks flushed red and he frowned and pursed his lips into a rigid line then flung himself back in his chair.

"God's blessing and mine," he said tightly. "You are dismissed to your duties."

He pointed to the butler. "Not you. Fetch me more wine."

He brought the palm of his hand down hard on the table.

Katherine sighed. Her husband was evidently ill-used to the mantle of authority and wore it badly.

The servants trailed out of the hall and Katherine sipped her own wine with slow thoughtfulness.

CHAPTER 3

THE UNSEASONABLY COOL, WET SUMMER DAYS wore on and tongues grew still. There was no more talk of poison mushrooms and death. Katherine pushed her own misgivings aside and busied herself with entertaining the constant stream of guests Nathaniel invited to Crenfeld. Despite the unrelenting bad weather, hunting, as always, was his preferred pastime and Katherine was ever obliged to make up parties to accompany him.

"Agnes, where is my grey mantle?" Katherine called out, a frown creasing her smooth forehead. "If Nathaniel insists on hunting in this vile weather I at least intend to be warm."

Her dresser pursed her lips. "The grey is being cleaned, my lady."

Katherine shut the lid of the garment chest and sat back on her heels. A pox on that husband of hers. She was of half a mind to feign illness. But she had invited their neighbours to the south and wished to make their acquaintance. They had evidently been great friends of Nathaniel's aunt and uncle and had stayed often at Crenfeld. So well known were they in fact, that the servants muttered darkly of Beatrice "the blister", whose ceaseless demands taxed even the most patient.

"My lady?" Agnes broke into Katherine's musings. "Lady Elizabeth's camlet mantle has been altered to fit you. It's lined with ermine and quite the warmest. Shall I bring it?"

Katherine brightened. "Wonderful. I had forgotten. Yes, get it for me. And be quick, Agnes. I fear I am late already."

Agnes was quick and Katherine rushed to the stable, arriving breathless and flushed.

Nathaniel was pacing.

"What kept you?" he fumed. "The boy cannot saddle that filthy beast of yours. Why you want an animal like that . . . "

Katherine stemmed the tide by stepping into the barn. Her black destrier was stamping in the new straw, tossing his head and arching his thick neck. He had pushed the stable lad into the side of the stall, pinning the poor boy against the boards. Katherine took hold of the lead rope and immediately the animal stopped his agitated prancing and stood still. His muscles quivered when she laid a hand on his neck.

"Sh-sh. There is nothing to fear."

Katherine rested her face on the horse's hard bristly cheek and stroked his flaring nostrils while the stable boy tiptoed gingerly around them, nursing a sore shoulder. Katherine led her coal-coloured mount into the ward.

"Might we saddle our own animals now?" Nathaniel threw a wary look at the black horse and moved to claim a chestnut gelding and two sorrel mares.

"That limb of Satan will kill us all," he complained.

"Pygine was father's war horse," Katherine said placidly, petting the horse's neck. "He simply has more spirit than any of your beasts."

Nathaniel sniffed and led the other three horses into the ward. Katherine clucked to Pygine. He followed her docilely onto the grass, where two strangers waited.

Nathaniel made the introductions.

"Sir Charles, my wife, the Lady Katherine, daughter of Sir Richard of Algincamp."

The baron bowed and eyed Katherine appreciatively. "I knew your father, my dear. England is the poorer for his passing."

Katherine smiled and offered a slim gloved hand. The baron's lips lingered overlong in the French mannerism and his wife stirred.

"Ah, forgive me. My dear wife, Beatrice, the baroness of Duncaster."

So, this was the much-maligned "blister" of the kitchen. Almost as tall as her husband, she shared his great girth and heavy jowls. Her broad flat face was thickly caked with whiteners and two startling red dots stained her flaccid cheeks. Beatrice's lips stretched into a tight grimace, folds of flesh making her hard black eyes almost pinpricks.

"A pleasure," she said, the ice in her voice belying the sentiment.

She was the type who instinctively mistrusted other women. Katherine had no difficulty accepting her suspicion for she could feel the heat of the baron's eyes even now. Katherine bestowed her warmest smile on Beatrice and deliberately and pointedly ignored her husband.

"I see you have altered Elizabeth's camlet mantle," Beatrice said shortly.

Katherine smiled and executed a half turn. "Do you like it?"

Beatrice gripped the reins of her horse, and with the groom's aid, struggled to mount the animal.

"It is very warm," she gasped, grunting with effort.

Astride the horse, she panted heavily. "My bones cause me great pain and kind woman that she was, Elizabeth loaned me that mantle on a particularly cold day. The warmth of the ermine greatly eased my discomfort and she promised it to me when next we should meet." She sighed. "Regrettably that day never came. And in any case," she observed, "you are a skinny thing so it is ruined now."

Beatrice clucked to her horse and it cantered after the two men, leaving Katherine standing alone beside Pygine.

Already, Katherine felt a great sympathy for her kitchen staff. Beatrice was indeed a blister. A blister she would like to lance. But no, she must hold her temper and her tongue. Katherine swung up into the saddle and prodded Pygine to move after Beatrice, wondering grimly whether it was the death of her friend or the loss of the warm cloak she minded most.

A light drizzle had resolved to steady rain by the time they reached the clearing where they were to eat a picnic breakfast. The hunting party tethered their horses and stood under the trees while servants set up tents and laid out a light meal. The huntsman and dog handlers set off with two of the hounds in search of spoor.

Presently, the tent was up and meat, wine and bread set out on a ground cloth. The small party sprinted the short distance from the trees to the tent and the servants retreated discreetly.

Nathaniel and Charles discussed the impending hunt between mouthfuls. Nathaniel ate quickly, darting his head forward with each bite, while his companion filled his cheeks to bulging before swallowing. Katherine thought he looked like a swollen squirrel. She nibbled gently at a slab of bread and turned her attention to the baroness.

"Did you know my husband's aunt well?"

Beatrice washed down a large piece of meat with a gulp of wine.

"Elizabeth and I were friends from childhood," she said. "In fact, Charles expected to be named heir to the manor after the unfortunate death of their poor son at Crecy. They never mentioned a nephew," she added in injured tones.

"Were you at the castle when they took ill?" Katherine's voice was light, her fingers busy separating a bit of meat from its bone.

Beatrice shuddered. "We were. Such a dreadful noise they made. My flesh fairly crawled with fear. The physic was sent for but it was too late for my poor Elizabeth."

The hand that stole to her cup trembled. Beatrice placed her other hand round the vessel to steady it and her lips quivered. The edge of the cup clattered against her teeth and her voice came hoarsely. "I pray I shall never hear a sound such as that again," she whispered.

Katherine eyed Beatrice speculatively. "Did the physic know how they died?"

Beatrice closed her eyes and drained her cup in a final gulp. "Something about the mushrooms from the kitchen. Poisonous in with the good. Something of that sort."

"Did he think it intentional? That someone meant for them to be poisoned?"

Beatrice's small eyes widened. "Oh, no. It was an accident. Although, there was that young wench who said . . . "

A perplexed frown folded her eyebrows, but as she opened her mouth to speak she was distracted by the huntsman's return. He conferred with Nathaniel in urgent undertones then disappeared into the forest. Nathaniel tipped back his cup once more then motioned to the servants to gather up the remains of their meal.

"They have a good sized buck in sight," he said, eyes glistening.

On his horse, he raised an ivory olifant to his lips and blew. The short series of notes threw the greyhounds into frenzied barking and lunging. They snapped at one another in their excitement and once unleashed, crashed into the dense underbrush. Nathaniel and the now mounted Sir Charles, urged their horses to follow.

Katherine was loath to leave the dry tent and the conversation, but the servants had started dismantling the canvas shelter around them. She tugged a heavy hood over her head and made sure it was fastened tightly before abandoning the tent. Beatrice complained a good deal over the thinness of her cloak and the soreness of her bones, but eventually sat her horse.

"They are a good bit ahead of us," Katherine told her. "Would you rather go back?"

"No, no," Beatrice panted. "We must be in at the kill. Hurry!"

Katherine groaned. She might have known Beatrice would be a huntress.

The woodland foliage sagged, heavy with rain. Leaves and fern fronds overturned their wells of water as the women pounded by. Their skirts were soon sodden and muddy. After a time they reached the hunting party where a great red deer was being kept at bay by the hounds. Its head was lowered, the heavy branched horns swaying from side to side, flanks heaving in convulsive spasms. One of the dogs leaped upon the horns, caution forgotten in its blood lust. The stag lunged forward in an attempt to escape and impaled the unfortunate hound on a nearby tree. Amid the agonized cries of the dying dog, the men let fly their arrows.

Heavily feathered, the hart's legs buckled and he sank slowly to his knees. He made one feeble attempt to stand but staggered as the life's blood pumped from wounds at his neck and chest, to puddle on the wet leaves covering the forest floor. He groaned softly, a shudder passed through his massive frame and Katherine saw his eyes fade to a motionless glare. He dropped, shaking the ground. There was a final gasp, a quiver of limb and muscle and then the stag lay still. Rain pooled in the curve of his flank, darkening the red coat and filling his gaping mouth.

Katherine regarded the dead animal sadly. The poor creature would never feel the warmth of the sun again or the triumph of horns locked in combat. She would have wished to protect him from the cold of the rain he did not feel. Foolishness, she knew.

As the men fell on the stag, Katherine turned away. She shivered and longed to be somewhere warm. Out of the rain and away from the shouts of the men and the snarls of the dogs. The horses were restless too, nostrils flaring, ears laid back. Katherine put a hand on Pygine's soft nose.

"You do not like it either do you, my darling. But you will not be its carriage. Nathaniel's own beasts can transport the poor creature for him."

The ride back to Crenfeld was no more comfortable than the ride out had been. Rain poured steadily, drenching them to the skin. Sally willows drooped under the grey sky, the rough thickets laid nearly flat to the ground by the heavy downpour.

Beatrice did not appear to notice the rain. She was fascinated by the buck's carcass and rode close to Nathaniel, where it lay across his saddle. She prattled excitedly and kept reaching out to touch the antlers. Nathaniel swelled under her approving eye while Katherine watched a rivulet of rain trickle down her husband's nose. She had never before noticed what a long nose he had, nor the slight hook at the tip. It was an ugly nose. She watched the droplet jiggle for some time before it fell onto the body of the deer.

Finally they gained the castle and cried for the gates to be opened. Amid the clamour of dogs, men and horses, Katherine slipped away to the stable with Pygine.

"Rub him well," she told the stable boy. "He is soaked through. Mind you give him no cold water. Warm it a little on the fire first. And two blankets."

The boy nodded and clucked his tongue tentatively at the black horse. But Pygine was agreeably disposed to cooperate and followed the lad into his stall.

Katherine picked up her muddy skirts and hurried across the yard into the great hall. She found the hunting party before a roaring fire. Joining them, she shivered and put out her hands toward the hot flames. Steam rose from her wet clothes and hair.

"There will be a feast, pet!" Nathaniel cried. "Day after tomorrow. The principal course will be my stag. Be sure the invitations ride out today and the kitchen is ready."

He grabbed the arm of a nearby servant. "Food, man. Food! We perish with hunger!" he shouted with hearty roughness, his eyes bright, then clapped the man's back to hurry him on.

"You should have sent for something to eat straight away, pet," Nathaniel scolded, pushing back a strand of thin, damp hair, "instead of wasting time with that beast of yours."

Katherine looked at his blond hair grown dirty in the rain, the uncommon flush of his pale face and said nothing.

Joints of meat, slabs of dark bread and jugs of ale were laid on a trestle pulled near the fire. The hunting party fell on it, tossing still heavily-meated bones to the dogs dancing hopefully around them.

Katherine sent for a kitchen maid and took her to one side.

"We are to prepare a feast of the stag for the day after next. Tell the cook to have ready these things also."

A small pucker formed between Katherine's eyebrows and she ticked a number of items off on her fingers.

"I think that will do."

The woman nodded and Katherine released her.

"We will have that rogue Victor of Stonehaven," Nathaniel said between mouthfuls. "I am told he has stirring tales of Crecy. We will hear them."

Katherine was not sure that a man such as Lord Victor would take kindly to being summoned so peremptorily to a lesser castle. She had heard much of the man since coming to Crenfeld, both from the servants and the townspeople. Lord Victor's holdings were vast, his power with King Edward, strong. Even in the far reaches of the kingdom, he was notorious for his prowess in battle and joust. It was only due to an injury he had suffered at Crecy that he had withdrawn from the king's war and the towns-people were proud that such a man had chosen to take up residence just a few miles west of Claringdon in Stonehaven Castle. In fact, he even held an interest in their manor, sharing it jointly with Nathaniel's uncle. Since his uncle's interest was now come to Nathaniel, Lord Victor might perhaps indulge her husband.

Uneasily, Katherine recalled a conversation she had overheard between the usher and a kitchen maid, remarking on the coincidence of Lord Victor's move coming just prior to the deaths of Lord Philip and Lady Elizabeth. The implication of their conversation was clear but surely a man of his great wealth and property would not covet a half interest such as theirs.

She smiled ruefully. Greed and ruthlessness was how most men acquired their wealth. Her own father had always seized every opportunity to increase his holdings by fair means, or if need be, by treachery.

Katherine yawned and chided herself for thinking such things. The day had been long and she was tired, her weary mind weaving a tangle of intrigue where there was none. Beatrice had been about to say something today, though. What, she would probably never know.

She watched the trio absently, Nathaniel pacing before the fire expounding on the hunt in minute detail, Sir Charles grinning and nodding, Beatrice following Nathaniel's every move and gesture with her hard bright little eyes, her hands clasped before her face as if in religious rapture.

They looked such fools. She had hoped the move to Crenfeld might improve her humour and make life more interesting. But the idle pace of castle life soon grew tiresome and she was as discontent as ever. She must rally herself. The feast Nathaniel proposed would be the first since their arrival. Perhaps she would meet someone other than the tedious round of courtiers and hunters. The record book had finally been located at the bottom of the chained chest in their room, buried under a pile of plate. After briefly satisfying herself it was more or less current, she placed the record book in the solar for later inspection. That would be something with which to exercise her mind. She yawned again, more broadly still.

"I believe I will wish you all good night," she said to no one in particular. "It has been a long day."

"As you wish, pet," Nathaniel answered distractedly, his back still to her and returning quickly to his conversation with Sir Charles and Lady Beatrice.

Katherine passed through the silent halls and gratefully crawled under the warmth of her miniver coverlet.

CHAPTER 4

ON THE MORNING OF THE FEAST, Katherine woke to the sound of humming. A little girl crouched before the hearth, trilling a cheery tune as she lay out the wood and set it alight. Her small face was framed in fuzzy blonde curls, her plump cheeks pink as new roses. The child paused intermittently to purse her red lips and blow up the flames. With the critical eye of a craftsman, she scrutinized her work, gingerly rearranging several pieces of wood. The child appeared satisfied and sat back on her heels, plucked the shavings from her skirt and clapped her hands together to shake off any dust.

"That's a wonderful fire, Alice," Katherine whispered.

Little Alice scrambled to her feet, her smile broad and proud, her blue eyes sparkling.

"Mama showed me, Lady Katherine."

The girl darted a quick look at the sleeping Nathaniel. His head was thrown back, mouth open, a rhythmic noise somewhere between a grunt and a puff emerging from between his lips.

"I help her in the kitchen too," the girl went on. "Most especially now, what with her hand. Poor mama cut it on a fleshhook."

Alice screwed her face up in a pained expression, then her features cleared. "You should see me. I do the bread."

Alice made vigorous wrestling motions in the air, punctuated by short jabs. Katherine's lips twitched.

"You must be a great comfort to your mother."

"Oh, I am," the child agreed.

The round eyes regarded Katherine for a moment then her little body swirled into motion once again.

"Mama will need me in the kitchen. Your basin is here."

She pointed to a bowl of water on the hearth. "I'll bring your breakfast after Mass. Excuse me."

Alice bowed with a grand flourish, beamed at Katherine, then skipped out of the room.

Katherine yawned. Such energy. Days like this were meant for keeping to one's bed. Through the bedchamber's rain-spattered window, the sky was leaden, the sun a vague glimmer behind black clouds. She sighed. Another miserable day.

Shivering, Katherine rose quickly and warmed herself before the fire. Gradually her exposed skin went from gooseflesh-white to rosy pink. On mornings like these she regretted the frailty of her frame, the closeness of flesh to bone. Katherine plunged her hands into the basin Alice had set before the fire. The water was warm now and she held her hands in the liquid until they turned pink, then washed her face. Looking about for her clothes, she noticed the edge of a sleeve dangling from the stone fire-hood. She stood on her toes and pulled, face hot as she stretched up before the flames, her thick red hair tumbling in heavy waves to her bare waist. Chemise, tunic and surcoat dropped into her arms. Even her slippers. Bless Agnes. She was a gem of a woman. Katherine dressed quickly, absorbing their warmth. Mass would not be nearly so uncomfortable.

It was, however, poorly attended. Nathaniel had remained abed and only a few servants stood on the wooden floor. Katherine observed the service alone from her second story recess. Even the chaplain and his lone attendant seemed anxious to have done with it, the chaplain muttering his Latin dully and with little interest.

Mass over, Katherine met the chamberlain in the cold hallway.

"Will you do something for me please, Peter."

The man stopped in front of her and waited.

"I am going to bring out the silver cups and spoons. I will leave them on top of the chest. Would you take them into the hall for the kitchen staff to put out?"

The chamberlain nodded curtly and without returning her smile. He was obviously still smarting from Nathaniel's poor treatment on that first day, no doubt reinforced in the intervening days. Nathaniel was proving to be a difficult master, alienating even their personal servants.

Katherine watched the chamberlain's stiff back disappear down the staircase, then softly entered the bedchamber. Nathaniel was nowhere about and she wondered briefly if Peter had been in their chamber. Nathaniel was always forgetting something and sending others off to fetch it. The room was different somehow. She could not put her finger on what it was, but it seemed changed. She frowned and shook her head, then bent over the chest and dug out the silver cups and spoons, closed the lid and set them carefully on top.

She was grateful to find her temmes loaf and wine already laid out on the hearth. The small loaf of dark bread was soft, and still warm from the ovens. The yeasty sweetness and rich aroma of wheat and rye set Katherine's mouth to watering. Unfortunately, the wine was not nearly as good and so gritty she had to sieve it between her teeth. Disgusted after only a few mouthfuls, she threw it on the fire. The flames lowered in a protest of sibilant hissing, then recovered with much crackling and popping. Efficient little Alice had already removed the basin of washing water so she could not even drink that. Katherine swept the bread-crumbs from her skirt and clutched her mantle more closely around her shoulders. It was time she visited the kitchen in any case, and was glad she had chosen to wear a woollen mantle. It was lined with rabbit fur, but still she shivered.

The air seemed not nearly warm enough for a summer's day and the long corridor to the kitchen was cold and dark and silent. Half-melted tallow candles guttered and flickered on wall brackets, her hurrying shape casting long, quivering shadows against the stones.

She hoped she had not made a mistake by waiting until morning to visit the kitchen. Yesterday had been taken up with the business of ensuring all invitations were made up and delivered. She quickened her step and was relieved when she reached the warmth and bustle of the kitchen.

It was a sizeable room in the rear corner of the inner ward. Three immense fireplaces stood against the long outside wall, all blazing hotly, orange flames curling around thick tree limbs. Partially burned logs, charred black on top and grey with ash beneath, lay on a glowing layer of pulsing red chunks. Two stone bread ovens stood along the shorter inside wall, faggots tightly tied and laid flat beneath them ready for firing.

A long table occupied the middle of the room and it was around this table that most of the activity was centered.

Kitchen staff was intent on pounding meats, blending a variety of sauces and preparing doughs and pastries. Bending to their tasks, they chattered and jostled one another in friendly fashion.

At the nearest fireplace a man with crooked shoulders and bandy legs looked up from turning a spit heavy with the stag's carcass. Katherine smiled at him and his grey-bristled jaw dropped in a lopsided grin.

She had met Old Henry the first time she inspected the kitchen and found, to her surprise, that the cook was a woman.

"Ah," Henry had sighed, "Jacko — him as was her husband — he was cook. Fine cook too. But she, she were ever railin' on 'im, 'til he fair leaped into 'is grave fer deliverance."

Katherine recalled the black look he had cast in Grace's direction. Tall and rawboned and strong as any man, Grace stepped into the position her husband vacated by his death as if it were her right. And according to Old Henry, "There weren't no man bold enough to take her up on it. So there she be, sharp-tongued viper."

The "viper" was further instructing little Alice in the complexities of bread making, her movements made clumsy by the heavy bandages hampering her hand. But Alice was an eager pupil and the dough received an alarming pumelling under her strong little hands. Grace clucked her approval and moved on.

Katherine watched Grace make the kitchen rounds, impressed again by her proficiency in managing its large staff. Grace checked on the progress of those at the middle table, nodding curtly if satisfied and barking her displeasure if not. She kindled the faggots under the bread ovens, tasted stews and soups boiling in great iron cauldrons suspended over the fireplaces by hooks and chains and angered Old Henry by telling him he must turn the spit faster. He muttered darkly and glowered, but leaned more heavily to his task. Katherine felt a pang of envy. Grace had something useful to do, while she . . .

Grace noticed Katherine standing in the doorway and executed an awkward curtsy.

"Come, come," she said, lumbering to one side. "We are readying for the great banquet."

Katherine smiled and moved into the kitchen, at once enveloped in the flavourful aroma of smoking and roasting meats, savory sauces and spiced pies. The hum of conversation slackened and the kitchen staff left off work to welcome their mistress. Some were inclined to be overlong in their greeting and received the back of Grace's big hand. Alice smiled prettily but did not leave the bread table. Katherine expected she would be cook when Grace grew too old. But would the vigorous Grace ever admit to being unable to govern the kitchen? Katherine thought it unlikely and smiled at the image of Grace, bowed and grey-headed, swinging switches at an ancient, but still defiant, Henry.

"Your daughter is a lovely child," Katherine said.

"Works right well," Grace replied gruffly. "Not like some."

She scowled at Old Henry who pretended not to hear.

"Has the butler brought in the wine yet?" Katherine asked.

Grace pointed to a row of jugs. "Over there, next to sink."

Katherine removed the knotted wooden stoppers, intending to decant a little wine from each. Sniffing the first she decided to forego sampling it. It was sour-smelling and thick with mould. The next two jugs poured out heavy and greasy and tasting of pitch. The last appeared to be from the same gritty swill served at breakfast.

Katherine was appalled. She had never tasted anything so deplorable. She stood up quickly, giving a none too gentle nudge of her foot to one of the jugs, that set it rocking.

"Is this all the wine there is?"

Grace shuffled over. "Why? Summat wrong with it?"

"It is undrinkable," Katherine said. "Barely fit for pig fodder. We cannot possibly serve any of this to our guests. Surely there are better wines in the castle. Where is the wine we have been drinking? This is not the same."

The cook rubbed her hands on her apron and frowned, then her face brightened.

"You'd be meanin' the wine as was served at high table, would you?"

"Yes, of course. And?"

Grace sniffed. "Father Simon has it. Only a few butts were left and they've been used up. So I had these . . . "

"The priest?" Katherine interrupted. It was her turn to look perplexed. "Why?"

"After your good husband's uncle died, God bless 'im . . . " Here she paused and executed a hasty cross on her chest. " . . . and the steward slipped off, dog that he were, father saw to running of manor. He took the wine." Grace sniffed. "Said he couldn't leave it for servants to drink."

Katherine heaved a sigh. She supposed that had been a wise precaution. The servants would have surely lapped it up. Still, she needed it and he should have returned it before now.

"This will not do for our guests," Katherine told the butler once he had been summoned. "Pour it out or mix it with the swine feed. Then take a cart and as many of the mesnie as can be spared from the wall and fetch back our cellar wines. Father Simon sheltered them in the church in the absence of the steward and has forgotten to send them back."

The butler smirked into his hand. "Yes, my lady. At once. Ah, my lady?" The man's sharp eyes were bright. "If the holy father is unwilling to return them?"

"Why should he be unwilling? They are our wines. Tell him I appreciate his foresight but it is necessary for the wine to be decanted before my guests arrive. As he is one of the guests, I expect he will not want any of this tar either."

The butler began to move away and Katherine called after him. "When you have the wines in the buttery, ask Grace for some table vessels. One of the butts should be sufficient. If not, you may unstop a second. Now, hurry on. There is only a short time to the banquet."

A bit later Katherine heard the portcullis groaning against the pull of the chains. Satisfied the wine would be returned in time, Katherine hurried back to her chamber. She wanted Agnes to help her put up her hair. When she entered the room, Agnes was in anxious conversation with the wardrober.

"See here, Hubert," she said. "That gown will wrinkle if you lay it like that. Let me."

Agnes elbowed the man aside and smoothed the sleeves and skirt with gentle fingers.

"You see," she breathed, eyes aglow. "Such a beautiful dress."

Hubert sniffed and bobbed to Katherine on his way out. Agnes dragged her eyes from the garment with difficulty.

"Oh, Lady Katherine. Never have I seen anything so beautiful. Lady Elizabeth had no such finery."

"Will you help me into it, Agnes? Our guests will be arriving at any time."

Agnes rushed to the hearth. "I'll just stir up the fire a little won't I, so you don't catch cold. Scarce seems like summer. So much rain."

Agnes poked the cinders vigorously and added logs until the fire was roaring.

"Good, good. Now it'll be proper warm."

Katherine slipped out of her morning clothes and Agnes consigned them to a perch, draping the plain woolen garments as carefully as if they had been fine sendal. Katherine watched, saddened by the inequities that caused poor Agnes to admire even her commonest dress. And yet she could not make a gift of it to Agnes, for her fellows would mock her and charge her with vanity, even though the dear woman had not a trace of jealousy in her character but served her mistress with devotion and contentment.

"Is something amiss, my lady?" Agnes fixed curious eyes on Katherine.

Katherine shook her head.

"No, no. It is nothing," she said briskly. "Help me with my gown."

Agnes all but clucked, fussing over her like a mother hen. "You fair take my breath away, you do," Agnes prattled. "Why you're thin as a twig. And your skin. Like new snow. You'll strike men dumb as stones," she said proudly.

Katherine caressed the pink damask fabric, her fingers gliding with pleasure over the raised embroidery of roses ornamenting the material. It was an exquisite dress, sewn with great care. The gown's neckline revealed the whiteness of her shoulders and throat and showed the slender softness of her figure to the hips, where the skirt fell full to the floor in ever-widening folds. The sleeves were close-fitting and buttoned from elbow to wrist with tiny white pearls. Four close-packed strings of pearls encircled her long, pale neck.

Katherine stood before the window, the black afternoon behind it and the glow of the fire before, transforming the glass into a mirror. She turned slowly, admiring the graceful lines of the heavy pink gown, skirts rustling richly with every move.

Katherine could see Agnes reflected in the window behind her, hands clasped in front of her face, completely unaware of the incongruity of her thick, roughly clad figure next to the splendour of her mistress.

"Agnes, would you comb my hair for me?" Katherine asked.

"Shall I coil it? Will you wear a gorget?"

"No, it will not stay. It slips out. Just this gold net, I think. And my circlet. Yes, it is pretty," she said, at the gasp of admiration from Agnes.

"My father bought it for me when I was a girl. He said the twinkling stones made him think of captured stars."

Agnes ran a comb through Katherine's thick hair, steadying her head with one hand and pulling the comb through briskly until the russet tresses gleamed. With quick, deft fingers she covered Katherine's hair with a thin gold net and gently settled the narrow jewelled circlet on her forehead. Agnes stepped back and cocked her head to one side.

"Lady Katherine, were I the king himself I could not imagine a more queenly consort."

Katherine gave a deep curtsy. "My liege," she said, fluttering her lashes extravagantly.

Agnes giggled then clapped a sobering hand to her mouth and dropped a curtsy in the direction of the doorway. Nathaniel had returned.

"Sir," she said, and slipped from the room.

"Where is my chamberlain?" Nathaniel cried in distressed tones. "It is time I was dressed. People are starting to come."

Katherine patted his shoulder. "Never mind. I will tend to them. Here is Peter."

Mounting clamour in the great hall reached to the bedchamber. The hall was indeed filling with guests. Appraising herself with the aid of a small round mirror, Katherine applied a little cheek rouge then gathered her skirts, swirled down the narrow staircase, through the short passage and into the hall. That heads turned was not, in fact, because she was mistress of Crenfeld. Could she but see herself as others did, she would see a slender young woman of elegant carriage. She would see the striking contrast of dark finely arched brows, brilliant green eyes and lustrous red hair against the milky whiteness of her skin. She would see softly rounded cheeks, an elongated tilt to the emerald eyes and an answering incline of delicate lips the colour of summer-ripened cherries. And she would hear the musical resonance in her voice when she paused for personal greetings among her guests.

But she did not see that. She saw crowds of people, all with eyes turned in her direction, making her nervous and self-conscious. She felt that she floundered through the throng and could not remember a single word she spoke to any of them.

At the high table, Sir Charles kicked back his chair, eyes bright. "My dear Lady Katherine. Pray be seated next to me."

Katherine hesitated then took the chair beside him. He pressed a damp hand over hers.

"You are indeed the loveliest of women," he whispered "And I your most humble servant."

Katherine concealed her discomfort with a smile and a polite lowering of dark lashes.

Beatrice looked tawdry in a vivid blue gown that pressed about her too closely, emphasizing the heavy folds of flesh accumulating down her back.

"I apologize for my lateness." Katherine smiled at her. "Nathaniel will be along presently."

Katherine did not recognize the man and woman sitting side by side to her left but knew them to be their neighbours to the west. So, he had come after all. Lord Victor was a great bear of a man with a tangle of unruly thick blond hair. His face was lean and brown, with clean-shaven cheeks and a deeply cleft chin. She was surprised. She had expected a sleek and crafty courtier.

Lord Victor looked on her with intelligent grey eyes and the hand he offered was hard and strong. Katherine winced in anticipation of his grip but barely felt a warm pressure before he released her hand. The beautiful dark woman with him gave Katherine a radiant smile. She was a gorgeous creature. All the richness of a painted tapestry; thickly plaited shining black hair, heavily lashed luminescent dark eyes, a lush figure encased in a brilliant crimson gown, jewels glittering around her neck and in her hair. And all her movements with the gentle grace of an ethereal.

To her right, save the empty chair reserved for Nathaniel, sat Father Simon, clad in the finest of ecclesiastical robes. A sweetish cloying scent wafted about his person, perhaps emanating from the thick bouquet of white roses nodding their delicate heads over the sides of a silver urn placed in front of him. Katherine knelt before the priest who offered a thin hand the unfortunate colour and texture of boiled whitefish. She stood just as Nathaniel made his entrance and took his place beside her. He loved to be the center of attention and Katherine had to admit that for all his shortcomings as a master, he was an excellent host. He beamed down on the assemblage.

"Thank you all for coming," he said grandly. "The hour grows late and I know everyone will be hungry."

He turned to Katherine and smiled down on her. "My wife and I welcome you to our humble feast," he said, then executed an abbreviated bow in Father Simon's direction.

"Will you return thanks, father?"

The priest nodded a solemn affirmative and rose carefully. He spread his robes over the arms of the chair, the gold threads running through the red samite glinting richly in the candlelight. He prayed at some length and in the Latin of the Church, allowing Katherine a surreptitious examination of the tables.

All seemed to be in order. The great silver salt cellar was well polished and shone in the centre of the head table. There was a sufficient supply of candles at all tables, along with smaller salt cellars. Each table bore a small nef, the largest in full sail before her. The little jewel-encrusted ships brimmed with the spices she had chosen this morning. The correct number of knives, spoons and drinking vessels appeared to be laid out. Katherine was satisfied and lowered her eyes for the remainder of the prayer.

Thanks to the Almighty having been given, the horn blew and kitchen servants bore basins and towels into the hall led by a minstrel playing gently on the viele, his bow merely touching the strings. It was a sweet tune and quieted the clamour while hands were washed.

Nathaniel leaned forward around Katherine to speak to Lord Victor.

"It is a great pleasure to have you at our table sire."

Victor looked up from scrutinizing already clean fingers. "I expect it is," he said drily. "One should always gild the hook and bait it so the barbs seem less painful."

Nathaniel's eyes widened. "I do not take your meaning, sir. You speak in riddles."

"Since the death of your uncle," Victor explained, "there has been a remarkable and considerable increase in the cost of doing business with your manor."

There came a barely perceptible rustling from the priest and he reached out absent fingers to caress the roses decorating the table.

"I am certain there is some mistake, Lord Victor." Nathaniel frowned. "We were unable to reach Crenfeld as quickly as we hoped and found the steward had abandoned his duties. If there is an error in our accounting to you it will be put right, I assure you."

Katherine listened intently. She had forgotten all about the wretched account book. It remained untouched in the solar.

"You see," the woman beside Victor laughed. "All will be well."

She turned her splendid black eyes on Nathaniel. "You must not mind Victor. He behaves badly. In fact, he has no manners at all," she continued airily.

Katherine smiled a rueful smile. They made such a handsome couple. One small and vivacious, the other a brooding colossus.

"Your wife is quite correct," Nathaniel said thinly. "Affairs of the manor will come later. This is a time for feasting."

Katherine and the dark beauty exchanged smiles. Lord Victor snorted.

"Wife? By all the saints I trust not. This silly creature is my sister, Ciscilla."

Ciscilla pouted good-naturedly at the slight and Katherine was relieved from the awkward moment by the arrival of the butler. Nathaniel nodded for him to pour out the wine.

During the discourse with Lord Victor, Father Simon had applied himself to his mazer. Once Katherine assured herself the wine was indeed that returned from the church, she turned to the priest.

"It was exceedingly prudent of you to house our wines, father. Few would think to guard another man's goods as well as he would his own."

The priest's pale eyes glinted. "Were I to know you required them, you would simply have had to ask and I would have sent them by my own butler," he murmured softly.

Katherine felt slightly rebuffed when he turned away to sip from his cup then look out over the company. She had insulted him somehow. She groaned inwardly. It was not only Nathaniel who antagonized the wrong people. She certainly had not intended any slight to the priest, but clearly he felt one. In future, she would try to think ahead at how her actions might be interpreted by others.

Katherine kept a watchful eye on the servants, scarcely touching a morsel on her trencher. The great hall rang with chatter and laughter. Candles flickered at each table, lighting up the steaming bowls. The blankmanger was thick and hot, each spoonful yielding a generous mouthful of chicken, in a broth of sugar-seasoned almond milk. The meat and fish pies were perfectly sauced with wine, mustard and carefully chosen herbs and spices. Peas and beans were sprinkled with onions and dearly-bought saffron. The *pièce de résistance* was borne into the hall; the stag's head cooked and replaced in its skin and still bearing the magnificent antlers. Chunks of venison were piled high around it. Spontaneous clapping erupted among the guests and Nathaniel and Katherine were enthusiastically toasted. The banquet was a success.

Charles took the opportunity to lay his hand over Katherine's once again.

"My dear Lady Katherine, you have outdone yourself."

Katherine forced her lips to form a smile. "You are very kind," she said.

"Indeed I would fain whisper more cordial compliments in your beautiful ears," the baron murmured, beginning to stroke the back of her hand with ardent fingers.

His attentions were noticed by Victor and Ciscilla. Ciscilla giggled into her own small hand while Lord Victor merely raised an eyebrow. Katherine snatched her hand away.

"Pray remember the presence of your wife. And my husband," she said sharply.

Charles rested smouldering eyes on her mouth, then heaving a deep sigh, fell back in his chair.

"You are right madam, of course. A more opportune time will present itself."

There would be no opportune time. Katherine pushed back her chair and stepped off the dais onto the hall floor where Nathaniel was already beginning to circulate among their guests. Most of Claringdon's merchants were in attendance. She put on a merry smile and spent the next hour moving from table to table accepting compliments on her gown and on the feast and exchanging village gossip.

When the kitchen staff began clearing things away and pushing aside tables, Nathaniel took a quick swallow of wine. He motioned for a minstrel to play some opening chords on the psaltery then began to sing a song of bygone years. His voice was somewhat reedy but he sang with great heartiness.

> *When I see winter return,*
> *Then would I find lodging,*
> *If I could discover a generous host,*
> *Who would charge me nothing!*

The guests laughed and stood and all joined in the familiar chorus as the rest of the musicians took it up on the harp, cornet and viele At the end of each refrain, the minstrel grasping a ring of bells, shook it as a dog would a rat.

When the tune was ended, games of checkers, back-gammon and chess were set up for those who preferred board games while at the far end of the hall two muscular men, naked to the waist, prepared to entertain with a wrestling match. They were eyed up and down, muttered over and had their arms felt of. Wagers were made and interested guests formed a ring about the wrestlers. The two men began circling each other for advantage.

This was an opportune time for Katherine to slip away to the solar and go over the records. She was not exactly sure why, but she was anxious to rectify things with Lord Victor, to clear up the matters that upset him and ease his mind. Tonight. Before Nathaniel might say something to him that they would all regret. No one would notice her. Certainly not Nathaniel, who was busy regaling wide-eyed townsmen with his hunting tales. The stag they had just consumed would have put up much more of a struggle from his tongue, than in truth and the number of dogs killed would increase immeasurably in the telling.

Katherine slipped through the crowded room quickly. She turned back at the doorway to satisfy herself everyone was occupied and noticed Lord Victor limping heavily on one leg and using a cane to steady himself. Katherine had not realized he was lame. It was a great pity an otherwise vigorous man should be so crippled. Many men returned from battle not quite whole and, even as fine a man as he, was not spared from such a blow. Still, it did not seem to bother the women all that much. They surrounded him like bottle flies. Nathaniel had paid a considerable amount of shield money to remain at home and away from war. The thought of any harm coming to his person horrified him, so the scutage was paid and he was spared any chance of suffering a like fate.

Katherine pushed open the door to the solar. A banked fire burned in the grate and the room was bare except for a small stool drawn up to a rough-hewn table. On the table sat a large book and a taper. Katherine poked a bit of floor straw into the fire and used it to light the taper. She seated herself on the stool, opened the book and studied its contents.

Earlier inspection of the manorial accounts seemed to indicate considerable overpayment for supplies and carting services. But as she sat and read, she realized things were far worse. Someone had made clumsy attempts to conceal outright theft.

She sighed heavily. Candles usually costing five pence a pound were recorded at eight pence a pound. Saffron, always an expensive spice, was recorded at twenty shillings a pound, double the usual cost. White wine, hopefully not the swill she had tasted in the kitchen, was recorded at a pound more a tun than previous purchases and carriage costs were outrageously high. It appeared too, that some expense had gone into repairs for the west wall of the outer ward. Brick prices were abnormal at twenty-five pence per thousand and artisan wages higher than was generally paid a master mason.

Katherine shook her head as she considered each page. Close scrutiny uncovered an increase in income from the sale of grain and ale, an increase not so cleverly diverted to personal pockets. Which pockets she could not tell, but undoubtedly the steward's. There would be no other reason for him to run off. She understood why Lord Victor was so angry. And they could likely expect more dissatisfaction among the townsmen.

She laced her fingers together, pressed the heels of her hands on the table and stretched weary arms. She would make an opportunity to pacify Lord Victor tonight and speak to Nathaniel about it tomorrow. She doubted, however, that Nathaniel had any experience in these matters. Perhaps she should speak to the priest. The Church had considerable holdings and must have suffered at least one dishonest steward. And Father Simon had looked after the day to day management for a short while just prior to their arrival. In any case, it was likely time she showed herself in his church. She had not attended the big stone church often, preferring the convenience of their own small chapel.

She remembered the first time well. It was soon after their arrival. Attired in a plain cloak and well-hooded, she had slipped into the sanctuary behind the rest of the worshippers. There had been none of the usual breaches found in other village churches. No rowdiness or stone slinging, no dripping of candle wax from the upper stalls. Only muted murmurings of conversation that ceased abruptly when the priest appeared. The congregation remained silent throughout the service, except to join in the Creed and Paternoster. Father Simon's pale blue eyes seemed lighted from inside with a fervour that was reflected in the intensity of his oration. The people stood in evident awe of their priest, and not of him only but also of the architectural splendors of their great stone church.

The skilled hands of an artist had been pressed into service on the walls of the chapel and presented superbly lifelike biblical scenes; the Last Supper, Daniel in the lion's den, Mary and the infant Jesus. Perhaps most eloquent of all were the clerestories high on the wall, depicting in startling detail the torments of the damned, writhing amid twining vines of red roses. It was disconcerting even in memory.

Katherine shook herself like a child shaking itself free after a roll in autumn leaves. The day was far spent and the guests would be hungry once more. She went to the kitchen.

"Would you prepare something for an evening meal."

"'Tis done, my lady," Grace beamed, pleased with her own foresight.

She pointed and Katherine saw that she had indeed. The center table was filled with steaming bowls of cut meats, lovage dressed in oil and vinegar, hot rampion boiled and sauced and huge baskets of strawberries and green and rewene cheeses.

Prompted by the odours from the kitchen, small groups of guests began trickling back into the great hall. The wrestlers were gone and a clump of noisy men pushed in from outside.

"Where have you been, pet?" Nathaniel's face was flushed. "The cocks fought well and I won every wager! A fine day, you agree?"

His heartiness continued throughout the abbreviated meal. Grace was mindful of Father Simon's disapproval of late suppers and his judgment that such indulgence made men gluttonous. Although he loosened his rigid restrictions at times like this, she had wisely kept the quantity to a minimum.

Once sufficient time had passed for all to taste of Grace's kitchen and the very good buttery wines, Nathaniel summoned the musicians. He bowed to Katherine.

"My dear," he said, with a nod to the man on the viele.

He drew Katherine to the center of the great hall. These were the times he lived for. Great crowds of people, all the attention, noise and excitement.

A sprightly tune romped from the strings of lutes and vieles. At a shout from Nathaniel, all joined in dancing a carole. Katherine had to admit he was an accomplished dancer. Their shoes rang on the bare floorboards and there was much good-natured shouting and hand clapping as they all sang and circled in the dance. The ladies' dresses fluted and floated like a multitude of colourful spinning tops and the men capered and leaped like youths.

The castle servants had been admitted to the hall to share in the late supper and Nory and Old Henry were drawn together by age and acid tongues.

"Dinner weren't same as when Jacko was in charge of kitchen," Old Henry grunted.

Nory thrust out her bony chin. "Was better."

Henry snorted. "That's as much as you know old woman. Ain't I been meat turner for both Jacko and Grace?"

Nory pushed her withered chest into his shrunken one. "And mighty poor job you've done 'em both ain't yer," she said, wagging a shriveled finger under his nose.

"I've heard Grace lashin' at yer. Lazy you is, through to the bone."

Henry skinnied up like a wizened fighting cock. "I won't be havin' that from you, old woman. I takes pride in me work. Best turner he ever had, Jacko said."

Nory sniffed and he glared at her.

"And don't I know right well where Grace comes by her sharp tongue," he continued. "You could cut stones with yorn."

Henry ensured the last word by elbowing Nory aside and quickly engaging someone else in conversation.

Nory grinned suddenly, her thin lips cracking. Nothing like a good set to. She stood considering a moment, then snatched up a joint of meat from the trestle table pushed against the wall and gnawed with gusto.

When the music changed and Katherine paused for a much-needed rest, she could not entice Nathaniel to do the same. He took another partner and, flushed of face and short of breath, he spun away. She found Lord Victor seated alone at a wall bench, his eyes on the flurry of colours swaying about the hall, a wine filled mazer cupped in his hands.

"May I?" she smiled, indicating the vacant spot next to him.

He stood slowly. "As you wish." He bowed in an absent way and reseated himself, continuing to watch the dancers and drink from his mazer.

Katherine cast about in her mind for a suitable way to apologize for the treachery of the steward. It would not be prudent to have Lord Victor as an enemy. Some of his income came from rents on property he owned in the south west quarter of Claringdon and he had certainly been correct about the prices charged him for carting and services. The steward had been particularly ruthless when it came to Lord Victor. For Nathaniel's sake she would do her best to be amiable. But it looked as if it might prove a more difficult task than she had anticipated. Victor Stafford did not seem inclined to talk, or even take notice of her presence.

"Your sister dances beautifully," Katherine ventured.

"M-m-m, she has been well schooled."

Katherine sat without speaking for some minutes, then blurted nervously, "My husband and I deeply regret any losses you suffered from our manor. It will be made right."

Victor Stafford bent forward, rested his elbows on his knees, cradled his mazer in his hands and turned to look at her. This posture brought his face uncomfortably close to her own and she could see a glint of mockery in the clear depths of his frank grey eyes.

"I will take the matter up with your husband another time, madam," he said.

Katherine became confused as he continued to look at her and words tumbled out of her mouth before she had time to gather them into coherent thought.

"It is only that I wanted you to know it was not Nathaniel's doing. The charges. They were not his fault."

She plunged on in agony, knowing she babbled and her face grew pink.

"The — the steward ran off before ever we came to Crenfeld. He was a greedy, unfaithful man. We — Nathaniel knew nothing of it."

Katherine grew even more uncomfortable as Lord Victor remained silent. Finally, when Katherine began to fear he would not answer at all, he took his eyes from her face, turned them back to the dancers, drained his mazer and stood.

"It is not for men's wives to defend them, madam," he said in a lazy, bland tone. "They must speak for themselves."

Katherine drew in her breath sharply. "I only meant to make our apologies and assure you it will be resolved," she said in a strangled voice.

"M-m-m," was all Lord Victor replied, staring past her to the dancers.

Katherine felt as if she might cry. She had tried to mollify the man but seemed only to have succeeded in giving him an opportunity to insult her. Her hurt immediately changed to anger and she had an impulse to swipe his cane out from under him so she could see him sprawl on the floor and know what it was to be as embarrassed as he had made her. He must have felt the fury in her eyes, for he turned a moment and the amusement in his own eyes made her seethe all the more. Although choking with repressed rage, Katherine fought to rise with casual dignity and walked stiffly out onto the crowded floor only to be swept up in some man's arms and danced around like a frenzied puppet.

The floor had become thick with drunken, boisterous men and women, plunging and spinning in wild abandon; the room grown warm with the heat of many bodies in motion. Katherine sagged dizzily in the arms of her partner, treading on his feet. The man frowned down at her through bleary eyes and thrust her at one of the other guests, a florid-faced perspiring man with fetid breath who crushed her to his hot chest. While she struggled to break free from his heavy arms, two men dropped to the floor almost beneath her feet, sprawling in a tangled heap of arms and legs. Beside her, still stinging from Nory's blistering tongue, Old Henry was taking offence at a remark made to him by a short, stocky man whose straight black hair hung limply over narrowed eyes.

"So little weasel," the short man spat. "Truth puts you in a pucker does it?"

"'Tis a black lie and I'll have yer eyes out for it!" cried Henry.

The dancing stopped. The minstrels faltered and grew silent. Henry's opponent swaggered out to meet him, hands on hips. Old Henry covered the short space separating them with surprising agility and dealt the heavier man a sharp blow to the chin. His opponent grunted and staggered, momentarily stunned. Henry leaped about cackling and pointing. With a roar, the man lowered his head and bore down on the old man. Henry was wiry and tenacious and although no real match for the stronger man, he fought on in grim determination.

The guests enjoyed this new diversion hugely. Someone began taking wagers and soon everyone was caught up in the brawl, shouting encouragement and bawling advice, accompanied by descriptive lunges and parries. The scuffle soon ended with Old Henry flat on his back and his opponent straddling him, his foot on his chest.

"See old man!" the victor cried. "You're no match for me. Save your talk for old crones and children."

Henry sputtered and squirmed but he was well and truly pinned. Finally the foot was removed and with a kick to Henry's ribs that set him coughing, the other man strode away chuckling and shaking his head. Those who had wagered unwisely followed the winner's example and toed the old man themselves before crowding the victor and joining him in a cup of wine.

Old Henry sat up slowly, gripping his side. Nory had moved to stand silently beside him. He saw her and glared through bloodshot eyes.

"Come to add yer boot to theirs, have ye."

Wordlessly the old woman extended her hand and kept holding it out until he grasped it with his own. They stared at each other for a moment or two and then carefully, Henry got to his feet. With Nory supporting him, he let her lead him to a seat. She left him briefly and came back carrying a cup of wine. Still saying nothing, she handed it to him. He looked puzzled but accepted the cup. As he tipped it back Nory scowled at him.

"Ye could have had him old man," she snarled fiercely. "If ye weren't so full of drink."

Henry gaped a moment then broke into a wide, foolish grin.

Katherine had had enough. Enough dancing, enough eating and definitely enough fighting. She did not care that Nathaniel had clapped the minstrels back to playing or that as mistress she was expected to stay. Everyone could dance and fight all night long if they cared to, she was going to bed.

She gathered up her skirts and stepped gingerly across the wine-stained floor. Nathaniel was flirting with the admittedly delightful Ciscilla, Henry and Nory sat in amazingly companionable silence, Lord Victor was deep in conversation with a pretty blonde woman and even Sir Charles had forgotten her and was dancing with one of the merchant's wives. Katherine felt neglected and peevish. With an impatient twitch of her shoulders, she sought the solace and quiet of her warm bed.

Sleep overwhelmed her almost at once, so she was barely conscious of Nathaniel clambering in beside her, nor did she hear his nasal snoring shortly afterward.

Quite suddenly Katherine's eyes flew open in a panic of suffocating fright. She had dreamed someone was choking her, the life being squeezed from her throat, leaving it sore and raw. But it was a waking nightmare. And it was not hands pressing the breath from her, it was smoke!

The green canopy over her head was in flames, a white-hot sheet, sweeping across the whole of the canopy in an instant. Sections of fiery cloth dripped onto the bedding and the heavy damask quilt began to smolder and puff into hungry orange teeth, eating great black rings in the material.

Galvanized with horror, Katherine clutched her night-clothes quickly and tightly to her body and flung from the burning bed.

"Nathaniel!" she screamed. "Nathaniel! Wake up!"

Katherine skirted the blaze, ran to his side of the bed and pulled at him frantically, pushing away the lead candle stand that had fallen across the bed. It crashed heavily onto the floor.

"Nathaniel! Nathaniel!"

Her husband lifted heavy lids, the leaping tongues of fire mirrored in his eyes. As they widened in terrified comprehension, he gave a wild shriek and drew his knees to his chest. Clutching his arms tight around his folded limbs, he began a high keening wail, rocking from side to side.

"No Nathaniel. You must come away! Hurry!"

What was wrong with him? Could he not see he would be burned? Katherine tried again and again to coax him from the bed but he seemed not to hear her. He continued to moan, his eyes wide and staring, his back pressed hard against the headboard.

The flames roared up the bedposts. Sparks snapped and arched off the blackening walnut lilies. Nathaniel stared with glassy eyes.

"The sons of the burning coal lift up to fly," he crooned, and reached out his hands.

Katherine grew frantic. She pulled at the fiery bedclothes and jerked them onto the floor, leaping out of the way. Tears furrowed her white cheeks and she started coughing as smoke filled and scorched her lungs. Blindly, she groped again for her husband, eyes cloudy and stinging, but the crimson tide had reached him and rent a howl of agony from his throat. His frenzied shrieks drove Katherine nearly hysterical.

"Take my hand!" she screamed. "Take my hand!"

The heat was intense and as Katherine plunged frantic arms through the flames, searing pain ripped tortured cries from her own lips. Screaming and screaming she tried to grab hold of her husband. But she could not reach him. Her vision dimmed and the rushing sound of a great wind filled her ears. Her knees buckled and she fell away from the bed to feel the rough planking scrape her cheek. A sudden draft of cool air blew over her inert body. She did not feel it.

CHAPTER 5

KATHERINE OPENED EYES DULL WITH PAIN. She blinked slowly. Her lids were blistered and swollen. They had put her in a bed in a corner of the solar. There was the table and even the taper by which she had read the account book. The account book, however, was gone. It seemed a long time ago.

She frowned and wished she had not. Her head ached. She glanced down at the arms lying on top of the bedsheets. They were completely swathed in bandages. Were they hers? She tried to move them, winced and was about to close her eyes again when the door opened and Agnes poked her head inside. Her somber face brightened.

"Oh, madam. You're awake!"

She turned and whispered briefly to someone behind her and then came to Katherine's side.

"We were so afraid for you. I've sent for the physic."

With gentle fingers Agnes brushed damp russet curls away from Katherine's forehead. Katherine ran her tongue over her dry lips. Her whisper was hoarse and weak.

"How-how long have I been here, Agnes?"

"Three days, my lady. Three days you lay as one near dead. You never moved."

"And Nathaniel? What of my husband?"

Agnes shook her head. "Gone, Madame. Gone," she said softly.

"Lord Victor tried to save him. He went back for him but it was too late. He couldn't reach him."

"Victor?"

"Yes, my lady. Most of the guests stayed that night. He and his squire were bedded in the stable. He heard the screams and . . . "

Katherine shuddered. The screams. Would they ever stop ringing in her ears? Poor, foolish Nathaniel. She was glad now she had not given him an heir. To bear a son as feckless as his father would be . . . Still. To be alone. She turned her face away from Agnes. Her eyes burned and she closed them.

Agnes observed Katherine's averted head and studied the hands in her own lap, unsure of what to say or do for her mistress. Just then, the physician entered. At the question in his raised eyebrows, Agnes shook her head.

"Now then, my lady," the physic said brusquely to Katherine's back. "We will look at those arms."

Katherine rolled over. The man standing before her did not look like a physician, just a kindly old man. She took in the plump, jovial face, the heavy black beard, thickly grizzled with grey and the shaggy head of unruly hair. His plain woolen tunic was aged but clean, his hose carefully mended where they had worn through at the knees. If nothing else, he cheered her merely by his heartiness. The smile he bestowed crinkled the edges of a pair of sparkling black eyes.

Katherine managed a weak smile of her own. "Have I given you much difficulty, physician?"

"You must call me Benjamin, my lady, and no, you have not. Now, let us see how those arms of yours look."

Carefully, Benjamin unwound her bandaged arms. Katherine gasped when she saw the red puckered flesh but the physician said nothing. He turned each arm with gentle hands and nodded approvingly.

"Yes, yes. I am pleased. They will be quite useful again."

"Such an ugly red," Katherine protested.

Benjamin nodded, "Yes, madam. That they carry the colour of the flames is regrettable but unavoidable."

"Will they — will they always be so?"

Benjamin considered, turning each arm slightly. "They may fade somewhat over time, but yes, the skin will remain much as you see it."

Katherine studied her crimson arms anew. Oh how cruel, how cruel! She swallowed hard, blinked back the tears clouding her sad, green eyes and spoke with effort.

"Thank you physician. Benjamin. You have been most kind. Will you replace the bandages, please?"

She held out her arms and turned her face away.

"No my lady. They do not require any further wrapping."

"Oh but surely, surely." It was a plea.

Seeing her dismay, Benjamin's black eyes softened. "You will soon grow accustomed to their strangeness. I am sorry I can offer you no greater hope. You must be thankful to God for your life, madam."

Katherine was not so sure. She watched the physician gather the soiled bandages and push them into a small leather pouch, then move to leave.

"I will look in on you again in a day or two. Oh, good," he added. "You have a visitor."

A tall figure loomed up beside the physician and Victor Stafford passed into the solar. Katherine slipped her hands and arms under the blankets and was rewarded with excruciating pain. She pressed her teeth deeply into her lips to keep from crying out. Victor pulled a stool to the side of the bed and searched her face with solemn grey eyes.

Katherine's own eyes had sunk into black-rimmed holes. Gone was the snap and glitter of fury he had elicited from their emerald depths only days ago. Her cheeks were hollow, their delicate bloom faded to a pallid hue. Lines of misery creased her pale brow and pinched in the corners of her mouth. Gone too was the sumptuous beauty of her hair. It hung about her tiny cheerless face in thick, lackluster cords.

"You are awake," he said simply.

Katherine could only nod.

"Do you have pain?"

Katherine shrank back into her pillows. "Some," she said in a low voice.

"I tried to save your husband, but . . . "

"I know," Katherine cut in. "I — am grateful you tried."

Victor ran his long brown fingers through the heavy thatch of hair at the back of his neck, then leaned forward and clasped his hands between his knees. He regarded her in silence for a few moments.

"Show them to me," he said at last.

Katherine opened her eyes wide. The colour came up in her face.

"What . . . what did you say?" she stammered.

"Show them to me. Your arms."

"I . . . I do not see why you want to look at them." Her voice was small.

"Because you do not want me to. You have hidden them."

How could he ask her that? To humiliate her? Suddenly her lassitude was replaced with anger and she snatched her arms out from under the covers, ignoring the shooting stabs of pain accompanying the abrupt movement.

"There! See them? Are they not beautiful!" she cried shrilly.

Then to her horror she began to sob. Great gulping sobs that shook her slender frame and blinded her eyes with scalding tears.

"Yes they are," Victor said, his own voice strained and hoarse. "Quite beautiful."

Katherine looked at him. She thought for a moment that his own eyes mirrored her pain, then he blinked and it was gone.

"Do you know why?"

Katherine shook her head mutely.

"Because they give witness to a selfless act of courage. You imperilled your own life for the life of the man you loved."

"But I did not save him," Katherine moaned, dropping her head. "I did not save him. Nor did I love him," she added bitterly. "I let him die and for my penance I am left with these."

Victor sat without speaking for a time.

"I will tell you a tale," he said suddenly, "of how I got this." He thumped his right thigh with his walking stick. "It was at Crecy. You may have heard."

Katherine nodded.

He cleared his throat and began.

"On August 24th and just at dawn, we crossed a ford called Blanche Toque. We waited for the tide to fall back and went in waist deep, barely ahead of the French van at our heels. Even as we reached the far side, French horsemen rushed through the morning mists. They captured a few wagons but nothing more. We marched on to Crecy, a little village between two small streams. South of those streams was a thick wood stretching across for ten miles. It was the only barrier between our army and the French. The king raised his standard near a windmill. You know the king. His pavilion was of such a magnificent size as to make the windmill look small." Victor paused as he recalled the scene.

Katherine smiled in spite of herself. The king was well known for his flourish. She could almost see the regal blond head of England holding court beneath the azure and gold silks as if in his own palace, calling for minstrels and draining flagons of wine with the scores of guests she heard he entertained in the wars. His flamboyance was much admired and indulged by his subjects. He was a popular king for he had hung, drawn and quartered the hated and vicious cuckold, Mortimer, who had seduced his mother, Isabella, and contrived the ghastly murder of his father, Edward II. The young king banished his mother from court for her part in the affair, ensuring her dower lands and holdings were returned to the crown and she herself removed to Castle Rising in a lonely part of East Anglia. But with his typical graciousness, Edward never permitted anyone to speak of his mother with contempt but only as Madam, the king's mother. The people loved him as much for this tender chivalry as they did for his military successes. Katherine knew men gladly followed him to their deaths, so proud were they to serve with their king.

Victor was continuing.

"The wagons were set up behind the king's pavilion, the campfires lighted. And we waited. Later in the day, word came that Philip of France was at Abbeville, beyond the Crecy wood and had amassed a huge army of one hundred thousand men. The odds were desperate but King Edward was unmoved. Seated upon his favourite white charger, he merely looked over the tops of the trees and said, 'This is the land of my lady mother's. We will wait for them here.' The night passed uneventfully, as did the following day. The sky was black and it rained heavily all that morning and afternoon. Close to four o'clock we heard the cry go up. 'Bowmen!' — and saw a line of Genoese archers rounding the end of Crecy wood.

"Just then, the rain stopped, the clouds moved aside and the sun shone down. On our backs and in the faces of the French. An omen, as it turned out. Thousands of mounted French knights fanned out behind the Italian archers, driving them forward. The archers tried to hold their ground and fire their first volley but the knights kept pressing against them. When finally they let loose their quarrels and we returned fire, some kind of confusion followed. The archers attempted to fall back out of range of our longbows but the French fools on horseback mistook their caution for cowardice and plunged through the poor beggars, trampling them underfoot and running them through to clear the way for the foot soldiers pouring in behind the knights. Madness overtook the French. They engaged us without forming proper battle lines and fought in a fever of undisciplined and disorganized frenzy. I cut my way down a slope thick with the bodies of men and horses. My own horse found it difficult to keep his footing on ground made so slippery with rain and blood. Suddenly, three men on horseback galloped up to meet me, their horse bridles tied together so they formed a solid wall. I was moving too fast to avoid them. We clashed, and I managed to get my sword into one of them before the man in the middle drove his blade through my leg, just here. I fell and rolled away and they pounded on up the hill. I tried to get up but there was no strength in that leg. I used my sword for support for I knew the French would be on me in an instant. A rider bore down on me even as I raised myself and cut my feet out from under me. I fell on my face and when I looked up he had dismounted. Even now I can see my blood on his steel and the triumph in his eyes. He smiled and raised his weapon. Then he froze. His face went slack and he crumpled on top of me. I could hardly believe my good fortune. One of our arrows was sunk between his shoulder blades. I was weak and by the time I pushed him off I became senseless. When I awoke it was to a deserted field, empty except of fallen men like myself. I could see a line of riders and footmen along the crest of the hill but could not make out if they were ours or theirs. Then I heard a voice asking me if I lived."

Here Victor laughed. "It was our physician, Benjamin. He told me we had carried the day, ordered a litter and had me moved into camp. That night a prayer of thanks was given to the Almighty with every fighting man who could, bent on his knees. The next day the dead on the field were examined and I learned that the man who gave me this was the king of Bohemia. He was quite blind and they found him amongst the bodies, still tied to the two knights who led him into battle. The French losses were heavy. Almost thirty-one thousand of their men lay dead on the field while we lost a few hundred only. And that is how I came to be the cripple you see now."

Victor could not help the bitterness that crept into his voice. "No noble combat. Felled by a blind man."

He looked her full in the face. "So do not be too ashamed of your scars. To try to save a man's life takes courage. And for a woman to make the attempt for a man she does not love, is nobler still. Do not be ashamed of your heart either, madam. You cannot help for whom it beats. Mine beat hard for my country and I failed to help her. That she was victorious while I lay in a stupor is little consolation to me now. I can never fight for her again."

"But you carry no shame," Katherine protested. "Your honor is intact. There were three men and you said yourself your blade found one of them. Surely you cannot expect more of yourself than that?'

Victor's lean face remained impassive and she thought perhaps he had not heard her. His eyes seemed fixed on some distant point beyond the little solar room. Suddenly he blinked and refocused on her face.

"Your honor also remains, madam. You did what you could. Now you, as I, must go on with life as God has given it. Bestir yourself. The castle and manor demand their mistress."

He leaned forward. "You do not want Father Simon to seize your wines once again to protect them from your servants," he said in a conspiratorial whisper.

Katherine laughed. It was painful but it felt good. "How did you know of that?"

Victor winked broadly and laid a finger alongside his nose. "Ah, madam," he said. "I have my spies."

Katherine laughed again. "They must be very good. I did not know myself until the day of the banquet. The banquet," she murmured. "Was it only a few days ago? It seems a very long time — a life time."

"Perhaps it is. You are the lady now. And without a husband you will need to be very shrewd."

He slapped his knees and rose. The small intimacy was past.

"I must be on my way. Business may wait for another day. When you are yourself again. But I will expect a reckoning of those onerous carting charges."

"You shall have it," Katherine promised.

Victor retrieved the cane leaning against her bed and limped out of the room, leaving Katherine to look pensively after him and wonder why he had no wife. He could be charming when he set his mind to it. But perhaps he found women dull company. He certainly had little patience for his lovely sister. Katherine smiled at the thought of the particularly ebullient butterfly that was Ciscilla. She needed a friend like that. Someone carefree and cheerful. Someone with whom to prattle away an afternoon. But Victor was right. Now she needed to get out of this bed.

Katherine found it was no simple matter to constrain her aching limbs to rouse. She groaned a little when she sat up. Agnes left the corner stool on which she sat quietly during Katherine's interview with Lord Victor.

"He ought not to have spoken to you so roughly," she fretted. "His sister is right. He knows nothing of how to speak to a lady. If you will forgive my saying so, he has few manners, even if he is a great lord."

"But he is right, Agnes. I feel far too sorry for myself. Here, help me up. It is time I saw where they have lain Nathaniel."

Agnes looked doubtful but assisted her mistress to rise and don warm clothes.

"Shall I come?" she asked.

Katherine shook her head. "No. It is something I need to do alone, Agnes. But thank you. And thank you for your kindness in tending me these past few days."

Although her disapproval was obvious, Agnes merely shook her head and withdrew.

Katherine made her way slowly through the great hall, into the ward and over the bridge. As usual these days, the sun glimmered but dimly through a screen of dark clouds. Katherine could have ridden out to the churchyard but the thought of having to grasp the reins in her hands made her wince. The wind was brisk and flayed her cheeks with welcome colour. The scent of the fresh, crisp air revived her senses, her spirits brightened and her steps grew more confident.

Upon reaching the churchyard she felt considerably strengthened in mind and body. The iron gate to the cemetery creaked in resistance and it took her several tries to force it enough for entry. The small enclosure contained a litter of listing rough wooden crosses, sprouting weeds at their bases, and sturdier stone markers standing inside individual short iron fences. The air was icy amongst the markers, the wind curling around the stones and crosses and forcing her to hunch her shoulders against its chill. Her muscles protested and a thread of pain coursed down her arms.

She found Nathaniel's grave easily, surrounded as it was by newly dug black earth. She stared for a long time at the freshly carved stone marking her husband's final resting-place. No emotion disturbed her mind or heart. No sorrow. No dread. Nothing. After a while she stepped closer and slowly ran her hand over its surface. 'Nathaniel Fendlay, died July, the year of our Lord, thirteen hundred and forty-eight'. So few words to mark a man's life on earth. Even though there had been no love between them, he had been kind. But who would know. There was nothing to tell of his hospitality, his grace in the dance, the care he took with his favourite falcon. Nothing, in fact, to recall him to mind at all. He was simply a name carved in stone. A name that would be forgotten amid other names on other stones as would her own when her time came. And the grasses would grow up and around the stones and cover them until even their names were lost.

She sighed, then turned to look at the stone beside his. It was a very small stone, older and crumbling a little. But there was a short verse etched on its rough surface. Her lips moved as she read it and tears stung the backs of her green eyes.

Oh, for the kiss of lips now cold, for the touch of a hand grown still.

Surely it took great sorrow of heart to inspire such an inscription. Could she ever love someone like that? Could anyone ever love her like that? She smiled a wry, sad smile. No, not with these hideously deformed arms. No one would desire her now. Victor Stafford could try to console her with noble talk of bravery. That was all right for men. They should bear scars of battle and acts of valor. But men wanted their women soft and unmarred. No, she would have to content herself with being both lord and lady to the people of Claringdon. She must throw herself into the business of the manor. If men would not love her, she would make them respect her. Katherine gathered up her skirts, turned her back to the graveyard and set her face toward Crenfeld Castle.

CHAPTER 6

FATHER SIMON WATCHED THE FENDLAY WOMAN in the graveyard with distaste. Her presence irritated him and he soon retreated from his vantage place at the sanctuary window to his private rose garden — an enclosed space accessible only through his living quarters. Father Simon had a great appreciation for beauty and he guarded this secret garden jealously, allowing no one to enter it. He breathed in the fragrant air, revelling in the sweetness that only he might enjoy. Walking slowly, he paused before each carefully chosen specimen, admiring the delicacy of one, the vibrant hues of another. It was a tranquil environment where beautiful things flourished under his hand.

As a young man, Simon came to terms with the fact that beautiful women found him repugnant and that he was permitted their company only as he became a man of power and influence. But the delicate beauties of the rose world made no such judgments and he gave himself to them completely, the pleasure of their company more satisfying to him than the company of his fellow man.

The sun had lowered in the sky, shadows slanting long and narrow when a small boy sidled just inside the garden, making sure he came no further than the entry flagstones.

"Woman in cottage by ale house is sick, father." he blurted. "Shall I get the physic?"

The priest grunted. "Is she?"

Tenting skeletal fingers, he brought them to his face and tapped his thin, petulant lips with the joined index fingers. The boy fidgeted, waiting for the priest to speak.

"No," he said finally. "Get the barber. Have him meet me in the tower room."

The tower room was a cramped little chamber on the west wall of the church. A single window allowed a sliver of light. On entry, Father Simon lit the wall sconce. Its lone candle made no appreciable difference to the gloom but the priest did not notice.

The only furnishing in the room was a ponderous high-backed chair, crafted of thickly padded sheep leather and tanned almost black with willow bark. Father Simon hunched his shoulders as he sat in the great chair, pale eyes slitted, lips compressed and rigid. He dropped his hands over the talons carved into the arms of the black chair, pressing his fingers between the claws, curving them to their predatory contours and waited, but not long. Few kept the priest waiting. Once summoned, most hastened to appear.

The tower room was designed to intimidate all comers and the barber was no exception. Arthur Bodwin hated this room. He hated the way Father Simon crouched in that great ugly chair, his heavy linen alb clinging to his bony arms and legs. Most of all he hated the dread shivering in his belly. A dread borne of long association with the priest.

Father Simon did not look around when the barber entered the room but rose instead and went to the narrow tower window. He gazed steadily on the village of Claringdon and drew his lips down in an ill-tempered grimace.

"It has come to my attention, Arthur, that Constance is of a peccant humour."

He spat the name out like rotten venison.

The barber said nothing.

"She has been making certain demands on me. Unpleasant demands."

Arthur bleated sympathetically but the priest stayed him with an impatient flutter of his hand.

"I have endured her long enough."

The barber shifted uneasily.

"A generous bleeding, Arthur," Father Simon's voice was soft. "Rid her of the evil humours."

Arthur paled and he shrank away from the priest's hard eyes when he turned to look on him.

"Do not fail me, Arthur."

It was a dismissal and the priest ignored the misery in the barber's face as he left on his less than merciful errand.

Father Simon returned to the window and considered the spires of Crenfeld Castle soaring skyward to the west of Claringdon. She was all alone there now. No husband to get in the way. His plans may yet come to fruition. From the corner of one heavy-lidded eye he saw a shadow fall across the room and turned.

"Oh, it is you," he said. "I see the woman in the castle still lives."

There was a sullen mutter from the other. Simon rested stretched out hands on the back of his chair.

"I had supposed the obstacle to be removed, but . . . " he shrugged. "The impediment remains."

"I have done as you asked. I will do no more," came the stubborn reply.

"I think you shall," the priest purred. "It would go hard on you should the magistrate hear the disturbing news of the part you played in our earlier endeavours. Endeavours you are quite unable to connect to me, I might add."

The other glowered.

"Return to Crenfeld and await my instructions."

Father Simon's visitor stood stupidly, while once again he went to the window. This time, the priest caressed the stained pictorial in the window glass. It was duplicate to the clerestory in the church sanctuary. He ran his fingers over the writhing flames, outlined contorted figures of demons and lingered on the gaping mouths of the damned, while the living damned picked up his worn cap and rubbed bony hands over his long, mournful face. His footsteps did not clatter on the stairs but dragged slowly, as if fettered.

Katherine had trouble lifting her head from her pillow after the short nap on her return from the churchyard. Perhaps it hadn't been such a wise thing to do after all. When she moved, a steady throbbing pounded in her temples. She groaned and Agnes, never very far away, rushed to her.

"What is it, my lady?"

"My head, Agnes. It is very painful."

"A small bleeding, my lady? Father Simon's barber is in the kitchen, just come from bleeding Constance."

Agnes lowered her voice to a whisper. "He's been making sheep's eyes at one of the kitchen maids but our Grace will soon run him off. Shall I fetch him?"

Katherine hesitated She had been bled quite recently and hated the prick of the needle and the sight of her own blood. A sharp stab of pain reminded her that she was being childish.

She sighed, "Yes, I suppose so. Yes."

Agnes scurried off and Katherine sank back against her pillows and closed her eyes.

White-faced and breathing heavily the barber brought with him the unmistakable stench of sickness. Katherine recoiled slightly.

"Arthur Bodwin, my lady," Agnes said, retiring a respectful distance.

Arthur Bodwin was a corpulent man, flamboyantly dressed as befitted a man of his station. Pearl buttons enclosed a splendid purple tunic and his hose were a bright green, as was the feather in the highly crowned beaver hat he removed. But what Katherine had always found most fascinating about the man was a small ugly wart on his left eyelid which had a strangely adhesive quality, causing the lid to stick to the brow bone when he blinked. It gave him a lopsided startled look.

The hand he gave her was soft and plump and as cold as the turbid waters of the moat. Katherine returned his limp clasp then quickly slipped her hand beneath the blanket. His thin smile did not quite reach those odd eyes. They remained unmoved and watchful.

Bodwin made a half turn away from the bed, stretched out his arm and snapped his fingers. Instantly, a boy appeared in the doorway. Panting under the weight of a large box, the lad dropped it heavily beside Katherine's bed. After a wide-eyed bob in her direction he took to his heels.

The barber opened the lid, revealing a disquieting array of sharp instruments, rumpled bandaging and closely covered containers. Katherine shrank back farther on her bed.

"What ails you, my lady?"

Katherine heard herself mumbling. "My head, the pain is . . . "

"Indeed. Indeed." Arthur Bodwin stroked his hairless jaw. He seemed to consider a moment, eyes cast upward.

"I would prescribe a liberal bleeding, my lady," he said gravely. "The weather is right, neither hot nor cold, and the moon is not yet new. It will be of great value."

"Oh, but only a small bleeding, surely," Katherine protested. "Why, the village barber bled me only a few days ago. See here."

And she thrust out her arm to show him the bruised skin and blood congealed furrow where the lancet had been inserted.

"It did nothing to ease the pain."

"Now, now, my dear lady," Arthur said, in the condescending tone Katherine expected he reserved for the most simple and difficult of his patients.

"In the hands of the unskilled, naturally one cannot expect beneficial results."

He bent over the implements in his case, rejecting the slimmer instruments in favour of a broader lancet.

Katherine eyed the lancet warily while the barber prepared the instrument. He sharpened the point, dipped it in a colourless liquid and wiped it.

"Now, please roll up your sleeve, my lady. The other arm would be more comfortable I think. Farther up. Past your burn."

He waited expectantly. Slowly, Katherine pulled up the sleeve of her dress to expose the bare skin.

Bodwin grunted, held the lancet in one hand and took a firm hold of Katherine's arm in the other. Katherine felt the lancet prick her skin and was suddenly afraid. She struggled to free herself but his grip only tightened, causing her to gasp in alarm and pain.

"Now, now. This will take but a moment, my lady."

Bodwin's teeth were clenched with the effort of keeping Katherine's arm still and he didn't notice Agnes stand up and move toward them.

"Is anything amiss, Lady Katherine?" she asked.

"Agnes, please. Tell him to stop. I have changed my mind."

Agnes swooped down and snatched up the lancet. Arthur Bodwin scrambled to his feet.

"What are you doing!" he snarled.

"She doesn't want it, sir. She's changed her mind."

Agnes arranged herself to stand between her mistress and the barber. It was evident that her thick solid body could well withstand his own, despite its great bulk. Bodwin stiffened and scowled at Katherine, his left eyelid stuck fast to the brow bone, lending it a glaring malevolence.

"You insult me, madam! You may be sure Father Simon will hear of this."

The barber banged the door behind him, cursing the luck that had placed the woman in his hands and just as suddenly wrenched her out of them.

Katherine slumped against the pillows, cradling her head in her hands, her fingers jumping in convulsive little jerks. Agnes sat beside her and rubbed her back gently, her own face pinched with worry.

"Pay him no mind, madam," she said. "That leech is too full of his own importance. I should have fetched the physician. I'm so sorry."

Katherine looked up, her green eyes cloudy with pain. "Do not fault yourself, Agnes. I will rest. Perhaps it will go away of its own accord."

"Yes, madam. I'll close the door behind me and tell the chamberlain. Shall I bring you some of Grace's soup?"

"Later, Agnes, please. Let me sleep now."

Katherine wished she did not feel so irritable. She closed her eyes and tried to keep her head motionless while Agnes crept quietly from the room and shut the door behind her.

In a cottage garden across from the ale house, a woman rose from pulling onions and nudged her companion.

"See," she whispered, her wide eyes straying to the other side of the muddy roadway. "He's bent t'ward the miller's house. To Constance without doubt."

The other woman shielded a snicker behind a work-worn hand, then drew in her breath sharply. "Look! He carries the sacred oil and holy waters."

Both women muttered grimly and made the sign of the cross, then hurried inside while the cassocked figure drifted into the cottage across the way.

Father Simon looked down at the wan face of the woman lying immobile on the pallet. Her breath was coming in shallow rasps through chalky parted lips. He said the required phrases, applied the oil and sprinkled the waters. Assuring himself with a quick look that he was alone, he lifted the pillow from beneath the unconscious woman's head, held it in his hands still watching her, then in a quick rush of movement pressed it down over the woman's face.

"Sleep well, Constance," he whispered grimly.

Her struggle was feeble and short-lived. Father Simon continued to hold the pillow against her face long after she'd gone rigid. Carefully he lifted it and gazed dispassionately at the starting eyes, distended neck muscles, the teeth bared in a last gasp for breath. With callous fingers he forced shut the eyelids. He looked at her neck and shrugged. It might appear thus in any case. There was often a frantic gulp for air at the end. He pulled the lips down over the jutting teeth and absently wiped his fingers on the bedclothes. Then he replaced the pillow under her head, studied the result and nodded to himself. A satisfactory end to an unsatisfactory woman.

Perhaps it was time to make the more permanent arrangement of a hearth-mate instead of taking other men's leavings. That woman now at the castle. It would certainly be a more agreeable solution to his difficulties and it would save him having to go through with his other plans.

While he was thus pondering his alternatives, the cottage door flung open and the miller, panting and distraught, burst into the poor little room. Father Simon composed his face into that of the sympathetic cleric. He laid a consoling hand on the miller and shook his head sadly.

"She is gone, Robert."

The miller sank to his knees with a groan and touched the cold hand of his dead wife. It lay strangely twisted as if seized at death by a sudden spasm. The miller eyed the hand fearfully. Had she felt the flame of the infernal regions even as she slipped away? He had tried so hard to spare her such an end. Hadn't he prayed for her wicked soul over and over and offered a penny at Mass only yesterday to secure her freedom from her sins. That she had often been unfaithful to him he knew. She'd admitted as much. In fact she'd mocked him with it on many a night when creeping into their dingy cottage where he lay awake waiting for her. Hadn't he begged her to repent of her ways and be the wife to him she ought? And now look at her. Damned to hell fire! He dropped his head on his wife's motionless body and wept like a bereft child.

The women worked quickly. Although they had prepared bodies for burial many times, it had not lost its horrors. Death was a shameful thing, stripped of dignity. All the while one felt as if one were violating a privacy the dead were helpless to prevent. That somewhere behind those fixed stares, they were protesting and demanding to be let alone.

The women removed Constance's thin shift and undergarments and, grunting under her weight, dropped her body into the bathwater. They scrubbed her briskly from head to toe then dragged her out onto the floor. Clean clothes had been provided by her husband and they hurried to redress the dead woman.

"Whatcher think of fire at castle?" one woman asked the other as she slipped a dead arm into a sleeve.

"Were a judgment on 'im, I'll wager," answered the second. "Fer doin' away with 'is uncle. Weren't no proper master, neither. Struttin' around like a peacock," she sniffed.

"I 'spect you be right," agreed the first. "Mistress were spared though, saints be praised."

They cross themselves solemnly, then one cried out, "Why, whatever is this? Look at this, will you."

She pointed to a large bluish boil under the dead woman's right arm.

"Didn't notice that when I washed her. Never seen the like, have you?"

Her companion leaned over the body. "No, but be careful it don't . . . oh, now you've gone and done it. What a horrible smell. And look at all that coming out of there. We're going to have to wash her all over now. My man isn't going to like this. Coming home for evening meal soon and me still at it. Come on, let's get her back in there. Not her fault, silly cow, but she'll need to smell better'n this or Father Simon won't let her in his church for her own Mass!"

That brought a chuckle from the other woman and together they repeated the bathing procedure. Both were panting by the time they had finished getting the dead woman dressed again and carried to her bed.

"Here, you take this end and we'll throw the water out behind. Come on now, let's heave it up."

The women staggered under the weight of the filled bathtub but managed to carry it outside. They set it down and tipped it on its side to let the water drain out, then wiping their hands on their aprons, left for their own homes.

Constance lay alone in the cottage. It grew darker and darker inside the still room until she became only a round black hump on the bed.

In the gathering dusk behind the house, two goats had broken their tethers, found the bath water to their liking and lapped it up. A young lad caught up to them there and dragged them back to their own yard with mouths still dripping, where they nibbled at what the cottage garden had to offer before being tied off to a tree for milking.

CHAPTER 7

KATHERINE FELT SOMEWHAT IMPROVED the next morning and was now comfortably ensconced in the window seat of her own chamber, plump green pillows supporting her back, red stocking boots warming her feet. The boots had been a surprisingly thoughtful gift from the old woman, Nory.

"Should have summat to snug yer toes, given yer yoke-mate's gone and cooked hisself," she had growled contemptuously.

Grown accustomed to Nory's forthright manner and frequently shocking observations, Katherine thanked Nory meekly and Nory went her way, bobbing her head and muttering darkly about the uselessness of men in general.

Katherine wiggled her toes inside the stockingboots and smiled. She had really grown quite fond of Nory and often found her stumping about the castle in the company of Old Henry. Since the night of the fire, a friendship sprang up between the two and in their simple way they took it upon themselves to be concerned with her welfare and that of the manor.

Many a slow moving servant had felt the sting of Nory's ash pole and Old Henry saved the tenderest and best from the kitchen for the private meals she took in her room.

Katherine looked up. The church bell.

"Agnes, what has happened?"

Agnes was bent over Katherine's new bed. It was plainer than the previous one, but still quite comfortable. The walls had been rewhitewashed and the little painted roses bloomed across them once more.

A rapt expression on Agnes' flat face made her look rather witless but her round arms and nimble fingers were still busily folding and tucking.

"That'll be for Constance, the miller's wife," she said over her shoulder.

The covers received a final pat.

"She took poorly yesterday. The barber cut her up fierce to loose the evil humors but when father went, she died."

Katherine shuddered at the memory of her own encounter with Arthur Bodwin and his lancets.

"Her poor husband," Katherine said.

Agnes sniffed. "Well rid of her. She was no proper wife to him anywise. Feet out from under the sheets with other men."

Katherine leaned forward to look out the window. The sun had gone in again and a mist of rain clouded the courtyard. She sighed.

"Did they ring the bell for Nathaniel, Agnes?" she asked faintly.

"Oh yes, my lady," Agnes assured her.

"And for Lady Elizabeth and Lord Philip?"

"Indeed, Tolled most mournfully and fair long. T'was an horrible thing, that," she added with feeling.

Katherine gave Agnes her full attention. "What was horrible?"

"Why, the way they died. Poisoned, my lady."

Agnes was gratified by her mistress's startled look.

"Yes, 'tis true," she nodded. "I was in the room only a short time before. The chamberlain, Peter, he'd put Sir Philip's mantle over his shoulders and was combing out his beard. I'd just turned down their bed and was brushing Lady Elizabeth's hair. It weren't like your hair, madam. Yours is most wonderful shiny and thick. And such a pretty red," she added wistfully.

Katherine gave an impatient twitch to her shoulders and Agnes blinked and went on.

"There was a knock and the little kitchen wench, Alice, brought in a bowl of mushrooms. 'From the kitchen', she says, flutters her apron and quits the room. Sudden like, it was. Madam weren't expecting no mushrooms. Anywise, Lady Elizabeth complained the mushrooms were cold, but no matter they'd eat them straight away. She giggled a good deal and said wouldn't Father be enraged if he knew."

"Father Simon allows as late suppers give rise to waste," Agnes explained.

"They ate up the fried mushrooms together and by the time I'd finished Lady Elizabeth's hair, they were done. I fetched the basin and Peter drew the bed curtains. They were still laughing and well pleased with themselves when we left their chamber."

Agnes paused for breath. "It weren't but a few hours had passed when I was wakened by the most terrible groans."

Agnes knit wispy brows together and shuddered.

"They were in cruel torment. My poor lady cried out for me and when I went to her, 'Agnes', she screamed. 'Oh, Agnes, the demons are at me!' and she clawed at her stomach as if fair to rip it open. Sir Philip had pulled down the bedcurtains and was rolling on the floor in them. Peter tried to help him up but Sir Philip's grip on the curtains was so tight and his shrieks so frantic that poor Peter turned quite white himself and fell away from him."

Suddenly Agnes' face crumpled into tears and she covered it with her hands.

"They died soon after that," Agnes went on in muffled tones. Her voice lapsed into a toneless drone.

"Benjamin, the physic, came and turned us all out. After a time he came from them, his face grave and angry. Scarce see the physic angry," she added with a kind of incurious wonder. "Said there were death cap mushrooms in the bowl and who had sent them to the chamber? The little wench said they'd been given to her at the door of the kitchen and hadn't really looked at the person who gave them to her so couldn't say who it was. She thought maybe a woman, but the person wore a cape and hood and she didn't see the face."

Agnes dropped her hands, her head still bent, her face blotched and red.

"Then Father Simon came and . . . and gave them the last rites."

"And no one knew where the mushrooms were from?" Katherine asked gently.

Agnes shook her head. "No. No one knew."

As silence fell between the two women Katherine grew conscious of a familiar persistent throbbing in her temples. The pain made her restless and she rose to pace the confines of her chamber. Agnes sat staring into nothingness while Katherine's skirts stirred the newly-herbed floor rushes, sending up the pungent scent of sage, tansy and costmary to prick their nostrils. Presently Katherine lay a hand on Agnes' bowed shoulder.

"My head has begun to ache again, Agnes. Where does the physician live? I must go to him."

Agnes started as if roused from a deep sleep. She blinked and clucked sympathetically.

"Shall I fetch him?"

"No, I'd rather go to him. It will be quicker."

When Katherine assured Agnes she wanted to go alone, Agnes gave her the directions she needed and added a warning.

"Mind you hurry on. It will be dark soon. I don't like to be caught out at night, I don't. And I wouldn't like to see you come to any mischief neither. The spirits is about on nights like this."

She pointed out the window. "Moon is full tonight. See it up there even now."

Katherine smiled patiently. Servants were more sensitive to such things. They could not afford the full protection and comfort of the Church. She set out in the gathering darkness and hurried on into the village, nodding to the women in their front gardens who looked up from pulling out something for the supper pot. The fields would be emptying soon, the men home and hungry after a long day.

Agnes had said three cottages past old Henry's rather dilapidated house, bending over the roadway at the far end next to the common field. One, two — yes, there it was and a glimmer of candle light flickered through its window. Katherine paused to glance inside. The physician was at home. She saw him sitting on a small stool, reading. So intent was he on the pages that lay in his lap that he did not hear her knock at first. When he did come to answer the door, he beamed in welcome.

"Do come in dear lady. Come in."

Katherine returned his smile and passed into the little cottage. She was surprised. It was a mean little room with only the barest of necessities and none of the luxuries she'd come to expect in a physician's house.

The floor was bare earth, with no rushes or mats to soften its surface. The fire was small and only a single pot hung over it. Two chairs and a roughly squared table made up its furnishings. No tapestries on the walls, no wall sconces. And a narrow bed of straw in a dark corner.

Benjamin gestured to what turned out to be a very comfortable straw coil chair. Katherine sat herself while he perched across from her on his hard stool, slipping his book beneath it.

The physician clapped his palms together and regarded her with his head tilted to one side.

"You are in some distress, madam?"

He brought a thumb and forefinger to her temples. "You pinch your brows together — so," he explained. "It pains you?"

Katherine nodded. "I thought perhaps you might have some little medicament."

Benjamin placed the flat of his hand on her forehead. His hand felt firm and cool. He grunted and withdrew it.

"A barber may be able to help you with a bleeding," he suggested.

Katherine shuddered. "I am afraid I refused Arthur Bodwin yesterday."

"You did? Refused Simon's own barber?"

Benjamin chuckled. "That must have stuck in his throat."

"Drove him near to apoplexy," Katherine said ruefully.

Benjamin slapped his knee with glee. "Never mind. I think I have something that will help."

He cast about him.

"Now where did I put . . . oh, here it is."

A much worn deer's hide satchel was drawn from beneath the table and a dark, round cake produced from its interior. He showed it to her. Katherine sniffed the little cake.

"This?" She eyed it cautiously. "What is it?"

"The juice of a lettuce, dried into powder and pressed so it may be eaten. As much or as little as you have need. I fear you must eat all of it. Unhappily it is ill-tasting."

He wrinkled his broad nose and made a face. "Phaph. What am I saying. It is terrible. But . . . " he broke into a grin and shook a stubby finger at her. "It will restore you."

Katherine made an end of the little cake quickly and shivered. The physician had not exaggerated. Something so hideous was sure to be curative. Katherine pressed a coin into the physic's hand. He accepted it with a grateful nod of his bushy black head.

"Thank you," he said simply. "Not all my patients have aught to pay."

His face broke into a smile that set his black eyes twinkling and he patted his slight paunch.

"I like my meals the same as the next man, I guess," he admitted.

"And so you should," Katherine said.

She rose, gathering her cloak around her.

"I will not trouble you further. I can see I disturbed your reading. I expect physicians must read a good deal about the ailments that trouble these mortal bodies."

Benjamin nodded.

"That is true. But just now I was reading of ailments that trouble the soul."

Katherine paused in the act of covering her red hair with the cloak hood.

"The soul?"

Benjamin withdrew the book from under his stool with careful fingers. He opened it and held it out to her. Katherine looked down and read, "'He that believeth on the Son hath everlasting life.'"

She gasped and drew back.

"But you are a Jew! Why do you read the New Testament? Jews do not hold to Gentile beliefs."

Benjamin chuckled. "This Jew does. I have a very good Gentile friend who attends Oxford University. He persuaded me to read some of the scriptures he copied out. As I read, I realized that almost all the books of the New Testament were written by Jews. Saint Paul wrote much of it and he came to believe in the Christ even though he was of the very strictest and most intellectual sect of the Jews, the Pharisees. I was fully convinced by his writings. However, my favourite book is the book of Saint John." Benjamin's eyes shone. "It is my most precious possession."

Katherine was horrified. To keep a copy of the scriptures was strictly forbidden to anyone outside the clergy and had been for over one hundred years!

"Only the Church is to have holy writ," Katherine cried. "It is on the List!"

Benjamin remained unperturbed. "See how beautifully my friend has copied it out for me."

"No, no!" she cried. "This is blasphemy. Father Simon will be furious. You are wrong to have such a thing."

She stared at him with wide frightened eyes.

"Why is that my dear, do you think?" smiled Benjamin. "St. John records the words of Jesus that tell us to search the scriptures for they testify of him and eternal life. Why would the Church forbid me to read what the Lord has instructed me to read?"

"He has not instructed it. He has instructed the Church. Only the priest should be reading this."

"But my dear, if you would just look. Jesus was not speaking to the Church at all when he challenged them to make a thorough investigation of the scriptures. He was speaking to those who were not sure who he was. They were to search and find out for themselves."

"No, no, I will not listen to you!" Katherine clapped her hands to her ears. "This is heresy. I beg you. Turn this over to Father Simon. Make a full confession."

Benjamin sighed and shut the book, closing the parchment between two heavy boards. He brought out a small leather case and set the book inside. Clasping the lid, he slid it back under his stool.

"I am sorry it discomfits you, madam," he said sadly. "That was not my intention."

He walked with her to the door.

"I hope you will be well."

Without another word, he let Katherine out into the now dark night and closed the door softly behind her.

Katherine looked anxiously up and down the street. Had anyone heard? But the road was deserted. Benjamin was a kindly man. She knew him to be devout, in his own way. But to harbour such heretical tendencies was to tempt the Church to retribution. She hoped he would keep his heresies to himself. Father Simon would certainly not hear of it from her. She did not know the priest well, but from the look of his pinched lips and rigid back, she did not believe him capable of any real compassion. Benjamin would feel the full wrath of the Church for certain. And Benjamin was a good man, if misguided.

Katherine shook her head and walked away from the little cottage. Fortunately, the moon was bright and she could see her way quite clearly along the empty streets. She decided to forego using the roadway and take the shorter route through the wood separating Claringdon from Crenfeld Castle.

Katherine pushed her way through the copse and into a clearing just the other side of the last row of yew trees. At its edge, she faltered. Two women turned to look at her, their faces bright against the glow of the candles they held aloft before them. Katherine started. They were two women, yet one, their features uncannily alike. But while one had brows knit in a kind of perpetual fretfulness, back humped and rounded, the other had wide, vacant eyes and a limp but unbent posture. Wimple and veil covered their heads and necks completely. Both wore shapeless woollen dresses in dull shades of faded sepia. She noticed the order of an unmatched set of buttons closing one woman's dress was repeated precisely in that of her companion's.

The women continued to watch her in a motionless silence Katherine found unnerving. Even the air felt strange, almost heavy. Katherine looked fearfully behind her, half-expecting to see the spectral form of a spirit floating toward her, meaning to envelop her in wispy folds.

Without a word to these strange women, Katherine hurried across the open grass to the safety of the wood on the other side and cast a furtive look back once she had gained the further trees.

The two women squatted over a collection of assorted objects grouped in a circle at their feet. Their thin downturned lips moved simultaneously in a low mutter.

"Mighty art thou, queen of the gods! Thee, O goddess, I adore. In thy godhead and on thy name I do call. Vouchsafe now to fulfil my prayers and I will give thee thanks. Come to me with thy healing powers!"

While Katherine watched, the women reached out together to pick up a single round object from the ground and carry it between their fingers to drop into a small cattle horn cup resting at the edge of the circle. A faint hiss came from the cup and a whitish mist puffed out. The women exchanged glances and nodded. Then one by one they retrieved the rest of the items from the circle. Katherine saw they took extreme care to have a hand on the same object at the same time and together deposit it into a pouch hanging from the long waist cord of one woman, then repeat the process for the next item, only putting it into the other woman's suspended pouch. They alternated this way until all but the last object had been retrieved. This last item seemed to cause some consternation between them. They muttered over it, then finally broke it into two pieces. It appeared to be a large mushroom of some sort and so divided quite easily. The halves were added to the pouches, again both of them handling the one half until placed in one pouch and then repeating the procedure with the second.

When they left the circle, both women raised their candles in their right hand simultaneously, turned in unison and glided across the meadow to be swallowed up by the night.

Katherine shivered. She was very tired. And frightened. The sight of these odd women who did not speak to her made her uneasy. Foolish, of course. They were probably simple-minded and harmless. And yet, she had felt something. There was something. She was sure of it.

Considerably refreshed, Katherine hummed contentedly on her way downstairs the next morning. Her headache was gone. Alice was laying the morning fire in the hall and singing to herself, bright as a spring sparrow. Nory rested in front of the hearth, while servants drifted in and out in pursuit of their daily tasks.

"Nory, have you ever seen two women in the village," Katherine asked. "Peculiar women who speak and move together like a strange kind of echo?"

Nory grunted and nodded.

"Who are they?"

"Hester and Nettie. Have the power. Can call up the spirits of the dead and work spells. Father Simon says they're sacred women, but I think they're just witches."

"They see things too," Alice broke in, looking up from the hearth. "Fall around on the ground and twitch and their eyes roll up inside their heads."

She attempted to demonstrate but only succeeded in crossing her eyes. She refocused. "Then they tell what they've seen in their visions."

Nory snorted and waved Alice back to her work.

"You never mind about all that. Seen 'em have ye?" she asked Katherine.

"Yes," Katherine nodded. "Last night. In the clearing just beyond the wood."

Nory nodded again. "They favour that spot. Most probably mixing up a potion or working at a spell. Mind how you speak to them, though."

"Oh, I did not speak to them," Katherine said hurriedly.

"Just as well," piped little Alice. "Gwendolyn, who used to have charge of the washing pots, spoke sharp to them one day for helping themselves to some herbs from her garden. They put a spell on her goats and they dropped down dead the very next day. Poor Gwendolyn was so affrighted she had father cleanse her house and garden of spirits regular for months. Didn't help though. Why only last week didn't her brother find her dead too. Lying in her bed, arms all black. And great ugly blue boils, filled with evil humours, broke and poured out demon odures when she were moved."

Alice shuddered and rolled her eyes magnificently. "So, madam, have a care of Hester and Nettie."

Nory grunted again and nodded soberly, then limped out the doorway to the kitchen.

Katherine digested this disclosure in silence. She wondered which they had been up to last night. Making a potion for some enamored young man or setting spirits at work. She recalled their eyes fastened on her. And their hands. Handling everything as one person, fingernails long and curved slightly upward, hands curling around that bone cup. She shook her head quickly. They were probably only gathering mushrooms by moonlight for some innocent purpose. Everyone knew certain mushrooms and plants must be taken under the moon to ensure their potency. Something stirred in her memory and then was gone. Katherine gathered up her skirts and moved to leave the hall. The usher waited at the door, his hand ready to swing it open.

"Alice," she called back. "Please tell Agnes I have gone for a ride on Pygine."

Alice executed a small curtsy. "Yes, my lady."

Katherine nodded to the usher, who bowed and heaved open the big timber door for her. She found the stable deserted save for the horses in their stalls. Pygine hung his head out over his enclosure and nickered gently into her outstretched hand.

"I have neglected you my darling," she said to him.

Katherine held out her arms, rolling up the sleeves of her cloak so the horse could smell them. His nostrils quivered. He whiffled softly over the red weals and Katherine felt his warm breath caress her puckered flesh. Pygine would accept her. He loved her despite her deformity. She lay her russet head against his black neck. Yes, he would always love her. And she him.

With no one about, Katherine had to ready him herself. Instead of being annoyed at the absence of the marshal and his grooms, she was grateful to be by herself. There was constant activity in the castle. One could never be quite alone. Out here in the stable it was peaceful. Only the crunching of horses at their oats and the sweet smell of fresh hay.

Katherine swung up on Pygine and sighed. It was good to sit on his back again. Good to do something. Since she had wakened from her long sleep, her mind had been in turmoil about what to do with the manor. Without a steward it would soon become an unwieldy and unprofitable holding. She had little understanding of the franchises of courts, rents, pastures, waters, mills and other things belonging to the manor. She knew nothing of how the demesne lands should be tilled or indeed even what crops they held. She had barely been able to ascertain that the livestock and swine were improved for the coming winter. The book, the account book, would have to be found. Within it she would find at least a list of the rents and services. What may have happened to it she could not think. She had left it on that table in the solar and that's the last she, or anyone else, had ever seen of it. She had assumed the steward was the thief, but perhaps it was someone else, or the steward had been stealing for someone else. She shook her head. She would think of it later. Now, she would ride!

Katherine walked Pygine through the outer gatehouse and over the drawbridge. He was difficult to control and his ears twitched back and forth with excitement. Poor Pygine. He hadn't had a run for a long time. She must try to ride him more often. Katherine ducked under the tree branches that clutched at her hair and held Pygine back to a canter until they were through the clearing where the two women had been last night. The horse sniffed nervously at the remains of their fire, snorted and shied sideways.

"Never mind. They are gone," Katherine assured him.

The rough grasses spread out wide and inviting before them and Katherine loosened the reins to give Pygine his head. His canter quickly turned into a gallop and his gallop into a run. His hooves pounded flat the untrodden grasses and she felt the ripple of his strong muscles against her legs as he reached out his neck to the wind. Katherine's fret came loose and flew away. She laid her head down on Pygine's neck and her thick red curls were whipped together with the horse's coarse black mane. All the world was filled with his heaving flanks, pounding hooves and sonorous breathing.

They went on like this for several miles. Katherine began to tire but was loath to pull him in. He was indefatigable and she knew he needed the exercise. So she let the reins go slack in her hands, relaxed and closed her eyes, letting her body go limp and allowing him to run himself out.

When Pygine came to an abrupt halt, Katherine's eyes flew open wide, she lost her grip and fell hard to the ground. Dazed but unhurt she got up from dusting herself off, meaning to scold him. But the great black horse was snorting and prancing around her on trembling legs, his eyes glaring and wild.

"Why, Pygine, whatever is the matter?"

Katherine put a steadying hand on his shoulder.

The muscles quivered and jerked under her touch and he blew out his nostrils, his ears laid flat. She took the reins to draw him forward a step or two to settle him, but he refused. Katherine frowned and stroked the velvet of his nose.

"What is it? Come a little ahead. I only want to throw a rope around this tree and . . . "

Her voice trailed off and she clapped a hand over her mouth to muffle a startled cry. There was a foot protruding from the underbrush and she had almost trodden on it. A naked foot, caked in dirt. She stepped closer, her heart hammering in her throat.

The foot belonged to a man who would not be getting up out of the thicket. She forced her eyes to travel up the length of his body. A muddy tunic had dried in stiff, hard folds. One arm was bent awkwardly under his torso; the other, reaching up and under his head, was crushed so flat it seemed boneless. His fair hair was thick with blackened blood, his eyeless sockets filled with dirt, his lips drawn back over broken teeth. A burial of sorts had obviously been attempted, but the relentless summer rains had washed the earth away, disgorging its gruesome secret and the body sprawled half out of a deep hole.

Katherine bit her lower lip, shuddered and backed away to lean heavily on Pygine. She pressed her face against the horse's side and closed her eyes. What should she do now? And who was he? Could it be the missing steward? The man who had run off with Lord Philip's money? If it was, he had not managed to get very far.

Katherine stood over the dead man. There was nothing for it but to bring him back with her. She could not leave him out here for the wild animals. It was too cruel an end even for a thief. If he was a thief.

He was not very tall. She drew off her cloak and laid it down. Gingerly, she climbed down into the hole with the dead man. The thought of having to touch a corpse made her heart start thumping again. You can and you must, she told herself. She clenched her teeth hard, closed her throat and pressed her tongue fast against the roof of her mouth so she would not inhale. Then quickly, before she lost her courage, she reached under his shoulders and pulled, steeling herself against the impulse to recoil at the feel of shrunken gristle and bone.

The hole was filled with mud and a nauseating sucking sound accompanied the operation. Once Katherine freed the body from the muck, it came out easily and she pushed it all the way up and over the edge of the hole. She was breathing hard after clambering out of the pit. Gasping a little, she bent and maneuvered the body until her cloak was completely under the dead man. Then she moved his legs to cross the feet and tied her cloak into a knot at the bottom, pushing the feet down hard against the knot. Gathering several thick tree branches she constructed a crude framework to carry the body, using Pygine's reins to fasten the transport to the saddle. She dragged the dead man up into the framework and secured his cloaked remains as best as she could.

Up on top of Pygine, Katherine regained a composure that had been slowly dwindling as she handled the dead man and the horror of her lonely situation mounted. Her shaking hands grew steady when she grabbed hold of Pygine's mane.

"Take us home," she whispered

After a few steps the big horse faltered and looked around, but Katherine patted him reassuringly.

"Think of it as an old stump," she soothed. "Or father's war cart."

Although they were losing the sun and she had no wish to carry her grisly cargo in the dark, Katherine tried to keep the pace slow and Pygine away from any notably rough terrain. But she could not shut out the sickening sound of the dead man's body thumping over the ground behind them.

Pygine moved too rapidly down the slope of the last hill that brought Crenfeld into view and the corpse bounded high into the air, dislodging the arms to drag and jump alongside the cloaked torso.

They must have seen her, for the drawbridge was down when she reached Crenfeld and the gates open so she rode straight into the ward. Many eager hands helped her down.

"We were just coming to look for you!" the marshal cried, his nut-brown brow lined in anxiety. He took a step past Pygine's haunches.

"What do you have there?"

He let out a slow whistle.

"I don't believe it. I don't believe it. Will you look at that, Peter . . . "

He motioned for the chamberlain who had his hand on Pygine's halter.

"Peter come and look at this. It's that cullion, Gerard. Done in good and proper too."

The chamberlain had begun to move toward the marshal but suddenly froze and turned deathly pale. His mouth dropped open and he backed away, slowly at first and then more quickly, until finally he spun right around and fled.

The marshal grunted and shrugged. "Seen worse," he said.

Agnes threw a heavy blanket around her shivering mistress and shook a finger at the marshal.

"Robert! Keep your vulgar tongue still," she barked.

Robert hung his head contritely. "Beg your pardon, madam," he said to Katherine. "Didn't mean to distress you."

Katherine gave him a weak smile. "I am not upset, Robert," she said, easing the sting of Agnes' rebuke. "Only tired, and . . . "

"I should think you would be," Agnes broke in. "It's not fitting for a lady to do such dreadful work," she said indignantly.

The marshal pulled the cloak completely away from the dead man's face and stared intently at it, unmoved by its disfigurement.

"Be wanting the physic, I expect. And Father Simon. Don't know as the father will allow a Christian burial, though," he added doubtfully. "Still, there may be something he'll do even for the likes of a thief like Gerard."

The physician and priest were sent for, the examination duly performed and at Katherine's insistence, Benjamin and Father Simon made comfortable in a corner of the great hall. They were sharing an uneasy silence when Katherine came in with a young serving lad bearing a tray of refreshments.

Benjamin looked up and smiled a welcome. Father Simon remained impassive. Katherine had changed from her dirty clothes and taken a restorative nap. She was now quite calm and untroubled at Father Simon's evident hostility.

He fixed Benjamin with his pale eyes. "You have not been to Mass for some time, Benjamin."

"I have not," Benjamin replied blandly.

"Nor observed the sacrament of penance," he pressed.

"No," Benjamin agreed.

"Not having made confession, your soul must be heavy," Simon went on.

"When it troubles me, I pray."

The priest frowned and was about to go on, when Katherine interrupted with a quick smile.

"Tell me. Was the poor man really the steward? And what happened to him? Can you do anything for him now?"

This last question was directed to the priest.

"Prayers for Gerard will not be made," Father Simon said in a harsh voice. "He has died in mortal sin and without repentance. He has gone straight to hell and our prayers will avail him nothing."

Katherine looked startled. "Surely, there is something."

"There is nothing. The Church is quite intractable on this."

"But if he was killed, his opportunity to expiate his sin was snatched from him."

Katherine appealed to Benjamin. "Was he murdered, physician?"

"Oh, most assuredly, my lady."

"You see," she implored the priest. "It is not his fault. He had no time."

"I am sorry," the priest said firmly. "There will be no prayers for him and he will not be buried in the churchyard either. Have your servants dispose of him elsewhere."

"That is very hard," Katherine cried.

"Nevertheless, it will be so." The priest rose to leave and Katherine and Benjamin stood with him.

"You will excuse me, Lady Katherine. I find the air quite close." He looked pointedly at Benjamin.

The physician merely smiled a bland smile and reseated himself once the priest was gone.

"Why must you provoke him?" Katherine groaned. "You can see he is displeased with you and your disrespect for him and the Church."

"I have only spoken the truth, madam. He made observations and I agreed with him."

"But he can do you grave harm," Katherine insisted. "Surely you can see that."

Benjamin grinned and leaned toward her worried face. "But his grey countenance takes on a healthy glow when he is excited. I do him good in spite of himself."

Katherine laughed. "You are a rogue. Tell me," she said, her features settling along more serious lines. "What *did* happen to the steward? How is it you know he didn't simply meet with an unfortunate accident?"

"It was unfortunate for him, to be sure," Benjamin answered. "But no accident. You are forgetting he was buried. And that was certainly no accident."

"No," Katherine allowed. "He could not have pulled the earth in on himself. But how can you tell what happened?"

Benjamin shook his shaggy black head. "Well, I am not sure I can. Not exactly. But it appears as if he were crushed beneath an extremely heavy weight. Now that in itself is no proof of evil intent. But then there are the marks of the ropes on his wrists and ankles."

"Were there? I did not see them."

"No, the skin was much too decomposed for you to be able to tell. The ropes have been there though. And were removed after he was dead. It could be there was no deliberate attempt made to harm him. He was simply trussed up and left alone and met his death quite by chance. Perhaps in a building that collapsed or behind a wall or a loaded cart that fell on him through no design of the person who tied him. But he was also hidden. And that would not be necessary unless he had, in fact, been killed. You see what I mean?"

"Yes." Katherine took an absent sip from the goblet in her hand. "So you think . . . what?" she said slowly. "He stole from Nathaniel's uncle and someone else stole from him?"

Benjamin shrugged. "It would seem likely. The money was missing and so was he. That is too much of a coincidence to be, well, a coincidence."

"Who do you think it was?"

Katherine regarded the pleasant face next to her with intent green eyes. "Do you know?"

Benjamin gave a short laugh. "No. There are many men whose greed could overwhelm them at any given moment. Even me."

It was Katherine's turn to laugh. "Forgive me, but if you were one of those greedy men, I think you would have provided yourself with better comforts."

"So I should have."

Benjamin slapped his cap against his knee. "Well, I must be off my dear. This is a puzzle for the magistrate. The coppersmith's wife is in the straw. Patience is a good midwife and careful, so the birth should go well, but the coppersmith has asked that I come before the naming of the child."

After Benjamin left, Katherine sat quietly trying to piece together the tangle of deaths surrounding her. Someone had taken the account book the night of the fire but the thief could not have been the steward. He was, by then, quite dead. If someone killed the steward, then perhaps, that same person also murdered Lord Philip and Lady Elizabeth and then tried to do away with both Nathaniel and herself. She shuddered, glancing down at the raised red weals on her arms. And almost succeeded.

She must cast her mind back to the night of the fire. See if she could remember anything that might help her discover the identity of her enemy. For she had one. Of that she was quite sure. As she mounted the winding stone stairs and listened to the hollow ring of her footsteps sounding down behind her, she whispered to herself.

"Think only of the room. Forget the fire. Was there anything different? Anything out of place?"

The room was dark and empty when she entered, the bed neatly made. A few coals glowed on the hearth and she lit a taper and set it back in the candlestand. She stared at the stand. It was made of lead and very heavy, having a circular base with three arms fused at equal distances apart from one another at the base and meeting at the top to form the shape of a cone. A small lead piece sat on top and extended to three hollowed out rounds for receiving candles.

The night of the fire she remembered pushing the stand off the bed. Everyone assumed Nathaniel had knocked it over, the lighted candles igniting the curtains. She had shared that assumption until just this moment, when she realized it could not have happened that way.

Katherine frowned and ran her hand down the main post of the stand. She had lighted the candles herself the night of the fire and the stand was at the foot of the bed. Nathaniel should have put them out when he came up, but he may not have. When the fire began, the stand was laying across the bed on Nathaniel's side. She remembered pushing it off. Katherine smiled thinly. And that stand was never on his side of the bed. His falcon had once burned her foot on it when it was still hot with candle grease. From then on he never permitted the stand to be anywhere but under the window on her side or at the foot of the bed. The chamber servants would never have put it there. They knew better. And she had not put it there. Yet that is where it ended up.

Katherine began a slow inspection of the room. She put her hand on the firehood — gingerly for it was still hot — and studied the hearth a moment. Then she circled the chamber, touching the furnishings, examining the window, peering into the corners. She went back to the bed. The new bed stood in exactly the same place as the former one. She crouched down and ran her hands against the wall, frowned a moment when her fingers found a deep groove, then bent to inspect it more closely. She rose with a sickening heaviness in her belly and a lump in her throat.

With trembling hands, Katherine dragged the candlestand over to the far side of the bed, braced the base against the wall so it would not slip back and leaned it out over against the bed. It caught the stand more than halfway to the base. Then she climbed as gently as she could onto her own side of the bed. Slowly she moved over to what would have been Nathaniel's side. The mattress began to dip and when she got farther to his side, the candlestand leaned into the depression. She rolled all the way over as Nathaniel would have in his sleep. The stand upended onto the bed with a bounce, scraping the wall and leaving a long black gash in the plaster. Katherine scooped up the lone lighted candle that fell onto the bedding before it had a chance to do any damage. She blew it out and flung it aside then knelt down next to the wall again, narrowing her eyes and running her hands over the fresh black gouge and the identical gash beside it, now covered in new whitewash.

It was true then. Someone had waited for them to fall asleep, came in, picked up the candlestand and carried it around to Nathaniel's side of the bed, knowing that eventually any movement he made would topple it. And it would have had to be a man. Someone strong enough to lift the stand. She and Nathaniel would have awakened if it had been dragged across the floor as she had done. Instantly, an image of Victor Stafford leaped into view but her mind recoiled from the thought. He had saved her. Surely he would not have done so if he was the one who set the fire. Unless some sense of remorse drove him to rescue her at the last minute. She squeezed her eyes shut and shook her head. No. It could not have been him. But in her mind's eye she saw the heavy muscles of his arms straining against the weight of the candlestand.

CHAPTER 8

KATHERINE PACED HER CHAMBER FOR SOME TIME, going over and over everything she knew. First, Nathaniel's aunt and uncle are poisoned. Their account book is tampered with. Money is stolen. It appears as if their steward has schemed against them, killed them, robbed them and then slunk away. There is a fire. Nathaniel dies in the fire and the account book vanishes. Has the steward returned? No, he cannot have done. He is lying in a hole far away from the castle. Someone has taken the record book, but not the steward. Someone has started the fire, but not the steward. The wretched Gerard is quite innocent.

So there is someone else, someone who comes and goes in the castle with perfect freedom and is responsible for everything. That someone may have altered the records; the steward discovered the discrepancies and was done away with because of it. But why? Even as her mind formed the question she knew the answer. The castle and income from the manor. Do away with all the heirs and it could be taken. The holding was not so large as some but the income was good. That much she had learned since she'd been at Crenfeld.

And now she was a woman alone, living among strangers. At the mercy of some faceless enemy who worked stealthily and invisibly.

And what of the record book? How could anyone remove it from the solar without being seen? It would have to have been removed the night of the banquet to safeguard the thief. She had been fortunate enough to find the answer to her question of how the fire was started. Perhaps her luck would hold and she would learn what had become of the record book. The solar might yet yield a clue to its whereabouts.

Her temporary bed was no longer in the little room off the great hall. In its place stood a large round tub half-filled with soapy water. Both the table and little stool remained as before. She remembered the day she awoke in this room. The day of Lord Victor's visit. He had been very kind. She did not want to believe he could be the one. That he would do such a thing. Yet he shared the income from the manor and he would have it all if she was dead.

Katherine shook her head. Never mind him. When I awoke, what did I see? She frowned. The table as now, the stool as now, the candle she had used and even the little puddle of fat scraped from the book and curled on top of the table. But the account book itself was gone. Some time between the night of the fire and when she regained consciousness, the book had been removed. She doubted it could have been taken while she lay in that room. Agnes would not have left her for very long. So it must have been done very quickly. And the easiest solution — burn it!

She sprang to the fireplace. The hearth told her nothing. Many fires had burned and been cleaned away by efficient little Alice. There was nothing there. The hearth was clean.

She rested her hand on the firehood and leaned in, twisting her head to look up inside the chimney. The chimney was thickly caked with soot. She reached behind her for the poker and ran it up the chimney, trying to stay out of range of the chunks of soot it dislodged. Once a good-sized pile had accumulated on the hearth, she put aside the poker, rolled up her sleeves and began the dirty task of sorting through the litter.

Her hands were soon as black as the inside of the chimney and it took some time to separate the sticky pieces. But her efforts were rewarded and eventually she sat back on her haunches in triumph, a scrap of grimy parchment in her hand. Carefully she rubbed it with the hem of her dress. The soot cleaned away, she made out a few words.

geese 10, already reckoned, oats, 3 quarters and a . . .

Too little left to betray the identity of the thief but at least now she was sure. Fearing discovery, someone had destroyed the book. A plausible chain of events unfolded to her. Not satisfied with what he had managed to steal from the manor, and emboldened by the ease of Gerard's murder, the murder of Lord Philip and Lady Elizabeth and even of her own husband, the deadly adversary would make her his next quarry. Once she was eliminated, he could move in to claim the spoils. Crenfeld Castle.

Katherine considered her plight grimly and a hard glint came into her emerald eyes. She was not about to be slaughtered like a feeble-witted sheep. Her enemy would not find the mewling coward he hoped for.

"This is my land," she whispered fiercely to the bare walls. "My land."

Many women had been pawns in the chess game of men's ambition. And as easily discarded.

"You will not find me so easy to dispose of, my black-hearted foe," she muttered. "Not so easy as you might hope."

Katherine started to wipe her grimy hands on her skirt, then caught sight of a soot encrusted wall hanging suspended next to the fireplace. The back of it might be cleaner. She pulled the dirty tapestry away from the wall, rubbed her hands on the rough back side and was about to let it fall into place when she noticed a line of loosened mortar running up a row of bricks. Curious, she pushed the hanging out of the way and used the poker to pry along the edge of the bricks. To her astonishment, a section of brickwork moved as a whole and suddenly she was looking down a black corridor. Katherine gasped and fell back a moment then moved forward to inspect the workings of the hidden door. Hinged on the inside, the framed-in brick door had a wooden pull attached by heavy lead bolts driven into the backside of the bricks. But how would one tug it snug to the long brick wall in the solar? Katherine searched the face of the door, holding back the hanging as she explored its surface. At the base of the door she found a small inconspicuous hinged piece of wood lying flat against the door. Flipped out, it was easily used as a pull handle and the brick door was once more flush against the wall. Katherine nodded in appreciation of the simple device, fetched a lighted taper, pushed open the door and stepped gingerly inside the wall.

The passageway was narrow and dank and she had to stoop for there was little head room. As she crept further along the corridor she heard the rushing of the river growing louder until finally she stood at the lip of an outside entrance, high on the cliff overlooking the Wyvern.

The river roared and frothed beneath her, boiling around the rocks.

She watched it for a few moments then retraced her steps, closed the entry from the solar and refastened the wall hanging that concealed it. She would tell no one of her discovery. It looked very dangerous. She wondered uneasily exactly how resolute her enemy might be and whether he was making use of this secret passage.

Over the following three weeks Katherine made a painstaking reconstruction of the account book. Nory turned out to be a wellspring of information with regard to the rents, having kept company with the long-tongued washerwoman. Married to a freeman owing money rents instead of most labour services, the washerwoman kept her sharp eyes on the rents owed by both villein and freeman lest she perceive any inequities to her disadvantage. Consequently she knew how much land each tenant was to plow and with how many oxen. She knew whether he was to use his own horse and harrow and whether or not he was free to fetch seed from Katherine's granary. All money rents received the same scrutiny and the minutest of details was weighed for balance.

Katherine gathered some of the more capable men to measure the demesne lands. She gave old Henry the position of overseer. Having lived longest on the manor, he was the most familiar with its holdings. He took his privilege seriously and she knew she could trust him to see to the accuracy of the measurement.

Katherine consulted those men who could tell her how and in what crops the land was tilled and she personally examined all the animals to see that she was properly stocked with cattle, sheep, oxen and swine. She also looked over the cart-horses to satisfy herself they were well cared for and strong enough to carry the loads to her barns at harvest.

Grace was very forthcoming with regard to the cost of those foodstuffs, spices and wines purchased by the castle. She had an excellent memory and Katherine doubted that much escaped her notice.

Old Henry's prying nature was put to good use and he was able to gather the information Katherine needed to complete her restoration of the records.

In the end, Katherine was grateful she had to go through the tedious piecing together of the accounts. Her knowledge of the manor was both accurate and personal. She knew each virgate of land in detail, from tilled fields to parks and forests. She had seen all the animals, become acquainted with the tenants and their families and knew the source of all off-manor purchase and expenses.

So it was with no little satisfaction that Katherine closed the new account book and placed it carefully in a niche in the small storeroom above the kitchen. The storeroom's few wooden steps brought her down to the bustle and smells of the kitchen.

She always enjoyed watching the kitchen activity. Lightly crusted loaves of bread were just being removed from the oven and she bent appreciatively to smell their warm, yeasty freshness. At the center table a side of beef was being cut into chunks for the pot. A pair of plucked geese lay on the edge of the table, their heads lolling limply over the side. Barrels of beans, carrots and shelled peas stood under the table. Overhead, clumps of onions hung from their dried and twisted stems. A pile of greens filled a large bowl at Grace's arm. Grace opened a bag of spices and poked her generous nose just inside the lip of the sack. She grunted and passed the bag to a woman stirring the big cauldron over the main fire. The contents were upended into the pot and the bag thoroughly shaken out.

Two women with their backs to Katherine were busy at the well. While one woman leaned into the well to steady the rope, the other worked the handle that wrapped the rope around the center pole bringing up the bucket. There was something familiar about them, but it was not until the bucket had been raised and detached that they turned around and she saw their faces.

Katherine stifled a small cry. What were they doing here? Those two odd women from the field. She drew Grace to one side.

"Why are those women in my kitchen?" she whispered.

Grace gave her a blank look. "Who? Hester and Nettie?"

"Keep your voice down," Katherine warned. "What are they up to?"

Grace looked even more perplexed. "Drawing water, madam. Is something wrong?"

"Why have I not seen them before now?"

Grace's face cleared. "Just began yesterday. They offered to take on the task seeing as the young wench whose duty it is took ill."

"But both of them? Surely, there is no need for both."

Grace chuckled and wiped her broad hands on her apron.

"Don't know about Hester and Nettie do you? They're twins. Born clutching one another and they're still at it poor things. Never apart, they aren't. Hester did once have a suitor. She is quite pretty. But he tired of Nettie's constant presence and Nettie became hysterical at the separation marriage was sure to bring. And so the man went away and Hester did not marry. They often speak together as if they know each other's thoughts and cannot bear to be apart for even a moment."

"How very strange," Katherine said slowly. "What a dreadful existence."

"They do not seem to mind. Nettie is something of a worrier and frowns almost all the time. Hester too is not quite right, but they seem content and work well as long as I don't forget to have them work together."

Katherine watched the two women curiously as they each took hold of one side of the pail and carried it to be poured into the cooking pot over the main fire. The fire was across the room and the pot was heavy so they moved slowly, giving Katherine time to study them. She began to feel a little foolish at her fright upon seeing them those few nights ago. They were pathetic really.

Grace was right about Hester. She had lovely large vacant blue eyes, a prettily shaped face and a slender, feminine form. But she also had a sad look of resignation that made Katherine think she was not nearly as happy with her lot as Grace had said. Nettie, for her part, was an extremely fretful looking woman. Her features were more angular, her eyebrows sloped and cowering over her eyes. And her figure was rigid, as if braced against some antici-pated misery. She felt a wave of pity watching them, bound hopelessly together by some mysterious and unbreakable cord.

Katherine wondered if they recognized her.

"Good morning," she ventured.

The two women looked up with a start and Nettie covered her pale, brittle lips with a protective hand. Hester kept her blue eyes fixed wide on Katherine. They were not vacant now, but frightened.

"Madam!" they cried in choked tones.

"I saw you in the meadow. Do you remember?"

The women nodded vigorously. "Yes, madam," they said in unison. "We remember."

"What were you doing?"

"Ah, that's a hard question, madam," Nettie replied anxiously and the two continued to stare at her in silence. Katherine was beginning to be annoyed by their reticence when Hester took her sister's hand in her own, squeezed it and the two exchanged looks.

"It is the lady, Nettie dear," Hester said to her sister. Nettie nodded gravely.

"We have the gift," Hester said, in such a bleak and despairing way that Katherine forgot her annoyance and frowned.

"The gift?"

Nettie lowered her eyes. "The changers gift," she whispered.

The women continued to hold hands and each supplied part of the rambling answer.

"When we touch things. Yes, when we touch them. If the person who eats or uses the thing we touch, if they have no evil in their heart, all is well. But if there is wickedness then it can make them ill or cause them to have an accident or even to die. Father Simon says we are very fortunate to have the gift."

"He does?"

"Oh, yes. It is a great blessing to have the gift, he says. Father Simon does not have it. Only us," Nettie said eagerly. "And," she added, "It makes people frightened of us sometimes and they call us witches. But it is only that we have the power. 'Tis their own hearts betray them."

"I see. So the things you were gathering?"

"Oh, for Grace, madam. For her hand. She is a good woman and so the remedy we made was sure to do her good. And she was not a bit frightened, which only goes to show she has a pure heart, doesn't it. Father Simon says we mustn't mind about what happens because it is only the wicked that are found out. It is hard not to feel sorry sometimes though," Hester finished. "Some seem so good and it turns out they are not." she said disconsolately. "Father says the heart is desperately wicked, but I was so sure that . . . ," she began.

Nettie clutched her arm in a warning spasm and Hester clamped her lips shut over the words already escaped.

"Pardon us, madam, but Grace will be wanting more water in the cooking pot. Please, may we go?" they begged.

Katherine sighed and nodded. She watched them hurry away and wondered what secrets were locked up in their strange, tangled minds.

Katherine left the scuttle and scramble of the kitchen somewhat reluctantly. Now the task of reproducing the account book was completed, with all the necessary interviews and inquiries, there was nothing for her to do. And she disliked idleness. Perhaps she would pay a visit to Stonehaven. She had not seen Ciscilla since the awful night of the fire but felt sure Ciscilla's gay company would do much to restore her own flagging spirits. And, of course, give her an opportunity to go over the accounts with Lord Victor. He had kept his promise not to tax her with correcting the errors in her records that affected his income from the manor, and she appreciated his restraint.

But she was ready with a reckoning and eager to dispense with any unpleasantness. She wanted to begin anew with Lord Victor; to wipe out the disturbing memory of his resentment over the unfair cost to him for manor services. And she was eager for an ally, even if she did not quite trust him. He was a man of power and if she could win him over and the time should come that she needed to protect her holdings, perhaps he would stand with her. He may even be persuaded to intervene on her behalf before the king.

Katherine opened her wardrobe chest and began choosing clothes for the trip.

It took most of the day to reach Stonehaven Castle and when it did not drizzle, the sun beat hard on Katherine's covered chariot. It was stuffy inside her wagon. Stuffy and hot. Katherine's clothes stuck to her in damp folds. Agnes fared no better and panted and fanned her face with the edge of her surcoat.

"Madam are you not parched? May we not stop for a drink from that stream?"

Katherine was thirsty too and consented to the rest, whereupon Agnes immediately leaned out the window.

"Roger, madam will stop here," she called to the driver.

Once the chariot halted, the two women climbed down into the outside air. The breeze, though warm, chilled Katherine to the bone and she was forced to shiver until the hot sun dried her dress.

Agnes got down on her hands and knees and drank greedily from the cold, rushing water. Then she filled a small pot and offered it to Katherine. Roger detached Pygine from his harness and led him and his harness mate to the creek for a drink. Their thirst slaked, Katherine and Agnes sank into a cool patch of corn cockles and caressed the silky purple flowers with absent fingers.

It didn't seem long before Roger approached them, fingering his hat in front of him.

"Madam," he said. "If you wish to reach Stonehaven before nightfall, we should continue."

The sun had almost left the sky when they made Stonehaven Castle. Katherine gasped as she caught sight of it in the twilight. Its appearance was like that of a magnificent waking dream. The castle had many tall slender walls and towers of sparkling white with fluttering red and gold banners on the topmost spires. The waters of the moat were of such sparkling transparency that the castle seemed to float atop its own rippling white reflection.

Katherine was relieved to see Ciscilla come smiling to meet her, hands outstretched to clasp her own warmly. Katherine had sent a messenger ahead but there had been no time for a reply.

"This is a wonderful surprise!" Ciscilla cried. "It is so dull without the company of a friend," she said and gave Katherine an impulsive hug.

Katherine smiled and followed her prattling, graceful friend indoors. The floor in this castle's great hall was not planked but made of tiles laid out in large squares of many colours. The stone walls were almost completely covered in thick, softly pleated red curtains that hung from thin gilded rods running just under the roof timbers. They were parted at intervals to make room for doorways to other parts of the castle. Above the open fireplace recessed into the wall behind the dais, the Stafford family crest was carved and painted upon an immense wall of wood.

Against a field of gold, two great red hawks spread their wings back to back, talons outstretched, beaks parted.

Mealtime being long past, the high table was empty as were the shorter benches and trestles on the hall floor. The laundress and her young ladies walked up and down the rows, removing stained bord cloths. They ceased their work and stood politely until Ciscilla and Katherine had left the hall. Agnes followed slowly, her eyes taking in the unaccustomed luxuries.

"Your sleeping chamber is just along here over the pantry," Ciscilla said. "Roger will have the chamberlain bring up your clothes chest."

Ciscilla pushed open the door of a snug, warm upper room. A pair of large-framed beds piled high with plump quilts stood at opposite ends of the room, small pallets made up beside each. Two women in nightclothes sat on a bed, one combing the thick blonde hair of the other. The woman whose hair was receiving attention looked up in surprise, a slow smile curving her lips.

"Ciscilla, I was not aware there were to be other guests."

Ciscilla dimpled. "Neither was I," she said, taking Katherine's hand and drawing her over.

"Katherine dear, this is Marjorie Clere." Here she winked broadly and arched a slender eyebrow. "She thinks to win the heart of my brother and make herself my sister-in-law."

"Ciscilla," Marjorie scolded. "You really must learn to be less direct. Your manners, darling."

"Oh, never mind, Marjorie. This is my friend, Katherine Fendlay. She has come from Crenfeld Castle."

A pair of very blue eyes regarded Katherine. "Crenfeld? I know that name."

"Perhaps, Miss Clere, because it is a shared manor with Stonehaven," Katherine suggested.

"Yes, of course. Victor must have mentioned the name to me. Claringdon is the village, is it not?"

"Yes, that is correct. Claringdon."

"Father Simon and I are very old friends." Marjorie said.

Katherine was surprised to hear anyone claim to be a friend of the priest. She had thought him rather reclusive and solitary. Perhaps Marjorie Clere was of some noble family. The Church and the nobility had long been close companions. That he should have friends as ordinarily as any other man seemed strange to her and she regarded Marjorie with greater interest.

"I hope you do not snore, Madam Fendlay," Marjorie said playfully. "The last time I shared this room, the woman made a dreadful noise."

Katherine laughed and shook her head. "We will be very quiet, Miss Clere," she promised.

Agnes thumped down on her pallet beside Katherine.

"Do you snore?" she muttered indignantly. "You are a lady. Of course you do not snore!"

Katherine raised herself on one elbow and giggled. "It was all in fun, Agnes. But mind you do not lay on your back." she whispered.

Agnes sniffed and rolled over to cover herself with her blanket. Katherine sank back down onto her bed and closed her eyes, passing the night with pleasant dreams of suitors lining up to beg for her hand. And as is usual in dreams, her hands and arms were perfectly white and unmarked, as if they'd never come near to a flame.

The next day dawned surprisingly warm and sunny. It felt good to wake up to no responsibilities and Katherine allowed herself the luxury of languishing in her bed in the quiet of the emptied guest chamber. Miss Clere and both servants were gone. She yawned and stretched and turned her face to the warmth of an unrestrained sun bursting in through the window. Agnes had removed all her gowns from the chest and arranged them on nearby perches. Katherine glanced lazily at each in turn and finally decided on the lighter fabric of a crisp white dress. Ciscilla had voiced a desire to play backgammon in the garden this morning and as it was a beautiful summer day, Katherine meant to be comfortable. She decided to do her hair in two side cauls and was just pulling some remaining strands through the open coils when Ciscilla tapped on the door and came in. She picked up the skirts of her rich green dress and swept over to Katherine's side.

"You do have lovely hair," Ciscilla cried. "Such a bright red. Here let me help you." Ciscilla tugged some hair through a caul and arranged the russet locks in front of Katherine's ears. Katherine thanked her and added a white goffered veil of the same fabric as her dress.

Ciscilla cocked her pretty dark head. "White suits you." She made a face. "You missed Mass you know. Marjorie was there with my brother. She means to be his wife," she sighed. "He does need a wife, but I do not think she likes me very much."

Katherine laughed. "Cheer up. It is only that you are different than she. Impulsive. Besides, you will marry soon and then it will not matter."

Ciscilla wrinkled her nose. "Silly, you mean." Then she shrugged and smiled and fluttered her long lashes. "I will be someone's wife soon, I think." She arched an eyebrow. "There are several young men who seem willing. They make sheep's eyes in the street and argue over dances at parties."

Katherine squeezed Ciscilla's arm. "You see. It will not be long now before one of them asks for your hand."

"They must get past Victor first. He can be hard at times. And for all that he disapproves of me, he does love me and will choose me out a good husband."

She turned sober dark eyes on Katherine. "What about you? Will you marry again, do you think? In time, I mean."

Katherine's laugh seemed harsh even to her own ears. "That will not be possible now."

Ciscilla's eyes widened. "But why? You are not old."

"Oh, it is not my age Ciscilla and in any case, nothing for you to fret over. Now, will you feed me or shall I perish with hunger?"

Ciscilla took Katherine's hand. "Come into the garden. There is bread and wine set out and I have even persuaded the kitchen to part with some very special sweet peaches for you."

Katherine reclined on one elbow beneath the dappled shade of an aged apple tree with a green skirt of vines creeping around its base. The heat of the sun brought out the heady perfume of the flower garden. Katherine could not recall when she had been more content.

"The peaches were delicious, Ciscilla. Thank you so much. It is restful here. And so beautiful. You *are* lucky."

"I suppose I am." She glanced around absently. " I never really think about it. I just enjoy it." Ciscilla gave an impish grin. "Are you ready for me to defeat you in a game of backgammon?"

Katherine held out her hand.

"Pull me up then and we shall see."

They played at a little table near the fish pond. While waiting her turn, Katherine enjoyed watching the trout break the surface from time to time. They were pretty fish. Occasionally she glimpsed the lazy drift of a long-nosed pike.

"Your turn, Katherine."

Katherine rolled the dice, considered her next move and made it. Ciscilla squealed and clapped her hands together.

"I have you now!" she cried. "You left all these unprotected, and I will not take pity on you!" She scooped up the dice and was about to roll them across the board when a small fair-haired child burst from behind a bush and scampered up to them on sturdy little legs. His tunic and stockings were covered with dirt and he was holding out a grubby little fist.

"Cissy, Cissy, look!" he lisped through plump lips.

Ciscilla laid down the dice and made room for him on her lap. "Come show me, Edward."

The lad scrambled up on her knees and opened his hand cautiously. A fuzzy orange and black ball unrolled itself and began inching its way across the little boy's palm.

Ciscilla pulled her head back. "A caterpillar!"

She lifted her eyebrows in Katherine's direction. "How nice!"

Edward began to open his other hand and three smaller versions of the first creature ventured out from between his fingers. "Her babies!" he cried triumphantly. "Would you like to hold them?"

Ciscilla closed the child's hands over the caterpillars and shook her head. "I think they would like it better if you took them home. Do you remember where you found them?"

The little boy looked at his prize doubtfully. "All right," he agreed with reluctance. "Yes, I remember."

The small boy slid back to the ground to gaze at Katherine with round solemn eyes.

"This is my friend, Lady Katherine," Ciscilla explained. "She has come to stay with us for a while."

"And who is this handsome young man?" Katherine asked.

The young man in question stood a little straighter.

"I am Edward Stafford. Lord Victor is my father," he said proudly. "Do you know my father?"

Katherine studied the chubby little face. "Yes, I do," she said slowly. She recognized the grey of the eyes and the beginnings of a cleft in his chin. Katherine frowned. But what of his mother?

Ciscilla spoke up before she asked the question aloud.

"Edward, please take these things into the kitchen for me. And ask the cook to give you a peach. Tell him I said you should have one."

Ciscilla tied up their breakfast things in a piece of cloth and Edward bounded off back the way he had come, disappearing into the shrubbery as nimbly as a rabbit down a hole.

"It is painful for Edward to hear talk of his mother," Ciscilla began. "You were wondering about her?"

Katherine nodded. "Yes, I was."

There were lines of sadness at the corners of Ciscilla's pleasant, upturned lips.

"Her name was Allota. She was not strong. Very frail and very pretty. With a soft voice and soft ways. Everyone was besotted with her. Allota died while Victor was fighting the king's war with Philip of France. In childbirth. The infant perished with her and we buried them together. It went very hard with Edward. And when Victor came home to the news that his wife was dead, he went away again to another part of England. We did not see him for months."

"He must have loved her very much," Katherine said gently.

Ciscilla's eyes glistened. "Yes, he did. We all did. But now Victor recognizes his little son's need for a mother. You have seen him. He lacks discipline and order. He needs a mother."

Katherine smiled. "He is a delightful little fellow. I am sure any woman would find him easy to love."

"I hope Marjorie thinks so. Right now she's more interested in Victor."

"That will change. You have to be a wife before you can be a mother. Once she is sure of Victor, she will have time for Edward."

Ciscilla nodded. "We have known Marjorie's family for a very long time and she's always had her eyes on Victor. He took no notice of her until recently. He is different now. Sad and distant."

"He is wise to choose his next wife from among familiar acquaintances. And perhaps a wife will cheer him and he will learn to be happy again," Katherine said.

Ciscilla nodded slowly. "Perhaps. She and Victor share many friends at court and she is a charming hostess. Marjorie will, I guess, make Victor a good wife."

They sat in companionable silence until the sound of voices and approaching footsteps roused them. It was Victor and the Clere woman. Marjorie had threaded her arm through his and was laughing up at him as they came into view. There was a faintly bemused smile on Victor's lips as he looked down onto her bright head and animated face. They stopped walking and talking when they caught sight of the two women.

"You. What are you doing here?" Victor was startled but Marjorie merely smiled contentedly.

"I did not tell him you were coming," Ciscilla whispered behind her hand.

"Surely you did not mean that the way it sounded, brother," Ciscilla said archly.

"No. No. Forgive me," Victor apologized. "Of course you are welcome here. I just wasn't expecting to see you." He ran his fingers through the fair hair at the nape of his neck.

Katherine had seen that gesture before, when he was uncomfortable and at a loss for words.

She smiled at him. "I followed your advice, Lord Stafford. I have taken care of the business of the manor and I thought to combine business with a visit to your sister. She has kindly welcomed me. I have made up a proper reckoning of the carting charges from your castle and will give the figures to your steward before I leave."

She turned to Ciscilla. "Come inside. We must give your brother privacy in his own garden."

When Victor did not reply at once, Marjorie spoke up. "We did not mean to chase you away, but thank you."

As Katherine and Ciscilla began to leave, Edward bolted from the bushes and collided against Katherine's knees, clutching at her skirts to steady himself.

She turned his hands palm up in her own.

"Taken them home, have you?"

The child nodded, beaming.

Katherine frowned. "You have scratched yourself, little man."

"Doesn't hurt," Edward answered.

She smiled and tousled his hair playfully.

She did not notice Victor bearing down on them, a frown on his lean face.

"Edward," he said sharply. "That is no way to behave. Running into the ladies like that."

The little boy's countenance fell in dismay and he hung his head contritely.

His father gave him a light tap on the cheek. "Now off to nurse to have your hands washed."

"She will be very angry that I am dirty. Again."

"If your father has no objection," Katherine interceded, "we can easily take care of them in the pond."

Katherine took Edward's hand and they looked up at Victor.

"Fine," he said gruffly, his eyes on Katherine's. Victor dropped his glance, then struck at a twig with his cane before turning to limp quickly back to the waiting Marjorie.

Katherine felt the same sadness she had before when watching him move. It must frustrate him to be crippled in this way. That whole men fought in the king's war while he was left behind. She felt a tug at her skirts.

"My hands. Will you wash them? Or shall I wipe them on the grass?"

Edward's rosy cheeks plumped when he grinned. Katherine shook a finger at him.

"Over to the pond. Quick as you can."

The little boy chuckled and hurled himself across the grass to drop flat out on his chest and dangle his hands in the pond water. He swished them around energetically, frightening the trout and sending them darting in all directions.

Katherine examined Edward's hands, pronounced them clean and sent him on his way.

"Try to keep them that way," she called out after him.

"He certainly has taken to you," Ciscilla remarked when Katherine rejoined her. She winked at Katherine. "You have bewitched him for sure."

Katherine gave a short laugh. "A conquest. My one and only."

"Why do you say such things?" Ciscilla complained. "There is no good reason for you to say that."

"There are two very good reasons, actually," Katherine said.

Ciscilla frowned. "What do you mean?"

"I mean — these." Katherine unfastened the sleeve buttons of her dress and pulled back the fabric on both arms up to her elbows in two swift moves. Then she thrust out her bare forearms.

Ciscilla's pretty dark eyes opened wide and she gasped and put a hand to her mouth. A perfect hand, Katherine noted miserably. Soft, white and delicate. Without a blemish.

Ciscilla lowered her hand slowly, seeing the pain in Katherine's eyes.

"Do they hurt? They are so red."

"Not any more."

"Will they always . . . I mean are they going to . . . "

"Return to normal? No. They will stay this way. The physician says they will always have the mark of the flame that burned them. Like a brand."

"I am so sorry," Ciscilla whispered. "I did not realize."

"How could you. I try to keep them hidden. And I mean to keep them hidden. I dislike pity."

"You showed them to me."

"Only because I want you to understand why there will be no husband."

Ciscilla regarded Katherine's sad face a moment then silently helped her refasten the buttons on her sleeves and tug them gently well down over her wrists.

She put her arm firmly around Katherine's shoulder and gave her a small hug.

"We will not speak of it again," she said in a soft voice. "I promise."

Katherine smiled. "You are a good friend."

The tragic confidence forged an unspoken bond between them and Katherine was glad she had told Ciscilla. A real friend was what she needed most. Someone from whom there need be no secrets. They passed the morning pleasantly, sunning themselves in an oriole window and chatting of nothing in particular.

Dinnertime brought another unexpected guest — Father Simon, returning from an audience with his bishop. The priest sat at the far end of the table and Marjorie Clere claimed the chair next to him. Victor sat beside Marjorie, then Ciscilla and Katherine. Edward slipped in unnoticed to plunk himself down in the vacant spot beside Katherine. While his father carved the joint he put a finger to his pink lips and leaned toward her.

"Don't tell father. But I cannot find nurse and I'm hungry," he explained.

Katherine warranted the search for his nurse had been none too diligent but smiled and nodded her agreement to be co-conspirator. He applied himself to the meal with great eagerness while Katherine listened to the table conversation.

"Was your journey tiring, father?" Marjorie asked.

"One must not complain when engaged in God's work, my dear."

"No, of course not." Marjorie broke the small loaf between them, handing him the larger piece.

"The business of the Church goes well?"

"Well enough. I was seeking advice on a matter recently come to my attention." He wiped his mouth carefully.

"It may concern you too, Lord Stafford and you, madam," he said, bending forward to look at Katherine. "How opportune that you should both be present."

"How so?" Victor asked.

"It seems one of your tenants has unlawfully procured a copy of Holy Scripture. Such a man can be very dangerous, both to himself and to any others he may defile with his heresy."

Katherine kept her voice even. "Do you know who the man is, father?"

Victor looked at Katherine and then at Simon.

"Do you?" he echoed.

Father Simon twined his fingers together on the table and regarded them with a frown.

"No. But I mean to find out."

His lips stretched in a pale grim line and his equally pale blue eyes turned cold and hard. "I mean to find out," he repeated. " The village has closed its mouth, but it knows. I'm sure of it."

"If no one is saying anything, father, perhaps it is because your worries are unfounded. How do you know anyone has done something so wicked?" Marjorie asked.

"One of the villagers had the effrontery to question me on a point of scripture from which I have never taught.

When I asked him where he heard the passage he became vague and evasive. It is a dangerous thing when men start to draw conclusions on their own without the guidance of the Church. They may fall into all sorts of error."

He looked sharply at Victor and then at Katherine. "Have you heard or seen anything of this?"

Victor shook his head. "No," he said. "I have heard no rumours and only my chaplain reads scripture at Stonehaven."

Katherine ignored the question and instead asked. "Why does the Church say men may not come to a correct understanding of scripture on their own? I know the law, of course, but I am quite ignorant of the reasons for it."

Ciscilla had lost interest in the conversation and was making faces at Edward around Katherine. The boy ducked his head and grinned at her from between his fingers. Simon's lips were pinched now. "There is no understanding of spiritual matters possible for the common man," he said. "The pope has declared it."

"The pope is a Frenchman," Victor pointed out. "He may be mistaken."

The papacy had fallen into disrepute with the appointment of Clement VI of France. His private morals were notorious and cast a shadow over the whole papal institution. He gave lavish grants while the luxury and waste in Avignon had reached the ears of all the world. He claimed that his predecessors did not know how to be popes and had begun an unscrupulous traffic in benefices that was causing some to regard him as the devil incarnate.

Father Simon's face turned an ugly mottle of red and white. That he held himself in check was evident by his short, clipped speech.

"He is not mistaken. He is infallible in matters of the Church and could no more be mistaken than if he were the Lord Christ."

"So then it is the Church's opinion that not even a learned man, if not of the clergy, could possess scripture without causing himself great spiritual harm?" Katherine asked.

"It is more than opinion, madam. It is decreed. Scripture is on the Index and will remain on the Index until mankind has benefited from the wisdom of the Church and become more enlightened."

"I see." Katherine looked steadily into the priest's pale eyes. She was not about to give away Benjamin's secret. Perhaps she was wrong and perhaps she would regret it, but Victor was right. The pope was a Frenchman and England was at war with the French. Rumours had reached even her own ears that Clement VI's loyalties lay more with the king of France than with the Church. She would not leave Benjamin to the tender mercies of papal authority.

Father Simon's eyes narrowed as he realized he would get no help from this quarter. But he would root out the heretic, with or without them. And if he could prove they *had* known . . .

He patted his lips one more time then pushed back from the table.

"I fear I must thank you for the meal and be on my way."

Marjorie laid a light, restraining hand on his arm. "Must you? I'd so looked forward to hearing of the goings on at court."

The priest's countenance lifted. "The gossip, you mean," he smiled at her.

Marjorie flushed but nodded and laughed. "If you insist, yes. The gossip."

"The bishop tells me the king has founded a new order, the Order of the Garter," the priest began. "Membership in the Order is limited to those with outstanding military careers. Those admitted are given a blue garter to wear on their sleeve."

Marjorie frowned. "A blue garter?"

The priest turned to Victor. "You may remember the beginnings Lord Stafford. It was at the banquet in Calais. The one to celebrate its capture. You were there, I think."

Victor nodded. "Yes, but I took little part in the celebrations. My leg."

Father Simon glanced down at the cane leaning against Victor's chair.

"Of course. But you must have observed the king dancing with the Countess of Salisbury. He was much in love with the lady."

"Yes, I remember."

"Then you must also have heard how her garter fell from her leg and that the king retrieved it and secured it around his sleeve saying, 'Evil to him who evil thinks'."

"Really!" Ciscilla cried. "Did he really do that?"

Victor gave a short laugh. "Either that or it was he who removed it from her leg in the first place."

Marjorie gasped. "Surely he did no such thing."

Victor smiled a patient smile. "Why do women think the king incapable of knavery? He had tried to force himself upon that very lady in her own home at Wark while her husband was a prisoner in France. Only her appeal to her honour and his own forestalled the king from taking advantage of her."

"She refused the king?"

Victor laughed once more at the incredulous look on his sister's face.

"Yes. And King Edward, to his credit, was so moved by her faithfulness to her husband that he ordered the earl ransomed and brought home without delay."

Ciscilla clasped her hands together, dark eyes shining. "Such chivalry. Did you hear that Father?"

The priest nodded. "Not many women could reject the king and still retain his favour. He was much impressed by the countess. And when she was so unfortunate as to lose her garter on the dance floor, no one touched it but watched the king stop to look at it. Everyone knew the blue silk trifle with its encrustation of jewels belonged to the Countess of Salisbury, and they knew of the king's feelings for her. So they simply smiled when he picked it up and put it on his own arm. And the motto of the order became, 'Evil to him who evil thinks'."

"That is a wonderful story, father. So romantic," Ciscilla cried. "But how could she refuse him after such gallantry?"

"I expect she loved her own husband." Marjorie suggested, her blue eyes fixed on Victor.

"Oh, love," Ciscilla shrugged. "It was the king."

Victor returned Marjorie's gaze. "And what about you?" he asked with a grin. "Would you be so indifferent to the heart of your husband?"

"It depends entirely on the husband of course," Marjorie answered. She smiled a crooked, flirtatious smile. "Some men incline a woman to loyalty."

Victor chuckled. "Really? What do you say about that Lady Fendlay?" Victor shifted in his chair to face Katherine. His lean face was creased in a playful grin.

Katherine felt her cheeks grow warm under his gaze, uncertain how to reply. Before the moment grew awkward, Ciscilla came to her rescue.

"What an insensitive thing to say to someone so newly bereaved. I am shocked you could be so callous to a woman's tender feelings."

Victor sobered immediately. "I forgot. Please, forgive me."

Ciscilla sniffed. "Forgot? How could you forget? You were there yourself when he died. And you forgot?"

Marjorie touched his arm. "You were? I have heard nothing of it. What happened?"

"You were not acquainted with those involved so I saw no reason to tell you. There was a fire. Lady Fendlay's husband died in the fire. It was an awful night."

"Oh, my dear." Marjorie turned a concerned faced to Katherine. "What happened?"

"It is a night best forgotten." Victor said firmly.

"You may tell her," Katherine's voice was soft. "I do not mind."

Victor studied Katherine's lowered lashes briefly then took a deep breath.

"If you are sure."

Marjorie's hand stole into Victor's and he gave it a small squeeze. With his eyes still fastened on Katherine's down-turned face, Victor cleared his throat.

"It was a feast day at Crenfeld Castle. A fine banquet with much good food, games, singing and dancing."

He turned to the priest. "You enjoyed it did you not father?"

Marjorie looked at Simon. "You were there?"

The priest closed his eyes and tented his fingers. "Of course. It is my village."

"Oh, yes. Go on Victor."

"It was a full day and I retired with my lad to the pallets in the stables. Some time in the night I heard screaming. It was still and dark and I saw nothing when I went outside to listen. The stables are on the other side of the castle from the lord's quarters and great hall and there were no flames or smoke to be seen from there. But I kept hearing the screams and some odd moanings. There was nothing to do but go inside and try to find the source. I smelled smoke as soon as I came into the ward. There was a tower window belching out flames and so I made for its stairway. The steps led directly to the lord's chamber. There I found Lady Fendlay trying to pull her husband from the bed. The bed was on fire, some floor tapestries were burning and there was smoke everywhere. I think Lord Fendlay had fainted in the smoke. Lady Fendlay collapsed when I reached her so I pulled her out as quickly as I could and then went back for her husband. But I could not reach him and it was too late by then anyway. A tragic accident," he added.

"It was no accident," Katherine heard herself say.

Victor's head jerked up and he pulled his hand from Marjorie's, using it to scrape his chair sideways to give her his full attention. Father Simon made choking noises and dropped his mazer heavily onto the table. Some of the wine spilled, spreading over the white cloth.

"What do you mean, no accident?" Victor cried.

Katherine looked at the startled faces around the table.

"Someone set fire to our room intentionally," she said flatly. "I think it was hoped we would both burn in it."

"Who would do such an unspeakable thing?" Ciscilla cried. "Surely you must be mistaken."

"No. I am not wrong. I wish I were, but I am not."

"How can you be sure?" Victor asked.

Katherine related her discovery of the scratches on the wall, the corresponding marks made by the candlestand, the bits of the account book in the solar fireplace; with the single exclusion of the secret passage, everything she had found the night she pieced it all together. When she finished, Victor let out a slow whistle.

"I commend you on your resourcefulness Lady Fendlay."

"Faced with a similar situation, any woman would have done the same."

Victor grinned. "In my experience, they would run for the first man they could find."

"That is not fair," Ciscilla cried.

"And not very wise either," Katherine added. "Not knowing who planned such a hideous end for my husband and I, I might have gone straight to the killer. How would I know whom to trust?"

Victor raised a brow and stroked his chin.

"You make a good point." He paused a moment and then held her eyes with his.

"How is it then, that you have told us? How do you know you can trust us?"

"I cannot know," Katherine replied candidly. "But it is highly unlikely you are all involved." Her eyes narrowed. "And if any of you are, you might as well know I will not die easily. I am on my guard."

She looked at Ciscilla's stricken face and rose abruptly.

"I have spoiled your dinner. I think perhaps I should not have come after all. Lord Victor, I appreciate your hospitality."

"But it is not safe for you at Crenfeld," Ciscilla cried. "You need protection. Victor. Please. Make her stay," she appealed.

Victor Stafford gave his sister an indulgent smile. "Precisely what would you have me do? Tie her up? Lock her in the strong room?"

Ciscilla leaped up and stamped her foot. "Victor! That's not funny. What kind of a man are you?"

"Apparently a very pliant one," Victor sighed. "Fine. I will escort the lady back to her home. And make certain she has a guardian. Will that satisfy you?"

"Excellent idea, Lord Stafford," Father Simon interjected. Then to Katherine, "I will join you in your carriage."

Mollified, Ciscilla nodded and put an arm around Katherine's shoulder. "Yes, that will satisfy me," she said.

"There is no need for all this," Katherine protested. "It is my problem and I will deal with it myself."

"You will not." Ciscilla said stubbornly. "You will accept my brother's help. Do it for me, Katherine," she pleaded. "No one will hurt you if you have Victor's protection. They would not dare."

Victor's eyebrows soared. "You give me too much credit, dear sister. But very well. It is settled, then. Collect your things, Lady Fendlay, and we will start. "

He grasped the head of his cane, used it to push himself up from his chair and motioned to a kitchen servant standing against the far wall. "Fetch me John Elder."

He noticed for the first time the now sleeping figure of his little son slumped down in his seat. He chuckled and called after the departing servant. "And the nurse. Her charge has escaped again."

He bent down and kissed the top of Edward's head, stroked his flushed cheek with gentle fingers then turned to Marjorie.

"I will not be long. A few days at most. Ciscilla will amuse you while I am gone."

Marjorie and Ciscilla exchanged doubtful looks but both nodded.

Father Simon rose and motioned for his travelling aide. Hastily, Katherine picked up her skirts and hurried to find Agnes and begin packing her things for departure. Such a lot of fuss for one day. She sighed, remembering she also had to locate the steward and make things right with him before she left.

The little carriage was crowded. Agnes sat beside Katherine on one side while Father Simon and his aide took the other. Their baggage lay under their feet to be used as an uneven stool. Lord Victor and John Elder rode on either side of the chariot and so the little procession made its way back to Claringdon.

The night air turned cold as they went and Katherine made no protest when Agnes folded a blanket around her legs and draped another over her shoulders.

"See if you can find a blanket for Father Simon," Katherine suggested.

"Thank you child, but my aide always brings a particular coverlet for me on our road trips. Hogarth?"

The priest's servant rummaged through the luggage and quickly came up with a heavy blanket lined with a blend of white ermine and fleece. He took great care to cover the priest to his neck and tuck in the edges around his torso and legs. He was still pressing the sides of the blanket against the seat when the priest frowned and grunted. Immediately the man withdrew his hands and sat back in his place.

"Well, Lady Fendlay," Father Simon began. "You were very shrewd to have discovered the source of your difficulties. Very shrewd indeed." The priest regarded Katherine closely. "You have no notion as to the agent of your shocking treatment?"

Katherine shook her head. "None at all. But whoever it is, I believe my manor to be the intended prize."

Father Simon's pale eyes narrowed and his chin sunk deeper into his chest. "Do you really? One of your neighbours perhaps." He watched her intently while she considered. "Are your nearest neighbours not that baron to the south of you, Sir Charles and I believe his wife, Lady Beatrice?"

Katherine made a face. "Yes they are."

"Could they? Would they, do you think . . . ?"

"I do not see why. Charles seems content enough with his own holding and besides, he and my husband's uncle were old friends."

"Ah, but greed changes many things," the priest purred. "With his friend dead perhaps he felt entitled to his friend's estate."

"Now that you mention it," Katherine began slowly. "Beatrice did say something of that sort to me."

"Did she?"

"Yes, she did." Katherine's green eyes widened in alarm. "She did."

"Look to that quarter then, child. Look to that quarter. I am sure the excellent Stafford will see to it you are avenged."

Katherine was startled. A priest advocating revenge?

Simon saw her look of surprise and his pale lips split in a thin gash of pink.

"Vengeance is mine, saith the Lord. But the instrument of his wrath may be Victor Stafford," he said softly.

"I think I will go carefully, father. I would not want to accuse the wrong person."

"Were they not at Crenfeld the night of the fire?" he persisted.

"Yes, of course. But so were a great many people. Why, even you."

"What about the night your husband's aunt and uncle died? They were there then too I think."

Katherine exchanged a glance with Agnes.

"You know about that?"

Father Simon sniffed. "The whole village knows. It is no secret."

Katherine ran her fingers slowly over the red weals on her right arm and stared blankly into space. Could it be those two? Her mind recoiled at the memory of Sir Charles touching her hand with his. Perhaps the same hand that provided mushrooms for the poisoning of his friend and the same hand that later moved the candlestand in their room. Nathaniel's screams and her own filled her head and she forced her hands against her ears and squeezed shut her eyes.

"Lady Fendlay. Is something wrong?"

Victor Stafford had his hand on the carriage window and was leaning down from his horse. His fair head filled the small opening.

"No, no. I am only tired."

"Might I suggest you rest awhile. We are several hours away."

Katherine swallowed. "Thank you. Yes, I will." She looked across at the priest. He had not moved and was still watching her. She shivered and pulled her blankets more tightly around her shoulders.

"Rest, my lady," Agnes whispered, pushing a pillow under her head.

Katherine gave her a strained smile. "Thank you Agnes."

Katherine closed her eyes and drifted into sleep, unaware of the priest's pale brooding eyes regarding her from under hooded lids.

CHAPTER 9

KATHERINE AWOKE SOME TIME LATER to find the bench across from her empty and Agnes leaning against the side of the carriage snoring softly, her limp head jouncing with each bump in the road. Father Simon must have disembarked while she slept.

Katherine looked out the window and squinted. There was light ahead and she could make out the windows of Crenfeld. The glow from the castle was at once welcoming and sinister. Did death await her behind those walls? Strangely, she was fascinated by the possibility. The part of her that was young and hopeful protested vigorously against such a thing. But the part that expected something from life had grown torpid. The years stretched out long and unfulfilling, merely something to be endured until they were ended. And yet she knew she would fight for life despite her despair. A strange paradox. To cling tenaciously to something you did not really care for. Perhaps it was only that she did not want some vile stranger taking her life from her.

The coach stopped in the ward and Victor opened the carriage door. Katherine tilted her head in the direction of the still-sleeping Agnes and smiled. Then she shook Agnes, who hiccuped and jerked her head away from its resting spot, smacking her lips together several times and blinking rapidly.

"Are we there?" she croaked.

"We are," Katherine answered.

Victor helped Agnes first and then reached in for Katherine. When his hands closed around her arms to help her down, Katherine was keenly aware of the warmth of his skin through her sleeves and the gentle strength in his hands. She stumbled. He gripped her more firmly to steady her and she began to tremble.

"You are cold," he accused and reached around her for a blanket. Why had her heart begun such a staccato? She smelled the night air on his clothes. His face was so close she felt the softness of his hair as it brushed her cheek. Katherine closed her eyes and swallowed hard. When she opened them, he was regarding her strangely.

"Here, wrap yourself in this." He turned to Agnes. "Help your mistress inside."

"Thank you," Katherine said, not looking at him.

While Agnes clucked and muttered about the journey being too long and hard for Katherine, Katherine clung to her and shivered. Victor watched until they went inside, then helped John and the driver unhitch the horses.

"A bath, my lady. To warm you." Agnes advised.

Katherine nodded dumbly and sank down on the cushions in the oriole. She stared at the yellow moon and the golden road it made into the courtyard, without really seeing it. She tried to close her mind to the memory of Victor's touch, but could not and an odd gnawing pain crushed her chest. This cannot be love, she thought frantically. But even as she willed herself to deny it, she knew it to be true. Victor had once told her that no one could help for whom their heart beat. How could this have happened to her without her knowledge? Of course he was handsome. Many men were handsome. And he would marry Marjorie Clere soon. But even if he did not marry Marjorie, what difference would that make? He had seen her arms. He knew her secret. She shifted miserably and closed her eyes. She must make sure he left soon. She wanted him out of her house. Then, perhaps, he would stay out of her thoughts.

But when Agnes returned to tell her that her bath was drawn, she also told her Victor had asked after her, and the glad leap of her heart betrayed her and she knew she wanted him to stay. If only so she could pretend for a little while that he was here because he wanted to be with her and not because of a promise he had made to his sister.

By morning she found Victor had gone early into Claringdon and left John Elder outside her door. She barely missed colliding with him when she left her rooms.

"Pardon me, madam," he apologized. "But I'm to stay with you until Lord Victor returns."

Katherine smiled at his anxious, freckled face. He was a long, raw-boned man with large knuckles, bony shoulders and knobby knees. And he had a loose way of walking that made it appear as if his joints might not quite hold him together. But he was a kind man, respected his master immensely and was very loyal.

"That is fine John. Has anyone asked for me?"

"Yes, madam. There was a messenger but Agnes wouldn't wake you. I have the note here in my pocket."

John reached inside the slitted opening of his surcoat and bent sideways to plunge his hand in deeply. He came up with a wrinkled page, folded and sealed with three drops of wax. He pressed it flat against his leg and handed it to Katherine.

She recognized the ecclesiastic imprint in the wax before breaking the seal. It was a summons from Father Simon requesting her presence in his private quarters. Today.

"John, I must go to the church this morning."

"I will accompany you."

Katherine smiled at his stern-looking face. He was taking his charge very seriously.

"Naturally," she agreed. "Please have Pygine ready for me. I have had enough of chariots for awhile."

When they reigned in outside the churchyard, Katherine knew a moment's misgivings. The big church was so quiet and its grey bricks reminded her of the grave-stones in the cemetery. She shivered and went in at the side door that led to the priest's quarters, John walking quietly beside her. A chapel boy met them and took them through. He said nothing and disappeared after leading them into a well-furnished room. The plank floor was almost completely covered in a variety of thickly-furred animal skins. There were several chairs and stools, an ornately carved chest and two tall candlestands. The window was large and conical. Lead pieces covered the upper part of the window in an undulating design and the window opening had the slightly greenish tinge that meant the priest had been able to afford some rather costly white glass. A small table stood before the window and on it three potted roses, one pink and two white. Their sweet perfume filled the air while a brisk fire warmed the room.

Katherine was not so naive as to suppose the priest lived simply, but such lavish comfort surprised her.

"Ah, here you are my child."

Father Simon rose from his place in a high backed chair, placed at such an acute angle that one could not see him upon entering the room.

She looked over his head and into the bedchamber just beyond an open alcove. It was sumptuously appointed in colourful brocades, silks and fine firs and seemed more like the possession of an eastern prince for the enjoyment of his harem, than the room of a celibate.

Simon noted the direction of her gaze and rose to block her view.

"It continues to be a disagreeable summer. Warm yourself before the fire, my child," he invited with a wave of his hand.

Katherine moved obediently to comply. The priest stirred behind her and she heard the soft closing of a door. When she glanced around, Father Simon was just releasing the folds of a heavy curtain from the braided ropes that held it. It fell in front of the little alcove.

The priest frowned in John's direction. "Our conversation is a private one," he said, smoothing his lace-trimmed sleeves.

And when John did not move. "Your mistress is quite safe with me," he added drily, dismissing him with the back of his hand and turning to Katherine.

John Elder hesitated but Katherine raised her eyebrows at him. He looked unhappy, but he withdrew.

The priest settled back in his chair, tented his thin white fingers together under his chin and gave her a threadlike smile. Uneasily, Katherine returned the smile.

"I have been considering your predicament," he said. "And I may have a solution."

He got up abruptly to stir the fire with a long lead poker. He stood beside her, silently stirring up the hot chunks and then, not looking at her, said, "I am a man as any other, child. You may think God and the church are enough for a priest but I can assure you, they are not. As a priest I cannot marry, of course, but I am sure you will allow that a man must at least have a hearthmate."

Alarmed at the direction this conversation was taking, Katherine clenched her jaw and gave an abbreviated nod.

"In any case, it may be that we can be a comfort to one another. You are alone and so am I. You are in need of a protector and I am well able to fulfill that role. You would have the protection both of the Church and of God. It would be a satisfactory arrangement, I assure you. And not to be too indelicate, I will only tell you that my demands would be both discreet and infrequent. Things could be much as they are for you now. In return for your solace from time to time, I would look after both you and the affairs of the manor estates. The domestic routines would remain in your care."

He was waiting for a response and kept his head down, warming himself in front of the fire.

Katherine could not believe what she was hearing. How could he make such a vulgar proposal? She looked at the nape of his wrinkled neck and rounded back and shuddered. The thought of his hands on her made her flesh crawl.

"I realize this is sudden," he went on. "But I think you will agree the arrangement has merit."

Katherine found her voice. "You take me by surprise, father. And although I appreciate your concern for my welfare, I cannot see that such a course of action would be in your best interest."

She saw him stiffen. Still, he did not look up.

"And why is that?" he asked in a thin voice.

"I cannot let you compromise your position in the Church or indeed, in the village."

He frowned. "In what way?"

Katherine moved forward slightly and into his line of sight, then slowly and with feigned reluctance turned up the sleeves of her dress and showed him her arms.

"I am greatly disfigured as you can see."

The priest's eyes widened and he recoiled slightly.

"You may lose the respect of your parish if people find your hearthmate to be blemished by a likeness to the flames of hell."

Father Simon drew away from her and she dropped her arms to her sides.

"Yes, you are right," he muttered. He paced behind her for a moment, then stopped. "There is another course of action you might consider."

He stepped closer again and brought his face near to hers.

"Sell me your holdings," he purred, watching her carefully. "Your enemy would become mine and you would be free to return to your family."

Katherine opened her mouth to protest, but he held up his hand.

"Think about it, my dear."

"I will not sell," Katherine replied.

"But if you should?" he asked softly. "If you should. May I have your promise that you will give me an opportunity to buy before anyone else?"

"Yes, of course. But I assure you, I will not sell my holdings."

"Things change," he said. "Things change. Now leave me. I have had a tiresome day."

"Yes, father. Thank you father."

Hastily, Katherine gathered up her skirts and crossed to the door. Her hand was on the latch when she heard his voice raised behind her.

"You will not forget your promise, will you?"

John looked up from his position against the wall when she burst from the priest's chamber.

"If I didn't know it could not be, I would say you had a fiend at your heels." he joked.

"Not far from the truth," Katherine muttered. "Not far at all."

John frowned and took her arm. "What happened in there? What did he say to you?"

Katherine gave her head a savage shake. "No. It is too humiliating. Take me home. Quickly."

After dismissing a confused John Elder, Katherine sat in seething silence in her own private quarters. She would not be mistress to an aging cleric. Never! She was mistress of Crenfeld and would stay mistress of Crenfeld. Did he really think she would be so frightened for her life that she would submit to such a liaison, or sell her holdings and run away like a rabbit?

The chamberlain found her still agitated and pacing when he came to announce dinner.

"Lord Stafford is returned, madam, and will join you in the hall."

Katherine gave Peter a distracted nod. "Thank you," she said curtly. "I will be down in a moment."

"Yes, madam." He coughed slightly. "Shall I wait, madam? To accompany you."

"No."

When Peter left her, Katherine snatched up a mirror and held it to her face. Her cheeks were still flushed a deep red. She looked feverish. She slammed the little glass down on her coverlet and roughly tucked her hair up inside a gold caul. The netting atop the burnished red of her hair glinted like knight's chain mail under a blazing sun. And she felt as combative as she looked.

The servants were moving quietly around the tables when Katherine took her seat. Agnes chose a place directly below and regarded Katherine with wide eyes. Katherine dipped her hands in the basin brought to her, then took a long drink of wine. It made her dizzy. She reached for a slab of bread and began tearing it up into small pieces, dropping them onto her trencher. The servants on the hall floor exchanged worried looks and ate in silence.

When Victor Stafford entered the hall the atmosphere relaxed. He spoke to several of the men he knew and then sat down next to Katherine. He looked at the pile of bread on her trencher and then at her.

"Not hungry?" he asked.

Tightlipped, Katherine shook her head.

Victor regarded her more carefully. "Is anything the matter? Your face. It is very . . . " He made an open-handed half circle under her chin.

"Yes, there is."

"Is there anything I . . . "

"I do not wish to discuss it."

Victor leaned back and stroked his jaw. "Indeed? Do you mind if I eat? No?"

He motioned to one of the servers. "A basin. And some wine and meat." He glanced at Katherine's plate. "And more bread."

Katherine slipped her hands off the table and clasped and unclasped them in her lap. Victor turned back to her, ignoring her restlessness.

"I have made little progress in the village. For some reason all the men I approached to act as guardian seem reluctant. Frankly, I do not understand it."

Katherine made a wry face. "I do. They have been discouraged by someone who thought to take the position himself."

"That would certainly explain things," Victor agreed. His grey eyes rested on her fidgeting hands, red cheeks and set jaw.

"So who is this chivalrous fellow?" He asked. "By your manner it seems you disapprove of him."

"It does not matter." Katherine's green eyes glinted and she frowned at him. "I have decided I have no need of a guardian. I will look after myself. I will bar my door at night and make sure I am not alone during the day."

"That will not do at all," Victor said cheerfully. "Remember, I promised Ciscilla and I plan to keep my promise."

Katherine made a small fist and banged the table, startling the servants.

"You will do as I say. I do not want a guardian!"

Victor raised an eyebrow slowly, tilted his head to one side and watched Katherine jump to her feet and run out of the hall. She bumped into a servant carrying a tray of fruit and sent apples and oranges rolling over the floor. When she had taken refuge in the adjoining solar, Victor remained staring after her for a moment then calmly resumed his meal. After he finished eating, Victor motioned for Agnes to approach.

"Do you know what is troubling your mistress, Agnes?"

Agnes shook her head. "No sir. When she came back from the church she was like this. Didn't want any of us near her. Just locked herself in her chambers. I am very worried about her, sir. Perhaps she will speak to you."

Victor blinked. "She went to the church? Why?"

"Father Simon sent for her. John Elder did not tell you?"

"No, I have yet to speak with him," Victor said slowly. "And what was the purpose of her visit? Did she tell you?"

"She told me nothing, sir."

Victor patted Agnes' cheek and smiled. "I will learn what ails her."

"Thank you, sir. It is not like her to be so angry. She is not herself at all."

"No, I can see that."

Victor stood, picked up his cane and limped across the hall and into the solar. He found Katherine seated on the hearth, staring into the fire with unseeing eyes.

"Well, madam. Shall you bite off my head or will I join you?"

He put a hand on Katherine's shoulder and bent down to look in her face, then sat beside her. The contact was too much for Katherine. The hard anger left her and she felt hot tears brim up and spill over her already warm cheeks. A strange look came over Victor's face and he swallowed hard. When he spoke, his voice was oddly hoarse.

"What has happened?"

Katherine stared into the fire. "Have you ever been made to feel as if you were as trivial as the stool under a man's foot? That your existence, if convenient, was welcome. But if not . . . " She swept some ash off the hearth with a slow and deliberate stroke.

Katherine kept her eyes averted from Victor's and reached up to scrub the tears from her cheeks. "Do you know who offered to be my guardian? My protector?"

Victor frowned at the bitterness in her tone.

"No," he said softly. "Tell me."

"Father Simon." Katherine looked at him then and the pain in her eyes made him wince.

"And do you know what he required in return for such largess? Me. Or the use of me from time to time."

"What did you say?" Victor growled. "Do you know what you are saying!"

Katherine's voice shook when she spoke. "Only too well."

She clasped her hands together tightly in her lap and rocked forward as if to relieve a painful belly. "I might be a trollop whose company may be bought for a few coins," she choked.

Her chest ached so badly she could scarcely draw breath without feeling the pain. Victor gripped her arm.

"He had no right suggesting such a thing."

Katherine looked at his hand on her arm and he let her go and glared into the fire.

"He said he would look after the manor estates, the rents, the carting and all those things for me, too."

Victor snorted. "I warrant he did. And expected some handsome financial compensation for it."

"He said nothing like that."

"Well you may be sure he expected it and would take it. A very acute man of business is our priest. Very canny. He holds numerous rents outside of the village and the Church's glebe has grown to an enormous parcel of land since he was installed in this parish."

Katherine turned to look at Victor. "He offered to buy the castle and manor as an . . . as an alternative arrangement."

Victor held her eyes. "And you said . . . what?"

"I did not know what to say. He took me completely by surprise. Completely. I did promise to tell him if I decided to sell."

Katherine brushed the tears from her cheeks, smoothed her skirt with damp palms and stood up.

"I do not intend to leave. It might be foolish of me to stay under the circumstances, but I am not running away. I like it here. I have grown fond of my people and I think they have of me. This is my home."

Victor stood too. "Yes it is and you should stay. The villagers hold you in high regard and so do your servants. Agnes is quite beside herself with worry."

Katherine gave a small smile. "Poor Agnes."

She looked up at Victor's sober face, the intelligent grey eyes so filled with concern. He was a good man. Marjorie Clere was a lucky woman.

"I will speak to Agnes. Thank you for coming after me. It did me good to talk to you." She smiled wanly. "You must think me silly, but I feared being forced into a very distasteful position."

"You will not be forced into anything contrary to your own wishes as long as I am here," Victor said grimly.

"But you will not always be here, will you." Katherine's voice was soft.

There was silence between them for a few moments. Katherine broke it.

"You should have no difficulty finding a man to act as my guardian now that Father Simon has withdrawn."

"I know," Victor answered. "And that concerns me even more. Who will protect you from Father Simon? Obviously, no one in the village can be trusted. I will leave John here. At least until I can send someone from among my own men at Stonehaven. My men do not fear the priest."

Katherine frowned and shook her head. "Do not be too hard on the people of Claringdon. Your men have no fear of Father Simon only because he is no danger to them. He owns much of the land my people live on. They owe him rents and services. Between the church tax and his personal whim, they fear penury more than most. I do what I can to ease the burden by giving them more time to work their own crops, but my manor must be maintained as well."

"The Church is a hard master," Victor answered. "And a greedy one. I would to God, England could be rid of her grasping avarice."

"Some day, maybe it will," Katherine answered. "But until that day comes we must be careful to keep on her right side."

"I suppose. In any case, I will return to Stonehaven in the morning. John can stay here with you until I send another man."

Katherine's heart sank with the realization that Victor would be leaving. She kept the disappointment from her voice and spoke lightly.

"Of course. I have intruded too much into the time you were to spend with your fiancée."

Victor grinned. "It will do Marjorie good to be alone with Ciscilla for awhile. She had best get used to that vain little butterfly." He laughed. "Marjorie has little patience with my sister but she may find, as I have, that underneath all the froth and gaiety is a fine woman."

Katherine nodded her agreement. "And a true friend." She smiled. "I had better go calm Agnes. Thank you again."

Victor bowed. "Until morning, then. Oh, and could you have someone from the kitchen come to my quarters and stew a little fruit for me later. I like a bit to eat before retiring."

"Certainly," Katherine said and went back into the great hall. It was vacant now except for Agnes, who sat alone in a corner, for all her bulk looking quite waif-like in the big empty room. She bounded to her feet when she caught sight of Katherine.

"My lady, is it well with you?" she asked anxiously.

Katherine patted her hand. "Yes, Agnes. Thank you. I am sorry I worried you. You are kind to be concerned for me."

Agnes looked shocked. "I need no thanks, madam."

"All the same."

Agnes's worried face relaxed. "With your permission my lady, I will have the chambermaid turn down your bed so you may take your rest."

"Thank you, Agnes. I must go to the kitchen for a few minutes and then I will be up."

There was far less activity in the kitchen at this time of day. Only one fire was lit and even that one was merely a pile of glowing chunks. It was quiet. The kitchen maids murmured softly to each other as they washed the pots and bowls that had been used during the day. Grace was picking through a bin of peas with her good hand while Alice worked on a table with a little mallet, pounding up a loaf of sugar. They all looked up and smiled a greeting when Katherine came in.

"Grace, could you have Alice bring some fruit to Lord Victor's room in an hour or so. He would like a few pieces stewed for him before bedtime."

Grace nodded. "I have some just here. She can take those up."

Katherine nodded. "That will be fine, Grace."

Grace grunted, screwed up her eyes and went back to sorting through the peas. Katherine was just helping herself to a particularly plump plum when a panting young man burst into the kitchen. The poor creature gulped to catch his breath, bobbed his head briefly and gave an anguished cry.

"Claringdon is burning! Come quickly!"

Katherine dropped the plum, grabbed up her skirts and made for the tower staircase. She turned back to the gasping servant.

"Tell Josiah I will need my horse. And tell Lord Victor what has happened. Hurry! Hurry!"

The young man bounded past her, bawling for a squire. Agnes met her halfway up the stairway with her mantle. Katherine flung it on, fastened the neck broach with quick fingers then swarmed on down the stairs and out into the ward.

Pygine was dancing with nervous anticipation while young Josiah clung to his reins. Katherine took the reins from him and used Josiah's cupped hands to mount the black animal. She gave him a quick kick with her heels and he reared once before plunging over the drawbridge. She immediately regretted the silkiness of her sendal skirt. It made her seat difficult. But she fastened her free hand in Pygine's mane and held on with grim determination. A pall of black smoke rose thick against the horizon and Katherine prayed she would not arrive too late.

CHAPTER 10

THE DAY IN THE FIELD PROVED LONG AND ARDUOUS. In the morning the men broke up dangerously close-packed damp haystacks into smaller ones to prevent heat build-up. The women performed the tedious job of loosening and reforming them. Even so, some of the stacks caught fire and part of the hard won crop was lost. The men quickly constructed stone floors for the hay. A deep layer of still-green bracken was thrown on the stones to discourage rats and the hay lain on top.

Hurrying through a midday meal, reaping resumed on an adjacent tract. The reapers moved forward swinging their scythes in grim silence. Old Henry was working with them today. He faltered, lost his rhythm and straightened up to press bony fingers into the small of his back. Ah, but this day was a long one. He fixed his eyes on the damp stacks in the bordering field, sucked at his remaining teeth and shook his head. They were too big. He had told them to keep the haystacks smaller or the wet hay would fire up again. He caught the attention of the man reaping next to him.

"They are too big, Guy," he fussed. "The stacks. Too big."

Guy Southell shot him a black look, his stride broken. "You old fool," he snarled. "Leave me be. Pick up yer blade and finish yer row."

He bent back over his own row, scythe swishing in short angry strokes. Not to be deterred, Old Henry gripped Southell's arm in mid-swing.

"Listen to me," he insisted.

Southell shook him off.

"Keep yer tongue in yer mouth old man, else ah'll wrench it out for ye."

He shook a meaty fist and returned once more to his work. But Old Henry was relentless. He trotted along beside the other man, continuing his harangue in a whining litany. Not a man of considerable forbearance, Guy Southell finally wheeled and dealt Old Henry a solid cuff, sending him sprawling to the ground. But the old man seemed not to consider that he was outmatched once again and scrambled to his feet, clenching shaking fists.

"I'll put out yer eyes!" he shrieked.

Southell crossed brawny arms, a faint smile twitching his lips. An almost casual extension of one arm felled the old man again. With a screech, Henry rushed at Southell, dragging him down. The other reapers crowded about to watch Guy Southell pummel the old man. He meant no real injury, just kept knocking him down every time he got up until finally he remained on the ground, panting and probing his bruises. Henry glared at the rest of the men. They smirked and shouldered their scythes.

The sun was fast sinking and the entertainment being at an end, the reapers quit the field. Most quickened their pace near town and went directly to the alehouse. Henry limped along behind the rest. He had no taste for ale or talk. The drink would be bitter under the jeers of his fellows.

He turned instead to a dilapidated cottage leaning hard against the common field. The whole structure listed badly. Henry shut the door behind him and squinted in the dim interior. Squatting on the straw covered dirt floor he started a meagre fire, not noticing that some of the rocks meant to contain it were missing and floor straw stuffed into the gaps. He hunched his bony shoulders against a cool draft that whipped aside the sack over the cot's only window, then chafed trembling hands and gingerly curled sideways on the floor, knees to chin, closed his eyes and slept.

The tiny fire gained strength as the old man slept, darting out from between the inadequate circle of stones and clutching at the floor straw with flickering orange fingers. The straw smouldered for a time, then glowed a brilliant white, routing all shadows from the corners of the room. A wall of flame shot up suddenly, rolling under the sagging roof timbers. Perhaps comforted by the unaccustomed heat, Henry slept on. At some point, sleep changed to stupor as the fire sucked up all the air in the tiny room, leaving none for the old man.

Clamour in the alehouse rose to near deafening proportions. The warmth of many bodies pressed close together was a comfort after such a troublesome day and the men waxed hearty in their relief. Those who could afford no ale promised a share of their crops to those who could buy and those who bought, laughed at the empty promises of the penniless. But none wanted to drink alone, so villein and freeman sat side by side, considering what evil spirit had bedeviled the weather, changing summer to winter.

Eventually the conversation turned to other things.

"Did yer see Guy give t'a old man a hiding?"

There were chuckles and tankards were banged on rough tabletops, the thick brown liquid slopping down the sides and pooling in frothy puddles.

"Whatever fetched up the lord and lady would do well to fetch 'im up, meddlesome old dripper."

"Aye," the men agreed, nodding and thumping their tankards.

"Did yer hear them two goats of Oren's turned up dead as mackerels yesterday. Good goats them was too. Lovely milk they gave."

Teeth were alternately sucked and clucked in commiseration.

"Ate 'em though. Had some meself."

"Down Melcombe I heard the whole town is dying of same pestilence the vile French was cursed with, spitting blood, faces black like death masks."

"'Tis a punishment on them sailors for trafficking with the French."

Heads were nodded in vigorous agreement but all the same the men became gloomy and not inclined to talk, drinking in introspective silence and wiping their mouths thoughtfully with the backs of their sleeves.

Tales of the pestilence had been told for almost two years. Of whole towns decimated by a great death all over France and even more horrific tales from Greece and Italy of heavy foul-smelling mists that rolled over the land and sea, blotting out the lights in the sky, wilting crops and rotting fruit on the trees. Wherever the mists went, famine and death followed. A loathsome visitation that had been kept at bay by the swift waters of the Channel.

At some length the men drank off the last of their ale, scraped back benches and began leaving for home and dinner. Shouts of "Fire!" brought all bursting out into a summer night choked with smoke.

Victor Stafford ran a finger around the rim of the silver-lidded mazer that contained his evening Bordeaux. The servant should be coming any time now to stew his fruit. He yawned and closed his eyes, leaning against the bed's headboard. His boots were off, his shirt buttons loosened and he was feeling pleasantly sleepy.

Loud banging on the door of his quarters made him grunt and open his eyes. A puffing, red-faced young man burst inside.

"Lord Victor! The village is on fire! Some of the crops are burned to the ground!"

Breathing an oath, Victor gripped the boy's arm with long brown fingers.

"What are they doing? Are they saving the fields?"

The boy winced free, rubbing his forearm.

"No my lord. They are putting out the fires in their cots. The fields are abandoned."

"Fools!" Victor roared. He muttered something incoherent and wrenched his greatcoat from a hook on the wall.

"My horse!" His tone was savage.

The lad was panting too hard to move quickly and Stafford gave him a thrust that all but knocked him down.

"Now!" he shouted. "And get me John Elder!"

Stafford's wrath was clearly evident to the guards and squires in the courtyard. They stood silently by the castle gate, scarcely daring to draw breath. Accustomed to the gentle ways of their mistress, Victor's rough authority petrified them into rigid mutes.

Shouting for the bridge to be dropped, Lord Victor spurred his mount across the drawbridge while it was yet being lowered, forcing the animal to leap across a wide expanse of moat. John Elder urged his own horse after Victor. When he drew abreast of Stafford, John glanced quickly at his face. It was red with exertion and anger. Elder opened his mouth to speak but closed it again and gave his attention to the road instead.

They sped on in a silence broken only by the laboured breathing of the horses and the pounding of hooves on the hard-worn path. The thunder of their passage sent large black ravens reeling and screeching from the trees.

Crossing a small wooden bridge they reigned in at the top of the hill overlooking Claringdon. Fields lay charred and smouldering. Several cottages were ablaze and frantic peasants scuttled to and fro while the church-bell clanged mournfully. A black horse and female rider stood in the midst of the melee. The woman was directing the frightened peasants with swift graphic arm gestures. Soft, barely audible commands accompanied each movement. From time to time she succumbed to a spate of coughing, then resumed speaking.

Stafford turned abruptly to Elder. "Is that Lady Katherine down there?"

John took in the billowing skirts, chestnut hair unconventionally loosed to the waist and the determined set of the tiny jaw. He grinned.

"It is."

"What is she doing?"

"With respect, my lord, I suppose she is trying to save the manor. It is half hers."

Victor snorted. "Women and property. It is a fool's law that ever gave them the right to it. Look at her. She is barely able to keep her seat."

John Elder thought it best to say nothing and did not answer. He much admired the plucky young woman, but this was not the time to voice such an opinion.

Katherine dispatched a few more people to tend to the cottage fires then sent the majority out into the grain fields to beat out and douse what was still burning. Her lungs felt ready to burst in the choking smoke. A violent paroxysm of coughing left her weak and shaking. She wished they would stop ringing that infernal bell. Her head already ached. She clutched at Pygine's mane but found no strength left in her arms or fingers after so long a time breathing in little but smoke and ash.

She felt herself slipping from the back of the horse. Sensing her lack of control, Pygine snorted and slewed his neck from side to side. His body quivered and he began an agitated prance, which only served to further weaken her feeble grip.

John Elder reached Katherine first and steadied Pygine so she could safely dismount. She sagged against the side of her horse, her eyes closed, alternately gasping and coughing. John Elder quickly scooped her up in his arms and carried her out of the heavy smoke. He lowered her onto a heap of loose straw some distance from the fire.

Victor followed him, meaning to chide Katherine for her foolishness. But when he stood over her, he made the disquieting discovery that his anger was founded, not in exasperation for her rashness, but in fear for her safety.

When he noticed John watching him, he turned away. "Get her some water," he said brusquely.

John nodded and Victor stalked off through the village streets and out to the fields. It was hard going. The rain had turned the roadways into a mud that sucked and pulled at his boots and clumped around the base of his cane. Townsmen, recognizing the lord of Stonehaven, bowed and nudged each other, backing away and giving him room to pass. Victor surveyed the damage intently and with grudging approval. The fire had been extinguished with remarkable swiftness, the loss contained to less than a virgate. The scorched land puffed blackly and Stafford looked about for some indication of where the fire had begun. His grey eyes travelled the perimeter of the burned out field, stopping briefly from time to time before moving on. They finally came to rest on what was left of a cottage collapsed into the farmland. He grunted and made his way to the smouldering husk.

Inside, the sequence of events was obvious. Victor kicked away some of the debris.

"Whose cot is this?" Victor squinted, his eyes stinging in the hazy interior.

"Belonged to Old Henry," someone volunteered.

Stafford gave the rubble a final nudge. "He will pay heavily for his slackness."

A cold voice from the doorway caught him by surprise. "He has already done so. He is dead."

Katherine leaned against John Elder, looking pale, but her voice was strong and her green eyes hard.

All at once there came a high-pitched keening wail from outside. John helped Katherine back through the door with Victor close behind them. They found Nory crouched beside the body of the old man with her eyes shut tight, swaying from side to side. Nory's hands were balled into fists and she had them pressed to either side of her head.

Katherine's throat constricted at the anguished sight. She dropped to her knees beside Nory and drew her into her arms, resting her cheek against the top of the old woman's head.

"There, there," she crooned softly. "Do not take on so. You will make yourself sick."

"But e's gone. E's gone. Were an old fool, but there weren't no harm in 'im. Why did he have to die? He were an old man. He would have died soon enough on 'is own. Tain't right," Nory added fiercely, scrubbing the tears from her face with angry fists. "Tain't right," she repeated.

"No, I suppose not," Katherine agreed.

She glanced down at the charred body and shuddered. Poor old man. The horror of her own brush with just such a hideous end engulfed her, and she found herself gritting her jaw against groans that sought escape.

"Come away, Nory," she said abruptly. "Here, let me help you up. This is no place for you. You can do nothing for him now."

The old woman allowed herself to be led away and Katherine left her in the care of the townswomen who gathered around her protectively. Katherine, Victor and John stood in awkward silence while Old Henry's body was lifted onto a handcart.

"Take him to Crenfeld," Katherine said.

The man handling the cart glanced at Victor. He nodded.

"Do as she says."

Katherine gave him a sharp look, then caught the attention of one of the townsmen.

"Go to Father Simon and Benjamin. Tell them what has happened and ask them to meet us at Crenfeld."

"Physic already knows, my lady. He came when we first pulled 'ta old man out. Tried to see if there were any life left in 'im but he were clean gone."

"Just Father Simon then."

Old Henry lay on a trestle table in the great hall, his body carefully covered with a clean bord cloth. Katherine, Agnes, Victor and John sat around the table in silence. Katherine stared vacantly through the doorway, her hands folded loosely in her lap. Agnes sat stiff-backed, her eyes fixed on the table. Victor relaxed back in his chair, arms folded across his chest, legs astride, eyes closed. John leaned forward on his elbows, turning his cap in his hands.

They heard scuffling sounds in the hall and watched Father Simon cross himself with deft, practised fingers before approaching them.

"Your loss is regrettable," he said to Victor. "And yours, madam."

The priest stepped closer and gingerly lifted a corner of the bord cloth. He grunted and lowered it.

"Old Henry, you say?"

"Yes, father," Agnes said in hushed tones.

"He lived alone? No family?"

"No family, father."

"I see. That is a great pity. Everything was destroyed in the fire?"

"Yes, father. He had little. But what he did have is gone now."

"And no beasts of his own?"

"No, father."

The priest pursed his thin lips together and cast his eyes to the ceiling.

"There is the matter of the mortuary," he told the roof timbers.

"He was an old man, father," Katherine said. "He ate at my table and had nothing for a mortuary in any case."

"I understand that, madam." Father Simon's lips lifted like curling parchment. "But it is necessary for the death duty to be paid before the funeral Mass. And if the Mass is not given he may not sleep in the churchyard with the Christians but must stay outside with the heathen."

Agnes wrung her hands fretfully. "Oh, father what shall we do? Nory thought a lot of the old man and will be so distressed if he should have to be buried without his funeral Mass."

"I am sorry, child. I do not see what can be done. If Nory will meet his obligations, he may have the sacrament of burial as a good Christian. Otherwise . . . " The alternative hung in the air like a curse.

"You may make your choice amongst my own beasts," Katherine said coldly.

Father Simon inclined his head. "Thank you madam." He coughed slightly.

"Any beast, madam?" he purred.

"Yes, of course. Any beast."

"I am inclined to choose that big black horse you ride."

Agnes gasped and Katherine looked startled. "Pygine?"

"Is that what you call him? Yes, Pygine."

The priest folded his hands together and regarded her expectantly.

Katherine's face grew anxious. "Surely you do not mean to take my own mount. I thought to give you a good beef cow. Perhaps a Galloway. The meat is excellent and I am sure you do not have one."

"No, but I have need of a horse and yours will do nicely."

"He might not let you ride him," Katherine protested. "He is accustomed to me. If it is a horse you want, I can certainly find a gentler beast for you."

"I have a man that will deal with your animal," Father Simon said. "He will soon be of a mind to take a new rider."

Katherine could not believe her ears. He actually meant to take Pygine from her. Hot tears pricked the backs of her eyes. How could she bear to be without him?

"Please," she pleaded. "He was a gift from my father and is all I have left that is truly mine."

"You did say any beast," he reminded her. "So if you could have him saddled for me, we can take the old man's body back to prepare him for his funeral Mass."

Katherine looked piteously at Father Simon but he only said. "If you would hurry, madam."

Katherine nodded, blinked hard and turned blindly toward the door. Of course a man's soul was of greater value than a horse. She knew that. But oh, not Pygine. She choked on the sob in her throat.

Victor stopped her before she reached the door and faced the priest with a grim look.

"You ought not to tease the young woman, father. She has suffered much these past few weeks."

"I assure you, I am in earnest."

"You intend to take her own horse as a mortuary? A mortuary for a man whose best beast might be a skinny milk cow? And when she herself is entitled by law to that beast and you to second best?"

Father Simon blinked and his thin lips set themselves in a rigid line.

"The Church has a right to the horse. She promised me any beast I named. Would she make a pledge to God and not keep it?"

Victor snorted. "She made no such pledge."

He beckoned to John Elder. "John, fetch the father the best Galloway in the field. Take his aide with you to help choose it, then tie it behind the father's cart for him."

Father Simon glared. "You are meddling in things that are none of your business," he warned.

"That is not precisely correct," Lord Victor replied mildly. "I have an interest in this manor too and so am permitted an opinion in matters relating to the disposition of its assets. The value of the horse is much too high. It will not be released."

The priest gave Victor a black look as he pushed past him, but said nothing.

"Thank you so much," Katherine cried and she would have taken Victor's hand, but he moved a step back and shook his head.

"No need for thanks. That priest has already taken far too many liberties with this manor."

Though hurt by Victor's refusal to accept her gratitude, there was something in his eyes that tempered the roughness in his voice.

Later, alone in her room, Katherine wondered if things might be different between them if she were not so scarred.

But she was and that was the bald truth of the matter. She must abandon such foolish speculations and apply all her energies to managing her holdings. And staying alive.

Early the next day, Katherine stood in the ward wrapped closely in her warmest cape. She rounded her slight shoulders against the cold and shivered when a puff of morning air blew over her face.

Victor emerged from the stable leading his horse. It was well packed and he had to swing up carefully to avoid sitting on the transport baskets. The panniers were filled with his clothes, along with some of Grace's good cooking for the journey.

Katherine walked out to meet him while John stood off at a little distance.

"I should be able to send a guardian within a couple of days," Victor said. "You will be safe with John until then."

"Yes," Katherine said quietly. "John is kind and I trust him."

Victor reached down. Katherine hesitated briefly, then gave him her hand. He held it a moment before speaking.

"You will be as safe with John as you would be with me. Do not be afraid."

"I am not afraid."

Victor released her and sat upright. "Perhaps you will visit Stonehaven again," he said stiffly. "Ciscilla would be pleased for your company."

"Yes, thank you."

They looked at each other in silence. When Victor found his voice, it was hoarse.

"I should go."

"Yes," Katherine agreed. "Marjorie will be waiting."

Victor blinked and snapped the reins. His horse cantered across the drawbridge and Katherine watched until he disappeared from view.

CHAPTER 11

VICTOR WAS AS GOOD AS HIS WORD and within the week Katherine bade John farewell and welcomed her new protector. Rowley was a short, stocky man with a swarthy complexion and a fierce countenance. But when he smiled, which was frequently, his square teeth exposed a slight gap in the middle, lending him a disarming charm.

He settled into the routine at Crenfeld nicely, doggedly falling in behind Katherine wherever she went. He had also made a conquest of the formidable Grace, who brightened considerably when Rowley followed Katherine into her kitchen. She bore all the marks of a captivated woman. Upon sight of Rowley, Grace's hands flew to her hair to make immediate repairs, her voice became subdued, her lips relaxed and her eyes softened with indulgent tenderness. When Rowley took Alice's hand and drew her away from her work into his lap, Grace made no protest but merely smiled benignly.

So Katherine found reasons to frequent the kitchen. She enjoyed watching the three of them together; Rowley playing little games with Alice, Alice hugging one of his sturdy arms and prattling happily in his ear, Grace offering Rowley samples of choice morsels of the day and waiting for him to smack his lips in approval and pat his ample belly. They were a warm picture of domestic serenity that Katherine never tired of watching.

One morning Katherine watched the contented trio in the kitchen out of the corner of her eyes as she bent over the inventory books from a stool in the open upper storeroom. She frowned. The numbers were not adding up. There should be twenty barrels of corn and she had only counted fifteen. She counted three times to make sure.

"Grace," she called down, "Do you have any corn barrels in the kitchen?"

"No, my lady. Used last of it yesterday."

"M-m-m." Katherine looked under her table. Nothing resembling a barrel at all. Just sacks of ground wheat.

"I will have to look in the lower storage, Rowley."

Rowley rose from his place by the fire to gaze up the stairs.

"Wait a moment."

Katherine waved him away. "No, keep to your bench. I will not be long."

Rowley hesitated briefly then gave in to Alice's insistent tug at his rough hand. "Call if you need me, then."

Katherine nodded, picked up her skirts and descended the long stairway opposite the short steps leading from the upper storeroom to the kitchen. She held a lighted rush and began inspecting the vats and barrels ranged around the cold basement room. She wrinkled her nose. The floor reeds smelled moldy. They needed changing. She held her light high and leaned over the barrels, buckets, sacks and casks, opening lids and scrutinizing contents. The torch threw flickering shadows against the stone wall, making it difficult to see where the store of goods ended. Muffled sounds from the kitchen floated down to her ears. Katherine was just beginning to loosen the knot on a sack mouth when she heard a slight sound on the stair. Without looking up, she called out.

"Rowley, is that you? I suppose I could use your help after all."

There was no answer.

"Rowley?"

This time she looked up. All was quiet. She felt the hairs on the back of her neck prickle and held her breath to listen. There was no sound, save the faint drift of muted voices from the kitchen. Her hands began to shake and despite the coldness of the room, she felt perspiration spring out on her body. Why had she been so foolish and come down alone? Fearfully, she eyed the bottom of the stone steps, but no one appeared. In her mind's eye she saw a shadowy figure braced against the wall in the darkness, holding his breath. And waiting. She looked frantically about. She should hide. Someone was there, just out of sight. She could feel their presence. Her breath began to come in short gasps. Calm down, she told herself. Calm down and think. Of course. The trap door to the unused dungeon. She could hide down there. Whoever it was had not brought a light with them. She would have seen it if they had. And if she slipped through the door in the floor and closed it, maybe they would not find her.

Katherine sprang to the trap door, wrenched on the ring and yanked it open. Peering down inside, she saw a faint glimmer of light straining in from a narrow slit cut into the thick outer wall. She squinted, yet could not make out the bottom. How far down was it? She held her rushlight out over the edge of the hole, but before she had time to consider, further sounds of movement on the stairs propelled her in a terrified plunge through the opening. The door banged shut behind her and she tumbled headlong onto a dirt floor, perhaps ten feet below. Sharp pains shot up her ankle. She bit her lip and winced.

It was a dank room and much colder than the cool storeroom above. Katherine crept into a corner and huddled against a bank of earth. Her light had gone out when she fell, so the darkness was total except for that afforded by the narrow slit in the wall. As her eyes grew accustomed to the gloom, she realized she could see quite well. The floor was a rough surface of dirt and rock. The stone walls were thick with moss. And it was completely bare. There was nowhere to hide.

She sat and listened to the sounds directly above her. Footsteps shuffled across the plank flooring and particles of dust floated between the boards and onto her head. She heard the scraping of barrels being shifted and the soft grunts of the person moving them. Fear was a noose around her neck, threatening to choke her. She gasped for air, trembling violently, her heart pounding in her ears.

And then the trap door flew open. Katherine had a glimpse of a mournful face thrust in briefly before a man dropped down beside her, his long arms outstretched. Her scream was bloodcurdling even to her own ears and, blind with terror, she beat off the hands groping for her, pulling herself away from her attacker and flinging herself to the other side of the small room. But there was no escape. He simply turned and reached out again.

Katherine found her face pressed up against the mossy wall of the chamber. The foul-smelling stuff squeezed into her nose and mouth and her arms were wrenched back painfully behind her. What the man intended to do next she never knew, for all at once the hole in the upper floor was filled with light and Rowley plummeted through the opening brandishing Grace's iron meat hook. He fell on the man at once, burying the hook in the back of her attacker. The man moaned, sagged against Katherine, then slid to the ground. Rowley pushed him away with his foot, took the now sobbing Katherine in his arms and carried her up a ladder that had been dropped down to them.

Grace stood aside as Rowley came up, casting wide fearful eyes below.

"Is he dead?" she whispered from behind her hand.

"He is," Rowley assured her. "Get your mistress something hot to drink. And bring a blanket. I will put her in front of the fire."

Grace ran up the stairs ahead of him, then down the short flight from the storeroom into the kitchen. She scooped a ladle of soup from the pot into a bowl, set it aside and ran for a blanket. Rowley lowered Katherine to rest on the floor before the great kitchen fire, raised her head and lifted the hot liquid to her lips.

"Drink this. It will make you feel better."

Grace hurried in and tucked a thick blanket around Katherine's quivering shoulders.

Katherine's teeth clattered on the edge of the bowl. "Who is it Rowley? Who is the man down there? I saw his face for a moment, and it looked like . . . " She shook her head jerkily. "But it could not have been."

Rowley leaned back on his haunches. "The chamberlain? It was. It was Peter."

Katherine passed a trembling hand over her eyes. "But why? Why would he want to hurt me?"

Rowley shrugged, made a face and shook his head.

"How did you know he had gone down after me? Did you see him go through the kitchen?"

"No, he slipped in without my noticing and I blame myself for that." Rowley frowned. "I should have paid closer attention. But I heard you call to me up the stairs and as I knew I was not there, someone else had to be. I waited a few minutes to see if you discovered your mistake, but when you called out a second time, I knew something was wrong. It took me a while to locate a makeshift weapon and Peter had found the trap door and dropped through by the time I got to the basement."

He grinned. "I heard you scream. Probably the whole village heard that scream. It was splendidly shocking."

Katherine gave him a weak smile. "Thank you, Rowley. For saving me. But I cannot think what Peter hoped to gain by my death."

"I don't expect he did. But whoever put him up to it likely had something to gain. And with Peter dead, we cannot discover who that was. Or, if he will try again."

"Oh, surely not," Katherine protested.

But Rowley only grunted and insisted on staying close in spite of Katherine's objections. He was unconvinced Peter had acted alone and the danger was past, so he remained watchful, lest another assassin be employed.

Not many days later as Katherine walked in the garden, enjoying the scent of the herbs and the ripening fruit trees, Grace burst from the kitchen and made straight for Rowley. He was, as always, a short but discreet distance behind his mistress, taking every bit as much pleasure in the sunny morning as she.

"Rowley, come quick!" Grace cried. "Hester has fallen down the well and we cannot get her out!"

Rowley darted a look at Katherine.

"Go at once," she motioned. "I will follow."

The kitchen was in an uproar. Nettie shrieked continuously, her arms outstretched over the mouth of the well as if somehow Hester could be transported into them. Many heads bent into the well, calling to Hester. The young kitchen maids paced to and fro wringing their hands in their aprons, while the menfolk plunged noisily amongst the pots and foodstuffs frantically searching for something with which to pull up poor Hester.

Rowley pushed them all aside and leaned far down into the well's mouth then straightened. "What happened? How did Hester fall?" He gripped Nettie's shoulders and shook her roughly. "How did she fall, Nettie?"

Nettie gulped and her eyes bulged. "She bent over the edge to catch hold of the rope. She were feelin' so faint. I told her not to. It made her dizzy. And she fell!" Nettie's voice rose hysterically and she covered her eyes with trembling hands.

"I need some light," Rowley demanded.

Quickly a candle was thrust into his hand. He took it and bent back over the well. Hester was wedged about half way down, her back against one side of the well and her knees buckled against the other. Her head lolled downward so Rowley could not see her face, but one arm moved feebly against the well wall.

"Can you hear me, Hester? It's Rowley!"

When there was no response, Rowley lowered the candle deeper into the well, then sucked in his breath and recoiled up out of the hole.

"Everyone back away from the well!" he shouted.

Startled, they all did as they were told.

"What is it?" Katherine whispered.

"She has the tokens upon her. It's the death come up from Melcombe port," he muttered. "No one must touch her. I will have to pull her out with hooks and ropes. We must not lay a hand on her."

"Is she dead?" Agnes cried, eyes wide with fright.

"Not yet, but she soon will be and I do not intend for her to take any of the rest of you with her," he said grimly.

"How can you be so sure she will die?" Katherine asked.

"Believe me, she will. I have seen this before. In Melcombe, nearly the whole town died and there were barely enough men left alive to bury the dead. It is a savage pestilence and it's here now. Send for Benjamin. He will know how to avoid infecting the rest. But keep everyone back. And keep Nettie away from Hester. It will mean her death."

Rowley padded the hooks they found for him with soft rags and worked the ropes down the well beside Hester. He was sweating heavily by the time he had manoeuvered the hooks into position under Hester's arms.

He wrapped both ropes around the well-pole and slowly turned the crank to raise her. When Hester's limp form cleared the well's mouth, Nettie had to be restrained from rushing forward.

Benjamin arrived as Rowley was about to loose Hester from the hooks.

"No! Do not touch her," the physician said sharply. "Leave her be and let me look at her first."

Rowley nodded and stepped back. Benjamin reached into his physic's bag and pulled out a jar. He poured some of its contents onto a cloth, held the cloth over his nose with one hand and approached Hester cautiously. The odour of vinegar wafted out as he moved.

Benjamin knelt alongside the stricken woman and studied her carefully. Using a small twig, he lifted her shift away from her neck and shoulders. It was already torn from her fall and most of her bruised side was exposed. A livid, purple bubo, as large as a common apple, bulged out from under one armpit. Her skin was rosy and small black pustules spread out over her arms and legs. Hester's pretty blue eyes were wide open but they glared in a fixed way. A low moan slipped from between her parted lips.

Benjamin sat back on his heels and groaned heavily. "If any of you are to survive you must leave here at once."

Agnes gave a small cry and Katherine paled. "Leave here?"

Benjamin nodded. "Yes, leave. This evil marches quickly. The miller's wife died of it. The women who prepared her body for burial are also dead. And several others in the village. It was not common knowledge. We were not sure. But now that I have seen Hester, I can tell you for certain. The Melcombe pestilence has found us. You cannot save yourselves if you remain. Everyone must leave."

Benjamin gestured toward Hester. "When she dies, pull her outside the castle walls with the same ropes and hooks you used to bring her up out of the well. Put her in a deep hole and spread quick-lime over the body. Throw in the ropes and hooks and cover everything well. Burn all her clothes and anything you know she has touched. Use sticks to handle them. Touch nothing of hers with your hands. I am sorry if this seems hard to you, but it must be this way if anyone is to be saved."

Katherine stared dumbly. This could not be happening. The sun shone, the perfume of flowers floated in through the kitchen on a light breeze and the birds sang blithe songs. Death could not be this close.

Rowley touched her arm. "I will take some of the men and dig Hester's grave," he said softly.

Katherine put her hand over her mouth and nodded. Rowley left and three men with him. Benjamin had backed away from Hester to stand beside Katherine and Agnes. Grace hugged Alice to herself and the kitchen maids and Nettie huddled together nearby.

They began their death vigil, watching the slow rise and fall of Hester's chest. From time to time she would start or moan in her delirium and then was quiet. When her breathing became ragged and it was clear the end was near, Nettie tore away from the grip of those who would prevent her and threw herself on top of her sister, sobbing violently. Alarmed, one of the women moved to pull her away.

"Let her be," Benjamin said quickly.

Nettie's heavy sobs turned to whimpers and she cradled Hester's head in her lap and stroked her hair, whispering all the while into the deaf ears of her sister. Suddenly there came a long, deep gasp for air, Hester's chest rose high and then collapsed and was still.

Rowley and the men moved forward to take Hester's body from the kitchen. They put on gloves to handle the ropes and hooks and tried to persuade Nettie to release her sister. But she clung all the tighter and in the end they had to drag them both outside to the freshly dug hole.

"Nettie, you must leave her now," Katherine said gently. "Hester is dead, Nettie. She must be buried."

Nettie shook her head stubbornly. "Nay, nay!"

"We must, Nettie," Benjamin said. "She is gone from you now. Let her go to her rest."

But it was no use. Finally, one of the men used his hook to pry Nettie's arms from her sister's body. Nettie howled frantically but he managed to keep her at bay while Rowley and the others lowered Hester's body into the pit. The sun glinted off her glaring, sightless eyes. A shovelful of quicklime was thrown down, the ropes and hooks tossed in and they covered it all with dirt before Nettie could struggle free.

Once Hester's body was well covered, the men slung their shovels over their shoulders and walked off. Nettie shrieked and threw herself face down on the dirt mound. She lay there motionless and without crying out any further.

Katherine gave Benjamin and Rowley an anxious look.

"There is nothing to be done for her my dear," Benjamin said. "She will not leave her sister."

"But she will . . . "

"Die? Yes, the distemper is sure to come upon her. Leave her some food and a blanket." He shrugged in resignation. "She may take them. She may not. Her grief is deeper than we can understand. She has lost a part of herself, poor thing. And I believe she would prefer to be in that hole with her sister."

Katherine looked sadly at Nettie. At the matted mouse-coloured hair, the sepia shift, shapeless over the round back. And she remembered the story of the disappointed suitor and the forlorn look in Hester's eyes. Would the unhappy Hester have married her young man if Nettie had been the one to die? It did not matter now. Katherine turned away and her steps were heavy as she went inside to make the necessary travelling arrangements.

"But Benjamin, surely you are coming with us!" Katherine cried.

The physician's dark eyes were solemn and he patted her hand gently. "Not immediately. Someone has to warn the others."

Katherine had forgotten. The poor villagers. Of course they must be warned.

"Tell them not to worry about their rents, Benjamin. They must get away. Their homes will not be lost to them. I see no reason to make things hard for them to leave, or to return once the pestilence is past."

Benjamin smiled. "Thank you, my dear. I am sure that will be of some comfort. I will stay in the village to tend those who need it. When the time is right, I will follow you. Do you mean to make for Stonehaven Castle?"

Katherine started. "I had not thought to, no."

"You must. It is farther inland. It seems that proximity to water hurries the sickness on, though I cannot think why. Make for Stonehaven. And drink only from swiftly running streams, not from any standing ponds," he cautioned. "If anyone develops the distemper on your way, you must leave them."

Rowley and Agnes stood beside Katherine and listened carefully to everything the physician said.

Rowley nodded dolefully. "Won't like it, but we will do as you say."

"And if any die . . . "

Agnes covered her face and Katherine turned away and closed her eyes.

Benjamin took Katherine by the shoulders.

"Look at me, my dear. This is important. If any die, they must be buried as we buried Hester. Use the quick-lime. Burn their things. It is the only way."

Katherine nodded in dumb silence and watched Benjamin hurry away. This was a crushing responsibility. How could she bear it? Look at all those frightened faces watching her. They wanted her to tell them what to do. Her. Her, to lead them to safety. And she was every bit as afraid as they were. Maybe even more so. She looked into Rowley's dark face and was comforted to find no fear in it. Lord Victor had given her a man of courage, like himself. God bless him. She put all the assurance she could into her voice.

"Rowley, take some of the men and hitch up all the wagons and carts we have. Load some supplies. Only take what we need. No beds or furnishings. Only food, clothing and blankets. Whatever horses we cannot use, turn outside the walls. The rest of the animals too. They will have to fend for themselves. Find a harness-mate for Pygine. He will pull my carriage. And tie the pigs up behind the kitchen wagon. We will need them. Do not let anyone make off with them in the night," she warned.

"No one will. I shall see to it myself."

"And make sure everyone that has no place in a wagon has a horse to ride. I do not want anyone walking, Rowley."

Rowley nodded. "Yes, my lady. Shall I drive the kitchen wagon?" he asked hopefully. "I will be better able to keep an eye on the pigs," he explained.

"Yes. The food will need to be closely guarded."

Katherine knew the real reason Rowley wanted to be in the kitchen wagon and Grace and Alice could not have a better guardian. She could attest to that.

"Have my things put into the chest over there," Katherine pointed. "Load it into the first wagon so I will know where they are. Put Agnes' things in with mine and make sure everyone knows which wagon their things have been put into and tell them to stay with that wagon."

Rowley did not move off at once and Katherine raised her eyebrows expectantly.

"Is there something?"

"Yes, my lady. Are we making for Stonehaven Castle as the physic says?"

Katherine sighed. "I suppose we must. But how Lord Victor will look on our intrusion, I cannot think. Disease-ridden as we might be."

Rowley grunted and shrugged. "Lord Victor is a soldier. He will deal with this pestilence as he would any enemy invader. He will put it to rout. You may depend on that," Rowley said with pride.

Katherine's smile was wan. "If you say so."

"Stonehaven it is then," Rowley said cheerfully. "We will be ready to leave by day's end."

Katherine thanked him, sent Agnes off to gather her belongings and separated herself from the hurry in the courtyard. She walked outside the walls and down to the north bluff. The river was subdued today. Usually it flung itself with fury against the cliffs, but today it merely churned around the rocks below. She watched the gulls tilting into the winds that always circled this far tower. They were lucky. They had no knowledge of the menace to all things living, bearing down on them. Would she be back or would she too die? Like Hester. With no husband to mourn her, no children to weep for her. Agnes and her friends would mind for a little she supposed. But life wins out and the dead are forgotten. She sighed and wandered back from the cliffs, while the gulls wheeled and shrieked overhead.

CHAPTER 12

THEY DID NOT TRAVEL FAR THAT DAY and they travelled without most of the manorial military personnel. All of the household knights and men-at-arms had remained behind to help keep order in the village. The porter and a few of the watchmen were all that were retained for the journey. It was slow going and most were exhausted before they had ridden for long. The strain of their forced flight, the threat of death and the urgent scramble to depart Crenfeld, had all taken its toll. Men were impatient, mothers harried, children whimpering. They unpacked only enough to make up places to sleep on the hard ground, then most fell into restless and weary slumber.

Rowley appointed watches by turn throughout the night, taking the first rotation himself. Katherine observed him from her pallet beside Agnes. He circled the camp slowly, peering out into the darkness from time to time, then sat with his back against a tree, a blanket pulled up to his chin. She kept her eyes on him for as long as she could. The sight of him was reassuring. Her lids drooped lower and lower till she slept.

With the first light of morning, the camp began to stir. The panic of yesterday vanished as the shadows of night fled before a bright sun. Grace had already supervised the building of a good-sized campfire when Katherine awoke.

Katherine yawned and stretched her cramped limbs, then pushed off her blanket and reached for a heavy cape. The sun may be shining but she was still cold. She threw the cape around her shoulders and fastened it tightly.

Rowley and Agnes were nowhere to be seen but that did not surprise her. The clearing was milling with men and women. The children had forgotten their tears and were busy poking twigs into the campfire. Uncharacteristically, Grace did not scold them. Though not indulgent, her grim smile and folded arms gave them consent.

Alice had not joined the other children but strode importantly to and from the kitchen wagon, bearing armloads of bowls and breakfast loaves. The loaves would only keep a short time so they would eat them quickly. No more could be baked until they reached Stonehaven.

Katherine accepted her share of the bread and Alice handed her a cup of wine to drink with it. A dimpled smile and a curtsy were offered as well and Katherine thanked Alice then sat down close to the fire. Rowley appeared, grinning in gap-toothed admiration at Grace, who blushed to the very roots of her severely contained hair.

"I have been up the road," he said to Katherine. "Seems clear enough for the pack horses. And wagons will have no trouble either. All going well, we should reach Stonehaven tonight."

As if waiting for Rowley's proviso, a wild howl went up at the outer edge of the camp. Katherine and Rowley dropped what was in their hands and bolted toward the source of the commotion. A woman stood over a small child huddled up against a tree. She brandished a stick in one hand and prodded the frightened youngster with it.

Rowley lunged forward, knocking the weapon from her hand.

"What are you doing to the lad?" he cried.

"He's got 'em," the woman snarled at Rowley. "He's got 'em. Look at 'is legs."

She pointed an accusing finger and Rowley and Katherine followed the direction of her glare.

Katherine's heart leaped into her throat. The child's skin had the rosy hue of fever and he bore on his body the same marks as Hester had on hers.

"Whose boy is this?" Rowley called out over the assemblage.

"He's mine, ain't he," the stick-wielding woman sneered. "Him as I suckled to these breasts." She thumped herself on the chest. "And now he carries the tokens. I gave 'im life and he will give me death." She spat on the ground and tramped off into the surrounding wood.

Katherine and Rowley stood in stunned silence. Rowley was the first to recover.

"Now this is a pretty pass," he said. "Didn't think to be leaving babes behind." He shook his head and frowned.

"We cannot leave him here all alone," Katherine cried. "Some wild animal may attack the child."

She looked at the youngster still curled up against the tree. He was in a pool of shade and shivered, despite his feverish look. The raised black spots on his arms and legs were red-rimmed and painful looking. The boy's eyes had begun to glaze over.

"Rowley," she said, not taking her eyes off the boy, "have Agnes go into my chest and bring me the little brown cakes wrapped in a cloth on top of my clothes."

Rowley nodded, returning a short while later with Agnes trotting behind him. He handed her the napkin-wrapped cakes.

"What are they?" he asked

"Benjamin gave me one of these when I had the pain in my head. This child is in a much worse state and I think if we could get him to take some he may not suffer so."

Rowley accepted one of the brown cakes from Katherine and considered it. Then he tossed it over to the boy. It hit him on the arm and he winced and whimpered, but his eyes refocused and he gave them his attention. Rowley pointed to the cake, opened his own mouth wide and pointed to the cake again, nodding slowly.

"Find him a blanket," Katherine whispered to Agnes. "A warm one."

The blanket, too, was thrown close to the boy. He took it and wrapped himself in it. But the cake remained untouched on the ground.

"Maybe he is of a mind we think to poison him," Agnes whispered.

"Surely he can see we mean to help him," Katherine protested.

They watched a while longer and slowly a childish hand stole out from under the blanket and drew the brown cake back beneath the cover to reappear at an opening under his chin. He sniffed the cake and made a face and Katherine was afraid he would refuse it. But, groaning a little, he seemed to make up his mind quickly and gobbled it down.

Katherine kept watch until he sank against the tree. His eyes closed, his mouth went slack and he toppled sideways onto the ground. But he managed to maintain a hold on the blanket and it still covered him.

Katherine looked back at Rowley and Agnes.

"He's only sleeping?" Agnes whispered fearfully.

"Yes," Katherine replied. "I think he will sleep until it is over. It cannot be long now."

Rowley looked around him. "Where is the boy's mother? Still in the trees? Leave some food for her near the boy. If anyone knows where their things are, they had better be left behind too. Let's finish breakfast and pack up."

Grace was already gathering up the used bowls and napkins. Katherine retrieved her own breakfast things and handed them to her.

"What is to be done about that little one, then?" Grace asked Katherine. "Right fine mother he has," she added with a sniff.

"Do not judge her too harshly, Grace. When people are afraid of dying, they can lose all reason. Are you not afraid to die?"

Grace lifted her broad shoulders. "Course I am. Be a fool and a liar if I said otherwise. But that is still no cause for handling your own child so viciously."

Katherine sighed. "You are a strong woman, Grace. Some are not so strong. I know not how brave I will be when my time comes," she said faintly.

"Brave as any of us, I expect," Grace said.

"I do wish I were not afraid though, Grace. I wish I knew where my soul went. Father says to purgatory and Benjamin says either straight to heaven or straight to hell. Into the arms of Jesus or into damnation.

Grace snorted. "Benjamin is a good physic, but he don't even worship the Mass so he has no right filling your head with his heretical ideas."

"Maybe," Katherine mused, unperturbed by Grace's disapproval. "But who is to say who is right? Father or Benjamin?" she argued. "No one has been to the other side and come back to tell us what is there. And I would like to know. Would you?"

"Nay, I would not. And never you mind about dyin'," Grace scolded. "You are not dyin' yet. You have plenty of time to think about that. You are young yet."

"Except for the pestilence, Grace. It does not care that I am still young. Look at the boy. Does it care he is only a child?" Katherine shook her head sadly. "It does not," she whispered.

Katherine picked up the edge of her skirt, gathered it off the ground and went to sit at a little distance from the sleeping child. She became oblivious to the activity in the camp, concentrating instead on the rise and fall of the little chest. Katherine looked at the boy's closed eyes, the long lashes over the plump feverish cheeks, the blond hair sticking damply to his forehead and thought of another little boy near his own age. The memory of young Edward brought a lump to her throat. Dare she go to Stonehaven? To bring this terrible plague so close to Victor's child? Surely it would be safer for them to make for some abandoned castle or manor house.

Suddenly the dying boy sat bolt upright, opened his eyes wide and gasped deeply. His gaze locked on Katherine's startled face and she could see the terror in his pain-clouded eyes. He clawed at his throat with frantic fingers, mouth gaping. Attempting to stand, he reached out to her and then toppled in a small heap, writhing feebly while Katherine looked on, temporarily frozen. She lurched up to go to him but Rowley came behind her and laid a restraining hand on her shoulder.

"No, my lady. Stay where you are."

"But someone must comfort him," Katherine pleaded, tears brimming in her eyes. "He ought not to die alone and frightened with no warmth and no kiss."

Rowley made no attempt to reason with her. "You can't," he said.

Katherine strained toward the stricken child but Rowley held her firmly until Agnes pulled her away. From the circle of Agnes's arms Katherine kept her eyes on Rowley when he went to stand over the lad, one hand held over his nose and mouth. He looked down for a few moments then stepped away.

"It is over," he said to Katherine. "The boy is dead."

Katherine groaned and covered her face.

"Oh, Rowley. I dare not bring this company to Stonehaven now. We would put them all in danger."

Rowley stood, grim-faced. "You have no choice. You must go to Stonehaven. You will be safe there."

"But will they be safe from us?" Katherine cried.

"I promised Lord Victor I would protect you from your enemy. That your enemy has changed does not alter the promise. He wants you protected."

"But Rowley," Katherine protested, catching his thick, rough hands in her own. "Think what it might mean to Edward. And to Ciscilla. What it might mean to Victor himself?" She shuddered.

"I have thought. And my opinion remains the same. They would not turn you away. If I were to take you anywhere else, I should only be sent to fetch you back to Stonehaven."

Katherine dropped his hands limply. "But why, Rowley?" She looked into his eyes. "Why? I am not of their family. Why would they risk their own safety for mine?"

Rowley gave her a steady look. "You must know that without their help you may die."

Katherine lowered her head. She had no wish for him to see the misery in her eyes. How could she tell him that the thought of Victor dying almost suffocated her with panic? That Ciscilla was the only one in whom she could confide her secret pain. That little Edward was to her as the child she could have borne but now never would. She would die for them. Gladly, die for them.

"Yes, I do know but they are my friends," she said faintly.

"And you would not want anything to happen to your friends. Well, neither would they want anything to happen to their friend." Rowley smiled at her incredulous face. "Why do you find that so strange? Ciscilla insisted you have protection and Lord Victor sent me to do just that."

"Yes, but this is so different. Their own lives were not threatened by protecting me. Now they are. They are safe inside the walls of Stonehaven. I cannot think that my fate would be more important to them than their own," she added, with slight bitterness.

Rowley snorted. "Now you are feeling sorry for yourself."

Katherine laughed in spite of herself. "You know, you sound like Lord Victor. That is exactly what he said to me after the fire. Stop feeling sorry for yourself and get up and do something."

It was Rowley's turn to laugh. "That's my master. He said the very same thing to himself when he came home wounded from Crecy. Could not walk on the one leg at all. He stormed and raged. And with his wife gone too — you know of that — well, it was more than he could bear. He went away and John and I went with him. Finally came to his senses though and scolded himself just as he scolded you. I never heard him utter another word about his leg, his wife, or how badly off he was left.

Katherine averted her eyes. "Has he married yet? Married Marjorie Clere?"

Rowley studied her downcast features and heard the resignation in her voice.

"No," he said slowly, aware of her soft intake of breath. "No, he has not. He seems reluctant to commit himself to a time. Miss Clere is, of course, perplexed. She expects to be married before Michaelmas and cannot understand why he delays preparations."

"What does he say? What does he give for a reason?" Katherine asked.

"He doesn't."

"I see." Katherine lifted her head and looked him steadily in the eye. "I am sure he has a good reason," she said in a firm voice.

"I'm sure he has," Rowley replied, watching her face closely.

Katherine lowered her eyes." At least we will not be intruding on his wedding," she said brusquely. "Once the child is properly buried, we will set out for Stonehaven then, as you say."

Rowley nodded and left to attend to the unpleasant duty of consigning the pitiful little body to the ground.

Katherine watched him go. Sadly, she realized that she did not even know the child's name. Would his mother come out of the woods when they had gone and cry over his quiet little grave? She shuddered and prayed she was not bringing this pestilence into Victor's home. If a woman could hate her own child for infecting her by accident, what would Victor's reaction be if she brought the fatal malady to him intentionally? But there was really nowhere else they could go, and be safe. They had been lucky so far in not attracting the attention of road thieves. That luck would not hold for long. Soon the sharp eyes of the lawless rabble would ferret out their location and wait for an opportunity to fall on them and steal their provisions.

Katherine looked over the camp, its many wagons and pack horses, its few men to protect it. They must move quickly to reach Stonehaven by nightfall. She hurried to help reload the carts and obliterate from the camp as much evidence of their passage as possible.

Rowley said nothing when he surprised her by climbing into the wagon beside her and taking the reins from her hands. With a set jaw he cracked the leather thongs over the backs of the horses and clucked his tongue. Obediently, the animals raised their heads and walked out of the clearing. The other carts and pack animals fell in behind.

"Grace prefers that I stay with you," he said at last. "She can handle the kitchen wagon on her own."

Katherine raised a thin eyebrow. "I am able to drive these horses, Rowley. She should not worry about me. Agnes will take over when I need to rest." She glanced behind her into the cart where Agnes lay asleep, her head nestled between two soft sacks.

"If Grace needs you . . . "

"She does not." Rowley clamped his mouth shut over the words.

Katherine regarded his grim face with concern. "Is something the matter, Rowley? Have you quarreled with Grace?"

He looked at her and she saw the hurt in his eyes. "Grace does not want the plague near to Alice. She does not want me in the wagon."

"Oh." Katherine sighed heavily and put her hand on Rowley's arm.

"Grace still cares for you, Rowley. She is only afraid for her child. I think any good mother would be. Please do not think badly of her for it."

Rowley made no reply. He just stared forward to some point on the road ahead of them. Katherine sat in sympathetic silence for a time then turned in her seat and looked behind at the line of carts and wagons. They were stretched out at widely spaced intervals, a thick fog of dust rising between them. Each wagon had a pack horse tethered to either side at the rear and the horses swung wide on their ropes to keep to the outside of the wheels, away from the choking powder of dirt.

Katherine strained to see behind the line, peering into the woods on the sides of the road. The possibility of an encounter with thieves made her nervous, but the only movement was a startled deer bounding out to watch them pass. She squinted at the sun. It was now high in the sky and getting hot. That would mean stopping to water the horses oftener. For once she did not welcome a warm day.

She looked up at the few wispy white clouds keeping a respectful distance from the hot sun, scanning the sky for the black clouds that signalled showers, but there were none. Katherine turned back around in her seat and looked at Rowley again. But his countenance remained impassive and aloof. Poor Rowley. Katherine settled back, keeping one eye on the angle of the sun. She did not want to spend another night out in the open. The jostling of the wagon made her sleepy and she closed her eyes and dropped her chin and leaned against the sack pressing into her back.

Katherine awoke when Rowley reigned in the horses and waved to the rest of the column. She sat up straighter and saw that they had come to the same stream where she and Agnes refreshed themselves on her first trip to Stonehaven. It seemed such a long time ago. Most of the party kept to the wagons and the horses were left in harness and led to the stream so they could drink. The pack horses were untied and brought around to drink beside the others. Several men filled jugs from the stream and brought them back to the rest, where cups of water were handed out to the thirsty travellers.

They stayed only a short time. Once the horses were satisfied, they began cropping off the tender grasses beside the banks. They were left to graze while the wagons were inspected for any loose wheels or unfastened packs. That done, the column stretched out once more along the dusty roadway.

The day wore on and Katherine was dismayed to see the sun sinking lower in the sky and still they had not reached Stonehaven. Rowley prodded the horses to greater speed, squinting into the underbrush as they passed. Katherine sensed urgency in his rigid posture.

"We will not make it before nightfall, will we?" Katherine's voice was strained.

"No, we will not."

Katherine grasped the sides of her seat and watched the relentless descent of the sun. It sank lower and lower, bathing the sky in bright pink before disappearing behind the trees.

Suddenly, she heard a shout from behind. She twisted around in time to make out a lone rider dart out from behind a stand of rocks some distance away to the rear and then dart back in behind them. But the sentinel posted at the end of the caravan had already seen him and was signalling the rest.

In the gathering dusk, they wheeled their wagons to form a tight circle; wagons and carts to the outside, horses to the inside. Some of the animals, frightened by the abrupt change in command, reared high in their harnesses, eyes dilated and ears flat. But Pygine and his yoke-mate responded quickly, pivoting to the inside in unison.

Everyone scrambled down from the wagons, pulled the panniers from the pack animals and propped the heavily laden baskets end on end to form a shield. Rowley ordered everyone but the most able men behind this barrier. Then he and the rest of the men unpacked the long bows and crouched beside the back wheels of the wagons to wait.

They did not wait long. Dark shapes emerged from the shadows; the heavy bulk of horses and the tall, narrow forms of men on foot. Katherine held her breath and watched the featureless silhouettes spread out beyond the border of the wagons. She could not tell how many there were. Night was closing in and they seemed to blur together. There was a whispered consultation between Rowley and the men and then she heard the ph-t-t of arrows being let loose. Cries from their pursuers confirmed when arrows had found their mark. Katherine ducked down lower and covered the head of the woman next to her. Small children whimpered. Some sobbed aloud. The women moaned and quaked, clutching their little ones close.

In the gathering gloom it was difficult to see more than a few yards away. When one of the men staggered beside Katherine, back arched and arm twisted to grasp an arrow protruding from his back, she shrieked at the same time as he dropped face down at her feet. Then without thinking, she snatched up the bow that fell from his nerveless fingers, yanked free his arrow bag and, keeping low, ran toward the place she had seen Rowley and the others.

With trembling hands Katherine armed the bow and screwed up her eyes, straining to see any outline of their attackers. She made out just the barest change in the thick surrounding blackness, took aim and shot. There was a hollow thud and a shift in the shadows.

Now Katherine could hear loud gasping to her left and realized, with panic, that their assailants were grappling hand to hand. They would be upon her at any moment and she cast about frantically for something with which to defend herself at close range. Finding nothing, Katherine took an arrow and broke off the hilt as far up she dared and still leave herself a handle. She held it in front of her face, panting hard now with fear. She twitched it back and forth as each fresh sound came to her from the darkness.

Suddenly, Katherine was knocked to the ground and felt a searing pain in her left shoulder. She lashed out with the head of the arrow and drove it with as much force as she could into her attacker. He grunted and fell hard on top of her. Hysterically, she tried pushing his bulk away from her. She knew she was screaming but she could not stop. She used both arms to thrust the man up until the agony in her shoulder became unbearable. The only way to stay conscious was to continue screaming and so she did. Again and again and louder and louder. Finally, the dead man toppled over. She scrambled dizzily to her feet, panting and gasping and clutching her shoulder with her good hand. Warm blood pulsed between her fingers and she began to stagger. Somewhere between where she had made her stand and the safety of the pannier wall, Katherine collapsed. She heard a rushing sound in her ears and the muffled cries of the combatants. Someone bounded out from the row of panniers and dragged her back behind the barrier, but Katherine had fainted and was not aware of Agnes's small bravery.

When she came to, her shoulder was heavily bandaged and she was covered in a thick wool blanket. Agnes held her head in her lap and she felt droplets of warm tears falling onto her face.

"Agnes," she said hoarsely. "Agnes. Please do not cry. I am alive."

A candle was lit and she made out Agnes's tearstained and blotchy face hovering over her own. In a moment, memory returned and she gripped Agnes's arm.

"Rowley. Where is Rowley? Is he . . . ?"

The familiar face of her protector swam into her line of vision. It was streaked with dirt and sweat but it was Rowley. Katherine relaxed back into Agnes's lap.

"You were not killed," she breathed. "I am so glad."

"No more than I." Rowley brought his grave face down closer.

"We are going to have to make a run for Stonehaven." he said. " We have lost three good men and we can't take another attack. This lot has either been killed or bolted but there will be more. I have two men with lights at the front of the column and two men behind. Agnes will stay in the wagon with you. I am sorry I could not keep them from breaking through and injuring you. I hold myself responsible."

Katherine tried to sit up. "No, Rowley. It is not your fault."

Rowley silenced her with a gesture. "We must leave at once. Rest as best you can. We have to make Stonehaven. It will be uncomfortable for you but better than being slaughtered like cattle."

Once the wagon jerked to a start, Katherine gasped and gritted her teeth. She slipped in and out of consciousness with Agnes doing her best to keep her arm and shoulder immobile. Katherine was not aware of reaching Stonehaven. By then she had fallen into a senseless sleep. Blood soaked through the many bandaged layers on her shoulder and dripped out into the courtyard as they lowered her from the wagon.

CHAPTER 13

WHEN VICTOR SAW KATHERINE all the colour drained from his face. He had her taken to his private chambers and put into his own bed then watched while Agnes removed the bandage, his jaw hardening at the sight of the ugly knife wound. He inspected it carefully, threaded fine gut into a clean needle, then with steady hands sutured the bruised skin while Katherine remained unconscious.

"Put a fresh bandage on it, Agnes," he said when he was finished. "It should not bleed any more now."

Agnes gripped Katherine's limp hands. "Will she live, my lord?"

"Only God knows that," Victor replied. "Your mistress has lost much blood. Pray for her." His face clouded. "If only Benjamin were here. I think God listens to him. Benjamin did not come with you?"

"No, my lord. He stayed to warn the others."

"Of the pestilence you mean? Yes," Victor nodded, "Yes, he would do that."

Agnes gazed down at Katherine's pale face. "She did not wish to come here and put you in danger. But Rowley insisted. Now look at my poor lady." Her voice broke and she clenched her fists in a handful of her skirt.

Victor rubbed a hand over his face. "I am glad he did."

Agnes looked up but Victor was already gone. Turning to her mistress, she sank to her knees beside the bed, folded her hands in front of her face and closed her eyes. Her lips moved noiselessly.

Safe behind the castle walls, the tired company settled down into exhausted sleep. Victor roamed restlessly through the halls, now and again putting his head into his own room where Katherine slept. As morning approached, he slipped into the bedchamber past the snoring Agnes to watch Katherine. He bent down close to her face until he could feel her breath on his cheek then leaned over and put his lips gently onto her forehead. Her brow was hot and dry and she moved slightly under the light pressure. Slowly he stood upright, watched her for a few more moments, then silently left the room.

When Katherine awoke, her shoulder ached and felt stiff but it was not bleeding. She touched the bandage gently. Not so bad. Only numb. However, when she sat up the arm throbbed painfully. She grew dizzy and lay back on her pillows, then tried again. This time she moved more slowly and was able to slip her legs over the side of the bed.

Agnes stirred and opened her eyes. A grin overspread her wide face and she went to her mistress, halting on joints made stiff from sitting all night in a hard chair.

"Here, let me help you," she said to Katherine. "Lean on me on this side so your shoulder can be free. How does it feel?" she asked.

"Not as bad as I thought it would and it does not bleed any longer either," Katherine answered.

"Thanks to Lord Victor," Agnes said.

Katherine frowned, not understanding.

"It was him as stitched the wound to stop it bleeding. This is his own bed, too. Would not have you laid anywhere else," Agnes said proudly. "You being a lady and mistress of Crenfeld."

Katherine digested this bit of news in silence. "Would you do something for me? Would you find Victor's sister and ask her to come to me, please?"

With Agnes gone, Katherine groaned inwardly. Would there be no end to her shame? She was more like a battle-scarred fighting man than a lady. She grew hot at the thought of having to face Victor. She had no wish to see the pity in his eyes.

Suddenly Ciscilla whirled into the chamber and dropped to her knees in front of Katherine, laying her head in Katherine's lap and hugging her legs.

"I was so afraid for you," she cried. "Does it hurt terribly?" Her dark eyes were wide.

Katherine smiled. "Some," she admitted.

"We have been so worried. And Edward cried and cried when he saw you being brought inside. He thought you were dead."

"Please tell him I am all right, Ciscilla."

"Why not do that yourself?" Victor was smiling at her from the doorway and Edward came around from behind his legs to bolt into the room. He put both his chubby hands on her knees, leaned forward and studied her bandaged arm with round anxious eyes.

"Will you die?" he wailed.

Katherine allowed herself a small chuckle. She bent down and touched his forehead with her own.

"No," she whispered. "I am really much stronger than I look."

The little boy's face brightened. "I am glad. Shall I tell Nory? Shall I?"

Poised for flight, he seemed to need this small errand. Katherine nodded.

Edward ducked between his father's legs and hurtled down the stairs.

"Mind you do not fall," Victor called after him. Katherine lowered her eyes, not knowing where to look. Ciscilla had chased after Edward, calling for him to wait for her and so the little buffer between Katherine and Victor was gone. She felt awkward and nervous.

"Your mistress will be wanting breakfast, Agnes. Perhaps you would go to the kitchen and bring something up for her."

"Yes, my lord," Agnes said. "At once." She knew when she was being dismissed.

Victor pulled up the stool across from Katherine. She kept her head down and waited to see what he would say. But he did not speak and when she could stand the silence no longer, she blurted.

"I feel such a fool."

Victor raised an eyebrow. "Why is that?"

"I should not have been hurt. It is all my own fault, anyway."

Victor frowned. "As I see it, if anyone bears the fault, it is Rowley. He was supposed to look after you and he protected every woman except you."

"Oh, but that is where you are wrong. If I had stayed where he put me I would have been quite safe." She looked at him then. "I did not stay."

Victor was perplexed. "What do you mean, you did not stay? Where could you go in the dark?"

Katherine thrust out her chin. Victor knew that look.

"I thought I could help."

His eyes narrowed. "And exactly how were you going to do that?"

"My father taught me to use the bow. He said I could shoot as well as any man. I saw an opportunity to give assistance and I took it."

"What did you do?" He paused and added drily. "To assist."

"I took the place of one of the men from our party who was killed," Katherine said defiantly. "I saw he was dead, I got his bow and his arrows and I joined the others." She lifted her chin. "And killed the man who did this."

Victor shook his head and ran a hand through his hair. "You amaze me, madam. Truly you amaze me."

His face turned serious and he glared at her. "Did it ever occur to you that you could have been killed yourself?"

"Yes, it did."

"And have you so soon forgotten Peter's attempt on your life?"

"No, I have not forgotten but I did what was necessary. I may not be the kind of woman you think I should be, but I am also not the kind of woman who sits back and lets others endanger their lives. Those were my people and it was my duty to help keep them safe, if I could. And I could and that is the end of it!"

She fell back in her chair, breathing hard.

"I am sorry to have upset you, madam," Victor said coldly. "You did what you thought was right."

"Yes, I did."

Katherine struggled to her feet. "If you will excuse me?"

She stumbled a little at the door, caught the frame to steady herself, then moved away and down the staircase. The stairs led directly to the garden where she sank down on the grass, ignoring the dew dampening her skirt. She closed her eyes and breathed deeply of the fresh morning air. Her shoulder throbbed more insistently now so she concentrated on watching the little birds gathering their morning meal of worms.

She loved the way robins tilted their heads to one side. Were they listening for the sound of the worms? They did not appear to have any ears. Or were their eyes very sharp and they could see the creatures wriggling up out of the soil? They had such beautiful red breasts and thrust them out with so much pride as they bustled purposefully about on the grass. If she sat very still, they would come quite close and so she tried to stay immobile.

Unfortunately, this reverie was broken by Marjorie Clere, taking a morning turn in the inner ward. She came around the corner of the stone wall, frightening the birds away.

"Are you well?" Marjorie asked with genuine concern.

"Well enough, thank you." Katherine replied. "Three men were killed. I am only wounded."

"There is plague in your manor?" Marjorie went on.

Katherine nodded. "And in Claringdon."

An anxious frown creased Marjorie's forehead. "I understand you had a death from the pestilence on your way here?" she asked.

"Yes, a young boy." Katherine admitted.

Marjorie took a step back and shuddered. "How awful." She swallowed hard. "Where will you . . . where will you set up your tents? Outside the wall?" she asked hopefully.

Katherine gave her a stony look. "No. Inside," she flared, suddenly annoyed at the fear in Marjorie's voice. But her anger quickly subsided as she recalled her own fright when faced with the horrors of the plague and its tragic victims.

"You will not have to share your quarters with me, Marjorie," she continued more gently. "I will remain in the tents with my maid. In fact," she added, "I am going to search them out now."

Katherine got slowly to her feet, feeling a little dizzy after the strained exchange with Marjorie. She steadied herself on a nearby tree and closed her eyes a moment. Her arm throbbed and ached and her face was hot. She needed to lie down. Cradling her shoulder, Katherine walked slowly out of the garden. Marjorie did not follow her but remained where she was.

"Do not get too close." Katherine muttered to herself bitterly.

She felt somewhat cheered when she came to the jumble of tents and wagons set up just inside the outer ward. The tents were arrayed against the stone walls in a tangle of colours, shapes and sizes. Katherine smiled when she saw the largest tent flew the Fendlay-crested flag. Inside, all was quiet and dim. Plump pillows and thick, soft bedding invited her to rest but before she could take advantage of their comfort, the tent flap was whipped aside and Edward grinned in at her.

"Here you are! You were not in father's room," he accused.

"Come in, Edward."

The lad obeyed with alacrity.

"I couldn't find Nory," he reported, then fixed her with solemn eyes. "I heard father and Rowley say there is a very bad sickness in England and that you came here to be safe from it. And I heard you tell father what you did. I think you are very brave. Father fought with the king in France. He was wounded too, like you. Only in the leg."

Edward sighed heavily.

"I have no mother," he blurted. "Did you know I have no mother?"

"Yes, I know. You must miss her very much."

A look of anxiety flitted across the little boy's face. "If I tell you a secret will you promise not to tell father?" he said earnestly.

Katherine hesitated. "Should you be keeping secrets from your father?"

"Oh, but I dare not tell him," Edward wailed, and to her astonishment, burst into tears.

"Hush, whatever is the matter?" Katherine soothed, drawing him into her lap.

Edward lifted his tear-streaked face and gave a loud sniff. "I cannot remember what she looks like," Edward confessed in a doleful voice. "Not being with her or talking to her. My mother. I don't remember her at all!"

"I see." Katherine laid her cheek on the top of his head. "Shall I tell *you* a secret?"

She felt him nod.

"I do not remember my husband much either. He died too, and when I go to his grave and try to think of him I cannot make out his face in my mind. Nor can I recall the sound of his voice. I am beginning to forget him altogether."

"But why do I forget my mother? Why can I not remember her? Father remembers her. Why don't I?"

Katherine kissed his damp cheek. "I think it is God's way of making room in your heart for you to love someone else," she said softly.

Edward pulled a little away from her so he could look into her eyes.

"Is that why you have forgotten your husband? God is making room in your heart too?"

Katherine smiled into the intent little face but had no chance to reply.

"Edward!"

The harried florid features of the little boy's nurse appeared at the tent entrance.

"You must not bother Lady Katherine," the nurse panted. "She is to rest. Come with me. Your father wants you. Come at once."

Edward heaved a tremendous sigh and slid from Katherine's knees. Then he put the palms of his hands on either side of her face and brought his own face very close.

"You will not tell father?" he whispered in a conspirator's voice.

Katherine gave him a quick kiss on the tip of his nose and smiled an answering conspirator's smile. "No. Now, be off."

Edward giggled and slipped past his nurse who tried vainly to keep up with him, calling after him across the ward.

With the vivid energy of Edward gone, Katherine fell into a heavy lassitude. She closed her eyes and sagged back onto the soft corner prepared for her, wondering vaguely if Agnes had thought to bring her miniver coverlet. She was at once ashamed for having a mind only for her own creature comforts while three men lay dead without

Christian burial somewhere between Stonehaven and Crenfeld, their bodies left to suffer the outrage of scavengers. Guiltily, she crawled under the blanket and pulled it up carefully over her shoulder. She winced and closed her eyes.

CHAPTER 14

AWARE OF MOVEMENT IN THE TENT, Katherine roused to see Agnes making up her own narrow pallet on the ground cloth next to her. Agnes turned to look over her shoulder while she tucked in the corners of the blankets.

"Did you sleep?" she asked.

"Yes, thank you. I feel considerably refreshed."

And she did. Her arm was merely stiff. Her head was clear.

"If you will help me, Agnes . . . " Katherine held out her good arm and Agnes assisted her outside where she breathed deeply of the warm fragrant afternoon, enjoying the heat of the sun on her face. She closed her eyes and tilted her head back for a moment, filling her lungs. Sighing appreciatively, she walked with measured steps among the tents and wagons, accepting greetings and commiserations as she went. She saw the pigs tethered at the door of one of the tents, grunting placidly and stepped around them to look inside. Rowley, Grace and Alice seemed every bit as contented as the small hogs. Grace sat close to the fire, busy with needlework. Rowley knelt over the firepit, poking languidly at the wood while Alice leaned against him, one hand on his shoulder, watching the smoke drift up and out of a hole at the top of the tent. So Grace had forgotten her foolishness and the rift was mended. Katherine was pleased.

They all saw her at once and Rowley made a place for her by the fire. She was glad no one asked how she felt. Instead, Grace offered her a bowl of hot broth from the cooking pot, along with a thick chunk of oat bread and salt. Katherine did not realize until then, just how very hungry she really was and accepted the plain fare gladly. She was finishing off the last morsel of bread when the tent flap moved and Nory sidled in.

"Nory!" Katherine cried. "I am so happy to see you."

"Yes, well," the old woman answered in gruff tones, shuffling unsurely at the entrance.

"Come in," Grace invited. "Come see your mistress."

Then aside she whispered to Katherine, "Were afraid you was to die. Won't admit it of course, but she were some feared for ye."

Katherine smiled at Nory. "Come sit by me."

Nory grunted and settled herself on the dirt floor. She gave a fleeting glance to Katherine's bandaged shoulder.

"Wounded, were ye?" she said blandly.

Katherine fingered the bandage and nodded.

"Hurt much?"

"Not much. It will be fine."

"Good, good." The old woman coughed gently. "Will we ge goin' back then?"

Katherine raised her eyebrows. "To Crenfeld you mean?"

"Yars. We be goin' back?"

"Was there something you left behind that you need? Rowley could . . . "

"No. 'Tis home is all. Don't feel right settin' here."

"No, I suppose not. But we are safe here. At least for now."

"Don't care much fer bein' safe. Think I might just go back home."

Katherine looked at her in alarm. "You must not return now. There is plague in the village."

"Don't be a fool, Nory," Grace added.

The old woman bristled and glowered at Grace. "Be careful who yer callin' a fool," Nory snapped. "I'm no more fool than you." And she narrowed her eyes in Rowley's direction.

It was Grace's turn to take offense. She came to tower over Nory, hands on her hips, chin jutting. She looked down the sides of her nose.

"What'cher meanin' then?"

Nory realized she had overstepped herself and shrank back in an exaggerated cringe.

"Don't you be threatenin' me, Grace. I'm an old woman and me bones is brittle. Don't you lay hands on me," she whined.

Grace snorted. "You're about as delicate as pressed leather but I shan't touch ye. Old Henry was right. Should have yer tongue cut out."

Katherine broke in quickly. "Enough, you two. We should be helping each other, not squabbling amongst ourselves. Whatever will Lord Victor think of us?"

Grace relented and went back to her needlework. Nory stood up unsteadily, her tone waspish. "I expect I'll be goin' then," she said to Katherine.

"But Nory. We need you here."

"For what? There is no use for an old woman in this place."

Nory stood arms akimbo, bony elbows stuck out. Tiresome as Nory was, Katherine loved her and wanted her to be safe. She frowned thoughtfully, her fine brow creased. Suddenly she brightened.

"I think I have something for you to do. Something you will take to. I must speak to Lord Victor about it first and then I will be back to fetch you. Stay right here and mind there is no more brabble."

Katherine looked hard at both women. Nory sniffed, tightened her arms across her chest and lifted her chin.

"Won't hear nowt from me," she said.

Grace merely raised an eyebrow and primly quickened her stitching.

It took Katherine a little time to find Victor, but she finally located him in the stables. He was leaning over the gate, admiring Pygine. She watched him uneasily for a moment, wondering if he was still smarting from their earlier confrontation but was relieved when he looked up and smiled at her.

"He is a handsome beast, Katherine," he said.

The black stallion had been eyeing Victor warily from a corner of his stall but nickered and came to the fence when he saw Katherine. He lifted his great ebony head over the top rail and snuffled noisily into her outstretched hands.

"Looking for oats, greedy one?" she chuckled. "And I have none. You must be satisfied with petting."

Katherine ran her hand down his soft twitching nose a few times then scratched his forelock and stroked the broad neck.

"He is a fine one." she agreed. "He was my father's. Father gave him to me as a wedding present."

Victor looked surprised. "A war horse for a wedding present?"

Katherine smiled at Pygine and gave him a final pat.

"Yes. Father knew I could not bear to leave him. He and I are fast friends. When I was a girl, I would go to the stables and watch the horses when I was upset about something. I liked how calm they were. Their quiet ways would quiet me. One day the grooms were being dragged about by this great black unmannerly beast. They were trying to put him in harness but he was having none of it and backed off every time they came near, pawing and snorting and rearing. Finally, someone managed to get a rope around him and Pygine pulled the poor fellow out into the ward and tumbled him over the stones like a sack. Without thinking, I stepped out in front of him, raised my arms and called for him to stop. He did."

Victor chuckled. "Positively amazing."

His grey eyes smiled into her green ones and she felt the colour rising in her cheeks. She turned her attention to Pygine, threading her fingers through his mane.

"Father said that as he seemed to be mine anyway, I should have him."

"Very wise of your father." Victor grinned, his lean cheeks creasing in long dimples. "Saved many a groom's dignity I should not wonder."

Katherine laughed and returned his smile then let her lips slowly relax along more serious lines.

"I came to ask a favour of you."

"Say on. If it is within my power, you shall have it."

Katherine took her hands from Pygine's mane and clasped them together at her waist.

"There is an old woman in my company who cannot seem to find a place of usefulness. I noticed that Edward's nurse seems overwhelmed with her charge and might welcome some help. May the old woman share the responsibility for him?"

"Is she a pleasant woman?"

"Well, no," Katherine said truthfully. "She has a sharp tongue and stubborn ways. But she has all her wits about her and would not easily be cullied by Edward's guile."

Victor chuckled. "She would be kind to the little fellow?"

"Oh, yes. She has great patience with children."

"Certainly, then. She has my warrant."

"Thank you, Lord Victor." Katherine put out her hand haltingly.

Victor took it in his own and pressed it gently. "It is a bargain then."

He held her hand a second or two longer, studying her small face and the anxious shadow in her eyes. He was aware that her hand had begun to quiver and immediately released it.

"I am sorry. I should have known your arm still troubled you."

Katherine willed her heart to stop its wild thumping and smiled wanely, swallowing hard to give him a steadier look.

Victor grinned playfully. "Which old woman did you have in mind?"

"I will take you to her."

Nory greeted Lord Victor with surprising dignity, dipping in a stiff shallow curtsy and lowering her eyes in respect. They were small brown rheumy eyes, but regarded him with sharpness when he addressed her.

"Your mistress tells me you may be trusted with the supervision of my young son," Lord Victor said. "Is it a duty to your liking?"

Nory looked at Katherine, who nodded encouragement.

"Yes, my lord," Nory murmured.

"It would mean staying with him nights in his rooms."

Nory flicked a glance at the thin tents billowing out slightly in the breeze.

"Yes, my lord," she agreed, barely able to contain her delight.

"May we go find the young rascal?" Katherine asked. "And introduce them to one another?"

Victor nodded. "Yes, of course. He should be in the garden with his nurse."

They found Edward sitting at the edge of the fish pool, wriggling his toes in the water and humming softly to himself. When he saw them, he gave a small cry, bolted to his feet and rushed toward them, startling his nurse who dozed gratefully beside him. He flung his plump arms around his father's legs and hugged them briefly. Then he released him and swarmed around Katherine's skirts, catching a corner of the fabric in one fist. He tugged.

"Come and see my fish. There is a big one . . . " The blue eyes grew round and he bent his head toward Nory.

"Who is she?" he whispered. "She is very old."

Nory gave a bird-like cock to her head, squinted and pursed up her lips.

"Lived many a year to be sure, young master. But many years mean many tales. Are you fond of stories, then? Of knights and ladies . . . " She paused. "And dragons?"

Edward gasped and wriggled in delight. "Dragons?"

"To be sure." Nory flapped a hand airily. "Scores of them."

"Do tell me one," Edward pleaded. He turned to Victor. "May she papa?"

"Of course," his father agreed. "Young men should be acquainted with dragons." He bent down and winked at his little son. "Since they may meet up with a dragon one day and be forced into battle."

Edward whooped, grabbed Nory's hand and all but dragged her into the shade of an apple tree.

"I do believe your companion is well chosen," Victor said to Katherine. "Edward has a great thirst for stories."

Katherine smiled at the two heads bent closely together. "And Nory has a great quantity of tales to tell. They should both be well satisfied."

Katherine massaged her arm with absent fingers and Victor glanced sharply at her.

"Would you care to sit by the pond? You can admire Edward's fish," he smiled.

Katherine nodded. "Thank you. I should like to sit for awhile. But I do not wish to keep you from your duties," she added.

Victor shrugged. "There is nothing pressing at the moment. The wheels of the household are set in motion for a tournament two weeks from the Feast of Transfiguration and my steward has things well in hand."

"A tournament?" Katherine lowered herself carefully on the soft grass bordering the pond. "Is that wise with the pestilence so near?"

Victor laughed and shook his head.

"Benjamin will be here well before the tournament and I can trust him to inspect everyone that comes. Except the king, of course," he added casually, watching her out of the corner of his eyes.

Katherine uttered a small cry. "The king is coming?"

"He is. And not only as a spectator, but as a participant. Actually, it was the king's idea. He has never faced my knights and is eager for the challenge. As are they. The king is a dangerous opponent but a few of my men will be a good match for him. Besides all that, it whets men's appetite for war. As war with France seems destined to be long and drawn out and Scotland ever waits to invade our kingdom, it is a good place for the king to attract recruits."

"You will not compete, will you?" Katherine asked anxiously.

The gaiety went out of Victor's tone and she was immediately sorry she had voiced her fears.

"No," was all he said.

He grew quiet a moment, his countenance downcast and drawn, but then he blinked and threw his fair head back.

"Have you ever seen a tourney?" he asked.

"No. My father claimed they were too bloody, although he was fond of them." Katherine stared into the rippling water of the pond. "I should like to have gone with him," she said. "We shared so little together and now that he is gone from me, we never shall."

She missed her father suddenly and felt very alone. Exactly why, she was unsure.

"I will go to your tournament and pretend I am watching with my father and seeing it through his eyes. I want to know what thrilled and excited him. Knowing will bring him closer to me and I will not feel so alone."

Victor frowned. "But you are not alone. You have Ciscilla and Grace and your old woman. And me."

Katherine smoothed out her skirt and began to fold it into pleats with her fingers.

"I am grateful for my friends, of course. But one needs someone closer than a friend. Someone who belongs to you. Like a father or a brother, or . . . "

"Or a husband," Victor finished.

Katherine felt her face grow warm. "Yes. Surely you understand what I mean."

"Yes, I know what you mean. I know that kind of loneliness. When I lost Allota it was as if someone had cut me in half and I was not whole any more. I thought I should die too. But I did not," he added grimly. "And now I do not want to be alone any longer. I need a wife and my son needs a mother. And yet . . . "

"What?"

Victor fingered his cane. "I had hoped to offer a wife a complete man, not a cripple."

Katherine heard the bitterness in his voice and chose her words with care.

"The physicians have done what they can?"

"They have," he replied shortly.

"I mean you no insult but why exactly can you not walk without your cane? Are the bones misshapen?"

Victor looked at the offending leg.

"No, the bones are fine. The leg simply refuses to hold me up. For a long time I was unable to put any weight on the leg and now there is no strength left in it at all."

"Have you asked Benjamin what he thinks?"

Victor grinned suddenly. "You are fond of him too? Yes, he is a good physician and a good friend. He was quite certain that I could walk as before if there were some way to strengthen the leg enough to begin to take my weight. Many times when I am alone, I try to force myself to put all my weight on the leg but I end up going back to using my cane within a very short time."

Katherine scrambled to her feet excitedly, forgetting her bandaged arm.

"But that is wonderful. I know what to do!" she cried, eyes shining. "I know exactly what to do."

Victor gave her a sharp look. "What do you mean?"

"I am going to help you, just as you have helped me. And you are going to walk again, and dance again, and . . . " She fastened the emerald of her eyes on his startled face. "Do you want to compete in the joust?"

Victor glared at her. "Of course, but that is not possible."

"Yes, it is," Katherine said firmly. "But it will be hard work."

She continued to stand over him until he shook his head and stood up himself.

"You really mean this," he said slowly. "You think you know a way."

"I do know a way. Just give me some time to prepare and you will be dancing at your wedding," she promised.

"As you wish."

"It is decided then," she said in a firm voice. "Now I must return to the tents."

Victor frowned. "What do you mean — return?"

"I have had my things brought to my tent for the night. I will sleep there."

"To make your bed with the servants? I think not!"

Katherine laughed at his outrage. "I am quite comfortable."

Before he could protest further, Katherine moved quickly away. And when Victor made to follow her she waved him off, leaving him to look after her, shaking his head.

CHAPTER 15

KATHERINE RAPPED SOFTLY AT VICTOR'S PRIVATE QUARTERS. The chamberlain opened the door, his eyes narrowing.

"Has Lord Victor come up yet?" she asked in low tones.

"No, my lady, he has not." The man bowed gravely and barred the opening, arms folded.

"Good. Good." Katherine motioned abruptly behind her. "Take it in. Be quick," she breathed, looking around.

The chamberlain did not move. Katherine waved her hand at him.

"Stand aside. We have something for your master."

"I am sorry, my lady. I do not mean to offend," the man apologized. "But I dare not let you bring anything into my lord's rooms without his permission. These are his private quarters," he said pointedly.

Katherine had not bargained on being denied entrance.

"Such foolishness," she mumbled in vexation.

The chamberlain bristled. Katherine groaned. What was she to do? The men with her had begun to pant and groan under their burden.

"Oh, put the thing down. And find John Elder."

John arrived in his loose-boned fashion and looked amused when she began to explain things to him. Then he grew interested and finally instructed the chamberlain to let them pass. The workmen deposited their load and left Katherine and John to regard it.

In front of them stood something that resembled a short double fence. A long pole was fastened horizontally between two thick upright poles. Parallel to this and with just enough width to pass through, was an identical pole and post assembly.

"This is how it works," Katherine told John. She moved in between the two poles and stood at one end.

"This is, of course, made for Lord Victor's height and not mine, but what he does is put his hands on the poles and begin walking, resting all his weight on both legs. As he tires he can lean on the poles and still remain upright. Then he can rest until he is ready to begin again. The poles will hold him up and he can go back and forth until his leg will hold him no longer. It is important that he not give up when his leg begins to hurt. And it will hurt because it is never used. You must push him, John. Keep him at it. It is the only way he will regain full use of his leg."

John stepped over to the wooden structure. "How can you be so sure it will work?"

"My father used just such a thing. He broke his leg and was unable to use it for a long time. When finally permitted to walk again, he found the leg too weak to support him. His physician constructed something like this to help him so I am certain it will work for Lord Victor. But only if he wants to be whole badly enough. He needs something to spur him on and I think the tournament may do it. He will not want to sit in the pavilion, a mere spectator, while his king takes part if there is a chance he may ride. Will he?"

"No, you are right. He will not."

"And he will not want anyone to see him using this either. That is why I had it brought in here. Marjorie does not have to know how he recovered strength in his leg and neither does anyone else. Except for yourself."

John's freckled face spread in a slow smile. He folded his lanky arms and leaned back on his heels.

"I do believe you have found a way. My lord is indeed fortunate to have such a clever woman as yourself lodged within these walls."

Katherine ignored the compliment. "But he must work, John," she warned. "You must make him work hard."

"Yes, my lady, I certainly will. You may be sure of that."

"Good. I will leave you to it then."

Victor was surprised to find John Elder grinning at him when he entered his private chamber.

"Victor, that marvelous Crenfeld woman has worked a miracle. A way for you to gain back the use of your leg. Come, I will show you."

He repeated Katherine's instructions and waited expectantly for Victor's response.

Lord Victor limped slowly around the contrivance, a slight frown creasing his brow.

"So this is what she meant. Do you really think . . . ?" He gripped the long poles and shook them. They remained steady.

John shrugged. "To try will do no harm. You are unobserved in your chambers. But the lady did say I was to encourage you rather vigorously. There will be pain, but she assured me she has seen it accomplished before."

Victor looked up sharply. "She has? When?"

"For her father."

"And you think I should do this?"

John lifted his shoulders again. "I can but speak for myself. I cannot speak for you. But I would, yes." He tapped one of the poles. "If only to prove to the lady that I am as determined as any other man," he said casually. "And as strong."

Victor grunted. But was he? Forced idleness had made him soft. To outward eyes he looked the same but he knew his muscles had slackened, his strength was waning. And if he failed? What then? John would know. And Katherine. But not Marjorie. Marjorie would not have to know. Not that she seemed disturbed by his weakness or ashamed of his cane. He glowered at the bars. Why did Katherine concern herself? Devil take the woman, why had she not minded her own business? What right had she to meddle in his affairs?

Victor took a vicious swing at the apparatus with his cane and felt the jar in his shoulder as it met rigid resistance. John raised his eyebrows but stood impassively with his arms folded, saying nothing.

Victor threw down his cane. It clattered on the rough planks. He grasped the bars, locked his elbows and leaned heavily. They took his full weight without bending.

"How many times do I do this?" he snapped, glaring at his feet.

John dropped his arms and stepped closer. "Until weakness. Then rest on the bars a few minutes and do it again until your legs will not hold you. If you keep your hands always just over the bars, you can catch yourself before you fall. Lady Katherine says if you do this morning and evening, your legs will be strong enough to ride in the tournament."

Victor snorted. "Lady Katherine says."

But his mood brightened. Three weeks. He could do this. If her father could do it, so could he. And then he would show that meddlesome woman. In three weeks time he would announce his engagement to Marjorie at the feast before the tournament and dance with the cursed woman to prove he had done it!

Resolutely, Victor stood erect between the two bars, his hands hovering above them. In measured steps he attempted a casual walk to the further end. He found it difficult to keep from limping. He had favoured the leg for too long and was sweating after only a few turns. He gritted his teeth and kept going. Each time he seemed about to give up John urged him on.

"One more turn, Victor. You can do one more."

Back and forth, back and forth. Victor sagged against the bars, panting.

"You are only resting now," John prodded. "Only resting. Take the weight off your legs for a few moments, catch your breath and begin again."

Victor's bad leg throbbed with pain, but he nodded grimly and began once more. Yet his walk quickly became a slow shuffle from one end to the other and before too long he was gasping and finally, even his arms gave out. He was just too weak. Too weak. His knees buckled and he collapsed on the floor.

John rushed to Victor, helped him on his feet and struggled with him to his bed. Victor groaned as he fell onto the blankets. His leg ached and pulsed. It was agony.

John unfastened Victor's hose and there was instant relief. The aching subsided and Victor trembled with exhaustion.

"Next time you will not wear those things," John mumbled and flung the stockings aside.

"Next time?" Victor moaned. "I will never do this again. Lady Katherine means to kill me."

John began massaging the offending leg. "Not so. She means to see you take your rightful place in the joust. She is a good woman," John said firmly. "A good woman."

Victor closed his eyes. He did not feel like arguing. A slender red-haired figure with emerald green eyes and smiling rosy lips swirled in the blackness behind his lids. She was dancing and holding her hands out to him, then turning away to sway to music he did not hear. He watched the world she danced in grow darker and darker, finally blotting her out.

Victor began to snore softly. John continued his gentle kneading a while longer then drew away and left Victor alone in his quarters. He would likely sleep better than he had in a long time, John thought. And thankfully, without any benumbing draughts of wine.

No one saw much of Victor over the next few days. He seemed inordinately weary at meals and many feared he was succumbing to the common malady. But Benjamin assured everyone that such was not the case, having arrived from Claringdon in time to witness the change in Victor's manner and be apprised of its cause.

Gradually, Victor's fatigue disappeared to be replaced with a heartiness not seen in him since his wife was alive. As the days drew closer to the impending tournament, excitement at the castle grew. Crushed and flattened floor mats were pulled away, planks swept and freshly-herbed woven rush mats laid out. Candle brackets were cleaned and additional spikes and loops installed near doorways and along dark halls. Tables and benches were repaired, wall tapestries taken down and beaten free of dust. Bord cloth linens were packed into deep barrels and strong lye poured overtop, then laid out to dry and bleach in the sun. When the laundress pronounced them white enough, they were carefully folded and laid away for exclusive use during tournament time. The mesne made frequent outings to a nearby plain considered level enough and large enough for the great melee that would begin the tournament. Carpenters accompanied them to construct the lists and pavilions. Heralds were dispatched to announce the appointed day.

August brought warmer weather and all continued placidly with no sign of plague amongst Katherine's people. They lived contentedly in their tents, having been given the freedom to hunt rabbit and small game in Lord Victor's forests. They worked alongside their host's fieldmen and ate frequently at the lord's table. News reached them of the devastation of coastal cities and villages as the ugly black cloud of plague rolled across the country, but the pestilence not being amongst them or their own, they paid little attention to the accounts. "Sufficient unto the day is the evil thereof." Adversity would not be borrowed from tomorrow. At times, they spoke of Claringdon and their desire to return, but for now they were satisfied with their lot. According to Benjamin, Claringdon was virtually deserted. Here, they were warm. They were well fed. They were not idle. And they would be at hand for the grand tournament.

In the week following Transfiguration, guests began arriving at the castle. A night of feasting and games was to precede the tournament and although only the nobility could attend, kegs of ale were carted outside the castle that men might join their betters in the celebration. Great bonfires were lit and lesser men employed their own revelry, while behind the castle walls, the great hall filled with guests and anticipation.

When a splendid meal was ended, Victor rose from his throne at the high table and clapped his hands for silence. Marjorie slipped up beside him. Ciscilla, on his left, laid down her spoon and whispered in Katherine's ear.

"What is he going to say?"

Katherine shook her head but cold fingers closed around her heart as she watched Marjorie slide her hand into Victor's. Seated beside Marjorie, Father Simon clasped his ringed hands together on the table and leaned forward slightly to listen.

"Good friends," Victor saluted, raising his goblet. "It pleases me to mark this happy occasion with two announcements. The first is that our king has left the palace and will join us tomorrow and take the field."

A murmur of excitement ran through the crowd at the mention of King Edward. Rumours were afloat that over half the king's retinue had fled for safety into the country after seeing the great death descend with impartial ferocity on even the highest born of the aristocracy.

"My second announcement is of a more personal nature. The Lady Marjorie Clere has agreed to do me the honour of being my wife. Our wedding will follow in the spring. So may the winter be agreeably short."

He smiled and put his arm around Marjorie's waist. Marjorie laid her head against his shoulder and the dinner guests applauded. Several men rose to shake Victor's hand and offer their best wishes. Ciscilla hugged her brother warmly while Father Simon nodded but Katherine found it difficult to smile and listened in silence as Ciscilla prattled on about wedding gowns and suitable locations for the wedding banquet. She dared not look at Victor. He was certain to see the sadness in her eyes. But was this not what she had anticipated? That Victor would marry Marjorie?

Katherine took a long, slow deep breath. When the dancing started, she was led into the steps by a young knight. Sir Gilbert was a good partner and as he guided her amongst the other dancers, Katherine caught a glimpse of Victor dancing with Marjorie. His leg was healed then. She turned her head away.

"My mother is acquainted with Lady Clere's family," Sir Gilbert was saying. "The Cleres have long favoured this match." He winked roguishly at Katherine. "Although why Lord Victor overlooked someone as lovely as you, my lady, I cannot understand."

Katherine made a small face. "There is no accounting for love, sir knight."

Gilbert laughed loudly and Katherine laughed with him but it sounded hollow in her ears.

When the dance ended, Gilbert held her for a moment before dropping his arms with reluctance. He bowed.

"Thank you, my lady. It has been my very great privilege."

Katherine returned a deep curtsy. "You flatter me, Sir Gilbert, and I thank you."

Katherine let the young knight lead her to a place near an outside door. A cool breeze floated in. The young knight bowed once more and left her.

Katherine followed the perfumed night air into the garden. Behind her, muffled by the walls, the musicians resumed playing. She wandered aimlessly about the grounds, bending to touch particularly pretty flowers and lifting the slender branches of trees that crossed the path she took to the pool. The air was cool and soft, the small sounds of nesting birds, soothing. It was a pleasant garden. A full moon reflected its golden face in the waters of the pond. She leaned over, her hands clasped behind her, and watched for the darting shapes beneath the water's surface.

"Here you are."

Victor was standing behind her.

"I want to thank you for the use of my leg. You promised I should have it and I do." He smiled and patted his thigh.

Katherine's face was pale in the moonlight.

"I am glad," she said simply.

Victor held out his arm. "Will you join me in a dance and see for yourself?"

Katherine hesitated then ran her hand up over his forearm and shivered.

"It is too cold for you out here. Come inside."

Katherine had to hurry to keep up with his long stride but in the hall they moved together smoothly.

"What do you think?" he grinned. "And now thanks to you, I will dance at my own wedding."

Katherine gave him a weak smile. "I can see you shall. Congratulations. I hope you will be happy."

"Oh, happy. What is happiness?" he said perfunctorily. "Edward needs a mother and the household needs a mistress. That will be happiness enough." He smiled down at her. "And what about you? Have you given up your notion of being alone? Will you consider suitors and marry?"

Katherine looked him full in the eye. "If I fall in love."

Victor frowned and tightened his arm around her waist as he guided her between the dancers. Katherine could not hear the music anymore. Her heart beat too loudly. She was aware only of his closeness, his warmth and his scent. He smelled of green trees and the sun.

"Only peasants and villeins marry for love," Victor said. "I, as you, were born to a great house. Marriage must be convenient — for all parties. When I marry Marjorie, it will be to join our two families and unite our fortunes."

"Yes, I know that kind of marriage," Katherine said. "I had that kind of marriage with Nathaniel. Our children were to have ample provision." Katherine lowered her lashes. "But there were no children. Perhaps because there was no love. Maybe only love brings forth sons. Did your Allota love you?" She looked at him then.

Victor's eyes clouded. "Yes," he said softly. "She loved me. And I loved her."

"How can you settle for less now?" Katherine murmured. "Once you have known love, how can you be happy without it? I want to know love. Real love. Love that consumes. Surely, you can understand that." She lifted her chin defiantly.

Victor's grey eyes held a certain pain. "Yes, I can. I can understand that. But you speak as if there is already someone. Someone . . . Your words hold a passion that . . . is there someone?"

Victor's blond head dropped closer to her own.

Katherine's heart pounded, her mouth went dry. "He does not care for me."

Victor lifted her chin. "A man would be a fool not to love you," he said hoarsely.

"Some men are fools then," she replied, not taking her eyes from him.

Their eyes held a few moments, then Victor glanced around. The dancing had stopped. People were looking at them with interest and he was still holding her in his arms. He released Katherine quickly. His bow was stiff and formal when he left her in the care of Father Simon.

Obviously, the priest had forgiven Victor's interference in the matter of Old Henry's mortuary. Put aside, no doubt, at the prospect of a handsome marriage duty and the opportunity to eat off the same trencher as the king.

"'Tis a pity you refused my offer to purchase Crenfeld, my dear," Simon said smoothly. "As it is, I suppose it has become a possession for the bittern."

He made clucking noises with his pale tongue. Katherine's green eyes widened, her dark eyebrows arching.

"You do not suppose I would desert Crenfeld. Or Claringdon. I intend to return, father."

The priest laid a cautionary hand on her arm. It was as cold as his flat look.

"The death has all but emptied Claringdon, my dear. There is nothing for which to return."

Katherine changed the subject. "How is it that you have escaped, father? You do not fear for your safety when giving men their last rites?"

Simon lowered his head and closed his eyes briefly. "Ah, God has been merciful to his servant and has protected me, my child."

The truth of the matter was that he had not attended even so much as a single death but rather sent base men into the houses to pillage while the victims lay gasping on their beds. In turn he gave the thieves the Church's protection and a share of the spoils. Greed made brave men of the lowest cowards and Father Simon was taking full advantage of that fact for his own gain.

"Will you join me in a game of chess, Lady Katherine?" the priest asked. "I see the board set up just over there." He used a skinny finger to point and Katherine nodded.

She was engulfed in a despairing weariness when she sat down to play. What had she thought? That Victor would realize he had no love for Marjorie and would not marry her? Well, it made no difference to him. Katherine sighed and moved out one of the exquisitely cut crystal chess pieces. That the chessboard was made of jasper and this very set once possessed by kings, was of no consequence to her present humour.

Father Simon was a careful player. He deliberated over each move at length, chided Katherine for her ill-considered play and reminded her that the game had been of King Solomon's own invention and meant to test the wisdom of the player.

Katherine paid scant attention to the priest. While she waited her turn, she rested her chin in the palm of her hand and glanced ruefully at the happy crowd in the hall. The minstrels' gallery was filled to bursting with red-outfitted musicians playing lustily on harp, dulcimer and bladderpipe. A small portative organ lent accompaniment, along with a pair of jingling timbrels. The musicians were hot and sweating, their faces as red as their costumes. Oblivious to their discomfort, they plied the instruments with broad exaggerated gestures.

The center of the floor was a colourful whirl in deep hues of red, blue and green. Everyone seemed bent on outdoing the other in brilliant dress. Even the warm weather had not deterred some women from wearing low cut gowns trimmed with ermine and other furs. It was a new and exotic fashion that caused a stir of envy among the less daring.

Side tables groaned under the lavish provisions of food and wine. Between dances many resorted to the great flagons and sampled rare delicacies imported from distant markets. A large noisy group of men and women were evidently occupied with common ribaldry and she could hear their coarse laughter above the even rhythm of the music. Others used the walls as props to hold them upright while they drained cup after cup of wine and followed the dancing with bleary eyes.

Katherine made another ill-advised move, setting Father Simon's sharp tongue to work again. She shrugged and looked away to catch sight of Victor standing directly across the room from where she sat. He was head and shoulders above most of the men in the great hall, now that his cane was discarded and he stood fully erect. He looked happy and confident. Just as she had hoped. And handsome. Her throat tightened painfully but her eyes lingered on the thick tangle of his blond head, the deep cleft in his lean cheeks and the curve of his mouth when he smiled at a guest. She envied those who received the warmth of his grey eyes. Not for the first time she wondered if another pair of eyes would ever penetrate so deeply into her being as Victor's did.

He had seen her. Abruptly, Katherine straightened and attempted to quell the tremble starting in her throat. She nodded to him with what she hoped was a bright and casual gesture and lowered her eyes in apparent concentration over the chessboard. Victor continued to watch her. He followed the line of her bent head, the flaming hair glinting like amber in the candlelight, the soft flush of her cheeks, the slender arch of her neck. One small hand reached out over the chessboard. His heart quickened. Impatiently, he frowned and turned away.

Where was Marjorie? Oh, there, in the corner. His eyes narrowed. And flirting with that oaf from Wasdale, if the tilt of her head and curve of her lips were any indication. He watched her for a moment as she dallied, now touching her companion lightly on the sleeve, now shaking her curls in mock disapproval at something he said, but all the while smiling in her most beguiling manner. Were all women coquettes who preened themselves before any man that paid them a compliment?

Victor shook his head and left Marjorie to her admirer. He pursued a meandering course around the perimeter of the hall, speaking to his guests. He appeared to wander through the crowds without purpose and in fact had convinced himself it was so, all the while keeping in view the table at which Katherine sat and moving ever closer to it. He spoke to this person and to that, laughed at a joke or two, remarked on several costumes and took compliments on his fine table. When at last he reached Katherine, Father Simon was just completing a move.

"Is your game going well?" he asked with a polite smile.

Simon frowned at Katherine. "The lady is not a serious adversary," he said to Victor. "She does not give it her full attention."

Katherine bristled at the slight but could not disagree. Victor chuckled.

"Young women are more interested in gaiety than old men's games, father," he said.

Simon grunted. "Find me an old man, then."

Victor smiled at Katherine and held out his arm. "Would you care to join me in the search, Lady Katherine?"

When she hesitated, he said. "I think it is your duty to find a replacement." His grey eyes twinkled and she let him draw her to her feet.

"I suppose so," she said doubtfully. Then to Simon. "If you will excuse me, father."

The priest fluttered an impatient hand. "Go. Go."

"You see. I am very good at rescuing damsels in distress," Victor whispered to Katherine as he led her away.

"Was I in distress?" she asked.

Victor gave her a sober look. "You seemed in grave danger of being bored to tears." He grinned. "Some gayer company is recommended. Perhaps my sister. Ciscilla always surrounds herself with interesting people. Some of the king's retinue have arrived with tales of court. Oh, yes. There she is with them now."

"But what of your promise to Father Simon to find him a chess partner?"

Victor shrugged his wide shoulders. "I arranged for that before I came to your table. See for yourself."

Katherine turned to look. Hunched over the chess-board across from the priest she recognized one of the merchants from Claringdon. He was a shrewd businessman and by the set of his jaw had placed a substantial wager on the outcome of the match. With money at stake both men would play with determination for both loved the feel of coins in their hands and the sound of coins in their purse.

Ciscilla greeted Katherine with a squeal of delight and a warm hug.

"You must hear this, Katherine. News from the palace. You will not believe what the king has been saying. Come, stand with me. Here is a cup of wine. Now listen."

Katherine listened. Some tales were humourous and some no doubt untrue, but it was a pleasant way to pass the balance of the evening. Already, she was impatient for tomorrow and the tournament. She hoped the excitement of it would overshadow her personal disappointments.

CHAPTER 16

THE MORNING DAWNED GREY AND CLOUDY but could not dampen the enthusiasm of either the combatants or the spectators. The participants and their attendants rode out early, the spectators following as the morning wore on. Katherine shared a carriage with Ciscilla and Marjorie while Nory accompanied the women as their aide. Edward was quite put out that he had to remain at home without his storyteller.

The ride was bumpy and dusty but eventually they came to a stop and alit with eager faces. Katherine looked around her. Salisbury Plain was vast and flat, an ideal location for the great tourney. The tournament grounds thronged with excitement. Katherine had never been to this place and wondered at a great pile of rocks projecting up out of the grasses in the distance. She pointed to it and turned to Nory.

"Do you know what is out there?"

Nory nodded. "Seen it afore in me youth. Sacred rocks, them is. Brought by Merlin's magic in Arthur's day."

Ciscilla's blue eyes grew round. "Really? Merlin? What are they for?"

Nory pinched her eyes shut, clasped her hands high up on her chest and opened her mouth in a hoarse singsong chant.

Stone voices cry out, Behold your God!
And turn their faces to the Sun.
Between their bodies God doth rise,
Immortal Sun in immortal skies.
We are Ramsees children, sons of the Sun,
Ordained to godhood at end of days,
Our souls to the Sun, our ashes at home,
Around this circle, back to stone.

She opened her eyes. "I remember that too."

Ciscilla clapped her hands. "I must see them. Come and see them with me, Katherine," she pleaded, then gestured toward the tents and pavilions. "They will not be ready for awhile. Let us see Merlin's magic circle."

She climbed back into the coach. Katherine smiled and joined her, but Marjorie shook her head.

"You two go ahead. I do not want to miss Victor's entrance. Hand me down a cushion. I will sit in the pavilion with Nory."

While Marjorie and her reluctant aide tramped to the tourney grounds, Ciscilla nodded to the carriage driver, who obediently made for the rock projection.

What looked to be but a heap of rocks from a distance, became an enormous ring of stones soaring upward almost six times the height of the two women. An outer ring of monoliths formed a complete closed circle with a continuous line of stone lintels joining them across the top. Inside the ring were five sets of trilithons grouped in the shape of a horseshoe. Katherine moved in for a closer look. Each trilithon was made up of two upright stones, capped across the top by a third crosspiece stone. The central trilithon rose upward much higher than the rest and faced the opening of the horseshoe. Katherine had to bend her head back to see the top. It was monstrous.

She and Ciscilla walked quietly among the giant stones, stopping at the center of the horseshoe where two stones lay on their backs, one on top of the other. The top stone had a rusty stain on it that made Katherine uneasy.

"It looks like an altar of some kind," she whispered to Ciscilla.

Ciscilla nodded and put her hand out to touch one of the rocks.

"How long do you think they have been here?" she asked.

"A long time."

Katherine examined the huge structures, puzzled that the faces of the rocks were blank. There were no carvings or inscriptions of any kind on them.

"Do you think Nory could be right? Are they, as the rhyme says, some ancient people turned to stone by their god? And did Merlin use his magic to bring them here?"

Ciscilla shivered. "I do not like this place. I want to go back."

Katherine agreed. A slight wind had blown up and the eerie sounds it made around the immense rocks were unnerving. Like voices murmuring to one another, sharing secrets they did not want the women to hear.

Katherine and Ciscilla returned to find large companies of knights, men-at-arms and noblemen grouped around the big tents. Nearby and tethered to long hitching posts, were row after row of horses, stamping and snorting, as impatient for battle as those who would ride them.

A cloud of dust announced an approaching line of riders displaying the king's colours. All stopped what they were at and a great cheer went up from the crowd when King Edward reigned in and waved his arm in a wide circle. Fair-haired and blue-eyed, he was quite the handsomest king in memory. Although not tall nor of the bulky frame of most great fighting men, he possessed the cool, clear mind of a formidable strategist. A mind so nimble in fact, that he could anticipate an opponent's move practically before the other had planned it, making him the greatest jouster in all of England.

Katherine saw Victor emerge from one of the tents and bow before his king. Holding the helm his blacksmith had been working on, he sank to one knee and lowered his head. King Edward dismounted and placed his hand on Victor's shoulder, saying something that only Victor could hear. Victor let out a roar of laughter and leapt to his feet.

"Your king!" he shouted. Another cheer, and then Victor led Edward to a private tent to don his armour.

The covered stands were constructed in such a way as to give the best view of the field on which the mock battle would be fought. About two hundred yards out, the king and his men would form ranks to the left and Lord Victor and his company would form to the right.

While the spectators conversed in excited whispers, the contenders emerged one by one, heavily clad in armour, to be helped onto their horses. Amid an array of bright banners, trumpeters, clowns and hunting dogs, they paraded around the enclosed tourney grounds to loud applause. Many of these men would also be champions in the forthcoming joust and each man was studied intently so appropriate wagers could be made. The wall that separated the spectators from the participants was not so tall that the view of the surrounding countryside was obscured, and when the broad gate opened to allow the riders to exit the field, all could clearly see the two sides gathering for battle at each end of the plain.

At a flourish from the herald, the two bands of horsemen commenced their charge. Lances were lowered in unison and the horses spurred ahead. Their hooves thundered. The men bent forward in their saddles, clouds of dust rising up behind each "army." They met with a terrible crash and a tumult of such ferocity ensued that one could not discern the roars of the men from the screams of the animals. The horses reared and struck out with savagery, baring their teeth and craning their thick necks. The skirmish, although intense, was brief. Suddenly, men began to fall from their horses and struggle for safety, impeded by the weight of their armour. The rest whirled and fled down the field with their opponents in pursuit.

Katherine strained to see if Victor had fallen, while litter-bearers rushed out to retrieve the wounded. Only a few men submitted to the ignominy of being borne in due to broken bones. The rest limped and clanked in, carrying their helmets and dragging their lances. Katherine was relieved to see Victor was not among them.

As the injured were removed for physicians to examine, the victors rode in ahead of the vanquished, to parade around the jousting field. The cheering was deafening. Their king had won.

"God save the king! God save the king!"

King Edward bowed in his saddle with a flourish, while his charger pranced and snorted. Katherine took heart in Victor's smiling countenance as he congratulated the king. He did not appear hurt in any way.

The mock battle, although a great spectacle, merely whetted men's appetites for the jousting to come. The champions left the field to ready themselves for serious combat. Heralds rode back and forth announcing the contenders, marshals established the positions of the players and the rules to be followed in the joust. Then the entertainment poured in at the gate. There were many displays to occupy the spectators. Jugglers and clowns, magicians and acrobats, kept them amused until the bannered wooden horns blared to signal the time had come. The tourney grounds fell silent and the displays broke up and made a hasty retreat.

The first two contenders entered from opposite ends of the field to confront each other, visors lifted, lances upright. The great gates crashed shut, sealing off further entry to the field and the horns sounded once more.

Each rider pulled down his visor, adjusting to the view from its narrow eye slit before taking a huge gulp of air and heaving upward on his lance. Throwing the wide steel flange onto his shoulder, he clamped the butt inside his arm and tilted the tip forward into proffering position. The horses were spurred into action. Lumbering closer, each combatant gradually dropped his lance, pivoting the flange to rest in strike position on the right side of his steel breast-plate. With the lance head pointed diagonally across the neck of his horse towards his opponent, he raised his shield to deflect the other's lance. The collision of iron and iron was so violent that both lances flew to pieces over the heads of the men and they were knocked heavily to the ground with a tremendous crash, amid wild cheering and stamping of feet.

When the second pair took the field, one knight miscalculated his timing, his lance dropped too far and stabbed harmlessly into the tourney turf before ever his opponent came near. Helpless now to raise the heavy weapon, it was an easy matter for the other to unseat him with a blow to his chest. He lay quite still and was carried off in a cart.

Katherine held her breath and watched in horror as champion after champion was carried from the field, either on a cart or on his own shield, unconscious or bleeding from mouth or nose. One unfortunate was knocked from his saddle and catching a foot in the stirrup, was dragged across the field and fatally injured. A brawl broke out between the fallen man's squires and the squires of his opponent and they took to each other with sticks and clubs. It was some time before peace was restored and the tournament could continue.

When Victor made his appearance in the lists, Katherine was in such a state of nerves she was barely able to draw a proper breath. He looked magnificent though, cantering onto the field, his mount enveloped to the fetlocks in a rippling gilded leather trapper emblazoned with the red hawks of the Stafford coat of arms. He held his crested great helm in front of him, resting it on the neck of the horse. His padded coat armour was made of golden cloth with pairs of red hawks circling the hem and shoulders of the sleeveless garment. His plated arm defences were edged with bands of decorative brasswork and his leg defenses ended in sabatons decorated with silver gilt on the toe caps.

He bowed theatrically to the crowd, and Marjorie was led onto the field to hand him up the family shield. She also gave him a bit of white fabric which he waved in the air before stuffing into the edge of his shoulder armour, where it fluttered against the steel. He lifted his great helm and slipped it down over his head to rest on his shoulders, attached the anchoring chain and flipped down the visor to signal his readiness.

Katherine leaned forward and gritted her teeth against the fear that gripped her as she watched him lower his lance into strike position and gallop to meet his opponent. Both men twisted in their saddles, receiving only glancing blows on the first pass. They whirled and faced one another again to heavy applause.

On the second pass, Victor's opponent caught him on the corner of the helm, knocking the heavy piece sideways, while Victor's own lance tore through coat armour to dent the chestplate of his competitor. Victor wrestled desperately with his helmet, trying to turn it far enough to the front so he could see through the narrow eye slit, but the heavy dent prevented any side-to-side movement. Quickly, he wrenched the helm straight back and it fell behind his head to dangle from a chain on the collar of his armour. But there was no time to replace the head piece. His horse had made the turn for the third pass and his adversary was surging down the turf toward him with lowered lance.

Unconsciously, Katherine rose to her feet along with the rest of the spectators. An expectant hush fell over the crowd. Although Victor still retained his basinet with its shoulder length curtain of mail, it was an open-faced helmet of much thinner material and would never withstand a direct blow of the lance. Katherine could see the grim set of his jaw and the concentration in his grey eyes as he galloped past the place where she stood.

Already, Victor's opponent was tilting his lance and his intention was clear. To aim for Victor's unprotected face. Katherine gripped the railing of the pavilion wall and sucked in her breath sharply, drawing a long speculative look from Marjorie. Victor was tilting his own lance. Lower. Lower. Would he lose control?

As he came within striking distance, Victor bent forward over the neck of his horse and with the butt end of the lance anchored firmly against his breast plate, plunged the weapon with force against the bottom of his opponent's lowered shield. The man was pushed back so powerfully that he lifted the reins with him, dragging his mount up in a rear, hooves flailing in the air. His lance rose skyward, he lost his grip and the weapon flew out of his hands to fall under the horse. The beast stumbled over the rolling lance and falling forward, brought his rider to shoot over his neck and thump to the ground in a crash of steel.

The silent crowd erupted into a roar. Victor clenched his fist and raised his arm in stiff salute, bowed, waved and left the field.

As Katherine allowed herself to breathe again, Marjorie and Ciscilla chattered with excitement while Nory grinned and nodded. Marjorie bumped Katherine's shoulder. "My cousin is next in the lists. He is a brilliant fighter," she said proudly, fluttering her fingers at one of the combatants.

Katherine gave her a small smile and looked dutifully in the direction of Marjorie's gaze. One knight looked much the same as any other covered in so much armour. He was tall though. That much she could tell. And his hair was black. She caught a glimpse of a dark moustache and beard before he dropped his helm visor. He fought well and unseated his opponent on the second pass.

Ciscilla laughed and clapped with abandon. To Katherine's ears, Ciscilla's laughter sounded shrill to the verge of hysteria. She took hold of Ciscilla's hand, worried by its feverish warmth. She was overexcited, her face pink and her eyes overbright.

"Ciscilla darling," Katherine said. "Come with me out of the heat. A cold drink would be refreshing."

Ciscilla ran her tongue over her hot lips. "Yes. Yes, perhaps you are right. I am feeling a little warm."

She smiled at Katherine, but her eyes did not quite focus. She used Katherine's arm for support to climb down from the pavilion, then drank long from the water dipper hung over the side of the drinking vat. Ciscilla's hair had begun to loosen, perhaps from her own body heat or simply from the warmth of the day. Katherine offered to rearrange it for her and sought a private place behind the tents.

She unfastened the pins holding Ciscilla's wimple to the plaits on either side of her head. As she removed the material from under her friend's chin she was worried at how damp with perspiration it had become. She took down Ciscilla's fillet and veil and dropped them in Ciscilla's lap. Using her comb she recoiled Ciscilla's hair, tucked in all the stray strands, replaced her fillet and veil and lastly, her wimple. Ciscilla had been drowsy and uncommunicative while Katherine worked. She sighed heavily, then opened her great dark eyes and smiled.

"I feel much better. Thank you, Katherine." Then she giggled and lowered her voice to a whisper.

"Do you know that Marjorie's cousin has been paying court to me these last few months. I think he means to ask Victor for my hand."

Katherine had not the heart to tell her that it was common knowledge, noised among the women at the tournament, that Marjorie's handsome cousin paid court to many women.

Ciscilla began to fidget with the sleeve of her red samite. Becoming more restive, she sprang up and gave Katherine a quick, tight squeeze. "Victor will not be pleased if I miss his match with the king. I must get back."

She darted her eyes about in a distracted way. "Where is Marjorie? I thought she came down with us. And your Nory. Where is she? I must find them."

She gazed absently at Katherine, then brushing aside Katherine's hand she lurched off, now to go one way, then changing her mind, to go another. Katherine followed her meandering with a frown. Whatever was the matter with Ciscilla? She must speak to Benjamin. Ciscilla had a fever. Benjamin would give her some of those little lettuce cakes. If she could just find him among all these tents. Surely he must be attending some miserable contestant with a broken limb.

She found Benjamin in the blacksmith's tent, although not precisely engaged in physician's duties. A man lay in full armour with his head across the anvil, great helm still firmly attached. While Benjamin held the man steady, the blacksmith attempted to cut him out of the head piece. No small feat, for the steel was thick and the heavy dents it had suffered made the risk of cutting its wearer very great. Eventually, the man was released and Katherine was shocked at the bruising to his face. But he grinned and shook the blacksmith's hand, so she withheld her sympathy.

Benjamin dusted himself off and stood up to see her. "Hardly seems a 'joust of peace' to you, I expect." He took

Katherine's hand warmly. "Gentlewomen rarely have much of a taste for battle,"

Katherine nodded. "It is certainly violent sport. But rather exhilarating, too."

Benjamin laughed at her answer then asked. "Were you looking for me?"

"Yes, I was. Ciscilla does not seem herself. I think she may have a fever. Could you look at her? She is with Marjorie Clere in the pavilion."

But Marjorie sat alone. Ciscilla was nowhere to be seen.

"She did not come back?" Katherine's voice rose in alarm. "Surely she must have."

"If she did, she did not sit with me. I have not seen her. Perhaps she has gone to congratulate my cousin," Marjorie said lightly and shifted sideways. "Could you move away. I have no view of the field."

Katherine retreated to the grass and shook her head at Benjamin.

"I do not understand. Her intention was to come back here. Where could she have gone?"

Benjamin shrugged and began to look around. "She must be here somewhere."

Katherine gazed out over the tents and onto the surrounding plain. She saw a flash of red far beyond the tourney grounds. Ciscilla was wearing red.

"Look," she pointed, "Out there. Do you see that? Is that someone moving out there?"

Benjamin squinted. "I do not see what you are looking at. These eyes are old," he apologized. He squinted again and became alert. "Wait a minute. I do see something. You are right. Why would she go out there?"

Katherine shuddered and grabbed his arm. "It is those old stones. She has gone to that place. Merlin's magic stones."

Benjamin scratched his grizzled head. "If Ciscilla is ill, she ought not to be alone. I will gather up my bag and we will fetch her back."

It took only a few minutes to cross the open ground. Katherine did not like what she saw. Ciscilla was dancing and whirling around the ring of monoliths, holding her skirt out and waving her head back and forth. So violent were her motions that her veil and wimple had worked their way loose and hung in limp folds around her neck. Her dark hair whipped about her face in a tangle of heavy black curls.

"She looks demented," Katherine whispered fearfully.

"Fever can take a person like that. Do not frighten her. Speak to her as we approach. Try to calm her."

"Ciscilla," Katherine called out. "We have missed you, darling." She kept her voice light but her knees shook and she was afraid.

"Come, let us help you back to the tourney grounds. You wanted to watch Victor and King Edward. Remember?"

Ciscilla looked up briefly at the sound of Katherine's voice then resumed her spinning. She was humming tunelessly as she went and Katherine heard her repeating the words of the old poem Nory had chanted to them. When they came closer, Ciscilla started convulsively and stood stock still, staring at them with dull, glaring black eyes. Her beautiful red dress was stained and torn and she had her legs and arms spread wide. Her chest heaved, her breath coming in wheezy gasps.

"Oh, Ciscilla," Katherine cried, reaching for her.

Linnea Heinrichs

Her friend drew back in a sharp spasm and both Katherine and Benjamin moved quickly to take hold of her. But they could not get a firm enough grip and she slipped from them, twisting like a serpent, and bolted out of the circle of stones. Katherine and Benjamin gave chase. Ciscilla ran toward the tourney grounds, outstripping them with each step. When she reached the grounds, Katherine was horrified to see her climbing the tourney field enclosure.

"Ciscilla! No!" she screamed desperately. "No! No!"

But her friend did not heed the warning and plunged over the side and into the path of the tilting contestants. Both men attempted to pull back their horses but it was too late. Neither animal could slow its momentum under the heavy weight of the armoured opponents and both bore down on her. At the final moment Ciscilla shrieked and fell beneath the horses. The animals collided with Ciscilla trampled under them. Somehow Katherine managed to scramble up and over the enclosure herself and raced out onto the field. Pandemonium had broken out in the stands and on the grounds.

"Get off her!" Katherine sobbed, pulling at the horse bridles with frantic fingers. She was swept aside and stronger hands restrained the beasts and sent them back. Ciscilla lay crumpled and still. Katherine threw herself down beside her friend and cradled her head tenderly, rocking and weeping.

"Ciscilla, oh my poor Ciscilla."

Victor appeared, features drawn and white. He motioned for Benjamin. The physician knelt alongside the fallen woman. Katherine put her hand to her mouth and held back her cries as Benjamin laid his head against Ciscilla's chest.

"Her breath is all but extinguished," he said at last. "She lives, but I know not for how much longer." He shook his head. "I am sorry."

"Oh no. Oh no," Katherine cried, clutching her friend more tightly.

She lifted her face to Victor to find her own misery mirrored in his eyes. Gently he unwound Katherine's arms from about Ciscilla and lifted his sister's broken body from the dirty field. Shock and horror muzzled the spectators and the crowd stood aside to let him pass. He turned briefly at the gate.

"The tournament is ended. Get the carriage at once."

Katherine staggered after him, blinded by tears. Victor took Ciscilla out of the hot sun and lay her in an empty tent. Katherine stood, helplessly crying, arms at her sides, hair and gown dishevelled. Victor turned from his sister to look at her. The pain in his eyes gripped her heart and without thinking she went into his arms to reach up and pull his head down and onto her shoulder. She pressed her cheek to his and stroked his hair.

"I am so sorry," she moaned. " So sorry."

Unexpectedly Katherine felt Victor's warm lips on hers. As if in a dream, she slowly closed her eyes and returned his kiss, a caress of infinite tenderness. And then it was over. As suddenly as it had begun. Victor backed away, blinking and shaking his head.

"I did not mean to . . . I apologize for . . . "

He pulled the tent flap aside. "I must see to the carriage for Ciscilla," he said hurriedly and disappeared.

She looked after Victor in a daze. What had happened? Then she cast guilty eyes at Ciscilla. Had she seen? Poor Ciscilla. Oh, that she would live. Katherine put her arms around her friend and held her close, letting her tears mingle with the dirt in Ciscilla's hair.

"Live, Ciscilla. Live," she whispered softly.

CHAPTER 17

SLOWLY AND CAREFULLY CISCILLA'S BATTERED BODY was transported to Stonehaven Castle where she was made comfortable in her own quarters. Katherine remained at her side except when exhaustion forced her to sleep and then either Victor or the physician took her place. They watched anxiously for any signs of wakefulness but Ciscilla's eyes remained closed for many days and only a slight trembling of her blankets gave them hope for her life.

The Stonehaven servants crept about on silent feet, saving their mirthful exchanges for the alehouse. It was as if the castle must hold its breath until Ciscilla's fate was known.

"She is a beautiful child," Benjamin said gently as he watched Victor take his sister's hand and kiss her pale cheek.

Victor gave a heavy sigh and glanced down at Ciscilla. "I still do not understand why she ran out onto the tilting field."

Benjamin drew his thick brows together. "I hesitated to tell you until I was certain but I found a single hard bubo on her back."

Victor's eyes registered the horror he felt and Benjamin added quickly. "Do not be alarmed. I was able to lance and clean the boil. If the bubos cannot be lanced, all is lost but if they can be drained of the evil, the patient usually recovers. Ciscilla's fever has abated and her delirium will be gone when she awakes. All we can do now is wait."

"But how came this pestilence upon her?"

"Ah, that is a question I cannot answer. The plague seeks out whom it will."

Victor pressed a hand to his eyes. "I am so tired. I have longed for sleep but it will not come."

Benjamin leaned forward, clasping his hands between his knees. "You are worried for your sister. That is understandable."

"Yes. But it is more than that."

"Can I help?" the physician asked.

Victor gave a short laugh. "No one can help me. Certain courses are set that are difficult to change and I fear I have made a mistake I must learn to live with."

He heaved a ragged sigh and got heavily to his feet. Benjamin stood with him and gave him a pat on the back.

"If you ever want to talk," he began, then looked up as Katherine entered the sickroom.

Her face was drawn with lines of fatigue.

"Perhaps you ought to rest longer, my dear," Benjamin suggested.

"Not until Ciscilla awakens." She turned to the sleeping Ciscilla. "Please, oh, please, wake up," she begged.

As if Katherine's plea had reached into the recesses of her friend's delirium, Ciscilla's eyes opened. They drooped then opened again and she smiled. "You are all here," she whispered faintly.

The worry lines in Katherine's face softened. "You have been returned to us," she said simply. "God be praised."

Life returned to normal at Stonehaven and Ciscilla grew stronger with each passing day while Katherine became restless at the idleness borne of confinement. She had no duties here and little news of Claringdon and her manor found its way through the castle's high walls. Fewer and fewer infected persons attempted to gain entry to Stonehaven. The world immediately outside the castle was quiet, the world inside, serene. But Katherine could not keep still. Early one morning she sought out Benjamin, finding him in the great hall.

"I would like to return to Crenfeld and assess its condition. Will you come with me?"

"Of course. If Lord Victor has no need of me at present, yes I will."

In another corner of the hall, Victor conversed in lowered tones with Father Simon but looked up at the sound of Katherine's voice.

"It is not safe, Lady Katherine," he called out. "You ought to remain here."

Katherine clenched her jaw. "I mean to go," she called back.

"We will make our survey and return at once," Benjamin said quickly.

Victor frowned. "Stay to the main roads," he charged. "Have contact with no one. And if you do not return in three days . . ."

Katherine cut him off. "We will."

Victor frowned again then nodded and returned to his conversation with the priest.

Katherine bristled slightly but gave a curt nod of assent.

"Lady Katherine and I will make our survey and return directly," Benjamin said. Victor nodded and returned to his conversation with the priest.

The carriage ride to Claringdon was grim. Near the village, they passed the bloated bodies of dead cattle lying in untended fields, while carrion birds circled constantly overhead.

"The village seems quite deserted," Katherine remarked uneasily.

Benjamin nodded. "Many are dead. And some have shut themselves in to allow no one near them. The rest are in the surrounding hills and caves."

Katherine shivered. "Let us go quickly. I only mean to satisfy myself that Crenfeld has suffered no damage."

The drawbridge was down, the gate yawned open and the inner courtyard looked desolate. Rotted fruits lay on the overgrown orchard grass. The mews was empty. With no one to tend to them, all the birds had been let loose. A few chickens fluttered around the yard, the hives lay broken on the ground, the bees gone, their honey stolen. The barns were deserted, with not even so much as a mouse to peep out at them from the dark corners.

"Benjamin," Katherine said suddenly. "I wish to see where Hester is buried. It will take but a moment. We left so quickly that day."

Benjamin smiled grimly. "Yes, of course. Come this way."

There was only the slightest rounding of the earth beneath which Hester lay. Nothing betrayed the recent gravesite save a thin carpet of sparse new grass marking the disturbed area. The surrounding course grasses were thick with thistles and wild flowers. Hester's grave looked barren, already forgotten. Katherine remembered the church cemetery and how, even there, time would erase those buried in it, despite their grave markers.

She looked around, searching. A thick branch lay on a pile of other orchard prunings. Katherine dragged it over to Hester's grave while Benjamin watched in silent curiosity. Standing the branch upright on the mound of dirt, she sank it in the soil a ways, then gathered a few large stones and grouped them around it for support. Sorting among the rocks, Katherine chose one with a sharp edge. She carved Hester's name through the still-green bark of the planted branch, then stepped away. Now, at least for a time, Hester's resting-place would be known.

"I wonder where Nettie is?" Katherine said. "I wonder if she has gone away, or died too?"

Benjamin took Katherine by the arm. "I know not what has become of Nettie, poor thing. I did not see her here when I returned from warning the villagers."

Katherine sighed and shook dirt from her skirt and shoes. "We should go inside," she said.

The castle was silent. Cold and dark and silent. The floor rushes smelled of mildew and their footsteps sounded hollow and distant, like echoes from footfalls in far off corridors. Examining each chamber they saw that anything useful had been spirited away. All the food, all the tapestries, all the furnishings. The castle was quite bare.

"At least the walls are standing," Katherine said ruefully.

Benjamin grinned. "You expected more?"

She made a face at him. "I suppose not. In any case, I have seen what I came for. We can return to Stonehaven. If we hurry, we can reach it before nightfall. There is nothing more to keep us here."

A dry cough made them turn around. Father Simon and four men stood in the doorway — a resolute phalanx. One man disengaged himself from the group. Katherine recognized him as her manorial bailiff. She opened her mouth to greet him but he strode past her and clapped a hand on Benjamin.

"Benjamin, the Jew, I arrest you for poisoning the drinking water of the village of Claringdon and this manor."

Benjamin gave the man a startled look.

Katherine confronted the bailiff. "What lies! You have no right to do this. I did not order his arrest. You answer to me on my estate and I say, let him go at once."

Father Simon cast his pale eyes on her. "You have no right to interfere in these proceedings, madam," he said coldly. "You abandoned this village and your manor. Other hands have taken up your duties and other hands will perform them."

"I have not abandoned the village or my manor. I have taken the household away for safety and will return with them when the danger from this vile pestilence is past. As you well know, father." Katherine advanced upon the priest, her small fists tightly curled. "Leave my home at once!" she demanded.

Unmoved by her outburst, Father Simon gave her a thin smile. "If you do not wish to be arrested as an accomplice, hold your peace," he threatened.

Benjamin shot Katherine a warning look.

She watched helplessly as the bailiff and his men led Benjamin way. She turned on the priest, taking hold of his sleeve. "You know he did not do this. Why, Benjamin is the one who recognized the danger and warned us," she cried.

"I know no such thing. He was heard to caution you against using your well water. Why would he do that unless he knew it was poisoned? And who better to know than the poisoner himself!" Simon finished in triumph.

"No, you are mistaken. It was because Hester had fallen down the well that he cautioned us. He feared the pestilence had polluted it."

Simon's eyes narrowed. "Ah, but is it not more likely that he poisoned the well himself? And that poor miserable Hester, an innocent maid charged with drawing water, was the first infected by it?" He shook off her hand. "Manor court shall be held in the church sanctuary tomorrow morning. Notice will be given at once and the village summoned to attend."

Katherine waved her hands in a circle. "Who is summoned? There is no one here!"

"There are enough. You shall see. There are enough."

Frightened by the menace in his tone, Katherine watched him in silence as he left her, his gaunt face fixed, his bony fingers tented at his waist. She stared after him, dumbfounded, until the shrill call of a bird brought her back with a start to the reality that she was now quite alone in this empty, hostile place. What was she to do? She could not go back to Stonehaven and leave Benjamin to face his accusers alone. She must stay and wait to hear what would become of him. These were serious charges. But how could they be proven? Who would speak against him? Surely, none would bring accusation against their physician. He had helped every one of them.

Katherine spent the afternoon pacing the castle interior and grounds. Would Victor become alarmed when they did not return? Would he send someone to find them? Would he come himself? As evening drew on she made her way to the alehouse. The "devil's chapel" did double service as an inn and would provide her with a bed for the night as well as some plain fare to sustain her until morning.

Katherine entered under the swaying sign of the "Hag's Head". Although the small ale room was filled with noisy patrons, her arrival caused but little stir. They raked her over with bright or bleary eyes without a break in conversation, then ignored her entirely. She was surprised to see so many people. She had thought the village to be deserted.

"Nay," said the innkeeper, leering hugely and patting his grubby apron. "Trade is good. The pestilence time is a good one." He winked at her. "It carries off the rabble. Thins 'em out as ye'd thin out yer geese at Allhallowtide. Mind you . . . " He leaned closer and put a finger alongside his bulbous nose. "No credit here. No debts. Pay fer yer drinks as ye drink 'em and yer bed afore ye sleeps in it. No one'll be cheatin' me out of me dues complainin' their head aches and their arm pricks so as to be sent straight off without payin'. Nah, there'll be none 'o that in my alehouse."

Katherine blinked at this long discourse, took out her purse and paid for a meal and a bed for the night.

"Wise, you is," the innkeeper smirked. "Payin' fer just the one night. Niver know when you'll git took off." He sucked his teeth over the payment then howled to someone she could not see to get her supper.

While she ate, Katherine feigned disinterest but kept her ears opened to the conversations around her. At one table sat a very grave looking fellow dressed all in black. He spoke in somber tones of the influence of the stars and the conjunction of certain planets which must necessarily bring sickness and distempers and consequently, the plague. All that sat around him nodded vigorously, for was not the plague among them even now? And they begged him to tell what would become of them and should they stay or go.

Another group discussed the various remedies, potions and preservatives offered by all sorts of conjurers and witches, dispensing "sovereign cordials against the corruption of the air," "the only true plague water," "the royal antidote against all kinds of infection." They spoke of eminent Dutch or Italian physicians newly arrived from across the sea and having choice secrets to prevent the infection and cure any who had the plague upon them.

"Aye," said one, "Dr. Benwick is said to direct persons how to prevent them being touched by any contagious distemper whatsoever. And to direct the poor for free." His fellows grunted and one querulous voice broke in.

"Nay, he's as subtle as the devil. He makes a great many fine speeches, examines their health and the constitution of their bodies and tells them many good things for them to do. But none of those things is of any great moment and no cure. Then, at the end, he says he has a preparation which if they take a certain quantity of every morning, they should never have the plague even though they lived in a house where people were infected. When I complained of the cost of the preparation and that his bills promised help for the poor for nothing, he replied that his advice was free, but not his physic!"

"Medicines are for fools," scoffed another. "This plague is the working of an evil spirit. See here. Wear this around your neck and the spirit will be kept off you."

Carefully, he unwrapped a paper affixed to a long knotted string. On it was written the word ABRACADABRA in the form of an inverted triangle; the word written in full on the topmost line, the next line omitting the last letter of the word, the third line omitting the next letter and so on until the bottom line contained only the letter A.

"You must tie it up in seven knots, like this, close your shirt up over it and you will come to no harm."

Those around him bent to watch how he manipulated the folding and knots.

"It is all a dream," said another young man seated amongst a less earnest sort. "Banish it from your mind. Fill your time with pleasant company and good talk. That is the way to escape infection."

Katherine turned to look behind her. A group of men had pushed their table under a window and were leaning out to watch the street. From without, she heard a rumbling and the cry, "Bring out your dead!"

At an adjoining window she viewed what passed below. The sight would haunt her dreams forever after. Isolated by the solitude of Stonehaven, she was not aware of the means required to cope with the multitude of plague victims that succumbed daily. Beneath the window rolled a cart with a bellman walking out in front. At the ringing of the bell he made his cry again, "Bring out your dead!" Doors opened and weeping parents appeared, bearing the bodies of their dead children. Buriers grabbed up the victims and threw them roughly onto the dead-cart as though stacking cordwood. Women dragged out dead husbands and men carried forth dead wives. Some were wrapped in linen sheets, some in rags, some were almost naked. All were heaped onto the cart, the buriers unmindful of the indecency of the naked thrown face to face; men, women and children indiscriminately piled one on top of the other. They were, in any case, bound for a common grave, so what did it matter?

It was as if the bell signalled the unleashing of tormented souls, for men and women poured into the streets behind the dead-cart in various stages of delirium and madness. Great shrieks rent the night air and the poor creatures babbled, raved and tore at their clothes, oftimes shaking violently, all the while chasing the cart.

Across the street, Katherine saw a young woman appear at an upper window and before her horrified eyes, scream hideously and gurgle and throw herself out onto the road to her death. A burier tramped back, took her up and heaved her onto the cart.

It was then that she heard the men at the window, chuckling and pointing at the grim picture of grief playing out beneath them. They nudged one another and mocked and jeered at the poor creatures.

One man, after handing up his wife and children, followed after the cart, his moans of agony so loud as to reach up to the windows of the inn. His deep mourning was evident and Katherine's heart turned within her. She leaned farther out to watch his progress with anxious eyes. The buriers tried to warn him off.

"Let me alone!" he begged. "I but want to see them into the pit and then I will go way."

The men at the table beside Katherine called out to him.

"You want some courage!" they taunted. "Why do you not leap into the great pit with them and go to heaven!"

Katherine turned on the drunken men. "Have you no pity?"

One of their number glared at her and spat on the floor.

"What are you doing out of your grave?" he snarled and banged his beer on the table. "You should be at home, saying yer prayers against the dead cart coming to your door?"

They laughed uproariously at her stricken face and called out all the louder, swearing in a dreadful manner upon the wretches staggering in the streets.

Filled with horror and loathing, Katherine thought better of confronting them further. Disgusted, she left her meal, found her room and sat on the edge of her bed, trembling with rage and fear. The ringing of the dead-cart receded into the distance and the noise in the street abated.

At length she blew out her candle, lay down on top of her bed fully clothed and fell into a fitful sleep. Some time in the night she was awakened by a thumping at her door and the slurred demand for "the wench" to show herself. But the lock was stout and the one on the other side of the door laboured in fruitless evil intent, muttering and cursing. She heard him being drawn away, another door banged and then all was quiet again. Dreams of corpses filled the rest of the night. Corpses lying thick in the streets, muscular men wading through them with big shovels and tossing them into slow-moving wagons.

CHAPTER 18

WHEN DAWN BROKE, Katherine was as tired as if she had never closed her eyes. She watched the sun come up over the empty street and marvelled at how the desperate anguish she witnessed the night before had vanished with the sunrise. How could the sun keep its appointed rounds in the midst of such suffering? Surely it must stop and hide its face, giving grief time to pass. But no, it would rise and fall and rise again in unchangeable constancy, unmoved by the plight of mankind.

She sighed, gathered up her few things and left the inn. Every street led to the great stone church at the center of Claringdon and so she turned her steps in its direction. Some of the cottages she passed had large red X's painted on the doors and a guard posted. She knew there was plague in these houses and that the guard was not to keep people out, but to prevent the occupants from escaping. Sometimes pale faces appeared at the windows and stared out in hopeless misery, but mostly she saw no one at all save the guards. The filth of man and beast filled the street. Occasionally, she passed a dead dog or cat and swallowed hard lest the stench cause her to gag.

In the church sanctuary, court was commencing. On a hastily constructed dais, Father Simon sat in the usurped place reserved for the lord or lady of the manor. Her place.

By his side was the court clerk. Benjamin stood in chains before them. He had obviously been beaten, for his eyes were blackened and his lips swollen.

The usher cried for silence. "Oyez, oyez, oyez! All those whose duty it is to be present, draw near!"

The body of jurors for inquisition having been assembled, the clerk read the charges.

"That you, Benjamin the Jew, physician of Claringdon, are arrested upon the charge of poisoning wells, springs and other places with the design of destroying and extirpating all Christians."

Katherine watched in disbelief, as two men from the village gave testimony to having seen Benjamin distribute poison in several places under stones near springs. One man gave an elaborate tale of intrigue, saying Rabbi Jacob of Aberwern had sent Benjamin, by a Jewish boy, some poison in the mummy of an egg and that it was a powder sewed up in a thin leathern pouch accompanied by a letter commanding him to throw the poison into the common well in Claringdon. Three men bore testimony to having seen the poison and described it as being of two colours, red and black.

"What say you to these charges?" inquired the clerk.

Benjamin licked his swollen lips and drew himself up as best he could. His shackles clanked together heavily. "I did none of those things," he denied in a weak, croaking voice.

The jurors were instructed to commence their inquiry.

"Can you prove your innocence of these charges, physician?"

Benjamin shook his shaggy head. "How may a man put forth evidence of something that has no substance? As you have found no poison on my person or in my house, you may conclude either that I never possessed poison at all or that I have since sprinkled it out into the waters of Claringdon. Given there is no poison, I can prove nothing."

There was some murmuring and then the next man spoke.

"Are you saying then, that these good men of the village are lying, physician?"

"And if I say they have not spoken truthfully, what then? Tell me, how is it that one may prove one did *not* do a thing? How can someone say they saw me not doing it?"

This line of pursuit being exhausted, the next man looked hard at Benjamin.

"Is it not true, physician, that you absent yourself from the true Christian Church and the Mass? Does not that prove your malignant intent against all Christians?"

Benjamin remained silent.

"You are aware physician, are you not," Father Simon spoke up, "that the scriptures are on the forbidden list? That none but the Church is to hold them in possession? How came you then to read them contrary to the laws of this realm?"

Katherine started. He had found out.

Benjamin paused. "The laws of the realm are contrary to the command of the Lord to learn of Him. The Church teaches nothing of the Christ save His passion. Her concentration is on sin and punishment and the sufferings of purgatory." He lowered his voice. "A man needs more hope than that."

Simon banged his knuckles on the arm of his chair. "The Church will decide what is fit for a man to hear from holy writ. Unlearned men come to great spiritual harm if left to themselves. The Church is his guide and shepherd. A man must have faith in that."

"A man must have faith in Christ the Lord," Benjamin contradicted.

"Strange words coming from a Jew," the priest mocked. "Your Messiah has not yet come. What care you for the Christian Saviour?"

"Yes, I am a son of Zion," Benjamin admitted. "Yet, a true Christian," he added gently. "Did you not know that the Pharisees wanted to kill Lazarus because Jesus raised him from the dead, causing many Jews to believe in Him? And have you not read how the Lord said that if one believes Moses, one will believe Him, also?"

"Where did *you* read this?" Simon challenged, lifting his pale eyes to the jury. But instead of the disapproval he expected, he saw thoughtful looks pass between the inquirers. He frowned.

"We have gone astray from the charge at hand," he said quickly. "We are not here to settle ecclesiastic matters." His thin lips curled. "Although should we be, you would stand condemned as an heretic. But we are here to expose the true facts concerning the heinous crime of poison. And the facts are that six men have given evidence against you and that you are unable to give any satisfactory support for the contrary part."

He gave his attention to the jurors. "The judgment of this man is at your disposition. The evidences of a crime are plainly to be seen. The village is sorely afflicted and good men and women continue to die. Shall their deaths go unpunished? What think ye? Do and ordain as ought to be done according to the will of God."

Benjamin stood with eyes downcast and hands hanging at his sides, weighed down by the chains. Katherine could see the resignation in his face and fear clutched at her heart.

The jurors whispered amongst themselves for only a short time, now and again casting agonized glances at both Benjamin and the priest. Clearly they felt they had little choice as to their duty and were loath to do it, but in the end they motioned for the clerk. The clerk heard the verdict, nodded, came back to Father Simon, whispered to him and then cleared his throat.

"Since you cannot show it to be otherwise and the evidence against you is conclusive, it is found by the jurors that you did indeed poison the wells, springs and other places with the design of destroying and extirpating all Christians in this manor."

Father Simon pushed himself up from his chair and leaned toward Benjamin. His eyes narrowed and a tight smile creased his lips. He spoke with cold finality.

"Because of the great hardness of your heart in carrying off men, women and children without mercy, neither shall you be shown mercy but shall on the morrow be burned at the stake and from there consigned to the common pit."

Benjamin groaned, yielded to the pull of the chains and sank to his knees. Both the jury and the spectators were stunned into silence. All eyes turned to Benjamin's six accusers who seemed every bit as shaken as the prisoner. One man turned deathly pale and retched miserably before stumbling outside.

Katherine seethed with impotent rage. False accusers, all! May they roast in eternal flames for their treachery! Many of the townspeople hissed savage curses at the jury as they filed past out of the sanctuary. Benjamin was pulled to his feet and led away. Katherine watched him go. Then she turned, white and tight-lipped, to face Father Simon. Her green eyes glimmered.

"Where will you take him?"

"To Crenfeld's dungeon," the priest replied with ill-disguised rancour. "It is the nearest."

"May I speak with him?" she asked.

Father Simon closed his faded eyes into slits and touched his fingers together in front of his lips.

"In time. He will be given room to confess his crimes and repent. You may see him after you hear the ringing of the bell."

Katherine did not relish the idea of venturing forth after dark when the dead-carts were out with their grisly cargo but she nodded and withdrew, spending the rest of the day in a state of agitation. Restless, she could not light in one spot for more than a moment. Eventually, she determined to make her way to Benjamin's small cottage and see if there were any personal items Benjamin might wish to have with him. Before tomorrow. She shuddered and pushed the following day from her thoughts.

Benjamin's hearth was cold and his meager belongings yielded little except a small blanket. She doubted he would be afforded any covering against the chill of the little chamber beneath the storage rooms. She folded the blanket carefully and put it to one side. Looking around the sparsely furnished room she saw the little stool and recalled it had concealed Benjamin's box, where he kept the forbidden writings. She was disappointed to find the space empty for she had thought to use it to induce the priest to drop the charges against Benjamin. He must have moved it. She searched a little more but found nothing.

Aware suddenly that she was hungry, Katherine collected Benjamin's blanket and made her way to the market. She purchased two small apples. The merchant held a vinegar soaked cloth to his nose and mouth and in muffled tones told her he would not take her money from her hand but she must put it into a jar filled with vinegar. He did not make change. As she had given him more than was required, Katherine filled a small sack with peas and took them away as well.

In the gathering dusk, Katherine spread out Benjamin's blanket at the side of the road leading out of Claringdon and ate her scanty meal. The apples were still quite green and hard but she had good teeth and their tart crunchy flesh satisfied her appetite. She shelled the few peas into her lap, discarded the pods and ate them one at a time. When she was finished, she shook off the blanket, refolded it, tucked it under her arm and began to climb the road to Crenfeld.

CHAPTER 19

WITH WEARY EYES, Benjamin regarded the cell into which he had been thrust. His bruised lip throbbed painfully and his wrists were numb where the chains cut into his skin. He shivered. The little room was very cold but a warm breeze came in at a small opening cut into the outer wall. He hobbled over to the window and squinted. He could see outside, but there was nothing to see save the stones of the curtain wall opposite. He leaned back on his haunches and closed his eyes, savouring a light gust that played across his face. It had a fresh, sweet smell that somewhat repressed the dank staleness of his moulding cell. He hitched his chains to a more comfortable position, looking up when the trap door opened and a rope ladder fell through the hole.

Father Simon glowered down on him a moment before carefully descending rung by rung, lantern in hand. Benjamin shuffled toward the priest and waited. Simon raised the lantern high, sending long slanting shadows scudding across the stone walls.

"Have you thought on your position physician? Are you ready to confess your sins against God and the people of Claringdon?"

Benjamin smiled slightly.

"You know very well I poisoned nothing. What is there to confess?"

"And you know I have the power to take your life or preserve it. If you make a good confession, I may preserve it."

"What is it you want me to say? That I did what I did not? Do you want me to lie and multiply sin against God?"

Father Simon circled Benjamin, now sunk wearily to his knees.

"As you seem adamant on the point of the poisoning, can you be so adamant about your possession of the forbidden writings?"

Benjamin gave a heavy sigh and licked his swollen lips. "I am not charged nor convicted of that."

"But you have them all the same and you defy the authority of God's Church," Simon spat contemptuously, arching his back to drop his face close to Benjamin. "Confess it!"

"Scripture is the voice of God. If I have listened to the voice of God, how can that be wrong?" Benjamin countered. "Ought we not to heed his voice?"

"Mother Church is the voice of God," Simon snapped.

"God is His own voice," Benjamin argued. "And He speaks to every one of His children in scripture, not just to the Church."

Simon's taut, pinched lips twitched. He set down the lantern slowly and deliberately, took a step forward and with the back of his bony hand, struck Benjamin a savage blow across the face.

"Heretic! Bloody heretic!"

Benjamin swayed slightly under the impact, his cheek split and bleeding. Simon moved in, grasped the front of

Benjamin's tunic and with an uncommon strength born of rage, dragged the exhausted physician to his feet.

"You heretic," he repeated. "I will strive with you no further. You stand condemned out of your own mouth! You defy me. You defy the holy Church. You defy God. You are a stench in the nostrils of the Almighty."

Benjamin looked steadily into the priest's eyes.

"Do what you will, Simon. I will read God's word and heed His voice as He commanded as long as there is breath in my body."

"Which will not be for long, physician."

With a quick exasperated jerk, Simon released his hold on Benjamin, retrieved the lantern and climbed up out of the little cell, leaving Benjamin in darkness.

The physician closed his eyes and leaned against a mossy wall. He lay there a long time, listening to the sound of his own breathing, feeling his chest expand and deflate. He felt his heart throbbing in his chest, the pulse in his throat. When he concentrated, he even perceived the coursing of his blood through his veins. He wanted to experience life while he could, for tomorrow it would be at an end.

He hoped it would be a grey day. It is a hard thing to leave the world in brilliant sunshine. At least he had often thought so when attending a deathbed. To see corruption overtake the human frame while all the world was vibrant with life was doubly distressing. Yes, he hoped it would be a somber day befitting death.

He was not afraid to die. In fact, now that his fate seemed assured, death had become a sought after friend. When not faced with imminent departure, a man gives little thought to such things. But as men know they breathe their last, there is often a period of panic and hasty confession, a futile clutching at one last heartbeat, one last gulp of air, the eyes staring and not daring to blink lest they fall closed forever. A short time ago, that man would have been him. But Benjamin had caught a glimpse of what lay beyond the grave and was convinced the splendours of heaven awaited him.

The dying part, though. Ah, that was a different matter. Death and dying are not the same. Death is leaving this world behind to go on to places unknown. That did not frighten him. Dying, however, is the often unpleasant and often grievous means to that end. And Benjamin faced the means with trepidation and mounting horror. Who could withstand the agony of the flames? He had seen men and women roasted and its recollection brought him near to fainting with terror. He wished to die bravely, as his Lord had done, not screaming for release. He covered his face with his hands and his lips began to move in earnest prayer.

Katherine heard the bell ring down below. Father Simon would be in his church. It signalled his return. Now she could attend to Benjamin. As she gained the castle courtyard it came to her that she had brought poor Benjamin nothing to eat. The priest would not waste food on a man about to die. It mattered not to Simon whether the condemned met his fate empty or full.

The apple trees were quite bare and there were no pears; the season for cherries and plums long past. The strawberry plants had died back and the raspberries were shrivelled up on their canes. Nothing. Ah, well, at least she had his blanket. That was something. She went in at the kitchen, down the storeroom staircase to face a guard planted beside the dungeon's trap door.

"Father Simon has granted me permission to speak to the prisoner," she said. Her tone and look brooked no argument and the guard gave her none. He merely grunted, handed her a dripping candle and heaved open the heavy wooden covering.

Katherine descended into the black hole. Her small light dispersed the thick darkness enough for her to make out the form of Benjamin huddled in one corner. The cold in the little cell was bitter and she immediately hurried to wrap him in his blanket. Benjamin's teeth chattered.

"Th-thank you," he said simply, clutching the blanket around his trembling shoulders.

Katherine set the candle down between them and crouched so that her skirts covered her feet.

"I wanted to bring you something to eat."

Benjamin shook his black head. "No need. I am not hungry."

Katherine looked at the bruised face of her friend and fear squeezed her heart.

"Oh, Benjamin, must you die? Can you not see it is only that you have insulted the Church? If you give up the forbidden pages to Father Simon and come back to the Church he will forget these ridiculous charges against you. I am sure he will," she begged.

Benjamin frowned. "Not you too."

A tear slid down Katherine's cheek and her green eyes clouded. "It is only that I do not want you to die," she said in a muffled voice.

Benjamin's face softened. "I know, my dear, but some things are worth a man's life. Try to understand."

"Then tell me, Benjamin. Make me understand. Why is this so important to you? How can you die for such a thing as this? What difference can it make for you to give up the writings?" Katherine dissolved into tears.

Benjamin's dark eyes filled and he groaned as he watched her shoulders shaking.

"Do you remember the young men you saw me with at Lord Victor's?" he asked gently.

Katherine nodded. She recalled seeing him with a small group just prior to the tournament.

"I have been reading the scriptures to them. If I give up the scriptures, do you think those young men will have the opportunity to read them again?"

Katherine shook her head. She knew that would never happen.

"In the Gospel of John, after telling how Jesus made the blind see, the lame walk and the dead come back to life, it says, 'these are written, that ye might believe that Jesus is the Christ, the Son of God; and that believing ye might have life through his name.' I would die to preserve the comfort of that passage for those young men. A comfort denied them by the Church. There are many priests within the Church who believe as I do but seek a temporary peace with the Church rather than everlasting peace with God. The Church has no soundness in it but is corrupted by wickedness from the sole of its foot even to its head. The whole of it is one great open wound of avarice, indifference and immorality. How then is it a fit likeness of the love and compassion of Christ? Only in the scriptures can these young men see the true power of God and the truth of God. It is in my hands to preserve God's word and the hope that is in it, and I am compelled by the love of Christ to do it. It is God who saw to it that my friend copied out the gospel of St. John for me and gave me the courage to read it and believe it. There is true life, everlasting life, in the name of Jesus. My young friends are beginning to see that and I will do nothing to keep them from continuing to learn that it is so."

Katherine regarded him through a haze of tears. "Can you leave us so easily?" she asked in a wistful voice.

Benjamin shook his head. "Not easily, no. But I pray I shall leave bravely." His lips trembled. "I do so wish to leave bravely."

Katherine crept closer to him and lay her head on his shoulder. She put her small hands into his shackled ones and pressed them firmly. "You shall, Benjamin," she whispered. The tears flowed freely down her face and into their clasped hands. "I know you shall."

Katherine left the candle with him when at length she climbed the ladder. She had not wished to leave at all but he insisted. He needed time to prepare himself, he said. And so she relented after hugging him close and gently kissing his bruised face.

"Watch for me, Benjamin. I will pray for God to give you strength."

"Thank you. You are a good friend," he said simply.

Katherine found her way back to the alehouse, paid for her room for the night and sank to her knees before the open window. To her knowledge she had never prayed outside of the church and her prayers had been only those she had learned and memorized. But tonight she felt emboldened by Benjamin's words to frame her prayers according to the state of her heart and she poured out all her sorrows and pleadings directly into the ear of God.

While she prayed, Benjamin shone his candle over against an inner wall. Loosening one of the stones, he removed it with care and reached inside to withdraw the box that held the forbidden book of the gospel of St. John. He read until his heart stilled within him and he grew calm, his mind at peace. He read until the tallow guttered and then replaced the box and its contents in the secret place, being careful to replace the stone precisely. He dragged his chains into a corner, pulled the blanket around his shoulders, lay against the dirt wall and slept the dreamless sleep of the truly tranquil.

When the bells rang for morning Mass, men who were wont to be absent left their stools in the alehouse and betook themselves to the church in hopes that Father Simon would take note of their faithfulness.

The host was elevated, the Latin intoned and men pressed forward to kiss the white linen altar cloth. Well satisfied with their own piety, they quit the sanctuary and, passing the great pyre being erected outside the church, rushed to sustain themselves with all the ale they could hold before the execution put them off their drink.

Their departure was a signal for the church rats to scurry out of their holes. With the candles extinguished, the sanctuary was plunged into a deep gloom. Furtive shapes darted in the shadows making faint rustling sounds. Although the host was securely locked away in its protective tabernacle, the rodents sniffed the edges of the altar cloth hopefully. Its hem was heavily stained with ale and grease from the lips of the townsmen and the rats chewed and nibbled contentedly until Father Simon returned to remove the cloth and shake them off. Not from any malevolence did the rats leave the true means of transmission of pestilence upon the edges of the cloth but, as the priest balled up the material to take it away, he felt the bite of fleas. Annoyed, he smacked the backs of his hands and the sides of his forearms, then scratched the little red swellings. He pulled his sleeves down further over his wrists, adjusted the thin chain and cross he wore at his waist and looked outside, still scratching.

Even now there were men dispatched to the castle to convey that miserable heretic to his deserved end. Father Simon was irritated at being unable to obtain the forbidden manuscript from the obstinate physician but at least he would be rid of his influence and the cursed Jew would lead no more away from the Church into apostasy. He was satisfied the burning would curtail the activity of further zealots.

Simon carefully gathered up spent petals fallen from a gilded vase of cut roses, backed away from the window and strode down the hall to his apartments. He must change his robes. To the red. He smiled thinly. Fiery red. Fitting.

Katherine rose early so she could see Benjamin before they took him away. Her face was drawn and pale. She had spent a sleepless night listening to the creak of the dead-carts in the streets, the taunts of the alehouse patrons and the shrieks of the doomed. It was as if she had been plunged alive into hell itself. With men and women dying in such prodigious quantities it seemed especially heinous to take the life of a good man who could help them.

Waiting in Crenfeld's kitchen, she straightened when she heard the drag of chains. Benjamin emerged with a guard at each arm and struggled to keep moving forward.

Katherine rushed to him and was waved off. He looked at her and tears welled up in his soft dark eyes, to spill out onto his haggard, welt-lined cheeks. He looked so frail. Tears clouded her own eyes and she eluded his guards to dart in and clasp him in a frantic embrace.

"Do not grieve my dear," he whispered into her ear. "The flames burn but for a moment, only a moment. Heaven is for eternity."

One of the guards pulled her roughly from him and as she was wrenched away, she felt Benjamin press something into her hand. Her fingers closed around it and she stumbled aside.

When he was gone, she went to stand before the glass windows in the apse of the chapel tower. She unfolded a bit of cloth and read, "Ever hath my hope of refuge been in thee. Under the chamber wall there lies the blessed book. The fox waxes wroth and would burn me in a bath of flames. Grieve not for my soul. In heaven I will be at peace. Farewell. Almighty God bless you, dear Katherine."

Katherine's lips trembled. He must have known it would come to this. But when had he hidden the box? Likely before he left Claringdon to come to them at Stonehaven. Crenfeld would have been empty and he would be undisturbed. He must have carried the note on his person, maybe even from that time onward. She shuddered. He had suspected this for weeks and yet his demeanour had not altered in any way. And had placed himself in the priest's hands when he agreed to accompany her to Crenfeld. She — she had led him to his doom. Katherine closed her eyes and pressed her hand over her mouth to stop a sob. He had carried the burden of it all this time and carried it alone.

She turned to look down into the village below. The stone church stood high and proud and cold at the village center. Just outside its walls where the streets met, stood a small wooden platform. A stout post ran up through the middle of the platform with a great pile of straw and sticks surrounding it. This is where they would bring Benjamin.

She put her hand on the glass and pressed her face up close to it to see if he had been brought yet. She saw no one. Then she opened her hand and read the words again, leaned over and held the cloth above the flame of a nearby walls sconce until it blackened beyond reading.

"Forgive me, Benjamin," she thought, "but no one else is going to die because of the banned missive of a long-dead saint. There is too much death already. I will not go against the Church, but neither will I give it to Father Simon to gloat over. It can lay in that little cell where you have hidden it for at least as long as I live, I can promise you that much. I can do that much for you. I can preserve it."

Now she must make haste. She had no desire to watch her friend die such an ignominious death. Her whole being shrank from it. But she wanted him to see her face. Needed him to see her face and feel her presence and her love with him in his final hour. She would not let him die alone, among the crowds of curious frightened townspeople, the indifferent soldiers and self-righteous churchmen.

CHAPTER 20

WHEN AT A SAFE DISTANCE FROM LIKE SUFFERINGS, men have a perverse fascination with the torment meted out to their fellowman. Accordingly, the hub of the village thronged in a congested knot, waiting the appointed time of execution.

Benjamin's desire had been granted. The day was indeed a dismal one. Clouds gathered in ever darkening clusters and with them the distant rumble of approaching thunder. What had begun as a gentle breeze was mounting in strength, whipping cloaks and dresses around the women's legs and flaying their faces with their own hair.

Katherine struggled to squeeze her way to the front of the onlookers. She wanted to be where Benjamin could see her. A hush fell over the crowd when Benjamin was led up to the platform and lashed to the stake. He turned to look out over the upturned faces. She knew he was searching for her and raised her arm, palm outward. His eyes fell on her and he smiled. A slow and gentle smile that tore at her heart and took her breath from her. She was not going to be able to bear this!

Suddenly Katherine felt a hand grip her shoulder and turned to find Victor behind her. He nudged the person next to her and came alongside. His jaw was tight, his grey eyes stony.

"You must come away from here," he said fiercely.

"No. No!" Katherine shook her head. "I promised him. I must stay."

She tried to pull away from Victor but he brought his arm behind her shoulder and held her with iron fingers. She felt the hardness of his forearm across her back.

"Please," she begged. "Let me do this for him."

Victor looked into her face and relaxed his grip. He nodded but did not release her. Instead he used his free hand to brush back the loose strands of hair from her cheeks and brow before turning to follow the proceedings. Katherine was grateful for the comfort of his presence and sagged back against him.

Father Simon raised his hands for silence, his skin a ghastly white against the flowing scarlet robes, billowing in the wind. Gold stitching caught the meager sunlight and glimmered faintly.

When all was still, the priest turned and pointed a dramatic and imperious finger at Benjamin. "For your crimes against God and this parish, you are hereby sentenced to death by burning. May God have mercy on your soul."

Lighted torches were touched to the straw, which immediately caught fire. The straw flared and snapped, leaving a black track behind as it ate its way to the sticks and branches piled high around Benjamin's platform and up onto his feet. The flames sprang around the limbs in a kind of dance, now high, now low, now this side, now that. With the wind gusting, the fire could only burn according to its breath on fragile but deadly orange tongues. Sometimes they were pushed flat, sideways across the pile of fuel and sometimes the sticks pulsed red as the flames billowed up and over the boughs and twigs.

Katherine kept her eyes on Benjamin and marked the strained tension in his face and eyes as he too watched the relentless climb of the hot jaws eating their way closer to him. Some of the women began to weep softly and hide their faces with their hands. But Katherine was transfixed as though held in a trap. She could not look away. The wind whipped the fire into a frenzied roaring. Sweat poured in heavy rivulets down Benjamin's heat-reddened face. The flames were all around him now. Thick black smoke rolled up over his head and he began to cough. His eyes watered but still no flame touched him. The wind seemed to divide the fire around the stake. He looked up once, and as he looked the tension drained from his face and an extreme calm settled onto his features. He sagged limply in his bonds and when his eyes found Katherine's, a palpable peace shone in their depths. Katherine had the distinct impression that he was gone from her and beyond all feeling. Beyond the reach of the flames. Beyond the agony of the moment.

Father Simon had been watching too. And waiting. Waiting for the screams of searing torment. Katherine could see it in the priest's face, which held a tension of its own that could only be relieved by an explosion of suffering from the man pinioned to the stake. But it never came. Even as the fire curled around Benjamin's bare feet, the singed flesh turned black and the repellant smell of burning tissue reached their nostrils, no sound escaped his lips. He merely turned his face upwards and slowly closed his eyes. Then the fire swallowed him and he was lost from view in the devouring inferno.

Katherine pressed her face into Victor's chest and began to cry while the sky opened up its own torrents. His God had been with him at the last. Exhausted by her own emotions, the tears coursed freely down her cheeks. At first she wept for Benjamin but gradually her heart began to ache for her own loss and the tears continued to well, brim up and overflow. She could not bear the pain any longer. The hurt was too great. She had lost Benjamin and Father Simon had stolen her home. Then there was Victor. Soon, he would marry Marjorie. He would have the wife of his choosing and Edward would have the mother he needed. And she? She would have nothing.

She must get far away from here. Away from the horror and the memories. Her uncle would take her in. He had said as much many times. And although he lived in a wild and desolate corner of England, she welcomed the peace and solitude such a harsh environment would afford her.

The crunch of wagon wheels lifted her face and opened her eyes. Two men took the weight of the shafts and Katherine recognized them as the young men she had seen with Benjamin in days past. Alarmed, she shot a glance at Father Simon but he was taking no notice. Cheated of his anticipated revenge, he was having Benjamin's charred body dragged from the fire with long iron hooks. He took some consolation in seeing his enemy's flesh flayed from his bones and his features blackened and distorted.

The priest's face was suffused and livid. "Convey him to the common pit!"

Hooks were used to grapple with Benjamin's remains and his body tumbled into the wagon.

Katherine pulled away from Victor. She wiped the rain from her face and clutched her wet cloak around her. "I am going with them."

Victor looked at the wet tendrils of hair plastered against her cheeks and forehead and the shaking fingers holding closed her soaking cloak and thought to protest, but the set of her dripping chin dared him to argue with her.

"Very well. I will walk with you."

"There is no need."

Victor made no reply but fell into step beside her. They walked in silence, save for the pounding rain, the grunts of the men at the shafts and the creak and grind of the wagon. A dead-cart approached the pit just ahead of them and was upended over the hole to empty its grim cargo. The present horrors had dulled Katherine's senses and she watched in detachment as the quick-lime was shovelled onto the faces of the dead and ruthlessly went about its work.

Katherine cast her eyes on a young woman that lay on top of the pile. Had some young man admired her curls, no longer lustrous but matted together with dirt? Had he been charmed by her clear, sparkling eyes, now sunken into her head and filled with soil and the small creatures of the earth? Had he kissed the plump red lips now so consumed that her teeth lay bare and snarling? It was a hideous death.

Katherine saw Benjamin's body join the rest. Even though his clothes had been burned from him and he was quite naked, he looked as though he were clad in a black robe. She was glad of even this smallest decency but averted her face when the quick-lime was thrown over him. It was done. He was gone.

Victor touched her shoulder. She looked up with vacant eyes and obediently followed his lead back along the muddy village streets. As they went, they came upon a group of men chanting hymns and psalms and continually making the sign of the cross. They were naked from the waist up, wearing only a linen cloth that reached from thigh to heel. Each wore a cap marked front and back with a red cross and each carried a scourge of three knotted thongs. Sharp points were fixed through the knots and they walked barefoot in the procession and struck each one the man in front of him on naked backs already swollen and blue and running with rain mingled with blood.

"The Brethren of the Cross," Victor whispered and pulled her to one side to let them pass. "They mean to take upon themselves the repentance of the people of England, believing this present pestilence to be a punishment for not keeping the Sabbath and that this is the only way to appease the anger of Christ."

Katherine turned frightened eyes on the bleeding bodies of the brethren and hastened her step. She had witnessed far greater sins than Sabbath-breaking in recent days and doubted the efficacy of their actions.

When Katherine saw the carriage waiting to take them back to Stonehaven Castle, she knew she could not go; that before she left Claringdon she must fulfil the commission entrusted to her by Benjamin. Since watching her friend die with such courage, her viewpoint had altered and she knew she would have no peace if she failed him and his young disciples.

"I am too tired to make the journey, Victor," she said. "You go ahead. I will stay over until morning."

Victor's eyes narrowed. "Where will you go?"

"The Hag's Head has rooms." She looked at him. "The beds are soft and the locks are thick. I will lodge there."

Victor glanced up at the dark sky, the grumbling clouds. The cold hiss of rain pelted his face. "You are right. It would be foolhardy to take the road in such weather."

"I did not mean for you to . . . " Katherine protested.

Victor ignored her objection. "It is settled, then," he said. "We shall stay the night."

Katherine followed Victor to the Hag's Head Inn, groaning inwardly. Somehow she must elude him in the night, return to Crenfeld, retrieve Benjamin's secret, find his young men and turn it over to them. And all before morning and before Victor arose. She frowned impatiently. It was not going to be easy.

Father Simon divested himself of his sumptuous robes and wrinkled his nose delicately. They smelled of smoke and would need to be cleaned and aired out. He laid them carefully on the back of the tall black-tanned chair in his chambers and donned a plain white linen alb, securing the cincture tightly. It pinched a little so he loosened it off.

He heaved a contented breath. The woman would be gone now. The castle was his. Yes, despite the many infuriating delays, the Lord had seen fit to ensure the Church increased her glebe, joining Crenfeld and its manor to her holdings, as well as rid the Church of a malodorous heretic. The pope was bound to be pleased when he heard of it and would likely improve his position within the Church. Perhaps even a call to the papal seat for personal congratulations. His flat, pale eyes took on a dreamy quality. Ah, Avignon. Joanna, countess of Provence, had only just sold the city to Clement VI and this French pope was to his liking. Yes, he had proven his value to God and the Church.

Father Simon drew near to the open pit that housed the plague victims, as well as his own. He was not afraid. He drenched a cloth in the finest imported vinegar and pressed it to his nose and mouth, before looking over the lip of the burial trench. Ah, there he was. He looked like a mound of coal. The priest's lips curled and he gazed with distaste on the mountain of humanity heaped beneath him.

Suddenly, his vision blurred and he blinked hard. The vinegar must be making him dizzy. He took the cloth away from his face and shook his head. Lifting a hand to rub his eyes, he felt a sharp prick under one arm. A cold wave of terror swept over him and he explored the area with shaking fingers. It could not be! In a nauseating panic of fear, he ripped open the sleeve of his robe to reveal a hideous livid purple tumour. His heart began a violent throbbing and a great heaviness invaded his limbs. At once there came a loud buzzing in his ears and the unsteadiness that first alerted him to his plight, returned with a vengeance. He reeled, lost his footing, felt himself falling and realized too late that he had pitched headlong over the edge of the hole.

He landed with a sickening thump upon a slippery mass of cold naked flesh. The priest struggled vainly to get to his feet. Nameless muck coated his clothes and he felt the sting of the quick-lime bite into his skin as he slid helplessly across the vast ocean of the dead.

His thoughts grew dull and confused. His eyesight dimmed. Finally, he ceased fighting, succumbed to the lassitude taking hold of his limbs and lay back panting and frightened. He was conscious of nothing but a hopeless despair and moaned in fear, eyes closed, fists clenched under his chin.

Slowly Simon became sensible of a soft white light, somewhere behind his eyes. It grew in brightness and his tense muscles relaxed. The roaring in his head quieted and peacefulness soothed his tormented thoughts. It was going to be all right. The light intensified and shed a warm glow down a long narrow tunnel. He felt himself lift effortlessly to glide down the tunnel toward the source of the light. His body weighed nothing; his mind was emptied of all confusion and unrest.

Someone came to meet him. It was a man. The man wore gleaming white robes and pulsed with a radiant glow. The man smiled a serene smile, a welcoming smile. An angel. So he was dying, then. He was ready. He had served God and the Church well; protected her name and her faith. His reward was assured. He knew a brief preening happiness that he was to experience the glories of heaven even before the Vicar of Christ himself. But no, that was a venal contemplation and had no place here. Brief anxiety took him as he thought of leaving his rose garden but drew solace from the certainty that heaven's roses would bloom in even greater loveliness.

He drifted silently closer to the man in white. There was no sound in this dazzling brightness, just a satisfying calm. The man was waiting for him and behind the man, the most beautiful bridge he had ever seen. It was all of gold. Pure and clear and almost transparent. Smooth and unmarred. He laid a hand on the golden bridge rail. It was warm to the touch. He felt himself smile into the face of the man. The man took his hand gently and encouraged him to join him on the bridge, smiling with benign affection back over his shoulder, while drawing him to the other side.

It was a little warmer on this side of the bridge and Simon grew uncomfortable. He would tell the man when they reached their destination. But for now he would enjoy the tranquility, the agreeable harmony. Ah, there were others here too. In the distance. Perhaps he knew them. They were waving to him. He could not make out their faces but returned their cordial greeting with an amicable gesture of his own. There would be only friends here.

The man's hand tightened, introducing a discordant discomfort. He opened his mouth in mild protest but no sound came. All was quiet. The greeters swam into view and he was alarmed to find not smiles, but grimaces on their anxious faces. And they were not welcoming him as he had assumed, but attempting to wave him away, to warn him off. He had seen them somewhere. He had seen them in the painted glass of the church clerestories!

The man turned and although his smile remained fixed in benevolence, his eyes were now hostile slits. Simon tried to shake off the man's hand but found he could not loose himself. The heat intensified and he saw that the heat was coming from the man himself. Where the man's feet touched the surface, flames sprang up and billowed around him. Still the man smiled and dragged him on. He was beginning to suffocate in the heat. No, this was all wrong. He should not be here! He had to escape. But how? How to escape?

Someone had once told him but he could not remember. There was a name. Something about a name. A name whereby men could be spared this place of torment. But what was the name? He could not remember!

Frantically, he searched the corners of his mind for the name, but there was nothing. Only a void. He opened his mouth and screamed. It was a desperate and pitiful scream but a silent one for there was no sound here. All was quiet. He gripped the man's hand and shrieked and shrieked.

A head poked out to peer into the monstrous grave and pointed.

"Lookit that one there, would yer. Lookit 'im. Floppin' all over like a hooked fish.

The cartman wiped his mouth on the back of his sleeve. "Ah allus makes sure they's dead afore I tosses 'em in," he said virtuously. "Don't want 'em climbin' back out."

He leered at his partner, who chortled and punched his arm lightly. A bell sounded in the distance and both men stood still to listen.

"Sounds like Ralph Fairjohn's old clangour. Back to it. More custom for the cart, I expect."

They winked at one another.

"Make right sure they's dead awright. Obscene, that is," they agreed, casting offended eyes into the pit.

Another bell tolled and they grunted and dragged their empty cart away from the burial trench, away from the feeble twitchings of the dying man sprawled on top of the dead pile.

CHAPTER 21

KATHERINE LISTENED AT THE DOOR. There were no sounds from the other rooms and the dead-carts had long since ceased in the street below. Victor slept in the room next to hers so she turned the lock slowly, pressing her body against it to muffle any noise. With great care, she drew open the door, slipped into the hallway and crept toward the staircase. Moving toe by toe down the steps, she paused to look back when a plank creaked in gentle protest, then continued on down.

Although the moon shone in from outside, it was still quite dark and Katherine could only faintly make out the shapes of the furniture. She slipped through the inn's gathering room, feeling her way carefully around the tables.

As Katherine fumbled with the front door, she jumped in terror when a hand fell heavily on her shoulder. She opened her mouth to scream then another hand was clapped over her mouth and she was pulled back. Eyes wide, she twisted her head to identify her attacker. Victor! Katherine grew limp with relief. It was only Victor.

"And just where do you think you are going?" He withdrew his hand so Katherine could speak.

She licked her lips and pried his other hand from her shoulder.

"You nearly frightened me to death," she complained.

"Is it your usual practice to creep about in the dark in the dead of night, madam?" Victor asked drily.

"My business is my own."

Her tone was dismissive and she turned her back to Victor and tried the outer door again. But he was not to be put off so easily and laid a hand on the top of the door once she had forced it ajar.

"Where are you going?" he repeated, undeterred by her continued tugging.

"And I say again," she answered through clenched teeth, "where I go and what I do are my own concern and not yours."

"That may well be, but a sensible woman does not prowl around at night on her own. Where were you going?"

He pushed the door shut firmly and folded his arms in front of his chest. "We will stay here until you give me an answer or until you go back to your room. It is your choice."

Katherine glowered helplessly. How could she go on now? She would either have to tell him or else abandon the whole enterprise. She set her lips.

"Since you leave me no option . . . " she began.

Victor jumped in to correct her. "Oh, you have a choice, Katherine. You can tell me or not, as you wish . . . "

"Since you leave me no option," she repeated, each word bitten and icy. "I will tell you."

"Good. I am listening."

"May we sit?" Katherine asked coldly.

"We may."

With a flourish, Victor lifted a chair and set it down next to her then took one for himself. He faced her under a window and in the moonlight she saw a smile playing about his lips.

Katherine took a deep breath and looked Victor directly in the eye. Her voice did not waver and she did not look away.

"Before Benjamin died, he gave me something. A note on a bit of cloth telling me where to find the forbidden scriptures for which Father Simon was searching."

Victor's eyes widened and he leaned forward.

So, he *did* have them."

"Yes. He hid them at Crenfeld. I do not know how he managed it, but he did. He wants the young men he was teaching to have them and he asked me to see the scriptures safely into their hands. I am determined to do so, though I was afraid at first." She gave him an earnest look. "I *will* do it, Victor. Now, or at some other time. But I *will* do it."

Victor stared at her in silence for some little while and when he found his voice, it had lost its playfulness.

"You are a good woman, Katherine. Benjamin was right to trust you with his secret. I appreciate that you have now entrusted that secret to me and although I admire your courage, I cannot let you embark on such a dangerous mission."

He raised his hand as she scrambled to her feet.

"I cannot let you embark on it — alone," he finished. "Since you have made it quite clear that I cannot dissuade you, I will join you. We will do it together."

It was Katherine's turn to sit in wide-eyed silence. He was not going to stop her!

She slumped back in her chair. "Thank you."

Katherine lifted her head to glance around the room. They were still undiscovered. Victor followed her gaze then held open the door.

"We will continue this outside, on the way to Crenfeld. Have you formulated a plan?"

She gave him a blank look. "Not really, no."

He grinned at her.

"Stop that! I was going to see how things were at the castle and then decide what to do."

"I will tell you how things are. The priest has left a company of guards to ensure no further plunder until he makes Crenfeld secure."

Katherine snorted. "There is nothing left to plunder. It is all gone."

Victor shrugged. "All the same, the guards are there. How do you intend to keep from being caught?"

Katherine paused mid-stride and put a hand on his sleeve. "Do you know where the guards are placed? Are they outside the walls?"

Victor considered. "I have no knowledge of their exact location but it is usual to keep at least one guard in the gatehouse at the far side of the drawbridge. The rest will likely be inside the wall."

"The portcullis will be down? We could not swim the ditch, climb up onto the bridge and get in that way?"

Victor was taken aback. "You can swim?"

"Yes, of course. Now, will the portcullis be up or down?"

"It will be as you say. It will be down. We cannot gain access through the front gate."

"Then we will have to go the other way," Katherine mumbled to herself.

"What other way? Are we to scale the wall?" Victor laughed.

"In a manner of speaking, yes. There is a secret entrance to Crenfeld. A difficult entrance. I had hoped not to have to use it."

"A secret entrance?" Victor's tone registered disbelief. "Are you certain? I have not heard of any secret entrance."

"That is because I never told you. I never told anyone. I found it while looking for the record book I thought to have been stolen by my missing steward. I did not know who my enemy was, then. I know now it was that priest, Father Simon. A wicked man," she finished bitterly.

Victor nodded and they walked on in silence a ways before he asked.

Where is this secret entrance to Crenfeld? You said it was difficult. How so?"

"It opens out into the solar adjoining the great hall. A tapestry concealed the line of stones that betrayed the passage opening. I discovered it merely by accident. But all the tapestries have been stolen and so I cannot be sure the priest and his men have not found the passage and followed it for themselves. It could be watched."

"Hm-m-m, that may be a problem, yes. I see your point. And the entrance from outside, where is that?"

Katherine swallowed hard. "On the cliff side of the castle. We have to climb down the rocks to find it. In the dark, the way will be hazardous. The boulders are slippery with moss and the river may wash us off before we reach the entryway."

"But you know where it is? You have seen it?"

"Yes. I followed the passage from the solar all the way to the river. It lies directly beneath the far tower, below the middle window, where the cliff juts out the farthest." She looked at him then and her eyes were anxious. "But I have not attempted the climb. In daylight it would be dangerous enough but at night and without a torch, it may well be fatal."

"Then we must pray for a strong light from the moon," Victor said cheerfully.

Katherine looked up. A strong light from the moon. Would it be enough?

CHAPTER 22

KATHERINE AND VICTOR CROUCHED behind a thick stand of trees at the edge of the wood. They could see Crenfeld Castle clearly by the light of a very full moon.

"But if we can see the castle, surely the guards can see us," Katherine whispered ruefully.

Victor grunted and studied the sky. "For now." He pointed, "Watch the clouds. They are moving swiftly. We will wait here until they cover the moon and then make for the other side of the gatehouse."

Katherine nodded. Her heart beat a little quicker and her hands felt clammy as she watched the shadowy outline of armed men pacing near the castle. She swallowed hard.

When darkness enveloped the moon and the castle disappeared from view, Victor put his mouth close to her ear.

"Now! And stay close to the ground."

Katherine snatched up her skirts and ran, depending on Victor to lead her in the right direction. With the moon obscured, she strained to keep his back in sight as he plunged into the night. Although tree branches clutched at her clothes and hair, she managed to duck and weave away from them. She held her breath when they slipped past the gatehouse, a pulse pounding in her throat until she finally felt safe enough to gasp for air. She sank to the ground, panting.

Victor crouched down beside her and put an arm across her shoulder.

"Are you all right, Katherine?" he whispered.

She bobbed her head, unable to speak.

"Do you think you can make the climb? Perhaps I ought to go alone."

Katherine gulped in air and found her voice. "No . . . no," she gasped. "I will come with you. I need only a few moments to catch my breath. Just give me a little time."

Victor nodded and dropped his arm.

"We must wait for the moon's light, in any case. We have the time. Rest as long as you wish."

When her chest stopped heaving, Katherine peered out over the cliff's edge. Rolling waves crashed against the rocks, the spray wetting her face. Dread overcame her and she felt the sweat of terror bathing her body. But Victor sat calmly and studied the sky from time to time. His peaceful demeanour stilled her fears.

"I am ready," she said at length.

And just in time too, for the moon had reappeared.

Victor leaped up and swung out over the rim of the cliff, feeling slowly for footholds. He glanced at the sky once, then at Katherine.

"There is not much time to find the opening. Watch where I put my feet and follow me as quickly as you can."

Katherine pressed her lips together and nodded. She hoped he did not see the fear in her eyes. Mustering all her courage, she slid down beside him, gripping the rocks with tension-stiffened fingers. Victor raised an eyebrow to signal his intention to go on, then began the treacherous descent.

Katherine felt beads of perspiration forming on her brow and blinked rapidly to keep the salty drops from falling into her eyes. She worked her way down inch by inch. The strain of holding onto protruding tree roots and moss-covered rocks made her arms ache. The river's roar grew louder and she cast anxious eyes beyond her trembling legs to the rough waters seething and foaming just beneath her feet.

Katherine clung to the rocks in grim determination. Hand over hand, foot over foot, she struggled.

Victor saw the opening in the rocks overhead and pointed upward.

"Just above," he encouraged her.

He pulled himself aloft with little effort and stood at the opening. Katherine tried to climb up after him but her arms merely trembled weakly. She had no strength left. She closed her eyes and hugged the cold rocks, feeling faint.

"I cannot make it," she gasped. "I cannot make it."

Victor lay on his belly and reached down. "Take my hand. I will pull you up."

Katherine shook her head. "I will not be able to hold on."

Victor looked at her bleak, exhausted face and immediately climbed back down beside her.

"Face me, Katherine," he said.

When she did not respond, he took her by the shoulders. "Now! Face me!"

Katherine twisted sideways wearily, trying to maintain her footing while at the same time keeping a hand on a thick tree root. Suddenly, Victor's arms were around her waist. She almost cried out as her fingers were ripped away from their anchor.

"Hold on to me," Victor ordered and Katherine clutched a handful of his tunic.

It was undignified but effective and they were soon standing together just inside the cliff entrance. Katherine leaned heavily against Victor.

"Th . . . thank you. I was so afraid I would fall."

She shuddered and turned away from the river to look deep into the black corridor behind them.

"We have no light. How will we see?"

Victor shrugged. "We do not need to see. Hold my hand. We will stay against the wall and follow it up to the castle."

After only a few steps, Katherine was glad to be in the dark so she could not see what brushed against her hair and face or crunched underfoot. When Victor stopped, he squeezed her hand and leaned close.

"This is the end of the tunnel. I can feel a draft, so the opening must be ajar. Be very quiet," he whispered. "I will see if I can find the gap in the stones."

He felt around the wall, tugging at intervals and grunting softly. Suddenly, Katherine heard a crumbling sound, then the grinding of stone against stone. A cool current of air wafted over her face. She shivered.

"Is it open? Can we get inside?"

Victor pulled her closer to him until his head was touching hers. He kept his voice low.

"Do you have anything with which to defend yourself?"

Katherine shook her head against his and felt him press something cold and hard into her hand. She touched it gingerly, exploring its shape. A small dagger. She closed her hand around it.

Victor led her out of the tunnel and into the solar where Katherine steadied herself against the wall. She would need to maintain her nerve. Although no fire burned in the grate, there was a light glowing from the doorway into the great hall so they had no trouble seeing their way. Katherine shrank back and her heart beat a little faster. Were the guards inside warming themselves before the vast stone hearth?

Cautiously, Victor stretched his head out into the hall. It was empty. A fire burned but the big room was vacant. Silent as ghosts, they drifted across the floor in the direction of the kitchen. If the guards occupied any room at all, it would be that one. But again, they found an empty room. Evidence of use was all around them. A keg of wine lay on the center table, its grey planks halloed in dark-ringed stains. Roughly hewn slabs of meat bled over the edge of the table. Dirty pots littered the floor. A single caldron hung over a struggling fire. Looking inside, they found an insipid brown liquid with a few onions floating on the surface.

Victor lifted the dipper and wrinkled up his nose. "They are no cooks," he whispered.

"This way," Katherine breathed, waving aloft the little dagger he had given her.

Victor dropped the ladle and it fell with a plop, then sank to the bottom of the caldron. He looked around quickly, snatched up an apple that had rolled out of its sack and rubbed it against his sleeve.

Katherine frowned at him. He shrugged and took a bite of the apple, following her slowly.

"The lower storeroom is through here. We will need a candle. It is much too dark below."

Katherine searched among the debris left in the wake of the looters, found a taper and ran back into the kitchen to light it from the fire. Shielding it with one hand, she hurriedly retraced her steps and led the way down to the lower storeroom.

"The trapdoor is there. Pull on the ring. It should come up quite easily. This is where Father Simon kept Benjamin."

Victor heaved the door open, took the candle from Katherine and leaned down to look inside.

"He kept him here?"

Katherine's tone was resentful. "Yes. And he did not feed him nor make any provision for his comfort whatsoever."

Victor looked at her sober face. The candlelight glowed against her skin and gilded her red hair. She was a beautiful woman.

Katherine grew uncomfortable under his prolonged regard and turned from him to reach for the ladder stored nearby.

"We can use this," she said, avoiding his gaze. "I will go down first. I am familiar with the cell."

Victor smiled. "As you wish. It is your castle."

"Father Simon's castle," Katherine corrected. "But he will not happen on Benjamin's secret by chance and feel he has won any kind of victory."

Katherine descended into the little room. Raising the candle, she shone it around the walls. When the light revealed a blanket discarded in one corner, a sob welled up in her throat. Benjamin's blanket. She knelt down and lifted it, rubbing the fabric softly against her cheek.

Victor watched in silence for a while and when it seemed she was lost in reverie, he touched her shoulder.

"Katherine?"

Katherine started and blinked, breathing in deeply. She looked down at the blanket with sad eyes, then folded it and set it aside, letting Victor help her to her feet.

"Where might we start, do you think?" he asked, glancing around.

Katherine held the candle high. "I am sure Benjamin read from it after I left him. There will be signs in the dirt, unless he had the presence of mind to obliterate them."

"We will inspect the walls one by one, omitting the outer wall. That just leaves these three. Lower the candle nearer the floor. I think I see marks here."

Katherine did as Victor instructed and knelt beside him. The earthen floor was cold on her knees. She shivered then bent for a closer look.

"Yes, I see them, too. It looks as if Benjamin dropped the stone right here. Is there a loose one above this spot?"

"Hand me the dagger I gave you. The point is thin enough to slip between the stones. Look, this one is moving. If I can just wedge the blade in behind here." Victor applied more pressure.

Once the stone was dislodged, he removed it and put his hand inside the recess. He drew out a wooden box and handed it to Katherine.

"Is this it?" he asked.

Katherine gave him a quick, excited nod. "It is."

Victor put his hand on the lid and raised his eyebrows. "May I?"

"Yes. Yes, of course."

Victor opened the box carefully. It smelled of oil inside. He unbound a small package secured with narrow deer's hide thongs. Ornate lettering, beautifully written and decorated in gold and red, declared the contents to be *The*

Gospel According to Saint John. Victor rebound the package and closed the box, handing it to Katherine.

"You have what you came for. We need to leave at once. The guards are about and although we have been lucky so far, I doubt our luck will hold for much longer."

Katherine nodded and held the box close. "You are right. We must hurry."

Once up and out of the small cell, they heard muted voices.

"They are in the kitchen," Victor whispered. "We cannot go back that way. Is there another way out?"

Katherine shook her head. "No. We have to go through the kitchen."

Victor rubbed his face and frowned.

"Stay here. I will take a look and be right back."

Katherine sank down to sit on the floor with her back against a wall. She was suddenly very tired. She closed her eyes. How she wished Victor was not involved in her foolish scheme. Now they might both be caught.

After a few minutes, Victor returned.

He sat down beside her, his shoulder touching hers.

"There are only three, that I can see. All of them are sitting at that big table with the wine keg." He grinned. "They are getting quite drunk and will soon be in too much of a stupor to give us any real trouble. I say we wait a while and then take our chance."

Katherine bent forward and set down the box, then leaned back against the wall. "I suppose you are right." She paused, then said. "Tell me about your family. Your mother and father."

Victor shrugged. "My father was a rigid man. We were all afraid of him. Except Ciscilla." Victor's face softened and a smile creased his face. "My dear sister charmed him completely and he loved her almost as much as he loved my mother, I think."

Katherine sighed. "My father loved me, too. Not that my mother did not," she said quickly. "But Father and I had a special relationship. I had no brothers and it made him very happy when I showed an interest in archery. And of course, you know about the horse. About Pygine."

Victor laughed quietly. "Yes, it must have thrilled your father to see you able to tame such an animal. Your skill with the bow, I know well enough," he added drily.

"What was your wife like, if you do not mind speaking of her?"

"No, I do not mind. I did once. But not now. She was a lovely girl. Always a little frail but with such a kind heart." He stopped a moment and a faraway look crossed his face.

"I am so sorry you lost her," Katherine said.

"That was a difficult time. But . . . " he added briskly, "now there is Marjorie."

"Yes, now there is Marjorie." Katherine's voice trailed off and she was quiet for a moment. "How did you meet?" she asked at last.

Victor leaned forward to rest his elbows on his bent knees. "I have known Marjorie most of my life. Her father and mine were friends from their youth. She has always had a calm spirit and in the years since her mother's death has become a very efficient and capable woman. There is not much that disturbs her peaceful nature and her father's household operates smoothly under her oversight. She is every inch a lady. I am a lucky man," he added.

Katherine hoped the bitterness she felt did not show on her face. How had she dared to entertain the notion that this man might have any deep affection for her? She was such a fool.

"Perhaps you should check the kitchen," she said in a strangled tone. "The guards may be sleeping now."

Victor nodded and disappeared. When he came back, he helped her to her feet. "They are snoring. I think it will be safe to pass through the kitchen."

Katherine collected the wooden box, held it close to her chest and followed Victor.

CHAPTER 23

OUT OF SIGHT BEHIND SOME EMPTY KEGS, Katherine peered around Victor's shoulder. The guards slumped on a bench pulled up to the kitchen table, sleeping amidst the litter of their meal, eyes closed and wine-reddened cheeks crushed against the planks.

Victor put a finger to his lips and Katherine swallowed hard. It was time. Keeping close to the wall, they slipped quietly across the floor. Katherine was certain the guards could hear the thudding of her heart and her alarm made her clumsy. In the final rush to the doorway, she tripped and fell face down on the floor. As she scrambled to her feet, one of the guards lifted his head. His roar alerted the others and she caught a glimpse of them feeling for their weapons as Victor pulled her through into the great room.

"We cannot go back the way we came!" he cried, urging her across the room.

"Make for the drawbridge!"

"But the portcullis is down! Our escape is barred!"

"Then we will raise it. Run!"

With a fleetness born of terror, Katherine bolted alongside Victor. They were both panting heavily when they reached the outer ward and could hear the guards close behind, swearing in loud angry voices.

"Here is the pulley," Katherine gasped. "I will help you. Quickly, quickly!"

But before they could put their hands to the chains, Katherine dropped the box as they were set upon by the guards who dragged them to the ground.

Victor struggled with two of them while the remaining man pinned her down. She was more afraid of his leer than the knife in his hand. She squirmed and writhed in seeming helplessness, all the while inching her hand closer to the dagger hidden beneath the folds of her bodice.

She knew the guard would not put her to the knife straight off. His design was evident in the way he slid the blade across her throat and down over the front of her dress before pinioning her arms.

Katherine willed her heart to be still and she turned cold in the man's hands. She lay motionless beneath his weight. When he released his grip on her arms to sit up astride her, her movement was so swift, he had no time to react. He could only gaze down in startled disbelief at the handle of her dagger protruding from his belly. He struggled to his feet, clutching the handle with both hands. Katherine jumped aside and crouched like a lioness keeping a death watch over her wounded prey.

Red-tinged spittle welled up in the guard's mouth and dribbled out over his chin. He staggered and as he staggered, Katherine darted in and pulled away the dagger. He made a feeble attempt to lay hold of her but fell down hard instead.

Katherine turned from him and threw herself with ferocity on the two men scuffling with Victor. Victor was weakening under their combined assault and she knew it was only a matter of time before a knife found its mark.

She plunged her dagger into the back of one of the guards who bellowed in pain and rolled away from Victor, grasping at the hilt with frantic fingers.

She jumped up and away and watched as Victor easily overpowered the remaining guard, dealing him a hard blow to the chin. Katherine heard a crack and the guard dropped instantly.

Leaping up, Victor grabbed Katherine by the arm.

"Quickly! There will be more of them! Help me with the chain!"

Together they hauled on the thick links, gasping in unison as the portcullis slowly gave to the chains and began its ponderous ascent. When it was half way up, Victor tied off the closest link.

"Far enough! We can get under it now. Run! There are sure to be more guards outside."

Katherine swept up the box and followed Victor. The drawbridge was down when they ducked under the portcullis. Evidently, the outer guards had heard the sounds of fighting and lowered the bridge to come inside and investigate. Katherine and Victor could see dark shapes on the far side, moving hurriedly toward them across the bridge.

"Jump!" Victor yelled. "Jump! You said you could swim. We will have to hope that they cannot. Let me take the box, and jump!"

Katherine cast a fearful look at the advancing guards, handed Victor the box and threw herself into the moat. Immediately, the weight of her dress began to drag her down and it was all she could do to keep her head above water. Victor swam alongside her.

"Grab hold of me!"

She put her arms around his neck. With swift strokes he made for shore. Dripping wet, they struggled up the embankment and sprinted for the safety of the wood, spurred on by the loud shouts of the guards.

When the clamour of their pursuers grew faint, they slowed to a walk.

Katherine stopped and held out her hand. "The box." she panted. "I will take it now."

Victor handed it to her. "After a night's sleep — or what is left of the night." he amended. "We will see that Benjamin's box is put into the hands of his young men as he wished."

Katherine nodded and they walked on without further exchange. The streets of Claringdon were empty and silent and they slipped into the inn unnoticed. Victor left Katherine at her room and proceeded on to his own. Before too long, however, there was an urgent knock on her door and the puffing innkeeper whined outside.

"Show yerself. Father Simon's guards be here to see yer."

Katherine opened the door slightly. The innkeeper, angry at being roused, pointed an accusing finger at her.

"Whatcher done, then? Wakin' honest folk in the middle of the night."

As he glared, he was pushed aside and another man scowled at her.

"You have been to Crenfeld," he charged.

"I have not," Katherine lied softly.

The man snorted. "How do you account for your countenance? You are as red as if you was boiled. And your clothes are damp. Where have you been?" he demanded.

Katherine arranged her features into confused innocence and slurred her speech when she answered "I have an ache," she complained. "Here." And she absently prodded beneath her arm. "My head hurts. And see how the sweat gushes off me like rain. I need a physic."

She reached out an imploring hand but the man's eyes widened fearfully and he shrank back and slammed the door in her face.

Katherine heard scuffling sounds and muffled voices disappearing down the hallway. She was safe for now. The innkeeper would not push his way into her room again tonight, but come morning, he would pay someone else to do the job. She listened at the door a few moments. Had Victor heard the commotion? She dare not risk alerting the innkeeper by knocking on Victor's door but could not remain the rest of the night in this room.

Katherine slipped the box out from under her bed, gathered up what little she had brought with her then tied her bedsheets together and hung them from the window ledge. She leaned out. They did not go all the way to the ground, but far enough. She swarmed down the cloth ladder and dropped the few feet to the road, jarring her ankles.

Closing her eyes a moment against the pain, she limped down the empty street in the direction of Benjamin's empty cottage. One of Benjamin's young men lived next to it. Her progress slowed by her aching ankles, light was beginning to break over the horizon when she rapped softly on the young man's door. She put a warning finger to her lips as his puzzled face registered first fear and then gratitude when he saw what she had brought him. Wordlessly, he clutched it to his chest, glanced quickly up and down the street then withdrew into his cottage.

Katherine let out her breath in a sigh of relief. She was glad to be rid of it. Catching sight of an old man driving along on a hay cart, she waved and asked if she might ride with him.

Seeing her limp, the man's eyes narrowed.

"Not sick, are ye?"

Katherine shook her head. "No, only tired. How far are you going?"

"Where you be wantin' ter go?"

"Stonehaven. Are you going that far?"

"That far and more. Hop on then. Can't say as it's fit for a lady, but hop on if yer have a mind to."

Katherine pulled herself up into the back gratefully and promptly fell asleep. The rocking of the cart was soothing and she was exhausted, so when the cartman prodded her with his whip, she roused with difficulty.

"There it is, over the next rise. What you be wantin'. Stonehaven."

Katherine sat up and looked. It was indeed.

"Thank you," she said simply and slid from the cart.

The old man nodded, clucked to his horse and continued to plod along the road.

Katherine was greeted with concern when she arrived at the castle, disheveled and still damp. Servants in the outer ward called for Agnes, who gathered her up and took her to her quarters.

"What has happened to you?" Agnes cried.

"It is a very long tale," Katherine replied. "And one I cannot tell you now."

Agnes shook her head but asked nothing further.

CHAPTER 24

BY MID-AFTERNOON THE FOLLOWING DAY, Victor arrived at Stonehaven. Upon learning of Katherine's return, he demanded to see her. Agnes relayed the message to Katherine, a frown creasing her brow.

"He seems very angry. Why is he so angry with you?"

Katherine sighed. "It is nothing. I will speak to him. Where is he?"

"In the hall. He is very angry," Agnes repeated.

Katherine entered the great hall to find Victor pacing before the fire, in long furious strides. She paused a moment to admire how well he walked without his cane, then made her presence known.

Victor's grey eyes blazed. "How could you leave like that?" he shouted. "I thought they had killed you."

"They came to my room." she said calmly. "They accused me of being at Crenfeld last night."

"You were not arrested?"

Katherine allowed herself a small smile. "No. I made them think the plague was upon me. They did not dare to touch me."

As quickly as Victor's temper had flared, it was abated. He threw his head back and roared with laughter.

"You outsmarted them, then?"

"Yes."

"And Benjamin's box? Where is it?"

"In the hands of his young men."

He nodded. "Good — good. And how did you get here?"

"In a hay wagon."

Victor laughed again and shook his head. "Very resourceful."

Katherine reddened at the admiration in his eyes. "It is over," she said brusquely. "Benjamin's wish has been fulfilled."

Victor sobered. "Yes. You did as he asked. I commend you. Now . . . Ciscilla is asking for you."

"I will go to her at once," Katherine promised.

Ciscilla welcomed Katherine gravely.

"Benjamin is dead?" she asked, her eyes cloudy with pain.

"Yes."

"You saw?"

Katherine swallowed hard. "Yes, I saw."

Ciscilla's face crumpled and she put her arms around her friend and sobbed against her neck. Katherine hugged Ciscilla close and wept with her, releasing all the anguish, all the emptiness.

"Enough sadness," she breathed at length and drew away, giving Ciscilla a kiss on the cheek.

Ciscilla sniffed. "Yes, you are right. I will always remember Benjamin." Her lip trembled. "I will not forget him."

"Nor I." Katherine agreed. "Nor I."

Ciscilla took Katherine's hand and led her into the garden. Katherine glanced around despondently. She would miss this lovely place, this sanctuary of peace and tranquility. They sat on the grass together.

Katherine regarded Ciscilla with anxious eyes. She hated to cause her friend further suffering but it was time.

"Ciscilla," she began, "I have an uncle in Astonborough. He has asked that I come to him now that I have lost Nathaniel and I have agreed."

With a sharp intake of breath, Ciscilla shook her head. "No. You cannot leave. Not now."

"It has to be now." Katherine said.

"But why not wait until after the wedding? You must be here for Victor's wedding."

"No, I must *not* be here." Katherine insisted.

Ciscilla searched Katherine's face and her mouth dropped slightly.

"I did not know. Why did I not see it?"

"I did not mean for anyone to know."

Ciscilla frowned. "Have you told Victor that . . . "

"Told me what?" Victor called out as he approached them, walking the winding footpath with Marjorie on his arm.

Both women looked up guiltily and Katherine was the first to find her voice.

"I am leaving Stonehaven," she said bluntly.

"Oh, but surely . . . " Marjorie began to protest.

Katherine managed to smile at her. "I have family in another part of England who have kindly offered to take me in."

She shifted her gaze to Victor. "I am unable to take everyone with me. As I have lost Crenfeld and my uncle has no need of further servants I must either release them to their own devices or find another place for them."

Victor digested this information in silence, then in tight cold tones said, "They may remain here if they wish." He paused. " You will not fight for Crenfeld, then?"

"Fight Father Simon? No, I cannot hope to win such a fight." Katherine answered wearily. "He has the support of the Church, while I . . . am alone."

Marjorie touched Victor's sleeve. "You must appeal to the king."

Victor's eyes still held Katherine's.

"I do not believe she wishes me to do so."

Marjorie looked puzzled. "But, why not? I am shocked at Father Simon's wickedness. He must not be permitted to do such a thing," she cried.

"He has done it." Katherine said with finality. "I will not fight him."

After a brief uncomfortable silence, Victor asked, "When will you leave?"

"In a few days. My uncle is sending his carriage for me."

Hesitantly, Katherine held out her hand to Victor. "Thank you for all you have done. You have been a good guardian for me and the people of Claringdon."

Victor dropped her hand. "I hope you know what you are doing," was all he said then he took Marjorie's elbow and led her away.

CHAPTER 25

KATHERINE'S HEART GREW HEAVY at the unmistakable crunch of carriage wheels in the outer ward. It was time. Farewells were exchanged and Katherine fought hard to maintain control of herself as Stonehaven disappeared from view. But her throat constricted and ached so badly she found it difficult to draw breath.

The carriage driver chose the shorter route to Astonborough — along a narrow track through the wood. They had bumped along for about two hours when quite abruptly the carriage halted. Katherine leaned out her window, intending to tell the driver she was not in need of rest, but saw him scramble down from his seat and run ahead on the path.

Puzzled, Katherine stepped out of the carriage. She gasped and a deep horror took hold of her. On the ground lay a litter of dead men with heavy black birds hopping clumsily from one to the next. The driver chased off the birds with his whip, lashing it out like a snake and cracking it hard.

Katherine approached him cautiously. "What happened?" she whispered. "Has plague taken them?"

The driver gave her a keen look. "Not unless the plague carries daggers, my lady."

He pointed. Each man's throat was cut with a savagery that left Katherine weak with fear.

"Who could have done this?"

Her eyebrows shot up. "And are they not the king's men?"

"They are."

The driver stooped to retrieve something lying on the ground. He grunted and handed it to Katherine. Unrolling a crumpled parchment bearing the king's seal, she read,

"An order to the King's dear and faithful man, William Stockwell of The Cheviot, Custodian of the King's Marches towards Scotland, that he should grant to that Knight of Scotland, Sir Stuart Bothwick, letters of safe and secure conduct so that he should be able to come to the noble joust at Stonehaven with men in his retinue, either footmen or on horse, up to the number of sixty persons, for the aforesaid purpose. Attested by the King at Westminster, the twelfth day of . . . " Katherine's voice trailed off. "There were no Scots at the tournament nor any foreign knights. What does this mean?"

"It means," snarled the driver, "that the enemies of England think us defenceless because of the pestilence and this Bothwick intends treachery, using a surety of truce to mount an attack on an unprepared English castle. Stonehaven. I have heard of Bothwick," he went on. "His clan swear oaths of fealty to him 'by the foul death of England'. He is a brute, a barbarian."

The driver bent down again, plunged a finger into the gaping neck of the man closest to him and grimaced.

"They are not long dead."

He jumped to his feet and paced the trail. "We should be able to see where they went through. The main group will have stayed on the wide road. Only a few — ah, here it is."

Once again he bent down, this time touching the ground and sweeping his hands over bowed and broken branches. He jumped up.

"If we hurry, we may be able to warn Lord Victor. Will you return with me?"

Katherine nodded vigorously. Of course!" she cried. "They are my friends! They must be warned!"

The driver took long strides back to the carriage. "Only the horses," he called over his shoulder. "The carriage is too slow. That is your horse roped at the back?"

"Yes, yes. I can ride Pygine. But there is no time to unload my saddle. Quickly! Untie him and help me up."

As she ran, Katherine grabbed a handful of her skirt and wrenched at it until it tore up from hem to waist. The driver's eyes widened but he made no comment as she swung up to straddle Pygine. The carriage horse was stripped of his harness and the driver sprang to his back, prodding the horse with urgent heels.

Together, Katherine and the driver raced along the narrow track. Time was precious and they wasted none of it. They broke the cover of the woods and bolted out into the meadow bordering Stonehaven to find a host of riders advancing about a furlong to the east. The blue and white flag of Scotland rippled over the heads of the front-riders. There was no mistaking their kindred or their intent. From the waist down every man wore a plaid garment in black, red and green and upon spying Katherine and the driver, a roar rolled up from their midst and the Scots surged across the field toward them.

Katherine let out a strangled shriek and kicked Pygine's flank as hard as she could. He lunged forward, quickly covering the remaining distance with his long, powerful legs.

"The Scots! The Scots!" Katherine and the driver shouted in unison as they made for the gates. Startled faces appeared above the ramparts and the massive gates began to yawn open.

Once inside the walls of Stonehaven, Katherine slid off Pygine and stood gasping while she watched the guards rush to drop the portcullis, slam shut the great gates and winch up the drawbridge. A volley of arrows arched across the wall, scattering Katherine and the rest in retreat to the inner ward.

Men-at-arms poured out of the great hall and swarmed up ladders to vantage points on the walls. Stonehaven was in an uproar. A tumult of men coursed through the inner ward, shouting to one another as they went. The stable disgorged its horses and every able-bodied man donned protective chain mail before mounting and being handed up a spear and battle-axe.

Victor emerged from the throng and strode directly to Katherine. He took her by the shoulders.

"You are not injured?" he shouted above the din.

"No — no!" She shook her head impatiently. "A bow! Give me a bow!" she cried.

Victor glared and her and held up his hand.

"Stay here! Look after the rest. Get them to safety! I cannot spare any men."

Before Katherine could protest, he turned on his heel and sprinted toward the stables. She looked after him a moment then wheeled and ran inside. The great hall teemed with terrified men, women and children.

"This way!" she shouted. "Follow me!"

They followed after her through the passages in a congested clamorous mass to squeeze out into the chapel.

Katherine raised her hands for silence. "You must remain inside! Bar the door behind me!"

Ciscilla and Marjorie separated themselves from the crowd, their faces white with fear.

"But where are you going? Surely you mean to stay with us!" they begged.

Katherine hugged them to her a moment.

"You must help keep the others calm," she told them. "I am needed elsewhere."

Even as she spoke, a tremendous crash reverberated off the walls. Katherine took to her heels.

"Bar the door!" she cried.

When she passed into the yard, Katherine knew what had happened. The outer gates had been breached! Heavy thuds now shook the inner gates. The Scots were almost inside! An image of the king's men and their cut throats galvanized her to action. She sped to the armoury, sorting quickly through the remaining weapons. The spears were too long for her to handle easily. There were bows, but they were hanging on a far wall. She needed something now. It would have to be a squat battle-axe.

She snatched one up, found Pygine alone in the stable and rode out into the yard just as the inner gates crashed open. A body of men forced their way inside, spears bristling. Katherine wheeled to face them, brandishing her axe. Screaming like a mad woman, she charged so fearlessly that the men broke up in surprise, temporarily stunned.

Victor's men closed in behind them and Bothwick's clansmen spun to face their enemy on the ground.

Katherine waded in, swinging her battle-axe wildly. Arrows sang past her face as she fought her way through the melee. Pygine attacked furiously, his hooves landing with deadly accuracy on the heads of the Scots. Katherine's axe found its mark time and time again.

When once the enemy realized she was a threat, one of Bothwick's men hefted his spear and threw it at her, piercing Pygine's belly. The horse's scream was deafening and he reeled in agony, slewing around with such violence that Katherine was thrown from his back to slam hard on the ground. Dazed, she staggered to her feet. Blood trickled down over her eyes in a sticky stream, making it hard to see. She blinked rapidly, clearing her vision in time to ward off a blow from her left. But on the ground, she was no match for fighting men. A black-haired snarling Scot loomed up close, his mouth open in a roar and the force of his fist lifted Katherine off her feet, hurling her aside like a doll.

She was nearly blinded with pain and crouched, panting helplessly. She had no strength left. All she could do was watch.

The fighting was intense. Men plummeted from the battlements; cries and shouts filled the air; the smell of burning pitch grew stronger and stronger. But Bothwick's men were being driven back. They were weakening. She was sure of it.

Suddenly, a loud shout rose up from the tops of the walls and Katherine heard the sound of hoofbeats receding into the distance.

It was over.

She sagged back, then remembered Pygine and scanned the ward with frantic eyes. He stood quietly in a corner, head drooping, froth ringing his mouth. Katherine struggled over to him, relieved to find his wound to be a shallow one.

Instantly, she was exhausted. The yard filled with people and she heard their excited chatter but felt no desire to join them. She was spent. She needed to sleep. To find a quiet place and . . .

"Katherine!"

She heard her name being called and forced open her eyes to see Victor crouching over her. She smiled weakly and was at once crushed in his arms. Victor's cheek was warm on hers.

"I will not lose you again! Do you hear me, Katherine? Never again!"

Then Victor's lips found her own with an urgency that quickened her heart.

"Victor?" she murmured against his lips in happy bewilderment. "Victor?"

Slowly, Katherine lifted her arms to twine around his neck and Victor gathered her up and stood cradling her, his tangled blond head lowered protectively. His rough coat felt good against her face. It bore the faint musky scent of him and she nestled against him contentedly. Victor hugged Katherine to himself a moment longer then made her comfortable on a pile of discarded blankets.

"I have sent for my physician," Victor assured her gently. "Lie still. He will not be long."

Victor kissed her, then stood and the bemused smile slipped from Katherine's lips. Marjorie stood a short distance away with Ciscilla, Nory and Agnes. But Katherine saw only Marjorie and the pain in her eyes. Victor saw it too.

"I am sorry, Marjorie," he said simply.

Marjorie gave him a thin smile. "I have known for a long time there was something between you," she said with a ragged sigh. "I did not want to admit it but I knew. Even after you insisted that too much emotion would ruin a productive union, make you rash, cloud your judgment, I saw how your eyes followed her the night you announced our engagement. I saw how distraught she became when you were injured in the lists. I saw it and I knew." Marjorie held his eyes a moment longer. "I will not hold you to your promise," she added and turned away. When the women were gone, Victor knelt back down beside Katherine. She tipped her face to his, her arms circling his neck possessively.

"Poor Marjorie. She loved you, you know."

"Yes, but as I told you once before, we cannot help for whom our hearts beat. Hearts have a will of their own. And yours and mine beat as one."

Victor kissed Katherine's forehead, then her eyelids, lingered momentarily on the arms encircling his neck, then pressed her lips with such passion that Katherine thought her heart might burst with joy.

The pale horse and his gaunt rider pause, as if listening. The great sword is sheathed. Horse and rider begin to move away. They are returning from whence they came, having carried off a third of the population of England in a single year and changed the face of society for ever.